The MILL of LOST DREAMS

The MILL of LOST DREAMS

A Novel

Lori Rohda

SHE WRITES PRESS

Copyright © 2020, Lori Rohda

All rights reserved. No part of this publication may be reproduced, distributed, or transmitted in any form or by any means, including photocopying, recording, digital scanning, or other electronic or mechanical methods, without the prior written permission of the publisher, except in the case of brief quotations embodied in critical reviews and certain other noncommercial uses permitted by copyright law. For permission requests, please address She Writes Press.

Published 2020
Printed in the United States of America
ISBN: 978-1-63152-719-7
ISBN: 978-1-63152-720-3
Library of Congress Control Number: [LOCCN]

For information, address:
She Writes Press
1569 Solano Ave #546
Berkeley, CA 94707

She Writes Press is a division of SparkPoint Studio, LLC.

All company and/or product names may be trade names, logos, trademarks, and/or registered trademarks and are the property of their respective owners.

This is a work of fiction. Names, characters, places, and incidents either are the product of the author's imagination or are used fictitiously. Any resemblance to actual persons, living or dead, is entirely coincidental.

To Annie Kenny, who saved me

Contents

1: Starting Over 1

2: Waiting for Violet 24

3: A Different Dream 64

4: Francois's Discontent 73

5: Samuel's Fire 78

6: Stolen Dreams 95

7: Promises 115

8: Transformations 141

9: Degrees of Separation. 152

10: Choices 175

11: Annie's Best Day 198

12: The Arrangement 217

13: Broken Promises 232

14: No Turning Back........................ 243

15: Coming to Terms........................ 257

16: Restitution, But a Gift Nonetheless.......... 271

17: Annie's Secret........................... 288

18: The Truth Doesn't Always Set You Free...... 298

19: Doing the Right Thing 303

20: Love Unraveled 325

21: Forgiveness Lost 356

22: The Final Dream 367

Epilogue 389

1

STARTING OVER

Guido and Angelina Wallabia, bound by tradition, devoted themselves without complaint to reclaiming the farm that had been in Guido's family for generations. Like so many Wallabias before them, they were barely sustained by the fourteen acres of stubborn, sunbaked, steeply sloped land in the tiny village of Gap, Italy. It was, as it turned out, a hollow inheritance.

Ironically, after years of focused but fruitless attempts at restoration, Angelina and Guido now personified their farm's depletion. Gone were the vitality, optimism, and enthusiasm—the signature hallmarks of their youth. It happened so gradually that each had failed to notice, which was, perversely, the only good fortune that had come their way. After years of joyless sacrifice, they had less of everything except debt.

Penniless, they now ate only what they could seduce from the farm's sour, compacted earth, and because that was sparse, Guido and Angelina were now dwindled, faded people.

But when Angelina met Guido four years ago, he'd had deep, liquid eyes, long lashes, and unruly ink-black hair that always seemed to fall across one eye. In fact, that was the reason she'd first noticed him.

It had been a market day in July, which meant it had to be a

Tuesday. Angelina always dressed more carefully on Tuesdays and arrived just as the caravan of wagons pulled into the village square.

By way of explanation, she'd told her parents that produce was always freshest early in the day before the sun had a chance to shrivel the corn's plump kernels and the ripe fruits and berries were bruised and picked through.

Of course, this was all true. It just wasn't *the* truth. Market days were a respite from the leached gray gloom and suffocating predictability of Angelina's life. She savored market days as a desert traveler, finding an oasis, savors the cool, lifesaving kiss of water.

Suspense and anticipation impelled her. She could not stay away.

It was her habit to walk from one end to the other, filling her lungs with the earthy scents of herbs, woodland mushrooms, and freshly dug potatoes. The spicy aromas of still-warm, meat pies made her salivate, while the heady sweetness of just-picked berries tickled her nose. Market days were sensual banquets to which Angelina responded with exuberance, the only times she felt completely unrestrained and fully alive.

On this particular Tuesday, she entered the square at her usual time just before six o'clock and took her usual seat in Donna Maria's outdoor café with its unobstructed view of the square. While she waited, she ordered her usual: a strong, black coffee and a warm, plump, almond bun drenched in sweet butter.

Typically, the café was deserted so early in the day. Today, however, she noticed a young man sitting under the faded blue striped umbrella at the table to her right. He was drinking an espresso—or rather trying to drink an espresso. She watched in amusement as each time he raised the dainty cup to his lips, an errant lock of hair dipped into the cup before he could take a sip and he swatted it away like a buzzing gnat.

Although seventeen, Angelina hadn't much experience with boys. She was an only child and frankly, between the ever-vigilant nuns at school and her overprotective though well-meaning parents, Angelina had few opportunities to observe boys, much less speak to them. Nonetheless, she gawked without embarrassment at this handsome young man with long lashes, full lips, broad shoulders, and tanned, muscular arms.

In such a small village, there were few opportunities for the young to socialize: a few religious holidays here and there and, of course, at planting and harvest times. More than any in his circle of friends, Guido relished these festivities: the music, the dancing, the flirting, and the antics of his comrades after a few beers. Inexplicably, he felt clumsy around girls, but he learned early on to hide his discomfort behind false bravado and public drunkenness. Despite a relatively placid exterior, Guido Wallabia always concealed a reservoir of powerful emotions: guilt about disappointing his family, fear at being found wanting by teachers, and grief for the dreams he'd already let die.

They married in 1843 when she was eighteen and he was twenty-three but only four years later his liquid eyes were dulled from exhaustion and malnutrition, his handsome face weathered and lined with disappointment, and the lightheartedness of his youth replaced by pessimism and irascibility. Like many who take self-pity as a lover, he began to brood—over his string of failed ventures and the bad luck that typified his young life and somehow still believed that he was as capable, if not more capable, than most men in Gap, worked harder, and had better business instincts.

From these unsupported beliefs, it seemed a small step to conclude that for some reason he was being cheated out of what was rightfully his. How else could he account for the fact that so many others in Gap had tasted prosperity and success while it had perpetually eluded him?

One morning, quite spontaneously, he decided to share this delusion with his wife. At first, her silence didn't alarm him, but as her pupils widened and the corners of her mouth slackened, he recognized her absolute disbelief and disappointment. While he couldn't really say what he'd anticipated her reaction would be, he'd certainly hoped for more than the muddled incredulity on her face. Red-faced, Guido turned on his heel and strode out of the kitchen.

Up until this point, her husband's unpredictability and voluntary exile from their neighbors had just confused and occasionally embarrassed Angelina, but now she felt deeply ashamed for ignoring the niggling premonitions she'd felt from time to time and reproached herself for underestimating the depth of his depression.

Truth be told, Angelina had changed as well. Walking into Donna Maria's café on that morning so long ago, she glittered like the stars when the moon is full. Her pale, square face and wide green eyes shimmered with happiness. The early-morning sun highlighted the luxurious auburn streaks in her thick hair, creating a radiant nimbus.

She's too tall for a girl was Guido's first thought as she took a seat in the café. But still, he was forced to admit, she had a quiet elegance and a dancer's graceful movements.

Indeed, he would never know anyone else who took as much delight in the humblest events: a lark's song, the winter sun's warmth on her face, the delicate green of new spring leaves. Angelina noticed the singular beauty of them all.

Angelina, too was a pale reflection of her former self. All the youthful shimmer had ebbed from her eyes, her skin had dulled and coarsened. Though she still carried her tall frame proudly, her once graceful movements were now languid. Unlike her husband, Angelina had always smiled easily and still did, but now it was a weary smile, devoid of pleasure.

To survive emotionally, she consciously fought off every disappointment, opting instead to expect less from her life, her husband, and her friends. She'd long since ceased believing in a benevolent God, in any god for that matter, and instead nurtured an unshakable faith in herself and in the power of focused, hard work. So, Angelina, just like her husband, carefully guarded a secret inner world.

On rare evenings, she and Guido would stroll to the local tavern with its nicotine-tinted air to listen to their neighbors' squabbles about this and that. There were always a few who bragged about some relative or friend who had emigrated to America.

"Every man who wants to work can find a job there," announced the bartender, authoritatively wiping up spills along the counter.

"He's right," confirmed a patron slouched at a corner table, draining his mug and signaling for another. "My uncle's cousin works in one of those mill places. He told my uncle that the owners provide housing for their workers, even those with big families."

"I hear men can make ten times what we can here and anyone who wants work can find a job," a disembodied voice from the darkest end of the bar declared.

Here in Gap, Angelina thought bitterly, no one would take such a risk and so nothing changes.

She refused to believe that ambition or wanting more was sinful. She believed that each person was responsible for his or her own destiny. With absolute certainly, she knew that her destiny was not in Gap and, regrettably it seemed, not with her husband. She was already planning her escape.

As in most things, Guido was slower to recognize the need for change. Until the last cow stopped producing and the dulled blade of his plow wedged permanently into a scree, Guido Wallabia never considered abandoning his farm. Four generations before him had lived, floundered, and died on this land. Leaving it would be disloyal.

"I don't know what we should do, Angie," Guido admitted one night during supper. "Can these stories about America be true? Could we really find work and earn good money?"

Angelina was so startled she nearly dropped her spoon.

"Of course, we have no people there," he continued, tipping his bowl to reach the last spoonful of broth, which, unbeknownst to him, had exhausted their remaining supply of onions and small potatoes. There had been no bread for months.

"The farm's a legacy from my father, my father's father, and my grandfather's father. It was entrusted to me, Angie. To just walk away? I don't know. It would dishonor them all."

"It would be a dangerous trip, and we have no family there to help us," Angelina offered. "On the other hand, it's good we have no children to worry about or provide for on such a journey."

He continued staring into his bowl, and she couldn't be sure he had even heard her. She sighed in frustration.

"Guy, I don't know what to do either," she said, deciding to try another tack. "Even if we could sell the farm, would there be enough to pay for our passage and make a fresh start? I just don't know about these things."

Since Guido was someone who could never be hurried, she stood and busied herself with small kitchen chores. "Oh, Lord, please let it be tonight," she prayed, and her face reddened as soon as she realized she'd asked God for something.

"You may be right," he reflected soberly, lighting his pipe and leaning back in his chair.

"This farm has never treated us fairly," he added with undisguised bitterness. "Thick calluses, bad backs, mountains of debt—that's all we ever got from it."

"If only Pa . . ." He trailed off as a circle of smoke formed above his head. "But Pa would never agree to try something different. Couldn't see the sense in it. He was old school. He had no vision."

Choking on anger, Angelina pretended to wash dishes at the sink as usual. Splashing cool water on her face, she thought, *The first thing my husband does is look for someone to blame because it's never, ever his fault.*

Disgust, like bile, rose at the back of her throat. *What a weak and cowardly man*, she thought. *He's never taken responsibility for a single problem.* She was tragically wrong about her husband but wouldn't know that for many years.

Finally, her composure regained, she sat down across from him. "Caro," she said softly, though she hadn't called him that in years, "I totally understand your loyalty to your father and to his family. I admire you for it, Guy. So, if you decide that staying here is the right thing to do, then that's what we'll do." She was shocked that her dishonesty only slightly embarrassed her.

Silence.

"What would we absolutely have to do to make this farm prosper again?"

She waited. Seconds passed, then minutes.

Slowly, he laid his pipe on the table and exhaled dramatically. "Too much," he replied gloomily. "Way too much.

"We'd need a lot of money, Angie," he said with forced confidence. "Just to fix what needs repairing: the roof, the paddocks, the well. We'd need a lot of money."

He shoved his chair back violently but sat there staring at the floor as if the solution was in the scuffed, worn planks. Guido reached for his pipe, tamped it down, relit it, and put it back into his mouth.

"But the soil," he said finally, "that's the biggest problem, Angie. That's the biggest problem.

"It's so poor. And the truth is I don't know how to improve it. Maybe some of our fields shouldn't be planted but . . ." Again his voice trailed off and he continued to examine the floorboards.

"Are you sure?" she asked, deliberately baiting him. "Because maybe we could try—"

His head snapped up. "I've been a farmer all my life, Angelina!" he shouted, slamming his fist on the tabletop. "And I can certainly read the earth. Our land, this farm, it has no more life. It's empty of life."

And finally, they both knew. Angelina moved back to the sink so he would not see her triumphant smile.

In April of 1847, Guido and Angelina booked passage on the *Humboldt*, a three-masted square-rigger out of Hamburg, Germany. Including crew, her total capacity was 240. All accommodations were in one of two windowless steerage decks, where people were crammed in as tightly as kernels of corn.

Below deck, the living conditions were crude. Rough, wooden platforms, two tiers high, lined both sides of the ship with a narrow aisle down the middle. Each straw-covered platform became the living space for an entire family. Primitive toilets were inconveniently situated at either end of the two steerage decks. Ill and frail passengers often relieved themselves in their beds if there was no one to help them to the toilets. Small children peed on the floor as they played and in their straw beds as well. By the end of the second week, the stench from steerage was detectable up on the main deck.

Every morning Captain Himmell, a short man with a toothy smile and brows resembling cedar shake, circled the main deck. Once a week, he ordered the encrusted steerage floors to be scraped and washed with vinegar water, which helped dilute the stench of vomit and urine for a day or so. But since there were no requirements regarding personal hygiene, the smell of unwashed bodies worsened.

In such unhygienic conditions, diseases spread rapidly, and lice and fleas were rampant. By the fourth week, twelve passengers had died from fever, cholera, or dysentery. Nine were children.

Despite the conditions, Guido felt surprisingly fortunate. "Angie," he whispered one night as they lay on their platform waiting for others to fall asleep, "how are you? Are you okay?"

"I'm good, Guy. Why? Are you sick?"

"No, I was just thinking how lucky we've been. So many sick people. The boat's rolling don't bother me like it does some of the others."

"I know. Isn't it funny, Guy? On the farm, we never had enough to eat and we had to work day and night just to get that. It toughened us, made it easier to endure this. Who would've thought I'd ever have something good to say about your farm!" They both laughed out loud. Angelina turned to kiss him and saw the tears in his eyes. "Guy, what?" she asked, alarmed.

He kissed her with a tenderness she'd long forgotten. "Angie, I'm so sorry. For everything." He cradled her and stroked her hair until she fell asleep.

Both ate every morsel of the unappetizing meals delivered in huge iron kettles three times a day. For breakfast, a thin porridge with hardtack biscuits, watery soup ladled over hardtack biscuits for lunch, and stew made with potatoes, dried beans, and pieces of fresh fish for supper. There was no fresh bread, just the hardtack biscuits. Unlike some passengers who, in futile protest, threw them overboard, Angelina and Guido soaked them in tea and devoured them.

At six every morning, Guido, like all the other male passengers, pushed and shoved his way to the front of the line to receive the day's ration of water. Because drinking water was stored in wood barrels that had been burned on the inside, its color was an unappetizing brown.

Rainwater was collected in other barrels and reserved for washing. Captain Himmell tried to declare a washing day once a week as no clothing could be washed or hung to dry in steerage. On washing days, all colors, sizes, and shapes of clothing dripped from every possible conveyance: over the sides and the stern, off the rigging and tackle, from the spars and masts, atop lifeboats and sculls. On these pleasant days, as the ship sailed, cleanly splitting the water, it resembled a long, colorful clothesline.

Before leaving Gap, Angelina and Guido sought advice from neighbors whose relatives had traveled long distances by ship. So, before they stepped onto the main deck of the *Humboldt*, they were better prepared emotionally and tactically than most other passengers.

Guido had been told to barter the few remaining farm tools for heavy, woolen clothing—men's caps, long winter coats, trousers, and blankets—because sleeping below deck, according to Mrs. Moretti's sister, would become intolerable.

By the end of the second week, the stench of vomit, urine, and unwashed bodies was indeed unbearable, so after others were asleep, Angelina and Guido quietly dressed in multiple layers of woolen clothing and crept up to the main deck, where, in hidden spaces, wrapped in several blankets each, they slept soundly in the fresh air.

Angelina heard from another neighbor that diseases festered on these ships, so in addition to medicinal herbs, she packed strong homemade soap, which many passengers had completely forgotten to bring or had assumed would be provided. Guido and she used a small portion of their drinking water to wash their hands twice a day.

On halcyon days, all able passengers poured out onto the main deck. Women, their heads covered in tightly knotted kerchiefs, sat on overturned lifeboats, tucking their long skirts tightly around their legs. Men in woolen caps and multicolored scarves huddled shoulder to shoulder, trying to smoke, which wasn't allowed below deck.

Sometimes, small groups who spoke the same language chatted amicably, but usually men and women sat or stood in silence, lost in thought, trying to stay warm and dry. Guido and Angelina never mingled.

Five weeks later, the *Humboldt* entered New York harbor in the late afternoon and was immediately quarantined and forced to anchor offshore. Outside, it was a chrome-colored day with warm, damp winds that bore new, unrecognizable scents, but the weather could not dampen their excitement. On deck, passengers jostled each other along the railing to get better views of the shoreline; some men bravely climbed the rigging until they had unfettered views.

Only Captain Himmell's sudden appearance on deck subdued the crowd's enthusiasm. He informed them that this place was called Castle Garden.

The captain cleared his throat dramatically and nodded to his crew, who had taken up positions around the deck. "Ladies and gentlemen," he announced in his clipped accent, "we've arrived at Castle Garden, but I've just been notified that the *Humboldt* will not clear customs today. Ships that arrived before must clear customs first. I'm sorry to say, but you are confined to the ship for at least one, perhaps two more days."

Slowly, as this announcement was translated into language after language, blank faces morphed into exasperated, incensed expressions. Currents of animosity encircled the deck and soured the air. Captain Himmell held himself erect, his face untroubled because he'd crossed the Atlantic many times ferrying tides of immigrants, so he understood his human cargo.

Regardless of their country of origin, these were people who had already endured circumstances and conditions that degrade the human spirit. In the end, they were pliant and compliant, like anyone who has been beaten into servility.

With an air of authority, he turned abruptly, shouted instructions to the crew, and strode to his cabin. As he'd predicted, within minutes passengers drifted away from the railing, most returning to their quarters in steerage, pulling the grayness in with them.

Captain Himmell decided not to reveal that the *Humboldt*, like every ship arriving with human cargo, had to be quarantined for three days because shiploads of poor, unwashed people could introduce diseases like typhoid and cholera into the city. On the third day, the quarantine was lifted, and passengers were herded onto barges and ferried to a quarantine reception station while their luggage was sent separately to the Castle Garden baggage room.

Without adequate explanation, women and children were

separated from men, and were screened and examined by medical teams for illnesses and diseases. Those deemed unhealthy were transported unceremoniously to the hospital on Ward's Island.

Those deemed healthy were escorted to the baths where women and small children, dozens at a time, could bathe in a huge pool. For most, it was the first time in over five weeks that fresh water or soap had touched their bodies. The effect was magical; trepidation and modesty were washed away along with sweat and grime. Sounds of playful laughter and splashing reverberated around the room.

Afterward, Angelina joined a long row of women seated in a comfortably cool rotunda. For three hours, she waited her turn to meet the man and woman seated at diminutive desks in the middle of the room.

Finally, it was her turn. A simply dressed young woman motioned Angelina to a nearby chair into which she slid, nearly fainting with apprehension. A disinterested man with a detached expression sat next to the interpreter, wearing a starched white coat over a dark suit and tie. Without looking at either woman, he asked a series of questions that the young woman then translated into Italian, which was meant to put Angelina at ease but failed miserably.

The first question: Eduardo's mother gives him twenty lire to buy three onions and a loaf of bread at the market. If onions are three lire each and bread is four lire, how much change should Eduardo bring back?

Wide-eyed, Angelina balked. *What kind of silly question is this?* she wondered impatiently. *And what does this have to do with Guido or me?*

Nevertheless, she forced herself to smile and answer respectfully. In the end, without ever establishing eye contact, the man held out a blue card and pointed to the door behind them. Angelina's knees nearly buckled as she stood.

The innocuous door opened into an exquisite, sun-splashed room with lustrous marble floors, arched doorways, and a magnificent fountain that cooled and refreshed the air. With one hand shading her eyes and the other covering her mouth, she stood motionless, breathing in the familiar scents of furniture polish, lavender, and tobacco.

Curved benches, upholstered in muted stripes and rich solids, were spread about the room along with groupings of small, mahogany tables and chairs. Some families were already feasting on fresh bread, honey, and bits of cheese purchased from a vendor in a distant corner. The aromas made Angelina's mouth water.

In the center of the room, the sun's playful dance with the fountain was mesmerizing. Backlit by the sun, the water from the ascending jets appeared as luminous filaments but returned as rainbows of shimmering droplets.

For the first time in her life, Angelina felt dazzled and completely overwhelmed, in a good way. *Our first day in America*, she thought, *and already such spectacular beauty!* Beaming and breathless, she'd totally forgotten about her husband until she spotted him across the room pacing, an unlit pipe in his mouth.

And this, she thought kindly, *will always be the difference between us*. She loved adventure and looked forward to change because she believed that with change came opportunity.

Guido, on the other hand, resisted even the smallest change because it made him uncomfortable. It was almost impossible to convince him that changing something might actually make it better, easier, or more enjoyable. He never had her confidence.

When she was close enough for him to hear her, she shouted to him. Guido's anxious face flooded with relief as he hurried to reach her and lift her off her feet in a bear hug. He too was overwhelmed by such unfamiliar, lavish surroundings, but in a bad way.

Together, they joined a line of passengers at the registration desk. Slowly people shuffled forward. Finally, Angelina caught a glimpse of the unsociable official behind the desk: middle-aged, smudged wire-rimmed glasses, receding hairline, full beard, angry red scar across his cheek. It appeared his only purpose was to ask each family the same questions and record their answers.

Because Guido understood so few English words and the man behind the desk did not apparently speak any Italian, the conversation was understandably difficult and frustrating for both. For his part, Guido labored to find the English words in order to answer correctly. In contrast, the registrar appeared less fastidious and even indolent as he scribbled something on an official-looking document, stamped it carelessly, and slid it to Guido seconds before shouting, "Next!"

For safety, Guido placed it in the inner pocket of his jacket, and it wasn't until they reached their final destination that he retrieved it and discovered the misspelling of his surname: Wallabee instead of Wallabia.

Angelina and Guido would never forget the sacrifices they made to come to America, but their most painful memory would always be of a place called Castle Garden, where, with a stroke of a pen, an apathetic stranger robbed them of their most cherished possession.

Carrying their entire lives in one worn suitcase, a battered trunk, and a large wicker basket, they boarded the Old Colony Railroad headed for a city called Fall River. All their lives, Guido and Angelina had known only arduous work, long hours, and self-sacrifice with little reward. So, perversely, they were perfectly suited for mill work. And indeed, there was plenty of work in the mills of Fall River in May of 1847.

The Quequechan River ran right through the city and in the last half mile dropped 132 feet through a narrow channel and eight consecutive falls—intensifying its strength and speed at each one. The Pocasset Indians called the river Quequechan, or Falling Waters, and the city had taken its name from the river—Fall River.

Cotton mills, iron works, printing factories, and bleacheries lined the river's banks, above and below the falls, using the powerful water to run their factories. Mount Hope Bay, ten miles long and three miles wide, provided a deep-water harbor, and the Fall River Line provided reliable steamship connections to New York, Providence, and Boston. The confluence of water power, a deep harbor, and a diversity of both transportation and natural resources made Fall River an ideal location for industrialization.

Mill agents, whose primary job was to supply the mills with a constant stream of laborers, waited at train stations and piers for immigrants who arrived by ship or rail. They recruited entire families to work in the mill with promises of steady jobs and clean housing. Angelina and Guido were recruited by Nathanial Wheeler, an agent for the Troy Cotton Mill.

They boarded Mr. Wheeler's carriage, but their baggage followed in an open wagon. In a daze, they gawked at the neat rows of shops lining cobbled streets and the towering, stately buildings along the old Granite Block. The driver stopped at the mill's front entrance. Over the front door, etched into the granite lintel was TROY COTTON AND WOOLEN MANUFACTORY, 1813.

"This is the oldest mill in the city," related Mr. Wheeler with some pride. "The original three-story building burned to the ground in twenty-one and was rebuilt."

It was indeed stately, with an attached granite bell tower dwarfing the mill proper and five stories of perfectly aligned windows set exactly three feet apart, which now reflected the orange-pink rays of the late-afternoon sun.

There must be hundreds of windows, Angelina thought in amazement. "My God!" she gasped. "How many people work here?"

"At capacity, ma'am, 'bout six hundred," Agent Wheeler replied proudly.

The carriage continued on, rounded the side of the mill, and proceeded uphill. "This is worker housing," Mr. Wheeler explained.

They're all the same, Angelina noticed immediately.

"And," she cried, leaning out of the carriage for a closer look, "they're all connected!"

She thought wistfully about their little farm in Gap, now so far away, where although everyone lived on a farm, rarely were two farmhouses exactly alike.

"Yep," said Wheeler, "four families in each, two per floor, all share a common staircase and a common front door. A few even have a usable basement."

"Here we are," Wheeler said, reining in the horses and consulting his ledger. "Wallabee, you're in number 709, lower floor," he said, handing Guido a key.

"You must report to supervisor Haley's office by five-thirty tomorrow morning. First floor of the Administrative Building, right side of the mill. You'll get your job assignments there. First bell rings at four-thirty. Don't be late."

The carriage, now empty except for Agent Wheeler, jerked forward and moved quickly downhill, leaving them and their luggage standing in the street.

At first, they couldn't find their apartment, then Guido noticed a small stairway at the back of the first floor which led to a locked door in the basement. Opening that door, he stepped into a musty, dim room.

Angelina walked carefully to a small window, the only window it appeared, and opened it. Immediately, a cooling breeze caressed her face. That window, half window really, would be their only source of natural light and fresh air. Fortunately, it faced the back of the building and looked out onto a small patch of woodland.

Guido lit the two hanging oil lamps. The kitchen was small but had the bare necessities: a few hanging cabinets, a long shelf, a sink, a stove, and a small ice chest. The bedroom was at the back of the kitchen, separated by a curtain. The bed was made and the sheets looked clean. A rough but sturdy, wooden shelf lined the entire wall and had small pegs just below it.

Over the next few months, they would learn that the dirt floor never completely dried until the dead of winter, so the apartment exuded a perpetual musty odor. The nearest privy hung off the first floor—depositing excrement directly into the Quequechan River.

But they were beginning a new life. They went to bed early and held each other tightly. Tomorrow they would begin working ten- to twelve-hour days, six days a week. It would be arduous, dangerous work, in deafening, dimly lit rooms. But they did not know that yet.

Because of his size and strength, Guido was assigned work in the carding room—the most dangerous job and the dirtiest room. Carders were the most skilled and, therefore, the highest paid employees. As an apprentice, Guido started at six dollars a week, the same as most male employees. But with more experience, he could, over time, earn as much as nine dollars a week. He could hardly believe his good fortune.

Angelina became a speeder tender, operating a machine that prepared cotton slivers for weaving. The noise of the speeders was so loud that most women put cotton in their ears. Because the yarn broke more often on hot, dry days, the windows remained closed and overhead nozzles periodically sprayed water into the air to keep the yarn moist. By noon the air was thick and hard to breathe.

Like Guido, she worked sixty to seventy hours a week, six days a week, earning four dollars a week, or about five cents an hour.

In May of 1848, their lives changed dramatically. Miss Gretchen Johnson, supervisor of Rose Cottage, left quite abruptly without notice. Rose Cottage was the smallest of the company-owned boardinghouses for unmarried girls.

The position paid only $3.50 a week, a lot less than Angelina currently earned, and would require her to live in Rose Cottage apart from Guido, but she would have her own room and three meals a day for free.

In a bold move, Angelina walked to the supervisor's office and offered to take the position temporarily while they looked for a permanent supervisor.

"Do you have some experience managing a houseful of girls?" asked Mr. Haley, the mill supervisor, who already guessed that she did not.

"No, sir," she replied honestly, "but I have managed a large farm and supervised a number of farmhands. I know it's not exactly the same, but it's not entirely different either. Wouldn't you agree?"

"Well, I don't know," he replied. "I suppose I could let you try on a temporary basis, but I could only offer you three dollars a week."

Angelina knew she was being underpaid and knew Haley's reputation for bullying workers and pinching pennies wherever he could.

"Well," she replied, "perhaps you're right, Mr. Haley. I don't have the exact experience you need. And I do make four dollars a week now. I wouldn't want to take such a drop in salary. I only offered so Rose Cottage would not have to be shut down while a full-time person was found. But thank you for your time, sir." She turned to leave.

"Well, hold on now, Mrs. Wallabee! I certainly don't want to discourage anyone looking for advancement. Perhaps we can have a probationary period?"

"I don't know," she replied calmly though her heart pounded. "What would that mean, a probationary period?"

"Well, let's see. It's May now. Why don't you take the position for six months at three twenty-five a week? At the end of that time, if your performance is satisfactory, I'd be happy to offer you three ninety a week."

Angelina understood that Haley was still underpaying her but did not want to press for more money. "Perhaps," she said, "if you could do me one favor?"

Now, Haley was annoyed with this foreigner, this "Eyetalian" woman, who continued to press him. "What?" he barked.

She took a deep breath. "My husband, who will now be living alone, suffers from the dampness in our basement apartment. I wonder if you couldn't find him an apartment aboveground for this probation period. Otherwise, I'm afraid my concerns for his health would be too great a distraction."

Given her age, her grasp of English, and her strong work ethic, Haley understood she was the right person, and, in a small way, he respected her determination. "Done," he said, "but you need to start tonight. Can't have girls unchaperoned after dark."

"Thank you, Mr. Haley. I'll move in immediately."

As house supervisor, Angelina was given a spacious, clean room on the first floor with indoor plumbing, allowing her to wash every day and avoid using the communal toilets on the second floor. Three windows provided lots of natural light and looked out onto the quadrangle formed by the Administrative Building and the mill proper.

The bedrooms were on the second and third floors. A large, rustic dining room, a spacious kitchen, and a comfortable parlor furnished with upholstered chairs and even a carpet took up the first floor.

Angelina's day started at four thirty when she rang the wake-up bell, set out a small, cold breakfast with tea, and made sure all the girls left for work by five twenty. Then she began preparing a more substantial meal for the girls' return for a forty-five-minute lunch.

In the afternoons, Angelina cleaned the first-floor rooms, inspected the girls' bedrooms for cleanliness and contraband (like cigarettes and matches), shopped for groceries, and prepared supper. At curfew, she checked every room to ensure that each girl was accounted for.

Sick girls needed to be taken to the clinic. Homesick girls needed comforting. Maintaining harmony was a daily challenge. Violations of the strict moral codes needed to be reported. Attendance at church was mandatory, and Angelina escorted them there and back every Sunday.

Rose Cottage thrived under Angelina's supervision. Tardiness and absenteeism were significantly reduced, which did not go unnoticed by Mr. Haley. The girls came to view her as a second mother and respected her guidance on most matters. They knew she was fair and, on occasion, would even bend the rules a bit for them.

Angelina's radiant smile was a beacon warming each of them home at the end of the day. Her many spontaneous kindnesses touched them deeply. Young women from other dorms began to request rooms at Rose Cottage, and there was, for the first time, a waiting list.

The mill's patriarchal boardinghouse system encouraged house supervisors to provide cultural activities to occupy their young women's free time. So Angelina, like other house supervisors, learned to invite local poets and writers to Rose Cottage. She also invited accomplished musicians as well as professors to lecture on art, history, and literature. She arranged for the *Daily Beacon* to be delivered and had one of the older girls read it aloud to the others almost every evening.

Occasionally, she arranged for them to tour a historic building, visit a lavish garden, or walk through the recently completed public library, the first one open to both men and women. She encouraged them to attend evening classes, speeches, and concerts. Whenever she could get away, she would join them.

She adored this aspect of her job and was surprised at how naturally it came to her. She got to leave the mill proper and learned how to navigate the city streets. She met and spoke easily with teachers, writers, and, occasionally, even a politician. She saw first-hand the power of education—it was the ladder to respectability and security, and she vowed to give her children that gift.

Samuel, the first of her three sons, was born in October 1849. Since Rose Cottage had become sought after, Angelina, who'd passed her probation period, was allowed to keep her firstborn with her. Three years later, she gave birth to her second son, Anthony. Once Anthony started to walk with confidence, though, her room was no longer suitable. She worried every day that such cramped quarters would be detrimental to their health, and she began to see that it was inappropriate to raise her sons in an exclusively female environment, so she gave Mr. Haley her notice.

During her years as supervisor, Angelina and Guido saved assiduously with an eye to leaving the squalid immigrant housing area called The Acre. In 1854, they rented a two-bedroom, third-story walk-up on Bedford Street, close enough so that Guido could continue walking to work. A year later she gave birth to her third son, Alphonso.

Unlike Angelina, all three boys learned to read and write, a fact that even Guido boasted about. Anthony and Alphonso, never good students, remained in school until they were twelve, then eagerly joined their father at the Troy Mill.

Samuel, however, was the real scholar of the family. He seemed addicted to learning. Despite the fact that the family needed extra cash, Angelina insisted that Samuel complete high school, although he worked in the mill every summer. For Samuel, she had a very different dream.

Over the years, Angelina had cultivated relationships with the many educators, poets, and writers she'd invited to speak at Rose Cottage. In Samuel's senior year, she sought their advice about sending him to college. In the spring of 1869, as a result of her bullish determination and unflagging persistence, he was awarded one, of only three, two-year scholarships that Harvard University earmarked for the sons of immigrant mill workers.

Much to her surprise, Guido objected vehemently. He pointed out that while the scholarship paid for Samuel's classes and room, it did not pay for the other things Samuel would undoubtedly need: food, new clothing, and books. These "extras," he argued, would strap the family financially just when he, Guido, had hoped to slow down a bit. As Angelina had predicted so many years earlier, Guido had indeed risen to supervisor, and now he hoped, in fact he had already put in a formal request, to work fewer hours. For a start, he'd asked for Saturdays off, he explained.

Angelina was stunned to hear his news. "What? Why would you do this to me? Why didn't you tell me? Guy, we didn't discuss this, we always discuss. I don't understand." She was frantic.

"Our son gets accepted into Harvard University—one of the best schools in the country, probably in the world. Only the smartest boys from the richest families get to go there. And you object? You want him to pass it up?

"He's our eldest, Guido. And he's a good boy. But more important, he's worked so hard for this chance. He'd be the first one in both our families to attend college! Do you understand what this means for his future and the future of our family? You want him to throw the scholarship back in their faces because he'll need a little money for books?"

Guido had never seen her so angry. She'd never spoken to him in that tone, and he was no match for her. He could have told her how tired he was, how difficult it was to draw each breath, how he could no longer climb the stairs to their apartment without stopping on each landing to rest. But he had resolved not to tell her or the boys what the doctor had told him about his worsening dry cough because, at this point, there was nothing to be done about it.

So, Guido accepted his fate and reconciled himself to working the rest of his days at the mill. "You're right, Angie," he said apologetically. "What was I thinking? The scholarship's a great honor and, for sure, Sammy deserves it."

On the morning of July 20, 1869, Angelina dressed carefully, choosing her favorite pale-yellow cotton dress with tiny embroidered rosebuds on the collar and cuffs. She polished her white Sunday shoes and purchased yellow ribbon to tie on her wide-brimmed straw hat. She wished she had a newer purse, but the worn black one would have to do.

She hugged and kissed Samuel repeatedly but was afraid to speak lest she cry. Just before Samuel boarded, Guido shook his son's hand and said, "We're proud of you, son. So damn proud."

Both parents stayed on the platform until the train slowly rounded a curve, dropping out of sight.

"Now this," Angelina whispered as tears slid down her cheeks, "this is why we came to America."

This would always be the proudest day of her life.

2

WAITING FOR VIOLET

One eye nearly swollen shut and the other almost blind, Violet Alysworth lay in the unyielding darkness of her bedroom, worrying about her children. Were they safe? Would they make it in time? She was desperate to hear the late-night train whistle, praying that she would hear it before Jean and Bridgette woke, because if she did, then her children had escaped and she would die knowing her revenge was complete.

While she waited, guilt, shame, and grief enveloped her like viscous fluids. Oceans of disappointment, deprivation, and humiliation were how she would remember her life, what little was left of it.

Perhaps it wasn't all William's fault. *I could have objected, tried harder*, she thought. But even if that were true, and she knew it was, William had failed her miserably. The man she loved, married, and risked everything for not only proved to be a self-indulgent fool, but worse, deceitful, cowardly, and callous.

To mitigate the room's deepening chill, Violet tucked her blankets more tightly around her, but her tremors continued. Pulling her knees up for warmth, she gritted her teeth against the pain because she couldn't risk moaning or crying out. Unfortunately, the effort only forced more blood to seep into her pillow.

"I never told the children what you did, William," she whispered, her voice a mix of pain and despair, "so maybe they'll always think kindly of you. But know this, you bastard, I'll never forgive you, and I hope you're burning in hell!"

William died on the bed of an open wagon before reaching the main logging camp, leaving his family inexplicably destitute. For the second time in five years, he was the reason she and the children had been callously uprooted from every comfort and security.

The emotionally and physically bruising journey six years ago from her parents' comfortable home in Quebec City to North Bay, Ontario, had become a metaphor of logging camp existence—mind-numbing, unrelentingly dreary, and crushingly lonely. To distract herself, Violet replayed bittersweet memories of her life when they all lived with her parents, Francois and Elanie LaFleur.

As a child, Violet had been easily frightened, embarrassingly bashful, and timorous. Her skittish gestures resembled a startled animal in danger of bolting, and frankly, both parents worried considerably and hoped that, over time, Violet's meekness would bloom into self-confidence and a sense of ease. Despite these shortcomings, she possessed a charming sweetness along with lovely blue eyes, porcelain skin, and cascading blond hair.

Inside her childhood home with its broad hallways, gleaming floors, and tiny-flowered wallpapers, Violet felt a bit more self-assured. The LaFleurs lived modestly but comfortably, and the house had space for them all, including the children. Francois and Miranda adored their grandparents, a passion that was fully reciprocated. Life there had been rich and delicious.

William, who had been raised on a farm in Ontario, never explained what had brought him north to Quebec City. Of medium height, with wavy brown hair and strong, muscular shoulders, William didn't have much of a presence. He was hard to read, and Violet's parents did not take to him the way their daughter did.

Violet came to observe that he was, like her, painfully introverted and loath to talk about himself or his past. Unlike her, he was parsimonious with both praise and money. Naïve and gullible at twenty-three, Violet felt a strange kinship with this shy, humorless, seemingly lonely man, and, over the vehement objections of her parents, she married him in 1846.

Except for farming, he had no work experience and not surprisingly drifted from job to job, never really satisfied or successful at any of them. Without any clear focus or direction, he meandered erratically for several years like a scrap of paper caught in a summer breeze.

Enigmatically, William had never been content. Not on his family's farm, not in her parents' pleasant, roomy home, and not in the primarily French-speaking city of Quebec. Violet would learn too late that William was one of those men who cannot be happy anywhere.

The pandemonium of the city exhausted him, and the tedium of life with his in-laws oppressed him. His restlessness and agitation drove him from the house almost every night—for hours and sometimes until dawn, he wandered the quiet city streets.

Their son, Francois, was born in 1848 followed by a daughter, Miranda, in 1852. Just after his daughter's birth, seemingly out of the blue, William began talking about moving north to cleaner air, open spaces, and the financial opportunities he'd heard were found in logging camps. Violet found it difficult to understand why he wanted to go and even more difficult to believe his arguments for doing so. However, she sensed the increasing urgency of his need to leave Quebec, and as a loving wife, that was enough.

So in early June 1857, Violet, William, Francois, and Miranda boarded the steamer, *Sainte Louisa*, on their way to a logging camp in North Bay, Ontario. Francois and Miranda waved frenetically to their grandparents on the pier below. Like their father, the children believed they were embarking on a marvelous adventure to find an elusive rainbow and its pot of gold.

Her husband's eagerness to "get a new start" was apparent in his broad smile and energetic waving as he hoisted Miranda onto his muscular shoulders. Violet, her slender fingers gripping the ship's railing, mirrored the stoic resignation of her parents and blinked back bitter tears until her parents and the crowd gathered around them resembled flotsam on the pier.

She had loved him then and prayed that his dream of a better life was attainable. She'd never anticipated leaving Quebec City, the home of the people she loved most and where her roots ran so deep and wide. She didn't understand William's desire for a "better life"—couldn't even imagine a life better than the one they were now sailing away from.

The *Sainte Louisa* took them down the St. Laurence River to Montreal. Their first-class cabin, a gift from her father, was comfortable and spacious enough for the children to play indoors. In Montreal, they boarded the Grand Trunk Railway to Ottawa.

At the Ottawa station, Violet, William, and the children waited for the outbound coach. When one finally arrived, the elderly matron on board did not disembark. Her crenellated bulk completely filled one of the two benches, and she was disgruntled by having to share her bench even with a small child. Fortunately, she alighted at the Huntsville station, the last stop before North Bay, their final destination.

At Huntsville, the family was allowed to roam the town for two hours while fresh horses were hitched, Huntsville's mail was unloaded, and the mail bags and packages bound for North Bay were secured on top.

As if released from prison, Francois and Miranda raced up and down the streets, chasing livestock and stray dogs until a townsperson shouted at them to stop. Violet found a small grocery where she bought cheese sandwiches, some small cakes, apples, and cups of hot tea, which she carefully carried back to the station. William, who was supposed to be watching his children, milled aimlessly about the streets before finally stopping at the local tavern for a drink.

When the stage started out again, everyone was in better spirits. The children devoured the feast Violet purchased but drank their tea slowly, caressing the hot cups for as long as they could. Francois was delighted to finally have a seat of his own, and his parents slept better without him across their laps.

Mist and drizzle arrived with the morning, dampening their spirits and their clothing. By midday, the children were quarrelsome and Violet was listless. She stared out her window, even though there was nothing to see except dense woodland on both sides of the road. For an entire day, there was not one animal, not one person on horseback, not one farm wagon or buggy—just trees.

Finally, in late-afternoon sunshine, they reached North Bay in July, 1857. From the station platform, Violet was relieved to see a general store with a two-story, narrow hotel attached to it and, further down, signs for a livery stable, a blacksmith shop, and a harness shop. Across the street, she saw a doctor's office, the sheriff's office, and, of course, a tavern. On a rise at the far end of the street, she could make out the gold cross atop a small white church steeple and rows of smaller crosses in the cemetery next door.

Two camp women came to meet their stage, helped load their belongings onto a wagon, and drove them to their new home—a modest square-log cabin, identical to all the others queuing both sides of a narrow lane. They passed small children, damp laundry flapping on low-hung clotheslines, and dogs barking from somewhere in the shadowy woods around them.

On their front porch a fragile wooden stool and a rusted bucket greeted them. The thick front door opened into a kitchen with two windows, a worn plank floor, a table, two chairs, and a wood stove in the corner. Two small, windowless bedrooms, each with crude, wooden dressers, could be seen off the kitchen.

Involuntarily, Violet sighed—a long, low sound more like a moan. Her neighbor, Sarah LaFontaine, patted Violet's arm gently. "It'll all get sorted out," she said knowingly.

Without a word, William left his family standing in the kitchen and walked back to town to find the administrative office, which turned out to be an oddly shaped building with a tin roof and a PUKASKWA LOGGING COMPANY sign carelessly nailed to the door. There he signed documents and was briefed by the owner, Amos Gallagher. Among other things, William learned that he would start earning only seventy-five cents a day for a six-day work week, much less than the ninety cents a day he'd seen advertised on the flyer in the Quebec post office.

More distressing, he discovered that no one was paid for days when work was canceled because of the weather—and this far north bad weather was as common as moss and could move in and settle for days or weeks.

Amos saved the worst news for last. Rent, six dollars a month, would be deducted from William's pay. Because the post office flyer affirmed, without clarification, that housing would be provided, William had assumed it was free.

Suddenly, the air in the room seemed too thin. Tugging at his collar, William felt faint as spots floated in front of his eyes. Head bowed, thoughts oscillating, he pressed the palms of his large, coarse hands against his temples. What about the advertisement he'd seen in the Quebec post office? He was sure that the flyer promised, boasted even, that this was the opportunity of a lifetime. Had he misread it? Misunderstood it? He'd brought his family all this way.

Squeezing his eyes shut, he tried to see the poster's words again but couldn't. What he could see, however, was that his optimism had been spurious. He'd been duped. He bent forward, trying to ease the sharp pain in his chest while his face flushed with embarrassment and helplessness. As wave after wave of humiliation rippled through him, the enormity of his disgrace became undeniable.

Stone-faced, he stared out the window, watching the dream his heart had cradled for years melt into the shadows outside and vaporize. Shattered, William took the pen Amos offered and signed the contract.

The next morning before either Violet or the children woke, William dressed quietly and left to join about three dozen other men seated in covered wagons that would take them deep into the woods.

William was gone for three weeks, and Violet learned that loneliness would be her most dependable companion. She never unpacked her mother's precious china or her grandmother's silver tea service—they were useless to her here. She learned to split wood for the stove, haul water from the well, and keep her children close to home. The woods were dangerous, especially in winter.

She measured the passing years in catastrophes. The first year, like many wives, she assisted in childbirths, many of which were stillborn. The second year she helped wash the dead bodies of husbands and fathers mutilated by equipment or crushed by falling trees. In her third year, an epidemic of diphtheria took the lives of eleven children. She helped nail together the tiny pine coffins, each time more ashamed of her relief that her children were still safe. But later that year when she received news of her father's death, she believed it was her punishment.

It was in her fourth year that she was assigned the most heartbreaking of tasks: keeping vigil with mothers whose children had simply vanished—carried off by animals or lost in blizzards. For this tragedy, there were no pine boxes. There was nothing to be done.

Through all these traumas and disappointments, Violet sewed. She bought remnants on sale, ribbons, and spools of thread. By hand-stitching strips of ribbon or embroidering borders on the plain linens stocked in North Bay, she replicated the more elegant linens she'd seen in Quebec and sold them in Amos's General Store.

In the spring she and the children planted a small garden. Camp women taught her how to preserve summer vegetables, dig a root cellar, and make jams from berry bushes that grew in the clearings. Violet's parents would not have recognized their daughter who was now resilient, self-sufficient, confident.

Of necessity, William's role in the family changed. For the first two years, William worked the outer camps, returning for only a few days a month—less in the winter if the snow was too deep for the wagons. In January of 1862, his fifth year, William was finally assigned to the closest site and could return home every night for supper. By then, though, his children and wife had fully adjusted to life without him. The void caused by his constant absence had closed and reformed into a more reliable family unit of three.

William was a stranger now, a ghost. Violet was startled but not overly apprehensive to see that he had become even more secretive and taciturn. But it seemed neither her life nor the children's lives were much impacted by his return.

At the end of that same month, Violet received a letter from her family's attorney in Quebec City:

Mr. Adam Howe, Esq.
350 Tremont Street, 1st Floor
Quebec City, Quebec
January 10, 1862

My Dear Violet,
I am truly sorry to inform you of your mother's death on January 8 of this year.
  Before your father passed two years ago, he'd wagered and lost a considerable amount in mining speculations. Upon

his death, I discovered those losses and unpaid bills going back six months. Your mother insisted that all bills be paid immediately and in full. She dismissed the household staff, except for Henri, and gave them all three months' severance.

She did not wish to trouble you, Violet. In fact, she forbade me to contact you. She was forced to sell the property and move into an apartment on Fredrickson Street. Unfortunately, a month ago she contracted pneumonia. As soon as I learned, I moved her to the hospital, but she did not recover.

As you know, your father and mother were proud, independent people, and contrary to my persistent advice, they refused to let me contact you for assistance—which, of course, you would have generously provided.

Violet, I simply could not tell your mother that she had exhausted her meager savings last month. I've paid her medical bills, for which I do not wish reimbursement, and sold the few pieces of furniture she kept in order to settle the remainder of her debts.

It distresses me more than words can say to inform you not only of her untimely death but also the loss of your inheritance.

With sincerest sympathy,
Adam Howe, Esq.

The news of her mother's death unmoored Violet, extinguishing her newfound resilience and casting her adrift in shadows—in and out of consciousness for four days and nights. On the morning of the fifth day, she woke to see William sitting on the bed and her dear neighbor, Sarah, who had no doubt been taking care of the children, standing behind him.

Slowly, very slowly, over several weeks, Violet's strength returned, but her mind didn't heal cleanly—at times there seemed a few empty places like an unfinished jigsaw puzzle, her thoughts sometimes seemed tangled and, on occasion, fissured. Violet seemed muddled and mortified when this happened.

She had no coherent memories of her breakdown after her mother's death in January or even of William's death in early April. When, just two weeks after William's funeral, Violet received notice to vacate the property, she crossed the lane to Sarah's cabin, holding the notice in her hand like a bouquet of flowers.

"I've nowhere to go, Sarah. No home to go back to," she sobbed, gripping the kitchen table so tightly her knuckles were nearly transparent.

Because Violet had been weeping since the day William died, Sarah wondered how her friend could have any tears left. From Sarah's point of view, crying was self-indulgent and never solved anything.

"Think, Violet!" she said sharply, her frustration temporarily getting the better of her.

"Violet," Sarah continued more gently, "there must be someone back in Quebec. A cousin, perhaps? An aunt? A good friend?"

"No, no one." Violet replied, shaking her head as her eyes darted around the room. Still gripping the edge of the table, she began rocking back and forth.

"Okay. What about William's family?"

"I never met them."

"But he did have family?"

"Yes, parents and an older brother. He didn't invite them to our wedding. I never really understood why. Actually, he never talked about them."

"So, where are they now?"

"How should I know? I just told you I never met them," Violet replied petulantly.

"So, where did William say he came from?"

"Ontario. Eastern Ontario, I think. The family's farm was near . . ." She paused and studied the floor as if the answer was written there. With her forehead deeply furrowed, she cleared her throat, pursed her lips, and offered, "Bonneville," but it sounded more like a question.

"No, wait, maybe it was . . ." She paused again before admitting, "I'm sorry, Sarah, I really don't remember the name, just that it began with a *B*."

"Lenny Boyes will know. Let's walk into town."

"Now?"

"Yes, Violet, right now."

As Sarah predicted, Leonard Boyes, the postmaster, had maps of the Canadian provinces with stage coach routes marked in red, but they were stuffed into a dusty overhead bin, and as he reached for one, they all fell out, rolling in every direction.

It took some time for him to gather them up and read each title, but, finally, he found the map of Ontario. Lenny was a bit of a character in the community: unfailingly polite and welcoming to everyone but oddly ignorant of many post office rules and regulations.

People who came to the post office didn't just come to send or pick up mail but to socialize. It was a place where people might run into and chat with friends or neighbors they hadn't seen in a while. Lenny was a very sympathetic listener, someone people felt they could confide in, and, as a result, no one had a better finger on the pulse of North Bay than Leonard Boyes.

Unfortunately, with his pock-scarred face, lank brown hair, and dark circles under his eyes, Lenny wasn't particularly handsome and had never married, but his easygoing manner, optimistic nature, and generosity with gossip had won him many friends.

Bending over the counter, Lenny studied the Ontario map fastidiously, silently sliding his tobacco-stained fingers back and forth, up and down, from one section to another.

"Okay," he said finally squinting up at Violet, tapping the eraser of his pencil on the map.

"So, we're lookin' for a town in Eastern Ontario, eh? And the town we're lookin' for begins with a *B*?"

"I think so . . . ," Violet confessed, biting her bottom lip, "but really, I'm not one hundred percent sure."

"Well, there's quite a few *B*s here, Violet, so let's just take a look."

"Okay, let's see," he pushed on. "There's a Belleville, Ontario," he prompted, straightening up and searching Violet's face.

Violet shook her head dismally, avoiding his eyes.

"No worries," he added quickly, bending over the map again, continuing his scrutiny, resuming his tapping.

"Yep, here's another one, Violet. How 'bout Bancroft?" He paused, leaning in, eyebrows raised.

"No, that doesn't sound right either. I'm so sorry to have troubled you, Lenny," she said quietly, pressing her fingers over her mouth, wishing she could fade into the background.

"Well now, don't go givin' up just yet, Violet," Lenny chastened but smiled kindly, revealing a cracked front tooth. "Let's see"—*tap, tap, tap*—"okay"—*tap, tap, tap*—"well now, here's another one, Brockville?"

"Brockville," Violet repeated the name quietly, tilting her head and squinting. "Yes. That's it! That's where William came from, Brockville."

Lenny smiled triumphantly.

At home in the evening's muted calm, Violet mulled over her situation. She had no family and no home to take the children back to. Her only option, despite never having met them, was to appeal to William's family for assistance. Doggedly, she wrote to tell them of his death and to ask for temporary refuge.

The next day, Violet asked Sarah to accompany her into town. Stopping first at the post office, Violet posted her letter to William's family, but Lenny waved off her attempt to pay him. That done, the two women walked behind the post office to the Pukaskwa administrative office to collect William's back pay and the balance in their account at the general store.

Fifty-two-year-old Amos Gallagher sat brooding at his desk, a ubiquitous cigar in his mouth that many joked was permanently attached to his mustache. His attempt to spring to his feet at their arrival was thwarted by the fact that his substantial bulk was crammed into his chair. At last, extricating himself, he greeted them effusively while motioning for them to be seated.

In truth, Violet had never trusted this self-satisfied, fleshy man with his hooded eyes and insouciant manner. She took a deep breath and explained why she had come.

Amos cleared his throat once, then again. "I'm sorry," he told Violet with a quick smile, "but there's no back pay coming to William and nothing in the store's account. Surely, you can't believe I would've kept a thing like that from you all this time?" He feigned distress and disbelief.

Violet flinched. She certainly hadn't anticipated this. "I don't . . . I don't understand what you mean," was all she could mumble.

Again, Amos cleared his throat theatrically, extracting the soggy cigar from his mouth.

"Well now, Violet, as you know, William got paid seventy-five cents a day. Every payday, after rent was deducted, the balance was deposited into your account at the general store. Whatever money was left in that account at the end of each month was returned to him in cash."

Violet's face was inscrutable.

"So, Violet." Amos shifted uncomfortably in his chair and tried again. "At the end of every month, your account at the general store was zeroed out, and William received whatever cash remained. So, you started fresh every month." He finished by stuffing the cigar back into his mouth, feeling self-satisfied, overconfident.

"Are you telling me that there is no money right now in our account?"

"That's correct," confirmed Amos, his facial muscles visibly relaxing now it appeared that Violet had finally grasped his meaning.

"And you're telling me that William has no pay coming?"

"Correct."

"How can that be?"

Emotional women always unnerved Amos, and sweat was already collecting in his armpits, staining his freshly laundered shirt.

"Well, William signed a new contract renewing his lease with us every year," he explained, making a show of unclasping the green ledger on his desk and flipping to the last page.

"And?"

"Well, as you know, he's paid only for the days he works. You were sick for almost three weeks in February. He stayed at home for two of those weeks. So, on the last day of February his pay was nine dollars."

"Only nine dollars," she repeated incredulously. "But that's not . . ."

Feeling beleaguered, Amos leaned back in his chair, crossed his arms over his chest, and tried to loosen his collar. His mouth was dry as dust and his cheeks flushed, but he pushed ahead.

"After deducting the rent, three dollars went into your account at the general store."

"The rent?"

"Yes. You rent your cabin for six dollars a month." He waited for a reply, but Violet remained taciturn.

"So," he continued, "that was February. In March, William worked the entire month and he cashed out your account at the end of the month. But William only worked nine days in April before his accident. So, his pay for those nine days was six dollars and seventy-five cents, and after deducting the rent, well, there was just nothing left to put into your account. I'm terribly sorry, Violet."

From the corner of her eye, Sarah saw Violet falter but managed to grab her before she slid completely to the floor. With Amos's help, Sarah hoisted Violet back into the chair, and Amos bolted in search of water.

Returning with a glass of water, he plopped back into his chair, relieved to see that Violet's eyes were open. Resting her head on the chair's leather back, she appeared lost in thought. Placing the glass on his desk, Amos did the only thing he could do. He waited.

Finally, Violet, her face the color of ash, turned to face him. "Tell me the truth, Amos," she insisted, her voice flat and lifeless, "no matter how much you think it might hurt me." She paused and swallowed. "Was there ever a month, a *single* month in the past five years that you did not return some cash to my husband?"

Amos took a deep, pained breath and shut his eyes. He was so dumbfounded by her question that he pretended to study the open ledger before retreating to the window behind her to stare at the street outside. What was she really asking?

Was it possible that William had acted so dishonorably and reprehensively? Now, when Amos glanced at Violet's drained face, he understood how completely shattered and disgraced she must be and how doomed her family was.

When he finally found his voice, he turned to face her, and his reply was muffled and contrite. "No, Violet," he mumbled, avoiding her eyes, "there was always cash left over at the end of every month." He paused a long while, then asked, "You didn't know, did you?"

"No, Amos," she whispered as her cheeks and neck reddened and her eyes started to tear, "I never knew."

The next morning, after sending the children off to school, Sarah brewed a strong pot of coffee and, pot in hand, crossed the lane. She found Violet curled up on the bed still wearing yesterday's clothes and shoes so the bedding was caked with mud.

"Here," she said, firmly handing Violet a steaming cup of coffee. "Look, Vi," she said kindly, "you need to get this off your chest and out into the open. It's clear as day that something Amos told you yesterday unnerved you. I'm here to listen. I'd never judge you."

Violet didn't think she had the strength to tell such a shameful story, but once she began, she couldn't stop.

"Oh, Sarah, we had such a good life in Quebec! My parents adored the children and they were so kind to William. Their house was warm and roomy and full of liveliness. But for some reason, William didn't want to be there—and his unhappiness spread like mold.

"One day, he saw some kind of advertisement about Pukaskwa Logging in the post office. He became convinced that he could make his fortune out here and give us a better life. But we already had a wonderful life, Sarah. I was such a fool. He wasn't thinking about me or the children. We didn't need a better life, William needed it.

"He talked about it relentlessly, we argued endlessly, and finally he wore me down, I admit it. I simply gave up. My children have suffered and will continue to suffer because of my weakness. We sacrificed everything so William could chase a dream.

"God forgive me! I denied my own children the smallest pleasures. I did everything I could to save money so we could leave this dreadful place. They've never worn new clothes. I fed them whatever canned goods Gallagher's had on sale. Even bought day-old bread. The only fresh food they've ever tasted was from our garden."

"You loved them, Vi," Sarah retorted, "and kept them safe. It's our duty to follow our husbands. Do you think there's any woman in this camp who wants to live here? You did what was expected of you. We're women, that's what we do."

"No, you're wrong, Sarah," she argued. "I didn't protect my children like I was supposed to. Did I ever ask William what he earned?

No. Did I ever ask him how much we had in savings, after all my penny-pinching? No. Did I ever ask him when we'd be able to leave? No."

Sarah's bafflement showed on her face, but before she could say anything, Violet continued.

"In Quebec, William told me he could earn ninety cents a day here. You heard Amos yesterday—William made only seventy-five cents a day. William lied about that, and when he assured me that housing was going to be provided, he never mentioned that we would have to pay for it. He deceived me for years.

"But that's not even the worst! My husband never saved one dime for us! He took that cash from Amos at the end of . . . every . . . single . . . month. Cash that was leftover because I had denied our children new clothes, shoes that fit them, even toys. It's unforgivable!" she cried, snorted in disgust, and fell back onto the bed, sobbing while Sarah held her hand.

Cloaked in grief and shame, the family left North Bay two days later on April 27, 1862, silently boarding the post office stage coach. Just as the stage was pulling out, Amos Gallagher came dashing around the corner, his large waistcoat flapping behind him. Winded and flushed, he yanked open the stage door and pushed a small envelope into Violet's hand. "I'm so sorry, Violet. Good luck."

This time the stage took them to Mattawa Pier on the Ottawa River. From there a small passenger steamer took them slowly through a series of canals to Ottawa. In Ottawa, Violet booked passage on the Ottawa-Brockville Railway, and when they finally pulled into the Brockville station, a perfectly brilliant, spotlessly clean May afternoon welcomed them. They sat on benches, enjoying the bustle of a town so much larger than North Bay while they waited over an hour to be picked up.

With growing concern, the stationmaster who had watched them disembark approached them. "Ma'am, may I help you?" he asked, removing his navy-and-gold cap and tucking it under his elbow.

Violet smiled timidly. "We're waiting for the Alysworths. They're expecting us. Do you know them?"

"Yes, ma'am, I do," he said quickly, but Violet saw something more than just recognition flash in his eyes. "I haven't seen them today though—least not here. And I would notice because they don't come into town that much."

"Well," Violet replied airily, "it's probably just a misunderstanding. How far away is the Alysworths' farm, would you say?"

"It's a ways, ma'am, 'bout three or four miles. It's the first homestead on the right. I could hire you a wagon if you'd like?"

"No, thank you," Violet replied quickly, worried about spending any more money.

With the sun warming their faces and lifting their spirits, Violet, Francois, and Miranda started out. The slightly raised dirt road was dusty, but here and there they came upon delightful clusters of hardy oaks just starting to leaf out and sometimes in the damper places, a few graceful birches. Violet loved the hopeful, promising color of new leaves. *New life, new beginnings*, she thought.

When they reached a plank bridge over a wide creek bed, they stopped to rest. Francois and Miranda chased each other up and down the creek bed and back and forth across the bridge. Violet didn't worry. The water, this early in the season, was barely a trickle.

"Miranda! Francois! Let's get moving!" she called finally.

"Are we almost there, Mama?" Miranda asked cheerfully.

"I really don't know, Mira. We're at least halfway there, maybe more."

"Why didn't they come to meet us, Mama?"

"I don't know that either," she replied, but, in her heart, she began to feel that something was amiss.

"Will there be boys my age there?" asked Francois, swinging the satchel back onto his shoulder.

"I don't know, Francois," she replied wearily, her agitation increasing. Again, she had a sinking feeling.

She scrutinized her children as they walked side by side in front of her. Miranda, now ten, was still painfully thin, awkward, and shy. Francois, like most boys his age, was full of bravado and biting sarcasm, and lately, a sad expression followed him like a shadow.

Francois cheered as he spotted a farmhouse in the distance. As they got closer, they could make out a two-story square-log house, a small barn, an enclosed paddock, and a henhouse—or maybe it was a rabbit hutch.

When they reached the sagging, barely attached front gate, they turned off the town road and followed a long, narrow, grassless lane up to the farmhouse. A front porch ran the entire length of the house at least six feet deep, but it was surprisingly empty—no benches or chairs inviting anyone to sit and rest. An untidy pile of firewood had been dropped under the windows on either side of the front door.

Some of the larger foundation stones had fallen out over time and still lay on the ground below the gaps they'd left behind. Sections of railing were missing and the mortar between the logs was deteriorating, especially around the windows.

It was almost seven thirty in the evening when Violet timidly knocked on the front door. A short, ruddy-faced, squared-off woman in her late fifties, presumably Mrs. Alysworth, opened the front door.

"Hello," Violet said, smiling meekly, "I'm Violet, William's wife. I wrote you . . . and these are our children, Miranda and Francois. Thank you for taking—"

"I'm Bridgette," the woman interrupted gruffly. Her greasy, blond hair was pulled into a loose bun, revealing the coarsened, sunburned skin on her neck. She was barefoot and wore an ill-fitting dark dress.

"Follow me," she said, stepping away from the door.

The door opened into one large room—a kitchen on one side and a sitting room on the other. The wide floorboards were grooved and faded with age. Oil lamps attached to wall brackets had not yet been lit, so the rooms were washed in dull, pearly light.

A pine table with mismatched chairs sat in the center of the kitchen. Faded cupboards and open shelves, crammed with an assemblage of metal tins and paper sacks, hung on both sides of a west-facing window.

Even at dusk, the view from that window was glorious—suffused in the softly spreading pinks of the setting sun. A substantial but unkempt garden could be seen in the foreground, beyond which were several previously furrowed acres now choked with weeds. Furthest away, some gently rounded, reddish hills slid all the way to the horizon.

An obsolete pot-bellied stove was positioned against the back wall, a scuffed copper kettle straddling its burners. As a reminder of more prosperous times, a delicately carved cabinet the color of warm buttermilk with its original seeded glass panes sat regally under the front window.

The living room's centerpiece, a round, mahogany game table with beautifully carved legs, stood near a window flanked by carved, high-back, mahogany chairs. The craftsmanship was superb and, like the buttermilk cabinet, hinted at better days.

Bridgette led them down a hallway at the back of the kitchen. It appeared that, at some point, a windowless lean-to had been added behind the kitchen. Shadows chased each other on the wall as an overhanging lamp swung from its hook. Two piles of straw, pillows, and two blankets lay on the floor.

"The kids can stay in here for now. Your room's down here," Bridgette said to no one in particular.

Like ducklings, they followed her to another room, where a needle of light pierced a single pane of a small window, the remaining three panes having been carelessly boarded over. To Violet's relief, this room had a door.

A rusty spring bed stood pressed against one wall, a thin mattress lay over the springs, and a sheet, a blanket, and a pillow were left in a pile at the foot of the cot.

"You'll have to make your own beds. I don't have time to wait on you three."

Miranda was the first to speak. "Where's the washroom?" she asked.

"Outhouse's in back. You can wash up at the kitchen sink. Bucket's next to the stove. Don't think I'm gonna be haulin' water for you."

"No, of course not," was all Violet could think to say.

"You missed dinner," Bridgette announced irritably. "We eat at six thirty here. I left bread and tea on the kitchen table."

She left them without another word. Her thickly calloused feet climbed the stairs to an upstairs bedroom—each stair sagging and groaning under her weight.

Violet leaned heavily against the wall, her exhaustion evident. Miranda steered her to the bed. "Here, Mama, lie down, rest a bit. Francois and I will get settled, then we'll bring in some tea."

Back in the lean-to, Francois plopped down on his makeshift bed but quickly jumped back up. "We can't sleep here—the straw's damp."

"Go sit with Mama then. I'll be right there."

Miranda found her way back to the kitchen, lit the lamp, found a bag of loose tea, and opened cabinets until she found three cups. When the kettle was steaming, she poured hot water into a teapot, added fresh tea, and carried it with the cups and bread back to her mother's room.

"Here, the tea will warm us. We'll all sleep in here tonight. In the morning, we'll sort it all out."

They woke slowly the next morning, unsure of the time but sore, hungry, and dispirited. From the kitchen they could hear Bridgette rummaging through cupboards and moving back and forth, but when they entered, nothing much in the way of food had actually been prepared.

A man, presumably William's brother, Jean, sat slumped in a chair, his rough hands gripping a steaming cup. He eyed them suspiciously as they sat down.

He seemed tall—a wiry man with muscular arms and arrogant, inhospitable eyes. His fingernails and coveralls were grimy, as was the limp, dirty kerchief tied around his neck. Violet thought he bore no resemblance to William at all.

"So," he snorted, "you're William's family, eh?" His voice was sonorous and mocking.

"Never laid eyes on you three before—or him since he went up north. Seems little brother didn't want to stay on the farm with his family. He wanted that big money up north. Guess that didn't work out, eh? Look at you all, not a pot to piss in. Scrawnier than our chickens."

He and Bridgette laughed heartily.

Bridgette poured anemic tea into the cups she'd set in front of their chairs. Then she scraped two greasy fried eggs onto Jean's plate, adding a slice of bread she'd toasted over the fire. Without another word, Jean began shoveling bits of egg into his mouth and swabbing the plate with his bread.

Miranda and Francois watched mesmerized as a rivulet of golden yolk ran down his chin, congealing in the considerable stubble on his face. Bridgette scraped the last egg onto her own plate and sat down. Violet stared at her in disbelief.

"I'm nobody's maid," Bridgette announced belligerently, throwing a defiant look at her husband. "You make your own breakfasts."

Violet, looking frightened and small, sank deeper into her chair and stared into her tea as if some answers lay at the bottom. Francois looked confused. Finally, Miranda stood. "Are there any more eggs?" she asked.

"I didn't have time to collect any this mornin'," a stone-faced Bridgette replied. "Don't know why I'm supposed to be cookin' for three more," she complained. "You ain't *my* family. How'm I supposed to do my own chores and wait on you three?"

Bridgette, it was becoming clear, was a woman unconcerned with the social niceties.

"What's wrong with you people?" Francois shouted, losing his temper. "You knew we were coming. Ma just lost her husband, we lost our father, your brother. We've traveled for days and days. We had to walk from the station carrying our bags because no one was there to meet us."

Francois knew he should stop, but the grief and fury of the past months overtook him. "Our rooms are dirty, the straw's damp, the blankets are soiled. If you didn't want us to come, why didn't you just say so?"

Violet stared at him in alarm. "Francois! I'm sorry, Jean, my son is tired and hungry—it was a dreadfully long journey. He has forgotten his manners and your kindness in taking us in."

Jean gulped the last of his tea and looked slowly from one to the other. "So, you don't find our accommodations to your liking?" he asked sarcastically with a smirk.

"Think I care that you're William's family? You think me and Bridgette has some obligation to take you in? William always thought he was better than us—he was above farmin'. You wanna stay here? You wanna roof over your head and food in your bellies? Fine, but you ain't gonna freeload offa us. As long as you're here, you'll earn your keep."

With this, he flashed an angry look to his wife. "And here's how it's gonna be. The boy here will help me in the fields. The girl'll carry water and tend the garden out back. And you"—he pointed at Violet menacingly—"you'll do laundry and clean this place up.

"Bridgette, you'll make breakfast and dinner for all of us from now on. And I don't wanna hear no complaints from anyone of you or

I'll take my belt to you," he threatened, and there was no doubt in anyone's mind that he would.

"Boy"—he pointed at Francois—"you grab that bread for our lunch and follow me." Jean opened the front door, glaring at Francois, who stood silently and followed him out.

Bridgette grabbed the water bucket from the side of the stove and handed it to Miranda. "We need lots of water every day, so you better make sure we don't run out. When you're finished, shovel some manure from the pile near the barn and turn it into the garden soil. We'll start planting in a week, and I want that whole garden fertilized by then."

"You," she said, sharply turning to Violet, "start washing the windows and floors in the kitchen and don't skimp on the soap or elbow grease. I'll start takin' down the curtains for you to wash."

At the end of the day when Jean and Francois returned from the fields, the kitchen was spotless. Bridgette had prepared a supper of canned beans, rice, and thin, sticky cornbread. She heaped Jean's plate first and then her own before pushing the skillet over to her guests. Violet divided what remained evenly but knew her children would still be hungry at the end of this meal.

After a strained silence, Violet asked, "Are William's parents still alive? I understand that this was their farm."

"Dead, both of them," Jean replied accusingly. "William shoulda kep' in touch better."

Looking Jean in the eye for the first time, Violet asked, "So your parents left the farm to you?"

"Like I said," Jean replied coolly, "William shoulda kep' in touch."

Violet decided to change the subject. "As you might imagine, Jean, we've had a long, dusty journey. We would like to take baths before going to bed. What do you use as a tub?"

"We don't have no tub," Bridgette replied, rising to put the dishes into the sink.

Violet ignored her and continued to stare at Jean, who finally said, "You can use the metal tub in the barn." When Bridgette started to protest, he flashed her a look that silenced her immediately.

"One other thing, Jean," she continued. "The children need proper beds. The straw is damp as is the floor because their room has no window."

"Bridgette'll see to it," he replied, flapping his hand in dismissal, and with that, he left the table and headed upstairs.

It took Francois an hour to haul and boil enough water to fill the tub, while Miranda and Violet scoured and rinsed it three times before being satisfied that it was clean. For privacy, they set the tub in Violet's room. By ten o'clock, all had bathed, and while they felt better having removed the dust and grime, they were still famished.

The three of them worked ten-hour days, six days a week. It was backbreaking and humiliating work with few opportunities for conversation because they were rarely together except at mealtimes and Jean preferred to eat in silence.

Painfully aware that they were no better than indentured servants, both children resented their mother's decision to bring them here and, worse, her insensible resignation to make the best of it, but most of all they were furious at her failure to protect them. If she noticed the welts on Francois's arms and back or Miranda's red face and swollen eyes, she said nothing.

Chronically fatigued, hungry, and afraid, both children would be scarred from living in such an abusive environment and would struggle with feelings of inadequacy, trepidation, and helplessness for the rest of their lives.

In May, 1863 nearly a year after their arrival, everything changed, although the morning started out like every other. As always, everyone ate breakfast quickly and silently, but when Jean finished, he cleared his throat instead of leaving the table immediately, as was his custom. Alarm spread quickly as everyone braced for one of his verbal assaults or worse.

"So," he announced in an almost pleasant tone, though his attempt at a smile more resembled a smirk. "Last year was a better year. We grew more and sold more." Jutting his chin out and rocking his chair onto its back legs, he scanned each face with exaggerated casualness.

"So yesterday," he continued quickly, trying to hold his excitement in check, "I went to the bank and took a loan for a new tractor!"

Still no one made a sound.

"Even settled our account at the general store," he boasted.

He paused and looked around, but no one had anything to say and he could feel his face getting hot.

"And still had some money left, so, since we all worked, I divided it evenly between us," he announced magnanimously.

"But," he quickly corrected himself, "first I deducted for the rooms and food Bridgette and me provided you three—then I divided it evenly." Jean made a show of fishing in his coverall pocket, pulling out some surprisingly dirty bills, and passing them to Francois, who sat closest to him.

Without looking at them, Francois quietly passed them to his mother, who did look—seventy-two dollars. Jean waited expectantly, but still Violet said nothing.

"Starting today, Bridgette'll take the girl with her when she goes to market—teach her what to do. After a couple weeks, the girl can go alone."

Immediately, Bridgette's face resembled a thundercloud. "Don't get no ideas 'bout holdin' back money either," she snarled at Miranda. "I been doin' this for years, so don't think I don't know exactly what we make on market days."

Jean, who had convinced himself that Bridgette would be pleased to have more time for herself, was confused by her reaction and then annoyed by her lack of enthusiasm. It seemed that nobody appreciated what he had done.

"Let's get to work," Jean growled as he rose and headed for the door, Francois in tow.

"No!"

Jean and Francois stopped with the door half open. Bridgette and Miranda stopped piling dishes in the sink. Violet rose slowly from her chair, stepped behind it, and straightened to her full height.

"No," she repeated simply.

"What are you jabbering about, Violet?" demanded Jean, calling her by name for the first time.

"The money," she replied flatly, her eyes the color of river stones, "it's not enough."

"What the hell!" he started to object, but Violet's raised hand silenced him.

"Who are we, Jean? Because if we're family, it's a custom, some would even say an obligation, for family to help one another in bad times, and that's why I asked for your help. You are my husband's brother, his only surviving relative and, unhappily, mine as well.

"We never intended to be, as you feared, freeloaders. We fully expected to share your workload, to help make your lives a bit easier in return. You have just told us that the farm was more prosperous last year, so we have succeeded, at least a little, and that pleases me. But we did expect to be treated fairly. So, it's unacceptable for you to hold back any portion of what is fairly due us for what you call our 'rooms and food.'"

He tried to speak, but his mouth was too dry.

"But, if we aren't family," she continued, "then we're just farm laborers and you're obliged to pay us a fair wage. William told me that your father paid seasonal laborers sixty-five cents a day. The three of us have worked six days a week for a year. Done everything you told us to do without complaint. Seventy-two dollars is absolutely unacceptable. It's not enough."

Francois, Miranda, and Bridgette stood frozen in place, hardly breathing. Jean looked stunned; his mouth gaped. Violet stared at him, waiting.

Jean felt everyone's eyes on him. *That ungrateful bitch*, he thought, but simultaneously her argument revealed an intellect and a courage he'd not expected—certainly not in a woman.

As he dug new post holes all morning, he replayed the scene over and over in his mind, becoming more furious each time. She'd challenged his authority. He had a score to settle.

Violet washed and dried the breakfast dishes, then heated buckets of water so she could wash Francois's and Miranda's dirty clothes. She washed them gently because they were so worn and rinsed them carefully before hanging them outside to dry.

Next, she stripped their beds of the sheets and blankets that hadn't been changed for almost a year—blankets she'd made from scraps of cloth when they lived in the logging camp. Adding more hot water and soap, she scrubbed furiously and rinsed them twice before the water ran clear. She hoped the children would be pleasantly surprised to have fresh-smelling, clean linens to sleep on.

Once more, she carried a heavy load of wet sheets and blankets out to the clothesline and began to hang them. As she hoisted and pinned one end of a wet blanket to the clothesline, she was grabbed from behind and lifted completely off the ground. At the same time, a rough leather glove clamped over her mouth.

Panicking, she twisted her body, but because her feet weren't on the ground, she couldn't get any leverage. The arm around her waist tightened, she could barely take a deep breath, and her screams were so muffled by the glove that only she could hear them.

Without a word, she was thrown to the ground, her face rammed into the softened earth until she feared she would suffocate. Suddenly, he was on top of her, the impact forcing the remaining air out of her lungs and pinning her arms to her sides. She felt her bloomers being ripped and her legs forced apart.

She tried once more to twist away, to strike back, to take a deep breath, but something hard and solid slammed into the side of her head. The pain was excruciating; she saw flashes of brilliant light and finally, thankfully, nothing.

When she regained consciousness, she didn't know where she was, why she was lying on the ground, or why her vision was blurred. Each time she tried to raise her head, a spasm of pain took her breath away. She lay there for a while, thinking, breathing, waiting for her vision to clear.

Finally, one hand gingerly swept the ground around her and felt the laundry basket next to her. Yes, she remembered, she had been hanging laundry, and then from the chafing and savage burning between her thighs, she knew what had happened, knew who had raped her. Didn't have to see his face—the stink of manure on his glove, his foul breath, and the heavy scent of chewing tobacco were all too familiar.

For the very first time since their arrival, Violet allowed herself to feel the full terror of the truth she'd tried so hard to keep hidden. All of them, but especially her children, were not and never would be safe here.

When Bridgette and Miranda returned in the late afternoon, Bridgette, the ubiquitous malcontent, asked Miranda, "Why's that wet laundry still in the basket? You'd better get it hung."

When Miranda knocked on her mother's door before supper, Violet called out that she was sick. "I'll be fine in the morning," she assured her daughter, "but I don't feel like eating. Please check in on me after supper."

Both children knew something dreadful had happened when they opened the door to their mother's bedroom after dinner. A putrid smell assaulted them. Their mother's face was the color of ash, her voice frail, and her pillowcase soaked with blood.

"Mother, oh my God, what happened? Who . . ." Francois was frantic.

Violet put her finger to her lips. "Close the door. Come sit by me," she whispered. Realizing that she could barely see them, that she was nearly blind, Violet knew immediately what had to be done.

Even in the dimly lit bedroom, Miranda and Francois could see the reddish- purple bruises on Violet's arms. The left side of her face was badly scraped, her nose was swollen, her left eye looked cloudy, and her hair was sticky with barely clotted blood.

"I have something to tell you, and I want you to listen carefully. Don't say anything until I finish. There isn't much time."

Without a word, both children sat gingerly on the edge of her bed.

"I'm ashamed that I brought you to this hideous place. I'm ashamed every day when I see how cruelly you are treated. I'm ashamed that I didn't try harder to support us myself—there might have been another way, perhaps someone else would have helped us."

Violet's tears spilled over and ran down her face. "But until today, I didn't see how impossible things were—how unsafe we are here, how evil these people are. Please, Francois. Please Miranda, forgive me."

Francois tried to speak, but she silenced him with her hand. Her eyes were glazed, and she turned her face to the wall to avoid their stares. With a stronger voice, she continued, "I'm responsible for this and I will make this right. You will do exactly what I tell you . . . exactly."

"If we stay here, we'll all die. I am absolutely sure of this. You must believe me and don't ask questions. We must all leave and you must leave first. Tonight."

"But Mama, where can we go? How? We have nothing, we're trapped." Miranda's despair was heart-wrenching.

Finally Francois spoke, his sarcasm and bitterness undisguised.

"But Mira, you're forgetting our recent windfall. We have seventy-two dollars! Did he do this to you, Mama?"

Violet pulled her blanket tighter and shivered, although the room was quite hot.

"Francois, that is not important right now. Yes, I understand what you want to do, what you think you must do, but I need you to take our revenge in another way."

"Mama, what do you want me to do?" he asked, his eyes wide with fear.

"This morning I washed your clothes. Heat some water and bathe. Put on the clean clothes, pack everything else into your suitcases. When you're certain that Jean and Bridgette are asleep, leave this house..."

She stopped to catch her breath and tried desperately to hide the searing pain in her head and the fact that she could no longer see them.

"Walk as quickly as you can into town. Go to the train station and buy a ticket for the very next train going north. I hear train whistles after dark almost every night, so there must be late-night trains running from Brockville all the way to Montreal," she said. "Francois, there is a small packet in the lining of my winter coat."

Francois lifted her coat from the wall hook, felt for the packet, and pulled out a tight roll of bills. "Mama, this is much more than seventy-two dollars. Where did you get this?"

"I saved every penny I got for Mother's china and Grandmother's silver. Mr. Gallagher and Sarah gave me some money when we left North Bay. But mostly, I stole it."

"What!" Miranda and Francois spoke at once, alarmed.

"It's a long story which we don't have time for now. Something Bridgette said at breakfast made me suspect that she takes a little bit for herself on market days. So, as soon as she left for market and before I started the laundry, I went into her room. I found money hidden in a false drawer of her dresser and in the lining of her Sunday hat. I took most of it. After Jean insulted us this morning with seventy-two dollars, I felt we deserved it. When Bridgette notices that the money's gone, she can't complain to Jean because she stole it from him.

"But Mama," Miranda protested, but her mother silenced her.

"Don't stop until you get to Montreal. It's a big city. Find yourselves a small, out-of-the-way place to stay. Leave a note with the stationmaster telling me where you're staying. Use my maiden name, LaFleur. I doubt Jean knows it."

"This is crazy, Mama!" Miranda was openly sobbing now.

"Yes, it's a desperate plan, Mira. If I'm still here, Jean will assume you'll be coming back. Which is why you need to be careful and secretive. I've held back enough money to take the train and find you—don't worry about that.

"Now start getting ready. I need to rest. When you're ready for bed, come and wake me—we'll say our good-byes then. One last thing, but it's important . . . when you get to Montreal, wait three days for me and not a day longer. Promise me, you'll wait there only three days before moving on."

Both children nodded solemnly. "Good," Violet whispered.

Neither Miranda nor Francois spoke. They did what they were told to do, and they came in to say their good-byes at bedtime. The three of them hugged, but none of them spoke for a long while. Finally, Violet said quietly, "I've failed you both. I love you both. Promise me you'll do exactly as I said."

They nodded, hugged her one last time, and went to their room, where they waited, fully dressed. When the house was silent and Francois could hear Jean snoring, he signaled his sister. They walked quietly, carrying their shoes to the front door, put them on, and gently closed the door behind them.

Violet heard them stop at the front door and held her breath. She wanted desperately to hold them close one last time, but it was too dangerous. She had no choice. Then she heard the front door close and they were gone.

With tears streaming down her cheeks and fresh blood still oozing from her head wound, she prayed, "Please Lord, keep them safe and please forgive me."

Though the May night was cold, beads of sweat formed on Francois's upper lip, his heart raced, and he felt light-headed with anxiety. Pulling off his heavy wool cap, he passed it to his sister, who was shivering. Silently, Miranda pulled it on, tucking her hair underneath and tightening her mother's quilt around her neck. Without his cap, Francois's wiry hair stood on end, his ears, always too large for his narrow face, now seemed enormous, and his brown eyes, once hidden by the brim, blinked rapidly.

Four years older but barely taller than his sister, Francois wore his dead father's overcoat, which, although definitely too long, fit him perfectly across the shoulders. As a consequence of the past year's forced servitude, he was muscular and strong, but his uncle's chronic abuse had broken his sensitive spirit. Now hypervigilant and morose, he was as alert and inscrutable as a soldier on guard.

While he pretended to appear confident and mature, Francois was, in truth, naïve, socially awkward, and much too young to be responsible for the safety of his sister—after all, he was only fifteen. But he'd promised his dying mother revenge and, despite the cruel circumstances of their lives so far, both siblings held fast to their father's assurances that a better life was their destiny.

Miranda, unfortunately, inherited her father's predilection for wishful thinking and his exaggerated sense of self. Despite the family's complete lack of ancestral pedigree, she was convinced that she was fated to become a lady of substance and importance, a woman respected in her community. Always convinced of the rightness of her beliefs, she thoroughly disapproved of this escape plan, and Miranda was never one to suffer in silence.

Although the narrow path was well trod, both stumbled often on its uneven surface. By day, the sun softened the earth, and by late afternoon, shallow imprints of work boots, wagon wheels, and livestock chronicled the farm's activities. The cold night air, however, stiffened those impressions forcing the siblings to step slowly and tentatively. It took them nearly twenty minutes to reach the front gate, which stood, as it had when they'd arrived a year ago, suspended by a single rusted hinge.

Finally, they turned left onto the town's dirt road leading into Brockville and the train that would carry them to freedom, but it too was badly rutted. Francois knew it would continue to be slow going but was grateful for the feeble illumination of the night's thin wafer of moon.

"I can't see, Francois. You're going too fast!" Miranda cried out, splitting the silence. Her voice quivered, and from under the brim of Francois's cap, her eyes were wide with panic.

Francois flinched and stopped. He knew Miranda couldn't possibly appreciate the danger of their undertaking, but he did. At any moment, they might be detected and returned to servitude, but, much worse, Mama would pay most dearly if their escape failed. As if emulating his foreboding, clouds began to drape the wispy moon, and as brother and sister stood side by side, the night folded in on them like an ominous, dark wall.

"Mira, you know we can't stop now," he said firmly. "Uncle will be up in a few hours. If I'm not sitting at the kitchen table, he'll come looking for me. We've got to get to town and on the train before he wakes."

"But I can't see, Francois! It's pitch black. I keep tripping and I'm really cold," she whimpered.

"I'm cold too, Mira, but we'll be warm on the train," he promised, regretting his earlier curtness. Squatting next to her, he slowly placed her right boot into a wagon rut that ran along the side of the road.

"Here," he said, coaxing her, "keep your boot in this groove, just slide it along. It's the wagon wheel's track from Bridgette's trip to market this morning, so it will lead us right into town."

"I can't," she snapped, placing her hands defiantly on her hips. "This isn't a good idea! I'm cold and tired. We need to turn back." Miranda was never easily appeased and, in truth, had always been a bit of a whiner, complaining about every little ache or inconvenience.

"I know. It's hard," he said, struggling to be sympathetic—knowing that he needed to if he wanted her to cooperate.

"Here, take my quilt. Just keep your foot in that rut. Now, you can be the leader. I'll follow you." Without waiting for her reply, Francois quickly fell in behind her, rested a hand on her shoulder, and firmly pushed her forward.

Her early attempts were awkward and spasmodic, but eventually they became smoother and more rhythmic. An hour into their escape, it started to rain—a steady, cold spring rain that quickly saturated their quilts and overcoats. As the road became spongy, mud sucked at their boots, Miranda lost her balance, fell with a thud, and screamed.

"Francois, that's it! We have to turn back, right now! I'm sorry. I know I promised Mama but . . ." She struggled to regain her footing, but her overcoat and hands were stuck in mud. Openly weeping now, her tears mingled with the rain streaming down her face.

"We can't turn back," he told her unapologetically, offering her his arm to help her stand. He was determined to ignore her distractions and focus on what he could do or say to overcome her objections and fear.

"Yes, we can!" Miranda shouted defiantly and would have stomped her feet but thought she'd probably lose a boot in the gelatinous mud. "Look," she said confidently, "we'll go back. Wait 'til Mama's better so she can come with us. Wait for the full moon and next time we'll bring a lantern from the barn. It'll be easier, Francois, and I promise I won't complain even once."

Francois was chilled, soaked through, and exasperated. His mother's instructions had been absolute. Miranda was his responsibility now; it was his job to keep her safe. He couldn't reveal that their mother was never going to join them and was, by now, probably dead. He had to find a way to keep Miranda moving, and he had to appear calm and patient.

"Mira, how far was the bridge?" he asked calmly.

"What? What bridge?"

"The bridge over Buell's Creek. You know the plank bridge over the creek. You cross it every time you go to town with Bridgette—it's the only one."

"Oh . . . yeah," she replied warily. "What do you mean 'how far'?"

"On your trip to market this morning, when the wagon passed over the plank bridge, did it seem that you were closer to town or to Uncle's farm? Think carefully! It's important."

"I don't know," she replied miserably but at least had stopped sniveling. "I don't know. What does it matter anyway? I just want to go back, Francois! Please, take me back."

Francois inhaled deeply, then exhaled slowly, forcing himself to speak more tenderly. "Because," he explained, squeezing his eyes shut, "if the gully under the bridge is dry, and it should be this early in the spring, we can rest under the bridge until the rain stops. We'll be safer there off the road and warmer."

He couldn't judge her reaction in the darkness. *If I'm not more forceful*, he thought miserably, *she's going to stop and whine every half hour.*

In a determined voice, more contrived than real, he added, "Miranda, we're not going back. And we're not stopping until we get to that bridge. We're wasting precious time." And without meaning to, he shoved her forward—hard.

She stumbled and almost fell again. "Well," she yelled, jabbing his chest with her index finger, "you can go on if you want, but I'm going back. You don't tell me what to do. If Papa were here—"

"But Papa isn't here!" he snorted, spittle forming at the side of his mouth. "And it's his fault that we're out here in the middle of the night in a damn rainstorm!"

Suddenly, Francois's head pounded with rage. He knew he should stop talking, right now, but his outrage propelled him forward.

"Papa left us with nothing, Mira." He spit the words out. "He forced us to leave Quebec, then dragged us to that awful camp. After he died, Mama found out he hadn't saved a penny for us. That's why we're servants now. I'm glad he's dead!"

Without turning to look at her, Francois strode ahead, his face burning with anger and shame. He couldn't look at his sister, so didn't see the incredulity on her small face or her beautiful gray eyes filling with tears again.

How could this possibly be Papa's fault? Miranda wondered in shock. *It just couldn't be Papa's fault. But why did Mama bring us to this awful place to live with such horrible people?*

Head down, Miranda plodded after her brother, so completely lost in thought that she felt neither waterlogged nor cold.

Ten minutes later, Francois realized from the sound of their footfalls that they'd reached the wooden bridge. Sliding down the gully, pulling his suitcase behind him, he inched under the wooden arch to find that, as he'd predicted, it was completely dry and discernibly warmer. Returning to the top, he took Miranda's suitcase and guided her under the bridge, where they sat on the ground, resting their backs against their suitcases.

"So now what?" Miranda asked, huddling next to him.

"We wait," Francois replied softly, putting an arm around her shoulder. "We wait and try to rest."

The rhythmic beat of the rain on the planks above them was

hypnotic. They were finally warm enough to remove their wet quilts and felt protected for the first time.

"Francois?" Miranda's voice was soft, her breathing quiet.

"What?"

"You're wrong about Papa," she murmured, and with her head pillowed by his arm, Miranda slid into sleep.

But Francois couldn't sleep—he needed to be vigilant now; he needed a plan. His thoughts eddied around him like dried leaves caught in a gust of wind. Resentment and rage brought bile to the back of his throat, but he forced it back down. There'd be time for that later. Right now he needed a clear head.

Maybe I'm wrong, he thought, his empty stomach growling. *Why did Mama bring us here? What did happen to Papa's money?* This was not the first time Francois struggled to make sense of the disastrous shift in their lives. And, in the end, what he could piece together—the "facts" as he saw them—were never enough. It was too bewildering and illogical, and with that thought, he too surrendered to sleep.

"Mira, wake up!" Francois shouted, shaking his sister roughly.

Begrudgingly, Miranda roused herself and stretched her arms over her head. "Ouch," she cried when her hands struck the underside of the bridge. She was confused. It was still very dark. She couldn't remember where she was.

"Mira!"

When she heard the alarm in her brother's voice, she remembered everything. "Francois, what's wrong?"

"I fell asleep. I didn't mean to. I can already see a hint of daylight. We have to hurry. The rain's stopped."

As he spoke, he pushed their suitcases out from under the bridge.

Slowly, painfully, he stood up, taking in deep gulps of cool, moist air. One by one he carried the suitcases up the slope.

Miranda used the side of the bridge to pull herself up the embankment. At the top Francois handed her a blue-and-white enamel cup which he'd filled with water from the creek.

"Bridgette's favorite cup," she said, smiling at him. "She'll be furious."

"Um, I suppose," he replied, but he was smiling too.

Francois dug around in his satchel and pulled out some bread. Pulling it apart, he handed the larger piece to his sister. "We'll eat as we walk."

The bridge was almost completely dry. A sliver of pink on the horizon welcomed them, and the sparrows cartwheeled across it to welcome a new day. The white ribbons of fog had disappeared, but the air was still softly moist against their faces.

Neither could make out much in the distance yet, but the road in front of them was clearly visible. Francois guessed, from the light on the horizon, that they had an hour, maybe less, before Jean rose for chores.

"Mira, I don't want to frighten you, but we need to get to the station and board a train in the next hour. Jean and Bridgette will be up by then and . . ." His voice trailed off.

"I know. We promised Mama," Miranda replied morosely, gulping the last of her water and finishing her bread.

She began walking briskly, then jogging until she was exhausted. Francois followed her, admiring her tenacity despite her awkwardness.

Finally, over the sounds of their own gasping, they heard a train whistle so shrill it stopped them in their tracks. When they could hear the hissing steam engine, they knew the train was very close; they had to be on the outskirts of town.

Fighting to catch their breath, they stared at each other for a long moment.

"Mira, give me your suitcase. Take my satchel." Francois took a deep breath. "Ready?" he asked, looking directly at her.

Her anxieties temporarily at bay, Miranda nodded bravely.

They broke into a run.

3

A DIFFERENT DREAM

"Francois, breakfast's ready! The four-thirty bell rang a few minutes ago. I'm to be at St. Anne's by six-thirty."

Miranda and her brother, Francois, moved from town to town for years but finally stopped running when they reached Fall River, Massachusetts in August, 1869. They changed their surname, convinced it would reduce their chances of discovery and give them a fresh start. On the surface, assuming the new surname, Davis, seemed simple enough. It was easy to pronounce, easy to spell, easy to remember, and, most importantly, very American.

What followed was curious. Miranda who immediately entered nursing school began, cautiously at first, to speak to some of her nursing classmates. Instead of rushing home immediately after class, as had been her practice, she joined some of them for tea in the cafeteria. If they were surprised or puzzled by her uncharacteristic friendliness, they didn't mention it. In fact, Miranda soon learned that her classmates thought her "one of the smartest" and "sure to go places after graduation."

All of which led Miranda to feel something quite alien—in a word, hopeful. At seventeen, she was experiencing, for the very first time in her life, the effervescent camaraderie of having a "best" friend. Petite, seventeen-year-old Maddy Walker, with curly, coffee-colored hair and wide-set brown eyes, was the yin to Miranda's yang.

Maddy was an unapologetic average student. For her, nursing school was simply a means to an end. She didn't yearn to save lives or alleviate world suffering; she simply wanted a reliable job that would pay the rent.

Miranda, who did, in fact, experience a real calling to the profession, tried not to disparage her friend for this minor failing. Maddy was blessed with boundless enthusiasm and irrepressible self-confidence, she relished any sort of adventure, and had a vivid imagination.

By end of first year, they were inseparable—gossiping, studying, daydreaming—each one desperate for a future more generous and less ordinary than her past. They envisioned themselves wearing the sophisticated fashions pictured in the magazines Maddy "borrowed" from her mother's dress shop. Over endless cups of tea, they scrutinized every design and, with exuberance, attempted to incorporate some small detail into their own limited wardrobes.

They daydreamed about the handsome men they would meet, and naturally, their weddings would be the stuff of fairy tales: romantic, elaborate, gauzy affairs held in marble cathedrals crowded with preeminent people and enormous mounds of flowers. As for their lives after their weddings, there would be travel to exotic places, shopping in the fashion capitals of Europe, and summers in Narragansett or Newport mingling with fascinating, influential people. Miranda Davis and Maddy Walker spun these airy, meringue dreams so often that they began to seem almost possible.

As Miranda moved into young adulthood, her early experiences, unfortunately, had already shaped her character. At her core, she continued to believe that people generally cannot be trusted and, above all else, she needed to be independent, a woman of consequence, someone who would control her own destiny.

Sadly, and only when it was too late, Miranda would understand how these beliefs shackled her emotionally and ultimately robbed her of a fuller, more harmonious life.

But now, staring out her kitchen window and marveling at the view, she felt content. This time every morning, she watched, with a mixture of incredulity and disdain, as hundreds and hundreds of uniformly colorless people poured out into the street from row after row of identical triple-deckers. Sluggishly, like sleepwalkers, they let gravity pull them down to the ravenous mills along the river, where they labored and disappeared.

Without turning from the stove, Miranda listened to her brother's footsteps. She poured him a cup of tea from the steaming kettle, added three sugars, spooned some thin porridge into a bowl, and set both in front of him.

"You look ragged," she observed, making no effort to hide her disapproval.

She studied him. His frizzy hair, never an asset, was completely flattened on one side, which almost made her laugh out loud. Up until their early teens, she and Francois had been about the same height. Now he was almost six feet tall and towered over her—but he'd not gained a single pound. So, he still looked like a praying mantis—her nickname for him as a kid.

He was unshaven this morning, and, as usual, his fingernails were lined with the black, oily residue from the spinning machines. Miranda always thought her older brother handsome, though not so much this morning.

"You were out late last night," she remarked.

"Mm mm," was all he offered. Then, suddenly and uncharacteristically, he shoved the bowl of porridge at her so forcefully it nearly slid off the table.

"You know I hate this stuff, Miranda," he announced without looking up. "I want a proper breakfast. How can you eat this slop after what we went through?"

Miranda exhaled. "We eat it because it's cheap and filling. We eat it because we agreed to be careful with money. Though you're out three or four times a week spending it."

"It's my money, Mira. I work hard for it. And if I want to have a couple of beers with my pals after work, I will. It's not like you're bringin' in any money," he replied petulantly.

"Yes, it's your money, Francois. That's a fact. I'm in school three days a week and at the hospital two nights a week, plus every other Saturday. I do the shopping and cooking, the laundry and cleaning. Then I try to find time to study. I don't go out with my friends at night. In fact, I don't go out at all. So, I spend almost nothing on myself."

He held up his hand to make her stop. "Mira, I didn't mean to . . ." He laid his head on the tabletop. *Damn it*, he thought, *I didn't want this.* Although his head throbbed and his stomach balked, he was being unfair to his sister and he knew it.

She sighed. "I'm honestly tired of arguing about this. I don't work like you do, but I do work, Francois. I'm training to be a nurse. I only have a year left and then I'll have a real job too."

He wanted to nod in agreement, but his head was too heavy. "I know, I know," he replied, but the words were muffled by his arms.

Finally, with effort he raised his head. "You do more than your share, that's a fact. But I just don't get it, Mira," he said, squinting up at her. "Why are you wasting all this time in school and workin' for free? You know I could get you a good job at the mill anytime."

"Because I want to be more than a mill girl, that's why," she snapped and immediately felt remorse. "I want to be able to take care of myself and not have to rely on you—or anyone. Nursing is a profession, Francois. Hospitals are clean, safe places to work. Doctors are highly educated and respected."

"You think you're better than me, don't you? You think I'm just another dumb, immigrant mill worker?" He regretted this immediately and had no idea why he was so out of sorts this morning—well, aside from his hangover.

"Ah, come off it, Francois, you know that's not true." She pulled out a chair and sat.

"Mira, maybe I wanted something more too. Do you ever think of that? But the last of our money went for your schoolin'."

"God, Francois, don't go actin' like I took advantage of you, because I didn't! You swore you didn't mind spending the money on nursing school.

"If you didn't tell me the truth then, well, that's on you, isn't it? Why is it that in our family no one seems to know how to tell the truth? I'm so tired of lies and broken promises."

She watched as splotches the color of port appeared on his neck and cheeks.

"Mira," he said angrily, "I promised Mama that I'd take care of you. I didn't break that promise, did I? Far as I know, I haven't broken any promises to you or her."

With the mention of their mother, Miranda softened. She hadn't meant to hurt his feelings like this. "I'm sorry. Of course, you've taken good care of me. You're the only person I can trust in the whole world."

He studied her and concluded she hadn't changed much since they left the farm six years ago. She was still long limbed, thin as a beanpole, with blond hair and skin so pale you could see the tiny blue veins at her temples and across the bridge of her nose.

Then he remembered the dazzling smiles she'd been so generous with as a child. *Now*, he thought, *her forehead's almost permanently furrowed by her constant worrying.*

"Francois?" she asked quietly without turning around. "Do you ever wonder why our life has been so—"

"No! I don't think about the past. What's the point?"

"Why didn't anyone want us, Francois?" she asked as she turned to face him. "Why didn't our own parents love us?"

He refused to look at her.

"Maybe you're right," she continued. "Maybe it's a waste of time to try to figure it all out. It can't be changed. But I'm going to make something of myself. In spite of them, I'm going to make something of myself.

"I don't look down on you for working in the mills," she added sadly. "I know how hard you work, and I'll never, ever forget how you've taken care of me. I'll make it up to you. Once I finish school, I'll get a paying job and you can go back to school."

"Ah, it's too late for me, Mira. I'm pretty content with what I have—a steady job, good chums, roof over my head. Most chaps my age don't have all that."

She reached for the kettle, refilled his mug, and added more sugar. Then, she unwrapped the cheese sandwich she'd made for his lunch, put it on a plate, and slid it to him.

"Mira, you're wrong if you think Mama didn't love us."

"No, I'm not wrong about that," she snapped back. "We waited for her and she didn't come. Maybe she never meant to come. Maybe she started a new life without us."

"She's dead, Mira." There, he'd said it out loud for the first time. He'd carried it for far too long. Now, he was released from the crushing weight of it.

"What? I don't believe you."

"She's dead. He beat her and I think he raped her. That's why she sent us away so suddenly."

Miranda sat silently, almost calmly, remembering how she stood behind Francois in that dimly lit room with that awful smell. Mama was lying on the bed, something dark on her pillowcase and her nightdress. She was trying to say something to them, but her voice was so weak, her face twisted in pain.

Miranda could see the reddish-purple bruises on her mother's cheeks and arms, the angry red gash across the bridge of her nose, and her left eye blackened and swollen shut.

"He raped her?"

"And beat her, badly. The blood on her pillowcase was still fresh, still oozing from behind her ear—her hair was matted with it."

"But she told us she'd meet us . . ."

"I know, Mira. She just wanted us to leave and go to a safer place. She told me to take her revenge by leaving with the stolen money and starting a new life. She made me promise to look after you."

"Why didn't you ever tell me this before?"

"I didn't want you to shoulder any more pain."

"And now?"

"I watch you, Mira, still carrying so much pain inside. I thought maybe if you understood what happened, you could put the past behind you, finally let go of it."

"Thank you for telling me, Francois," she said softly.

He paused, "I didn't mean to tell you this way, but I'm glad you know. I'm sorry but I really need to go, I'm already late." He grabbed his old satchel and ran out the door.

She noticed the cheese sandwich untouched on a plate and regretted he'd have no lunch today. God, she wished Francois didn't have to work so hard. She wished he'd find other work. She loathed the Troy Mill—she loathed them all.

She'd brought him lunch once and would never forget it. Hundreds of pounding metal looms made conversation impossible. She was terrified of these howling machines with their bone-crushing gears and racing leather belts that could grab your hair or clothing in an instant.

Unbelievably, Francois seemed at home there, greeting this or that operator, slapping some of the men on the back. He proudly introduced her to his boss, Guido Wallabee, a stooped, graying man with a kind, creased face who spoke with an accent. He seemed so pleased to meet her and shook her hand firmly in both of his. This man clearly admired her brother but, for some reason, called him Frank.

God, the place reeked! Rancid oil, smoking metal, damp wool, and sweat. Empty-eyed operators, the men in coveralls, the women standing shoeless by their machines as if for inspection. That Francois stopped to chat so amiably with them disgusted her. No, this was not her destiny—not in a million years!

The truth was that she did think less of her brother because he chose to work in a filthy mill and because he chose to be with those kinds of people.

She glanced at the clock. "Damn!" she shouted as she grabbed her nursing manual and hurried out the door.

"Good morning, Miss Davis. You're right on time. I appreciate that. If you report to Ward B, you'll get your schedule for today."

"Good morning, Sister Madeline. I'll go there directly."

Sister Madeline liked this girl, Miranda Davis, about whom she'd had serious doubts a year earlier. Sister Madeline had spent the bulk of her sixty-two years working in hospitals, the last seven supervising the nurse trainees at St. Anne's Hospital. Her first impressions were usually quite accurate.

Sister Madeline had thought Miss Davis, who she guessed was nearly twenty, too young and skittish for nursing. But she had been wrong. It had taken a while for Miss Davis to settle into the routines, but she was totally reliable, very responsible, clever, and eager to learn. Sister Madeline imagined that, in time, Miranda Davis might be supervisor material.

Miranda, wearing the pale blue, long-sleeved, floor-length dress with a white floor-length apron over it, took the stairs to Ward B. She loved how the hallway floors gleamed in the soft lighting; she loved the smell of wax and polish.

But she didn't like the smells on Ward B, Obstetrics. Rows of pale women in various stages of pre- and post-birthing huddled on cots, groaning, sweating, sometimes screaming. None of them, even those who had finally delivered their babies, looked particularly happy. Most looked exhausted, resigned, and scared.

Sister Francis, younger and stouter than Sister Madeline, greeted Miranda with a quick nod, passed her a sheet of paper, and said, "Miss Davis, your assignments for today.

"Rounds in five minutes," Sister Francis continued. "We have two patients close to birthing, though one may need surgery. Dr. Waterman's on call, he'll join us for rounds. If you need to use the bathroom, do so now."

"Yes, Sister," Miranda replied politely, walking to the nurses' locker room across from the bathroom. Miranda carefully placed her belongings in her locker but had no need to check her reflection in the bathroom mirror—Dr. Waterman was married.

4

FRANCOIS'S DISCONTENT

Francois met Alphonso Wallabee, his supervisor's youngest son, a week after he started a job in the carding room of the Troy Mill in August. They were inseparable ever since.

When spring returned with delightfully warm days, the spiraled chartreuse leaves slowly started to open and perennial beds were just starting to bloom. If they weren't on Sunday's duty roster, Maddy and Miranda always took a picnic lunch to the pavilion in South Park, and it wasn't long before Francois, Alphonso, and Alphonso's brother Tony decided to join them, because food was always a motivator and free food was magnetic.

Miranda was mesmerized by Tony's brilliant smile. Unlike other boys, Tony was always interested in hearing about Miranda's and Maddy's work and plans. He was easy to talk to and calming to be around.

On September 30, 1871 Miranda passed her final exams and Sister Madeline offered her a full-time nursing position at St. Anne's, which she gratefully accepted. Maddy passed her exams as well and decided to take a live-in position at St. Vincent's Orphanage.

"It's perfect for me, Mira," she reasoned. "I'll have no living expenses. I'll have my own little apartment, and I'll eat all my meals with the kids. I'll be able to save almost all of my salary."

"I'll really miss you, Maddy," Miranda admitted. "I'll miss our chats. Will we still get together?"

Maddy's big eyes filled with tears. "Of course, we will," she said confidently. "On our days off. My apartment's small, but you can come by anytime for tea. A few years from now, who knows? Maybe I'll have saved enough to get my own place. Think of it, Mira, me with my own apartment. Maybe we could live together, if you're not married by then."

Miranda hugged her dearest friend tightly. "I'm never getting married, Maddy. You'll always be my best friend. We'll both save up. That way we can be roommates sooner!" Together, they had managed to turn even this sad moment into another adventure.

Miranda and Maddy invited Francois, Alphonso, and Tony to their graduation capping ceremony. The three of them applauded and whistled enthusiastically as first Miranda and then Maddy crossed the stage to accept their diplomas and new white caps with broad navy stripes, signifying their status as professional nurses.

Afterward, they treated the girls to a celebratory dinner at the Mohican Hotel. Other than an occasional tavern meal, none of them had ever eaten in a restaurant, much less such a grand one. It was also the first time they ever tasted champagne, which was sent to their table compliments of the hotel. Its lively effervescence made the girls giggle and its dryness made the boys yearn for warm, yeasty beers.

Miranda replayed this magical evening over and over before she fell asleep. She couldn't imagine what it'd cost the boys. She was grateful to have such good friends and now, finally, a respectable profession she could depend on.

Six months later, though, she noticed that Francois seemed more distant, at times even distressed. She was concerned about him and worried that he might be in some kind of trouble at work or that his pride might be wounded because, as a full-time nurse, she earned a little more than he did after three years at the mill.

Blissfully content with her work and her friends, Miranda was not eager to invite even the smallest adversity into her life. Believing that her good fortune might be transient, she avoided anything disruptive, which included a confrontation with her brother.

As it turned out, it was Francois who initiated the dreaded conversation. "You look tired, Mira," he said on one of the rare nights he ate dinner at home with her. "Everything okay?"

"Sure, yeah, things are great! But it's you who seems troubled, Francois. I get the feeling something's bothering you."

Putting down his fork, he exhaled dramatically and announced, "I want you to break things off with Tony."

Her eyes widened in disbelief. "I don't understand. You want what?"

"I want you to break things off with Tony." His tone was as calm as if he'd simply asked her to pass the salt.

"For heaven's sake, why?" She smiled now, convinced he was teasing her.

"Because Al's my best friend."

"I'm not following . . ."

"Al's my best friend, Mira. When you break it off with Tony, I'm worried that it will come between me and Al. So, the longer you wait, the harder it will be for Al to stay friends with me."

She was speechless; her gray eyes, hard as harpoons, bored into him. "So," she said sarcastically, taking time to carefully fold her napkin and place it on the table, "this isn't really about me, is it? This is about you."

"No, Mira, this isn't about me," he denied, then recanted, "Well, not just about me. I don't want you to do something that will jeopardize my friendship with Al.

"But," he added quickly, "it's also about hurting Tony—someone who's always treated me well. Someone I like a lot. And, just for the record, someone whose father is my boss."

"I really don't know what to say, Francois. What does or doesn't happen between me and Tony is just that—between me and Tony."

"No, it isn't. And I think you know that. How do you feel about Tony, Mira?"

"I like him," she said, caught off guard. "He's kind, funny, a decent man."

"So, you'd marry him, if he asked?"

"Don't be silly. We enjoy each other's company. We've only been seeing each other a few months! We're friends, that's all."

"No, Mira, that's not all. Would you marry him?"

"I wouldn't marry anybody right now. Why would I? I've just finished nursing school, just started my first real job."

Francois inhaled deeply and slowly exhaled. "Tony's a good man, Mira, you're absolutely right about that. But I'm guessing he's not the kind of man you'd ever consider marrying?"

"And why not?"

"He works in a stinking mill, Miranda. His hands will always be dirty. He comes from an immigrant family. He's not particularly well educated. He's a working-class man and that's all he's ever going to be."

She started to interrupt, but he talked over her.

"I know you pretty well, Mira, and I bet you've set your sights much higher. A doctor, maybe. A professor, maybe. A mill worker, never."

"Are you accusing me of being a snob? Are you implying that I'm just using Tony?"

"Mira, my dear sister," he said gently, sincerely, "you are a snob. It's not a crime! But you are a snob."

"I am not!" she replied emphatically.

"Yes, you are! As long as I've known you, you've always wanted

Francois's Discontent

more than we had. Wanted to do more. Wanted to have more. I've never understood what drives you, but it seems like you're never satisfied with where you are or with what you have."

She couldn't look at him. "So why are we having this conversation right now?"

"Because if you continue to accept his dinner invitations every week, you're giving him the impression that he's someone special. Someone you care deeply for. And he isn't, is he?"

"You haven't answered my question. Why are you bringing this up now?"

"Because Al told me in the strictest confidence that he thinks Tony's in love with you. He overheard Tony talking to his pa about needing to get a promotion.

"Tony said he needed to make more money and admitted he's thinking of starting a family and getting a place of his own."

"Oh, God." Miranda's stomach felt soapy.

"Al, of course, didn't say a word but couldn't wait to tell me. He wanted to know if you'd mentioned anything like that."

"And what did you tell him?"

"I said you hadn't." Francois waited for her to say something, but she didn't. "Has Tony asked you to marry him, Miranda?"

"No, of course not," she said, swallowing hard. But, in fact, Tony had hinted at it more than once.

"What do you want me to do?" she asked, suddenly feeling trapped.

"Mira, I'm only asking you to think about your situation . . . and Tony's."

"You're pressuring me to walk away from someone who makes me happy right now?"

He picked up his plate and put it in the sink. "Think about it, Mira. That's all I'm asking. My fate is tied to yours." He left, letting the door slam shut behind him.

5

SAMUEL'S FIRE

Blinking back tears, Samuel Wallabee, nineteen waved good-bye and boarded the train to Cambridge. He thought about the costly sacrifices and hardships his parents, especially his mother, had endured so he could be here today—on a train bound for Harvard University. The formidable weight of her pride and the vibrancy of her expectations unnerved him. By the time he stepped off the train in Cambridge, he was riddled with anxiety and self-doubt.

Fortunately, even as a child, Samuel seemed to have a natural ability to compartmentalize his emotions and concentrate on whatever needed to be done at the moment. By fourteen, he habitually read in bed until the early morning; five hours of sleep seemed all he needed. Whether genetic or learned, both abilities would be invaluable now.

As he walked to the university, Samuel could not have imagined that the series of tedious summer jobs he'd held at Troy Mill would have any relevancy here. Nor could he have foreseen how advantageous and lucrative those experiences would ultimately become.

He'd begun working at the mill the summer he turned eight and because of his age was not allowed to operate machinery or lift heavy bales. Like other boys and girls his age, he started as a sweeper, clearing debris from floors and machines. At ten he was a doffer, removing bobbins from spindles, tying them into bundles, and delivering them to the weaving room.

By fourteen, he'd memorized the production process and had worked on every floor. Because he was sincerely curious and respectful, operators and supervisors enjoyed his company and often took the time to explain what a particular machine did and why.

At fourteen, Samuel worked in the carding room, the first job his father, Guido, had been assigned. He hated it. It was dangerous work. The sharp, swiftly revolving teeth on the carding machines literally tore apart the cotton, removing any remaining debris and converting what was left into pencil-thin loose strands called slivers.

In just a few hours, the carding machine and the men who worked there shirtless and shoeless were shrouded in cotton dust. The air was sticky and congested with lint. The stink of soggy cotton, sweaty bodies, and unctuous grease was nauseating.

From there the cotton went to the web drawing room, where large frames straightened and stretched these slivers by running them through a series of metal rollers called speeders. Samuel was a speeder tender the summer he turned fifteen.

Afterward the straightened slivers were fed into a roving machine, twisted again to increase the strength of the yarn, and then wound onto wooden bobbins. These bobbins were collected, usually by children, and taken to the spinning room, where a throttle machine twisted the threads one last time and wound the finished yarn onto as many as seventy-two wooden bobbins. When one of the threads broke, which happened many times a day, the operator had to stop the machine and retie the broken ends by hand.

The more experienced operators, usually women, tended multiple machines and spent the entire day walking up and down rows of machines, repairing broken or snagged threads. At seventeen, Samuel worked in the spinning room and could retie broken threads faster than any woman. More importantly, though, he enjoyed the company of women better than men. The women, frankly, had much better hygiene and, just as important, did not spit on the floor as the men constantly did.

By nineteen, Samuel decided he wanted to become a part of this industry—a big part. And so, on this humid July morning, he arrived at Harvard University to pursue that dream. After locating his dormitory and depositing his one suitcase, he went directly to meet with his assigned advisor, Dr. Paul Everett.

"Good morning, Dr. Everett. May I come in?"

Without looking up from the file on his desk, Dr. Everett pointed to the chair opposite him. Absentmindedly, he lifted a china cup to his lips, grimaced, and quickly replaced it on its saucer.

The professor was a sizable man in his late fifties, stout but not overweight. His dark, neatly trimmed beard was at odds with his tangled eyebrows wisped with gray. His black woolen jacket and vest were spotless, his starched collar stood at attention, and his eyes, behind wire-rimmed glasses, were weary.

"Do you plan to sit, boy? I'd like to get started. I've other things to do today."

"Sorry, sir," Samuel replied, quickly taking a seat. He feigned interest for what seemed like hours while Dr. Everett launched into the same uninspiring lecture he'd probably delivered to new students for years.

Finally, Dr. Everett handed Samuel a written list of the courses he was assigned this semester. Although disappointed that he'd had no input into his class selection, he doubted any comments at this point would be appreciated. From what he'd seen so far, Dr. Everett did not appear to be someone who exchanged pleasantries with students. He was precise and thorough but certainly not sociable.

"Any questions?" Dr. Everett asked, his perfunctory tone neither inviting nor anticipating further discussion. Clearly, in his opinion, the interview was over.

"Yes, sir, quite a few," Samuel replied with enthusiasm. "I wonder, though, if you might be interested in walking around campus while we talk. Stretch your legs a bit? Get some fresh air? Seems your coffee's cold—perhaps you know where we might get you a fresh cup?"

Dr. Everett's head snapped up, and he examined this boy more closely, noticing that Samuel did not flinch under his gaze. *Well*, thought Paul Everett, *a young man who's observant, thoughtful, and not easily intimidated. Unusual qualities in a freshman. How curious.*

So, they strolled, the stout academician and the gangly new freshman, crisscrossing the quadrangle on cobblestoned walkways beneath antique chestnut trees and passing old, granite buildings with gleaming white marble columns tinted pale green, here and there, from generations of moss.

As they walked, the professor delighted Samuel with the history of some of these stately buildings. Samuel peppered the professor with questions but was increasingly frustrated by the professor's annoyingly succinct replies.

"Sir, I'd like to inquire about taking extra courses in business subjects."

"Not possible for freshmen."

"Well then, I'd like permission to audit them."

"Only juniors can audit."

"Professor Everett, I was hoping I could carry a heavier course load in order to graduate sooner."

"That's not something we recommend."

In frustration, and clearly without thinking it through, Samuel blurted out, "Sir, do you ever intend to say yes to anything?"

"Absolutely, boy. I intend to accept your offer of coffee." Dr. Everett hadn't the faintest of smiles on his lips, but his eyes looked amused.

They stopped at the faculty dining room and were shown to a table for two in front of a massive floor-to-ceiling window. Almost immediately, a male waiter wearing a stiff black-and-white uniform brought them coffee. Both waited in silence as the waiter poured the steaming dark brew into two china cups, placed a small silver tray with a sugar bowl and creamer in the middle of the table, and retreated without a word.

Dr. Everett brought his cup to his lips, inhaled greedily, and sipped. He closed his eyes, savoring the aroma and taste. Samuel, who had never seen anyone so enamored with a beverage, waited in silence. He would learn soon enough that coffee was one of Dr. Everett's passions.

"Ah, wonderful!" exclaimed the professor. "Yes, it's all in the roasting, my boy! Too little and the brew is weak. Too much and the brew is bitter, not stronger—that's a myth. You haven't touched yours, Samuel. Do you take cream or sugar?"

"No," Samuel replied, avoiding the professor's gaze.

"Ah, I agree. Why dilute the flavor? Black, hot, unadulterated—that's how I enjoy it."

"No, sir," Samuel corrected. "I meant that I've never actually tasted coffee. So I can't say whether I'd need sugar or cream." His cheeks reddened with embarrassment.

"Really? You can't be serious," the professor blurted out and was immediately shocked by the thoughtlessness of his remark. He could see clearly how chagrined the boy appeared.

"Well, Samuel," he continued, trying to recover, "you're quite an unusual young man. You're observant, thoughtful, and you don't drink coffee."

The professor smiled a little but then added in a serious voice, "Maybe it's time you told me about your family. But first, please, try the coffee."

By the end of their first meeting, Paul Everett understood why this young man was so remarkable, so unlike the other, more privileged boys he'd interviewed over the years. The pride Samuel felt in his parents was touching. In example after example, Samuel described their courage and endurance in the face of unimaginable adversity.

They were unpretentious and dignified people who worked long hours doing dangerous, backbreaking work in a mill. Dr. Everett was stunned to hear how little they were paid. In fact, these were honest people, caring parents, who sacrificed every single day; who went without the smallest luxuries that most, in Dr. Everett's circle, took for granted. These were people who had experienced few, if any, comforts but somehow, incredibly, were not beaten down—they continued to have hope.

Paul Everett felt burning shame. He had so misjudged this boy. He'd withheld simple kindness from him, offered instead only the minimum of guidance, and almost dismissed him entirely.

When Samuel finished his story, he sipped his now lukewarm coffee again. *Must be an acquired taste*, he thought. Such a strange bitter flavor, not entirely unpleasant, but definitely not as calming or fragrant as a steamy mug of sweet tea.

Dr. Everett finished the last of his coffee but held on to his cup while seeming lost in thought. "Well, Samuel, I think I've a better understanding of your earlier questions. Perhaps we should discuss them a little further.

"I have an early appointment in the morning, but why don't we meet around ten thirty? Let's see if we can find some additional courses—more aligned with your business interests—along with the required ones, of course."

Samuel smiled broadly and stood. "Terrific! Your office, sir?"

"No, let's meet here. I feel a need to educate your palate as well as your mind." This time he did smile. "Just one last question?"

Samuel stopped.

"What do your friends call you?"

"Sam."

"Okay, Sam, I'll see you tomorrow at ten thirty sharp."

"Yes, sir." As he walked away, Samuel thought, *That man will change my life.*

As in all things, Samuel was a voracious learner. He understood the routines of academic life. Spongelike, he absorbed dates, facts, numbers, and ideas, believing that any day might be his last, which, realistically, was true.

The scholarship he'd received covered all his expenses until the end of his sophomore year, which he was just completing. He worked five nights a week bussing tables in the dining room, where he was allowed to eat leftovers. He worked an additional four hours a week as Dr. Everett's assistant. Samuel hoarded every penny and, by the end of his sophomore year, had almost enough to finance his junior year.

In June 1871 his entire family came for a visit. He'd not seen them for almost a year. As his mother hurried along the platform, her arms wide, there were tears in her eyes. Even his father, always the more somber parent, gave Samuel a bear hug rather than his usual handshake. His brothers looked the same, only taller.

Samuel carried the picnic basket as they strolled along the Charles River, looking for a spot that would please his mother. He was shocked to see how aged they were. His father appeared almost feeble and walked unsteadily on the grass. Guido's eyes were ringed with red and he had a coughing spasm that bent him double, forcing him to stop walking.

Samuel recognized that cough. He'd heard it a lot around the mill, especially in the carding and spinning rooms. While he didn't understand what caused it, he knew that it was a harbinger of something serious.

Angelina picked a spot on the grass under a tree nearest the river. She had the boys spread the blanket so that part of it was shaded and part was in the sun.

"Mmm," Sam said, munching his second sandwich of thinly sliced pork with roasted peppers. "This is delicious, Ma!"

"There's plenty more," she said. "Don't make me carry any home." She was clearly pleased that her son still enjoyed her cooking. She couldn't imagine what he ate at that "cafeteria" place where he worked.

After the feast, while both parents rested on the blanket, the three brothers explored the boathouses and stood on the bridges, watching the crew teams practicing on the Charles River.

The late afternoon was still warm and pleasant, so Samuel took his mother for a stroll along the river while his father dozed and his brothers roamed about, hoping to meet pretty girls. He tried to raise the subject of their health, but Angelina swept his concerns aside like she'd done all his life.

"Ah, Sammy, you worry too much about us. We're just getting old, is all. We're doin' fine for two old people!" She laughed then, that clear, joyful laugh he remembered and treasured from his childhood. He couldn't help smiling at her as she linked her arm with his.

After seeing their train off, he returned to his room more concerned than ever about his parents and more motivated to finish early so he could begin to provide for them. He did not know that the next time he saw them would be the worst day of his life.

Though the fall semester of his senior year hadn't officially started, the professor and Samuel continued their habit of meeting every Monday afternoon in the faculty dining room to discuss the upcoming week's schedule and, of course, to savor the coffee.

This Monday, as Samuel scanned the room for his mentor, he was surprised to see two other men sitting with Dr. Everett. Not wanting to intrude, Samuel stood in the doorway until Dr. Everett waved him over.

"Sam, I'd like you to meet Dr. Thomas Walker, dean of Arts and Letters, and Dr. Erwin Douglas, chairman of Business Studies. Gentlemen, this is my assistant, Samuel Wallabee. He's the young man I've been telling you about."

Nervously, Samuel shook their hands but remained standing until the dean invited him to sit.

"Well, Paul," said the dean, "I'll get straight to the point, then, shall I?"

"Absolutely, before my young friend here hyperventilates!" Dr. Everett replied, laughing.

"Don't worry, Sam, you're not in any kind of trouble. I've asked Dean Walker and Dr. Douglas to join us because, as it turns out, some of us on the curriculum committee are thinking—"

Dean Walker interrupted. "Yes, Sam, in a nutshell, some of us on the committee believe that what we teach could be more relevant. The university has always prided itself on providing the very best liberal education across a wide range of subjects.

"But lately, there's been some concern that too much of the coursework is past-focused and not readily applicable to today's challenges and opportunities."

"Perhaps an example might illustrate," interjected Dr. Douglas. "Manufacturing, textile manufacturing in particular, is a good example. Though we in academia are sometimes accused, and many times rightly so, of living in ivory towers, we've not failed to notice that this industry, still in its infancy, has become a major driver of economic stability and prosperity, especially here in the northeast.

"Given its increasing diversity and localization," Dr. Douglas continued, "some of us believe that students might benefit from more depth, academically speaking, in this area."

"The curriculum committee," Dean Walker interjected, regaining the lead, "is considering making such a proposal to the faculty. But we feel we need to educate ourselves first to ensure there is merit to such a proposal. And of course, we anticipate that there will be many who simply won't support making any kind of change."

Samuel remained silent.

"Apparently," the dean continued, "you and Dr. Everett have had many conversations about your work in a textile mill. He believes that you have quite a bit of knowledge about the industry in general and mill operations in particular."

"Perhaps, we should get to the point, Thomas," coaxed Dr. Everett.

"Yes, of course," the dean replied. "We were wondering if you might be willing to share with us, in a more formal setting, whatever knowledge and thoughts you might have on this subject.

"Your opinions would be helpful and your first-hand experience invaluable. What, if anything, should our students know about the industry? Would more specificity be important preparation for future students? We'd like to have the benefit of your experience as we decide how to proceed."

"I'm flattered, Dean Walker. But I'm just not sure I'm the person you need. Wouldn't a mill agent or even a mill superintendent be a better person to advise your committee?"

Dr. Everett came to his rescue. "I know it's a lot to drop on you, Sam. Tell you what, why don't you and I continue discussing this over our coffee. If I know you, you have a lot of questions, and I'll do my best to answer them.

"Then," he said, turning to his colleagues, "let's give Sam a day or two to think about what might work."

"Fair enough, Paul," said the dean, smiling as he stood to leave. "Appreciate your help. Good to meet you, Sam. Hope we'll be seeing you again. Irwin, I'll walk back with you if you're heading to the quadrangle."

For the rest of that summer, Sam met weekly with the curriculum committee, which, as it turned out, had three additional members. After introducing Samuel to the rest of the committee, Dean Walker turned the meeting over to him and Sam stood.

"I decided to start with a short history and description of the Troy Mill because that's the only mill I've worked in. Other cotton mills might be smaller or larger, but, at least for now, the process of turning raw cotton into cloth is pretty much the same. I think you should understand what happens in each department and on every floor.

"The Troy Cotton and Woolen Manufactory, to use its full name, was built on the Quequechan River in 1813. Initially, it was a three-story building. The lower story was stone and the upper stories wood. At the time, it was intended to operate about two thousand spindles.

"The original mill was destroyed by fire in 1821 and rebuilt using granite instead of wood. In 1843, an additional granite building, of the same proportions as the first, was adjoined at right angles.

"Finally in 1860, the oldest part was completely torn down and replaced with a five-story granite building 296 feet by 72 feet. It was intended to operate 39,500 spindles, 888 power looms, and employ over four hundred people."

"I'm afraid I don't understand your references to spindles, Sam. I'm assuming that the larger a mill is, the more cloth, or whatever, can be produced. Is that correct? Oh, sorry, Sam, I'm Silas Fiske from accounting."

"Yes, sir," replied Sam. "You're correct. The use of 'spindle counting' is confusing. I'm afraid I don't know why or even when the practice started, but it is a standard now. The capacity of a cotton mill is determined by the number of spindles in operation. I believe but will check to be sure that the number of spindles is also used for valuation and tax purposes."

"I see. Thank you, Sam."

"I was allowed to study some of the earliest records housed in the Boston Public Library. In 1860, for example, the total number of operating spindles in the entire city of Fall River was 192,620. So twenty percent of the total number of spindles in operation was located in the Troy Mill."

"Impressive indeed," replied Silas.

"Yes, but things changed dramatically with the introduction of the first steam engine," Sam explained. "By 1862, the Troy Mill had incorporated some auxiliary steam power, but its primary source of power continued to be the river. But, over the next eight years, by slowly increasing the amount of auxiliary steam power, the mill was able to increase the number of operating spindles to 52,500. Which is what the mill has now.

"The introduction of steam power was more important than just additional spindles because for the first time mills didn't have to locate near water, they could be built anywhere."

"The sheer size of the mill is rather staggering," replied the dean, shaking his head. "It's hard to imagine how one manages so many people and tasks."

"A cotton mill is more than just a place to work, sir," Samuel explained. "It's a community. To entice workers, the mill provides all employees and their families with housing built on the nine acres surrounding the actual mill."

"That's an unusual practice, isn't it?" asked Dr. Plimpton, Chairman of Curriculum Development, "For an employer to supply housing?"

"For most industries, yes, but not textile manufacturing, at least not on this scale," replied Sam. "It benefits the mill more than the workers because the housing is far from luxurious. In fact, most would say it's substandard at best. Keeping the work force so close reduces commuting time and allows for a longer workday, which increases productivity."

"Not to mention that when your home belongs to your employer, it's more difficult for you to make demands or complain," the professor added.

"With so many families clustered together, people need convenient access to food, religious services, education, and health services. So, in addition to building housing, mill owners also located churches, schools, grocery stores, bakeries, barber shops, and even taverns in the same acreage."

At the next meeting, Sam drew a detailed floor plan of the mill and broke down the operations floor by floor. Raw cotton began its processing on the first floor, was hauled to the second and third floors for more refinement, and was finally made into yarn on the fourth floor. The final process, weaving the yarn into cotton cloth, took place on the fifth floor.

For the next few meetings, he walked them through each step of the complicated production processes by which a bale of raw cotton weighing about 470 pounds becomes cotton cloth. The Troy Mill was an efficient one and could produce seven yards of cloth for every pound of raw cotton—almost nine million yards of fabric a year.

He shared what he knew about the nature of the industry, where the cotton came from, and where the finished goods were sent. After some amount of research, Samuel was able to provide very basic information about some of the costs. For example, in the previous year, the mill purchased 3,500 bales of cotton at twelve cents a pound. A typical monthly payroll was almost $300,000.

For their last meeting, Samuel described the working conditions, although no one on the committee had asked about those. He asked them to imagine the physical effort it would take to stand at or bend over fast moving machines for ten to twelve hours a day, six days a week, making the same repetitive motions. It caused such swelling in the ankles and feet, he explained, that most women worked barefoot or wore boots one or two sizes larger than their shoes. There was no place to sit except on the floor.

He could not replicate the deafening sound of eight hundred metal looms but explained that the noise left many workers with permanent ringing in their ears, blinding headaches, significant hearing loss, and, in some cases, deafness. It was common to see workers at their machines with cotton stuffed in their ears.

To operate the machines safely required such total concentration, he told the group, that socializing and conversation were impossible. The machines moved so terrifyingly fast and the rooms were so dimly lit that hands, hair, sleeves, and occasionally arms were regularly snagged and pulled into the machine before the operator could shut it down, causing serious and sometimes fatal injuries.

"Although the windows are large and closely spaced to maximize natural lighting, the slender threads break more easily when the air is dry, so the windows are kept closed, even in the summer. Sometimes, steam is piped in or the room is sprayed with water from overhead nozzles to keep the air moist. In the end, regardless of the weather outside, the work rooms are always warm, humid, and filled with floating cotton lint.

"For ten to twelve hours a day, workers breathe in fumes from oil lamps, perpetual lint that swirls about as thickly as snowflakes in a blizzard, and cotton dust from the machines. Many doctors think that the combination of dampness and lint cause the eventually fatal respiratory disease called brown lung."

"So," Samuel concluded, "these are the circumstances under which men, women, and children work, ten to twelve hours a day, six days a week. They work between sixty and seventy-two hours a week and are paid about five cents an hour.

"Dean Walker," Samuel turned to face him. "You once asked me what students should learn about this industry. I would urge you, all of you, not to forget these people in your lectures, these strange, uneducated foreigners who provide the backbreaking labor upon which the mills and ultimately our city flourish. I appreciate having this chance to tell you about them. Thank you."

"Thank you, Sam," replied the dean, who stood and handed Samuel a check from the committee for what dean Walker called Samuel's consulting. It easily covered his expenses for his senior year.

At ten thirty on the night of October 5, 1872, as Samuel sat reading at his desk, there was a soft, hesitant knock on his door. He was not surprised to see Dr. Everett standing in the hallway as he often stopped by Samuel's room to discuss one thing or another, but mostly Samuel suspected, just to talk.

"Dr. Everett," said Samuel, "good to see you." Dr. Everett's face was terribly flushed.

"Are you ill, sir?" Sam asked with genuine concern.

"May I come in, Sam?" The professor's tremulous voice frightened Sam further.

"Are you ill, sir?" Sam repeated with greater trepidation.

"Sam!" The professor used his classroom voice. "May I come in?"

"Yes, certainly. Sorry, sir." Sam opened the door wider and quickly emptied the only other chair of the books and papers piled there. "Please, sit down, Professor." Samuel took the chair behind his desk.

Dr. Everett removed his gloves, then his spectacles but not his coat. He stared out the window behind Sam and finally said, "Sam, I'm afraid I have some very bad news. Dean Walker sent me a message a while ago concerning the Troy Mill. There was a fire this afternoon, and it's still burning."

Samuel stopped breathing as his ears filled with the thumping pulse of his heart. Dr. Everett's mouth was moving but the sound was garbled, as if he, Samuel, were under water. Finally running out of air, Samuel coughed and gasped to fill his lungs.

"Tell me, Professor."

"Sam, it's important to remember that there's still so much confusion at the mill, it's hard to separate fact from rumor. You absolutely need to return home. I've booked you on the eleven sixteen to Fall River. I'll take you to the station."

"Tell me!"

Dr. Everett's big frame sagged, his face grayed, and his deep, sorrowful eyes filled with tears, which he swiped at with the sleeve of his overcoat. He inhaled and exhaled slowly.

"Dean Walker made several inquiries, trying to learn the facts before we told you. So far, what we know is that the fire spread quickly, but it's not been determined where it started. Because the floorboards were soaked with oil, it burned hot and filled rooms with thick smoke. It seems that some windows, especially on the upper floors, simply could not be opened."

Dr. Everett's voice was hoarse. "Sam, I'm so sorry but, so far, your father's missing."

Silence.

Covered in sweat, Samuel violently flung open his window and vomited. Long after the contents of his stomach emptied, he continued to retch and, finally, slid to the floor, sobbing.

Dr. Everett, openly crying now, had no words to comfort his student; he could think of nothing that might ease the suffering of his young friend. He could not speak, knowing he had caused so much pain. His mouth was so dry his lips stuck together.

From the floor, under the window, came the question he was dreading most. "My brothers?" Sam croaked. "What about my brothers?"

"Again, nothing is certain, Sam. But the dean's note did say that your brothers are alive. They're injured. I don't know how badly."

Samuel slumped forward, his head on his knees, sobbing in great, shuddering gulps.

Dr. Everett stood. "We need to leave now, Sam."

He tried to lift Samuel off the floor but failed. Using the most authoritative voice he could muster, he said, "We need to leave now Samuel! I'm going with you, but I can't carry you. Your mother needs you and your brothers need you. So, pull yourself together. You can rest on the train. Now, stand up!"

6

STOLEN DREAMS

Twenty-four year-old Frank Davis, formerly Francois Alysworth, had always lived in shadow, around the edges, afraid to want or need too much, which led naturally to not depending on or connecting with anybody. And, until recently, he had no regrets.

Alphonso Wallabee changed all that. When he met Al, he saw someone much like himself, someone who had chosen—for different reasons perhaps—to remain detached, to stand on the sidelines. In Al, Frank discovered something that he had not known he so desperately needed—kinship. They came to trust and rely on each other. They understood each other. Their bond was as indestructible and as immutable as the granite mill where they worked. Until Miranda threatened it.

After the unexpected confrontation with his sister neither he nor Miranda had made any attempt to reconcile and the unprecedented antagonism between them remained.

From Ward B in the early afternoon, Miranda heard an ambulance's bell followed soon by a second ambulance bell and then a third. Although she was curious to know what was going on, she couldn't risk leaving her ward. Within a few minutes, however, Sister Madeline appeared.

"There's been a disaster, Nurse Davis. I need you to work in the emergency room for a while."

"What's happened, Sister?" Miranda asked.

"There's a fire. One of the mills, I think. The ambulances are bringing in people with second- and third-degree burns."

Miranda's stomach lurched. "Do you know which mill, Sister?" she asked urgently.

"No," Sister Madeline replied curtly, her mind already on the next problem that needed her attention. "I need to move more nurses," she said as she walked away. "Go there directly. Do what you can to help. I'll join you later."

The emergency room was congested and chaotic, orderlies carried in stretcher after stretcher of burn victims, their bodies grotesquely twisted, many dying on the way to the hospital. Miranda directed two orderlies to move all of the dead to the morgue. Then she gathered four nurse trainees who were standing outside the ER and instructed them to administer morphine to any patient that doctors indicated could not be saved.

"Nurse Newbury," she said, addressing the oldest of the four. "Make arrangements for all those patients to be moved to Ward C. Stay with them and continue to administer morphine as needed. As the day goes on, I'm afraid there will be many more, so rearrange the ward if you have to."

To the remaining three she said, "Each one of you will assist a doctor in the emergency room and do exactly what they instruct you to do. This will be a long day for all of us."

Miranda started to leave but saw the raw fear in their eyes.

"I know you're afraid," she added more gently. "I know it will be difficult to do your job today. But this is what we've chosen, isn't it?

I truly hope you won't have many days like this one. But this is what we have to do today."

As Miranda headed back into the emergency room, the smell of burnt flesh assaulted her and she gagged involuntarily. The screaming continued. As word of the fire spread, hysterical family members began to arrive, storming the emergency room, pulling back curtains, and shouting for their missing husbands, wives, and children.

Miranda quickly grabbed a metal basin and hammered it on the countertop until the entire group fell silent.

"If you continue to do what you're doing, people will die," she shouted, "perhaps someone in your own family. We must have a sterile environment to keep those who are burned from getting infections—which will almost certainly kill them.

"I know you're sick with worry. I understand that. But I'm sure none of you wants to contribute in any way to someone's death.

"Now, I want all of you to go back outside and take the door into the main lobby. Give the receptionist your name and the name of the person you're searching for. I give you my word that as soon as we identify anyone, I'll have the receptionist post that name.

"Now please, you must leave." People quietly shuffled out.

For the next few hours, ambulances continued to deliver casualties. Miranda's apron was spattered with blood and sticky bits of charred skin. The stench of death and acrid smoke seemed permanently lodged in her nostrils.

Around six o'clock, Dr. Patrick looked up at her across a stretcher. "You need a break, Nurse Davis. Get some fresh air, something to eat, and bring me back a cup of strong, hot coffee."

Dazed, Miranda headed to the small kitchen off the first-floor nurses' station, followed by two other nurses. She made herself a cup of tea and grabbed an apple from a basket on the counter.

"Here," said one of the nurses gently, handing her bowl of soup to Miranda. "By the looks of you, you've been in the thick of it. You need this more than me. It's almost over now anyway."

"What do you mean?" asked Miranda.

"Ambulances are being turned away now. We've no more room. They're being sent over to The Union Hospital or City Hospital. What a God-awful day!"

Summoning all her courage, Miranda asked, "Do you know what mill's caught fire?"

Both nurses shook their heads. "Sorry."

Miranda finished her soup, poured a cup of black coffee, and headed back to the emergency room. Dr. Patrick, still bending over a stretcher, straightened and accepted the hot coffee, gratefully emptying it in seconds. He'd barely finished when the emergency room door was kicked open. Two gasping firemen entered, almost at a run. Between them, they half supported, half dragged a third fireman whose jacket was saturated with blood and who appeared to be unconscious.

Doctor Patrick looked at Miranda. "Stop the bleeding, Nurse Davis. Then come find me or one of the other docs to examine his injury."

"In here," Miranda instructed the firemen. "Put him on that table." She cut away the sleeve of his jacket so she could get a better view of the wound which was pulsing blood. She needed a tourniquet. "Get his belt off," she ordered.

In one swift movement, she wrapped the belt around his upper arm, pulled one end through, and cinched it as tight as she could. The bleeding slowed and finally stopped.

"I'll get a doctor," she said. "You stay here. If the bleeding starts again, pull the belt tighter."

Both firemen nodded; they were clearly dazed and exhausted. One pulled a chair from the corner, slid it up to the table, sat down, and rested his head beside his bloody comrade's leg. The younger fireman sat on the floor in the corner where the chair had been, his elbows on his knees, his head in his hands.

Miranda hurried back, Dr. Patrick in tow. He took over immediately, shouting instructions to the nurses and the orderlies around him.

Miranda took the firemen to a small room off the nurses' station. "Sit here, I'll be right back." She returned with a tray and steaming bowls of soup with crackers on a plate.

"Thanks, ma'am," said the older man, "but we need to get right back."

"And you will," she assured him, "just as soon as you eat something." She placed the tray down between the men and looked away discreetly as they devoured the food.

"Which mill is it?" she asked, staring out the window, her back to them. Her voice was composed, her tone casual as if she were simply making conversation.

"Troy. It's the Troy Mill, miss."

As she slipped to the floor, the last thing she saw was Francois's accusing face. When she came to, Dr. Patrick was kneeling beside her. "You fainted," he said. "How do you feel now?" he asked with genuine concern.

"Fine. I'm fine," Miranda replied, struggling to her feet, red-faced with embarrassment. "Really, I don't know what happened."

"Nurse Davis, there's too much going on right now for me to worry that you're unwell or unfocused. Go home. Go lie down. Do what you need to do." Dr. Patrick was direct, as usual, and firm, but his tone was gentle and his eyes kind.

Miranda felt her light-headedness returning. "Yes, Doctor," she replied. "Perhaps I do need to go home."

It was eight o'clock. She gathered her belongings from her locker and walked through the lobby on her way out. Thankfully, it appeared empty, but then she noticed someone seated in the darkest corner.

As she moved closer, she could distinguish the outline of a woman. "May I help you?" she asked.

The woman looked to be in her late forties. Wearing a black coat, still completely buttoned, she held rosary beads in one hand and a damp handkerchief in the other.

"I'll be right back," Miranda promised, throwing her own coat on a nearby chair.

Returning with two cups of tea, which she placed on the tiny side table, Miranda gently unbuttoned the woman's coat, placed a cup of tea in her hand, and sat on the chair next to her.

"Who are you waiting for?" Miranda asked.

"My family," the woman replied softly.

"Oh, are they coming to get you?" Miranda asked, flooded with relief.

"No," replied the figure in black flatly. "I'm waiting for them. I can't find them. They all worked in the mill. Do you know where they are?"

"No," Miranda said sadly, "but let me see what I can find out. What are their names?"

"Guido, Anthony, and Alphonso Wallabee. My husband and my sons."

Miranda's cup nearly slipped from her hand, and hot tea spilled onto the hem of her uniform and her shoes. She rushed to the reception bulletin board where names of the identified had been posted and found Anthony and Alphonso Wallabee assigned to Ward C. She reread the list again but could find no mention of Guido Wallabee or her own brother, Francois.

"Mrs. Wallabee, your two sons are on Ward C. I can take you there right now if you'd like."

As they neared the room, Miranda said, "I'm afraid neither boy has regained consciousness. Would you like to sit with them for a while?"

Mrs. Wallabee nodded. "Why don't they wake up, Nurse? They don't look too badly hurt."

"Their injuries are mainly internal," Miranda explained, "and they are quite severe, I'm afraid. Their lungs were badly damaged by heat and smoke. Alphonso's lung was punctured, so he's having trouble breathing. Both boys have ruptured spleens and may be bleeding internally."

Angelina leaned over Alphonso, her youngest, and gently brushed back his hair. She held his hand for a long time, then kissed it and gently tucked it back under his blanket—tears sleeting her face the entire time.

Moving to Anthony's bed, she sat on the chair beside it, staring at the face of her middle child with an expression so profoundly anguished, so emotionally devastated, that Miranda had to look away.

"Nurse, can I stay with my sons a while longer?"

"Of course, stay as long as you like, Mrs. Wallabee."

Returning with a blanket, which she wrapped around Angelina's shoulders, she said gently, "I'm leaving now, Mrs. Wallabee, but I'll look in on you and your sons first thing in the morning."

Angelina continued weeping softly and staring into the faces of her sons—willing them to wake up, not yet able to give up hope. Not once in her life had Angelina given up hope. Not once.

Despite cutting and removing what was, or would likely become, infected, despite stanching, disinfecting, and transfusing blood, despite hundreds of invisible stitches and cartons of sterile bandages, eighty-six souls died before her shift ended. At least that many, probably more, lay unconscious in hospital beds, anchored to life by mere filaments.

Battle-fatigued to her core and defeated in spirit, Miranda stood outside the hospital where the October evening's cool moisture had already coated the cobblestone street. Agitated, unnerved by the day's demonstration of human fallibility and imprecision, she walked to a nearby bench, brushed the quilt of muted leaves aside, and collapsed, the weight of dense, complex emotions pinning her there.

It seemed inconceivable to her now how she revered this "science" as her teachers had called it; how they carefully built her conviction that medicine was a comprehensive body of knowledge, rigorously authenticated and legitimate. And its doctors, those godlike, infallible practitioners, were actually flawed, indecisive, and most definitely human. It shamed her to think of how many times she'd boasted to her poor brother about the honorable profession she'd been preparing to enter, with men so noble, so scholarly, and, by implication, so much loftier than he.

She saw herself clearly for the first time—egotistical, self-righteous and sometimes imperious. It was her vanity that allowed an unbreachable rift to form between her and her only brother. Now, he might be dead and she could never make things right between them, never thank him properly, never beg his forgiveness for the disgraceful things she'd said. Never.

Like a siren's song, the saffron silhouette of the burning mill drew her. She lingered on the outskirts, watching charcoal smoke drift like dust and huddle in low-lying spaces, brilliant flames spurting here and there in the pitch blackness and embers glowing like ripe ruby plums.

Now fully prostrate, gutted, and singed, the blackened walls stared back at her. Hundreds of massive windows that had, for decades, faithfully reflected radiant dawns and flamboyant sunsets were now sightless rectangles whose jagged shards littered the ground and scrunched underfoot.

She drew closer. Firefighters fanned out in the giant cavity, systematically poking and prodding smoldering piles of debris. Miranda heard someone shout, "Look out, miss!" But before she could react, somebody yanked her back as the heap of rubble nearest her reignited.

"Thank you," she said meekly as the bucket brigade propelled past her, heading to the wheelhouse to refill their buckets. She carefully examined the hem of her coat for burns and suddenly lost her footing on the spongy ground. If two stout-armed women hadn't grabbed her from behind, she would have fallen.

"Bring her here," a raspy voice instructed. Miranda was half dragged, half carried to some large trees, which miraculously seemed to have escaped the blaze. Under their canopy, a group of ten or twelve women sat on decaying leaves and a few dilapidated benches.

A woman stood, offering her seat to Miranda, who gratefully accepted it. Another pushed a cup into her hand, explaining, "It's just water." Miranda drank it down so quickly that another cupful was pressed on her.

"You're not wearing shoes!" Miranda exclaimed, pointing to the bunioned, misshapen feet of an old woman on the bench beside her.

"There wasn't time," the old woman replied cantankerously while trying to hide her feet under her long apron.

"Most of us don't wear no shoes while we work," a slender woman offered. "Then our feet don't swell so bad. Jenny probably didn't have time to grab her shoes." The woman's voice trembled and she was clearly shaken, but she fidgeted with the pockets of her apron while she spoke and wouldn't look up.

"Hell," rebutted the woman referred to as Jenny, "I couldn't even see my shoes!"

"I'm so sorry," Miranda said earnestly. "Are any of you hurt or burned? I'm a nurse."

"We're okay—just a few cuts and bruises. We're the lucky ones," the slender woman answered wryly, continuing to examine the contents of her pockets.

"Luck had nothin' to do with it," asserted Jenny pugnaciously. "If it wasn't for Mr. Wallabee pushin' me down those stairs, I'd be dead. No doubt."

"A lot of us would be wasn't for him," another woman with wildly disheveled hair acknowledged authoritatively.

"What happened?" Miranda asked.

"Can't really say," the wild-haired woman replied. "First thing I heard was a scream. I just figured one of them young girls got caught in a belt again. I looked down the line, but all's I seen was smoke. Then, something exploded behind me and the beam over my machine started to crackle. I kept shouting for Anna, my sister, but I couldn't see her 'cause the smoke had got so thick." The woman turned to scrutinize the charred ruins in the distance, no doubt desperate for a glimpse of her sister.

"Why were you pushed down the stairs?" Miranda turned to ask Jenny.

"Couldn't hardly see the stairs, just kinda felt my way along the floor. It was so hot. Hard to breathe. Thought I'd pass out. But then the landing appeared just in front of me, but smoke was pouring out and, well, I was too scared to move.

"Mr. Wallabee and his assistant, they was already on the landing trying to stop the people from upstairs tryin' to get into the staircase before us. Mr. Wallabee, he just wedged himself in—trying to stop them from coming down, but he wasn't strong enough, so then his assistant wedged in too, and finally the girls from our floor could get into the stair tower.

"Those narrow stairs was jammed and smoky. Everybody was yellin'. Then the pushin' started again and some girls fell. God, it was awful. I can't—" Jenny stopped abruptly, sighed deeply, and turned to look at the charred remnant of the stair tower. No one spoke.

"I just stood there nailed to the floor," she continued after a while. "Couldn't move. A piece of metal crashed to the floor right beside me and I screamed. Mr. Wallabee, he seen me then, grabbed holda me, and shoved me down them stairs. Last thing I seen was a burning section of line shaft crash onto the landing right where I'd been standing, blocking the landing and the stairwell. Nobody could go up or down after that.

"If Mr. Wallabee hadn't pushed me when he heard that coupling fall, I'd been trapped up there just like the others. God, I never even thanked him." Even in the dim light, Miranda could see how Jenny's quiet tears had furrowed the soot on her face.

"Sadie and me was on the fourth floor," a shy voice from the back offered. "Cause the looms are so loud, we always stuff cotton in our ears so, at first, we didn't hear a thing, but when we seen the smoke, we all stopped our looms. Then we could hear the fire cracklin' below us. Everyone began rushing around, but there wasn't nowhere to go.

"One of the mule spinners ran over, grabbed the metal lever off my machine, and broke some windows on our side. And for a little while it seemed better."

"Tony," declared Sadie, who looked the youngest, thirteen maybe fourteen.

"What?" asked her friend impatiently.

"The mule spinner who broke the windows for us," Sadie repeated quietly, as if to herself. "His name's Tony."

"By then, two ladder companies were outside," her friend continued, "and that guy, he stood out on the window ledge and waved for the firemen to bring the ladders. But the ladders didn't quite reach us, so he straddled the ledge and held on to each girl's arms until her feet reached the first rung and a fireman could grab holda her."

"So most of the girls got out?" asked Miranda hopefully.

"I don't know. The smoke was so thick by then, and it took so long for even one girl to get down the ladder. Some girls were too afraid to step out onto the window ledge. Sometimes, that guy Tony had to lift them kickin' and screamin' and hold them out the window 'til someone could grab 'em."

"There were two ladder trucks?" Miranda asked.

"Yeah. A bunch of guys from the fifth floor rushed down to our windows, trying to get onto the ladders ahead of us. That mule spinner yelled at them, waving the lever, trying to keep them back. Then another guy, younger, ran over to help, and I heard that Tony guy yell, 'We gotta get them down quicker.'

"So, the younger one broke another window, straddled the ledge, then started grabbing one girl after another, holding on to them until a fireman on the second ladder truck could grab them.

"Once I got to the ground," she explained, "a fireman pulled me away from the building. I saw Sadie by these trees, so I ran to her just before the third floor collapsed. It was a horrible, horrible sound. Smoke and heat poured out, choking everybody, and the ladder trucks had to be pulled back."

The silence was contagious. Every woman, including Miranda, appeared preoccupied with thoughts of someone dear—someone who hadn't yet been seen, someone each prayed had gotten out in time.

Unable to continue sitting passively, a few women separated from the group and wordlessly wandered into the darkness. As if on cue, the rest rose one by one and headed for home.

Miranda wasn't able to leave. At first, timid tears slid quietly from the corners of her eyes, but before long she was sobbing and gulping for air, her heart splitting into a hundred little pieces, as if in a hall of mirrors. Miranda tumbled into herself, into an abyss, just as her mother, Violet, had done years before.

When Maddy's doorbell rang, just after midnight, it didn't wake her because she was sitting, legs tucked under, in the overstuffed chair her mother had given her as a housewarming gift. She'd heard about the fire just before dinner and, since then, waited, sick with worry.

An exhausted young fireman covered in soot stood on her porch with her dearest friend cradled in his arms. "Sorry to disturb, miss," he said, "but this is the address she give me."

"Oh, God," Maddy cried, "is she hurt? Put her on the bed. Where did you find her?"

"At the Troy Mill, miss. She was lying on the ground under some trees. If she hadn't been crying, I might not a seen her. She keeps repeating something, but I can't understand her."

Miranda lay on the bed, her eyes open but empty. Maddy covered her with blankets to keep shock at bay, then lay beside her, gently rocking her, like she always did when one of the orphans was sick or scared.

"I'm here, Mira," Maddy whispered, holding her more tightly. "I'm here."

In shock, Miranda drifted in and out of consciousness. For two days, bloody, grotesque images splintered her sleep, causing her to wake as if in mortal danger—panting, wide-eyed, heart vibrating like a hummingbird, skin oily with sweat. Then she would cry out, but whoever or whatever she needed was indecipherable. Finally, exhausted, the thick blackness swallowed her again.

She clawed her way back and woke on the third day. Easing herself to the edge of the mattress, Miranda reached for and found a woolen shawl at the foot of the bed, wrapped herself in it, and walked barefoot to the kitchen.

Maddy, who was working at the kitchen table, filled the kettle, placed cups on the table, and worried that she would say the wrong thing.

"Before you say anything, Maddy," Miranda began, startled by the tremulous sound of her own voice. "I want you to know how grateful I am. Really, truly grateful. I had nowhere to go. I couldn't have survived without your help.

"I must have been in a terrible state. I'm not even sure how I got here. I don't remember much of the last few days, but I know I must have frightened you. You're my dearest friend, Maddy. I can never thank you enough."

"Mira," Maddy said, pouring tea into their cups, "you'd have done the same for me, no doubt. Please, Mira, tell me what's happened."

"There was a terrible fire at the Troy Mill," she said finally, concealing her face.

"Yes, I know."

"Al and Tony are in critical care, but there's little chance they'll survive. They may be dead already."

"Oh, my God," Maddy whispered, wide-eyed with fright. "Both of them?"

"Hundreds of workers were still unaccounted for when I left the hospital, including Tony's father and dear Francois. Almost fifty were brought in so grotesquely burned that no one could identify them. They died in such agony and we couldn't do a thing for them. People were screaming for help.

"The operating rooms were full until late evening, but the injuries were so severe, so beyond anything we'd ever had to deal with before. Most of those victims will die too, if they haven't already. We were so helpless, Maddy, so unprepared. I can still see their faces."

"Oh God, I'm so sorry, Mira. I can't even imagine it. It must have been awful, so terrifying. I wish I could have done something, anything, to help you."

"I'm never going to be the same, Maddy."

"It's too soon to think that, Mira!" Maddy interrupted. "We're nurses. We know things like this take a long time to heal. I wasn't there, but I know you and I know you tried your best and never gave up."

A charged silence crackled between them until even the air was permeated with electrifying sorrow.

As Miranda entered St. Anne's, the blue-black pouches under her eyes were the only visible signs of her ordeal. Inwardly, though, grief had emptied her—she was as clean and fragile as an eggshell.

Remembering that the names of those admitted to the hospital were posted just outside the waiting area, she stopped there first. The names of those who'd died had been hastily crossed off—as if they'd evaporated. Her eyes stung at the sight of so many names with crosses through them.

Remarkably, neither Tony's nor Al's name had been crossed out. She went directly to Ward C. Tony and Al were still there, still unconscious, but alive nonetheless. The back of Tony's head had been re-bandaged, but the swelling was profound. His pulse was faint, his breathing shallow. He was losing ground.

Across the small room, Al's breathing was labored and erratic. His eyes, arms, and most of his right leg were covered with ointment-soaked gauze. Despite the bandages, she could see that the burned flesh was inflamed and weeping.

She returned to Tony's bedside, remembering how handsome he was, trying to recall the wide smile that used to take her breath away, to hear his deep laugh again. Bending down, she gently lifted his hand and softly kissed it. "I'm so, so sorry, Tony," she whispered. "Francois was right, you deserved better."

Though it was quite early in the morning, she stopped in the waiting room and was not surprised to see Mrs. Wallabee, rosary beads still in hand. There was a man huddled on the seat across from her, and Miranda hoped that it was a friend. No woman should be alone while she waited for her children to die.

"I've just checked on your sons, Mrs. Wallabee," Miranda reported gently. "There doesn't appear to be any change, I'm sorry to say."

Without looking up, Angelina replied softly, shaking her head slowly, "No. No change." Then, she glanced up, and her face softened as she recognized Miranda. "I'm sorry, Nurse, I didn't recognize you at first."

Reaching for the hand of the man across from her, she said, "Sammie, this is the nurse I was telling you about. The one who found Tony and Al and let me sit with them. She showed me great kindness.

"Nurse"—she turned to look at Miranda—"this is my eldest son, Samuel."

Miranda was startled because she had entirely forgotten that Tony had an older brother. This young man had Tony's handsome face, but, unlike Tony, his deep-set eyes were bright hazel, although he did have the same lovely, long lashes. But his unruly, carrot-colored hair left her speechless. It seemed incongruous, knowing the other Wallabee boys as she did.

Samuel stood and extended his hand, his gaze steady and watchful. He was indeed taller than both his brothers. "Nurse Davis, I'm pleased to meet you," he said sincerely. "Thank you for taking care of my mother until I could get here."

"Your mother is being kind, Mr. Wallabee. I did nothing out of the ordinary. It was a horrendous day for us all."

"Please, call me Sam. Only my father is called Mr. Wallabee."

"I've been off duty for a few days, Mrs. Wallabee. Has there been any word about your husband?" Miranda asked hopefully.

"No," Angelina replied simply.

"We still don't know much about my brothers," interjected Samuel, who had remained standing. "We've been hoping to speak with a doctor about their condition."

"Yes, of course," Miranda replied. "I need to attend rounds, but right after that, I'll bring a doctor to meet with you and your mother."

"Thank you."

Forty minutes later Miranda returned with Dr. Patrick. Angelina, who had fallen asleep, was snoring daintily, her head propped against the back of an adjoining chair and Samuel signaled them not to wake her. "She really hasn't slept since the fire," he whispered.

They moved to the other side of the room, and Dr. Patrick

explained the seriousness of first Tony's and then Al's injuries. As was his nature, he did not sugarcoat the information, nor did he say more than he felt was needed.

"They are gravely ill," he told Samuel plainly but gently. "Both have serious injuries and neither has responded to treatment. In fact, I would say that both of them have worsened in the past twenty-four hours. I'm sorry to have to tell you this, Mr. Wallabee, but I don't expect either to regain consciousness."

Dr. Patrick paused, assuming Samuel would want to say something or ask a question. But Samuel remained silent, looking very, very pale.

"Well, please excuse me, Mr. Wallabee," Dr. Patrick continued. "I have more patients I need to check on."

"Thank you, Doctor," Samuel whispered before walking back to where his mother still slept.

Despite her detachment, Miranda's heart ached for this stranger—this young man with a strong, handsome face who now wept openly, curled up beside his mother like a small boy.

Like her brother, Francois, an unpredictable event had been thrust upon him—an awesome responsibility, a liability that he hadn't contemplated, wasn't equipped for, and certainly wouldn't have chosen for himself.

Seated on a bench with her back to the pavilion, Miranda was forced to pull up her collar and stuff her hands deep into her pockets as the wind whipped her hair. When she could no longer feel her hands and feet, she stood and automatically headed to what was called The Shelter—the irony of its name not lost on her. Though it overlooked the river and was open to the weather, the massive trees and overgrown shrubbery below seemed to redirect the wind.

Once inside, she lowered her collar and rubbed her hands together briskly until their color returned. This had always been her place of refuge, a quiet, solitary retreat. She favored the south side with its sweeping views. But as she approached, she was startled by a lone figure huddled there. As her eyes adjusted to the dimness, she saw someone she recognized.

"I'm terribly sorry, Mr. Wallabee, I didn't know it was you. I sit here myself sometimes but don't wish to disturb." She turned to go.

His head snapped up. "Nurse Davis. Sorry, I was lost in thought. Please," he said, pointing to the empty bench beside him.

"Has there been any change?" she asked with trepidation.

"In my brothers? No."

"Mr. Walla . . . Samuel," she corrected herself, "I've heard something about your father, but I don't know if it would comfort your mother or not."

"Please, Nurse Davis, if you know where he is, tell me!"

Flooded with anxiety that telling him might make things worse, she pushed ahead before she could change her mind. "I believe he didn't survive the fire," she told Samuel as gently as she could. "He saved others, but then he was trapped."

Samuel looked at her in total disbelief. "What? I mean, how do you . . ." Wide-eyed, he stared at her as if she were an apparition.

"On the evening of the fire, Samuel, I walked to the mill. It was very late," she explained. "I met some women huddled on the perimeter. Women who worked in the mill that day and had survived the fire."

She told him what she'd learned about his father's heroism. How he had saved so many of the women on his floor. She told him how the landing became entirely blocked by a burning beam too heavy to lift . . . and that no one could use the stairs after that.

Samuel was crying so quietly that, until she turned to face him, she hadn't heard him.

"I always knew my parents were courageous people," he said. "My mother told us so many stories about their life, if you could call it that, in Italy. How they risked and sold everything in order to come to America. I can't even imagine it. Selling everything, leaving everyone you know, going to a place you've never been to before."

Miranda could think of nothing to say.

"Thank you, Nurse Davis, for telling me. It's a great comfort to finally know what happened and how courageous he was. My mother will feel some relief, I'm sure of it."

"There's a bit more, Samuel."

"Yes?"

Miranda told him about how a young mule spinner named Tony had broken windows and lowered women onto the fire engine's ladders before the building collapsed.

"You might want to ask your mother if your brother, Anthony, was a mule spinner. Unfortunately, that's all I know."

Miranda left him then, dazed and weeping, hoping she'd done the right thing. She didn't help Francois, but perhaps she could help Samuel?

Both Alphonso's and Anthony's names were crossed off the admittance list the next morning. Miranda walled this fresh pain, as she had the old, in the basement of her mind. She did not attend the funeral, did not even ask to, although she knew with certainty that Sister Madeline would have given her permission.

As she did most afternoons at the end of her shift, Miranda walked to The Shelter, where she sat quietly, hands in her pockets. Occasionally, if she was lucky, she'd see her brother in the distance or hear him laughing with his friend, Al, as they headed off for some adventure, and she would smile for these treasured, fleeting moments of connection.

She looked up to find Samuel standing in front of her.

"I wanted to thank you for all your help," he said sincerely, "I couldn't leave without thanking you again."

"You're going back to school then? That's good. Is Mrs. Wallabee going with you?"

"No," he replied. "She's decided to share a home with her friend, Mrs. Haggerty. The Haggertys lived upstairs from us and helped my parents learn English. My mother will have a companion and Mrs. Haggerty will have a little money coming in. It's a good arrangement, I think."

"I'm so pleased to hear that she'll have a companion whose company she enjoys," replied Miranda. "It'll be good to move away from the mill and the sadness attached to it. Not that her grief will be erased, of course, but perhaps moving away will give her a little relief."

"Yes, I think you're right. I hope you are," Samuel replied. "Well, I've a train to catch. Good-bye, Nurse Davis."

"Be well, Samuel," she said kindly as he took the path to the train station.

7

PROMISES

Two weeks after the funeral for his father and brothers, Samuel Wallabee returned to Harvard University. He'd been gone nearly a month. A month spent in a purgatory of his own creation, consumed with reproach, self-doubt, and regret. Outwardly, he looked much the same, a little thinner perhaps, but no one would ever guess he was completely unmoored.

Striding from the train station, oblivious to rain pouring from low, lead clouds, he stopped when he found himself outside Dr. Everett's office. Rain that sleeted off his coat and oozed from his shoes formed a dark puddle that spread like an ink stain on the polished floor.

"Sam," cried Paul Everett, finally sensing his presence. "You're back! I'm delighted to see you. Now, tell me, how is your mother?"

"She's doing well, sir," Samuel replied too quickly. "No, of course she's not," Samuel said despondently. "I didn't mean to suggest . . ."

He stopped, took a slow breath, and began again. "She doesn't really say much, to be honest, sir. She doesn't talk about them at all."

Both men fell silent, the only sound from a small pendulum clock on the bookcase.

"For the first time in my life, my mother's inaccessible. It's as if she's gone to some other place—a place she prefers to stay." Unwittingly,

Samuel's expression exposed the enormity of his anguish, and the professor felt compelled to look away.

"I am so very sorry, Sam, for you and for your mother. Is there anything, anything at all, that I can do to help her . . . or you?"

"I'd like to get right back to work, Professor," Samuel declared. "I'm her sole support now. I might even need to cut back on my coursework."

"I can't imagine that it would be a problem, Sam. Did you just get back?"

"Yes, sir. Came straight from the station. To be honest, I didn't have anywhere else to go."

Paul Everett winced to see Sam's eyes brimming with tears and hear the desperation in his voice.

"Well, that's good timing then," he announced brusquely. "I'm up to my ears in midterms. Grades due end of the week. Could definitely use some help, if you've got time?"

"Absolutely, sir!" Flushed with relief, Sam peeled off his soggy coat and flung it over the hallway bench. "Where would you like me to start?"

At the end of his senior year, as in previous years, Sam stayed on to help the professor correct freshmen and sophomore exams, grade senior papers, and post final grades with the registrar. But this time, December 1872, his last, was bittersweet.

Once he booked his train home, the relief and buoyancy he'd anticipated failed to materialize. Instead, a sense of dread, more oppressive than the swollen winter sky, swaddled him.

It was his first Christmas with just his mother, and he'd come to accept, without a snippet of self-pity, that a Dickensian gloom would muffle the upcoming holiday—and, most likely, every holiday for the rest of his life.

In this context, the professor's invitation to a celebratory lunch at the Faculty Club before he left was as welcome as a lighthouse beacon to a hapless skipper in a fierce Atlantic storm. Samuel was determined that the entrenched melancholy he'd worn like a coat these past months would not mar this final meeting with his mentor and champion.

Over the years, their teacher-student relationship had morphed into a collegial one. Samuel could never repay this honorable, dignified man with impeccable manners, a self-deprecating sense of humor, and an addiction to coffee.

"So, Sam," Paul Everett asked as a waiter cleared their plates and poured coffee, "what's next for you?"

"Don't have much of a plan yet, except to find a suitable position near Fall River so I can take care of my mother."

"Well, Sam," the professor said, glancing at his watch, "there's another reason why I invited you to lunch, although celebrating your graduation was certainly reason enough. But this matter pertains to your future and since, as you say, your plans are not completely firm, there is something I'd like you to consider over the holidays."

"What is it?" Samuel asked, placing his cup into the rim of its saucer. He too had become quite the coffee gourmand over the last few years, another legacy of the professor's largess.

The professor sipped his coffee and replaced his cup to its saucer. "Well," he began, "it's a long story actually—so hear me out before you bombard me with questions, yes?"

"Okay," replied Samuel, his curiosity now fully piqued.

"Sam, there's a small group of investors who are in negotiations to purchase and rebuild the Troy Mill. They've made a series of inquiries through intermediaries and it appears that the current owners seem agreeable to the idea of selling—although a price is not firm as yet.

"I'm talking about a diverse group of investors, successful

businessmen for the most part, who, after evaluating the mill's numbers, have put together a proposal. But I suppose you're wondering what all this has to do with you? Or me, for that matter?"

Samuel nodded.

"Well, assuming we can get the price we want, we'd like you to consider managing it."

"Manage what?"

"Manage the mill, of course."

"Manage the mill?" Samuel repeated each word slowly, weighing it, as if the idea was as improbable as being asked to take over the university's presidency.

"Now, don't reject the idea outright, Sam," the professor cautioned firmly, "at least without knowing all the details—which I have here."

The professor extracted a large envelope from his briefcase and passed it across to Samuel. "The details are spelled out quite clearly, but, in a nutshell, you'd be paid a salary and a small percentage of the profits once the mill is running again. You'd be one of five managers, in charge of the day-to-day operations.

"You will have an option, as will the others, to buy out any of the investors at an agreed upon price, thereby increasing your profit percentage by his.

"We'd want to hear, one way or the other, after the New Year. If you are willing to consider the offer, we'd be most agreeable to discussing any specific concerns you might have. In fact, we would look forward to that."

Sam was absolutely dumbfounded. "You can't be serious, Professor? Are you telling me that you know a group of men who are financially able to buy and then totally rebuild the Troy Mill? Why that would take thousands, tens of thousands of dollars."

"Yes, I imagine it will," replied the professor. "And clearly you are astonished. No doubt, you're wondering how I could garner that kind of financial backing or how I came to acquire such business connections. Am I right?" Dr. Everett asked, a bemused smile on his face.

"I'm so sorry, Professor, I didn't mean to imply . . ." Ruby blotches started to spread across Samuel's cheeks.

"Ah, my young friend, I totally understand your dilemma." Paul Everett was smiling broadly now. "As it happened, my parents were quite comfortable financially. My father was quite well respected in the shipping industry, and my mother was an accomplished pianist who was invited once to play at the Paris Conservatory."

"As their only child, I inherited their property and assets when they passed some years ago. Now, don't misunderstand, Sam, I certainly don't disparage them for surrounding themselves with elegant possessions. But, after they passed, I didn't need such things and sold most of them, investing conservatively, but wisely, I believe."

"So, you're buying the mill?" Samuel asked, his mouth agape.

"Oh, no, absolutely not!" Dr. Everett laughed so heartily that he began to cough. "Though you do flatter me to suggest I'm financially able to do so on my own. I'm one of four investors, Sam. You'll meet the others if you decide to seriously consider this offer—which I sincerely hope you do.

"Now, Sam," he said, laboring to extract his ample frame from the delicate Victorian chair, "you've got a train to catch, and I've got some last-minute holiday purchases to see to.

"By the way, Sam, whatever you decide about the mill, I can't leave today without telling you how very proud I am of you. Safe journey, my boy."

Flushed with pride, Sam extended his hand, expecting the usual handshake, but Paul Everett leaned in and gave Samuel an awkward hug, slapping his back heartily. Then, he quickly turned to go.

Dr. Everett stopped short and turned back. "Sam," he said gently but firmly, "you're no longer my student. My friends call me Paul. Do you think you might become comfortable with that?" He flashed a brief smile, turned, and strode out, without waiting for an answer.

Samuel read and reread the professor's proposal on the train. He pulled out a notebook and began making a list of names and questions. By the time the train stopped at the Fall River station, he'd filled twelve pages.

The Christmas holiday was, as Samuel expected, a disconsolate time. His mother, who continued dressing in heavy mourning clothes, compulsively pulled rosary beads from her pocket whenever she sat. Her clothing hung on her, and her pale face was as translucent as onion skin, taut across her cheekbones but slack at the corners of her mouth.

Christmas Day arrived blustery and frigid. He was relieved that his mother did not mention attending Christmas services, and, in fact, Angelina remained in her room most of the day. Samuel worked at the kitchen table all morning and ventured out for a short walk just after noon. Although well bundled, he returned with blazing cheeks, frozen tears in the corners of his eyes, and a thin icicle on the end of his nose.

He had such fond memories of Christmases past. Angelina would decorate every window with red bows and hang a sheaf of pine branches on the front door, branches he helped her choose and carry back from the woods. For weeks ahead, she baked—dozens of gingerbread cookies, which he was allowed to help decorate, cranberry-nut loaves, and, his favorite, jam-filled shortbreads. Whenever he came home, the sweet smells of warm cinnamon, spicy clove, or tangy ginger would assail him.

Not today. Angelina prepared only a simple hash, using leftovers from the day before, although she added a fresh sausage. Samuel was bitterly disappointed and then annoyed that she'd made so little effort. He was, after all, still very much alive.

While Angelina seemed unaware of his company, he attempted to entertain her with some of the professor's travel stories, but she remained silent and lumpish. Tired of his own monologue, he finished the tasteless meal in silence.

Despite the storm, Samuel went out again after dark, deeply troubled and hoping the icy wind would clear his head. He took quiet pleasure in the familiarity of his old neighborhood streets, their edges softened by the nebulous glow of streetlamps.

Why was his mother's continued grief so vexing? he wondered. How could he have thought her pathetic and heartless? What kind of son thinks such things about his own mother? A mother, who, without complaint, had risen at four every morning for a decade, put on a crisp, white apron, and made breakfast for thirty girls and one red-haired, sleepy little boy.

This tall, graceful woman who seemed to glide, rather than walk, across a room; this courageous woman who, despite exhausting days, made time to learn how to read and write. He'd never met another woman like her and doubted he ever would.

She'd set him on a different path before he could even read. Once he entered high school, she'd begun preparing him for college and, in particular, for a place called Harvard University, describing its majestic buildings, its ancient shade trees, and cobblestone walkways encrusted with moss so thick it muffled the footsteps of all who passed by.

While he, personally, had never seen or heard about this Harvard place, he never doubted her. She was utterly unassailable in her belief that he belonged there and forecast that he would, in fact, be accepted there. And in the end, it happened exactly as she had predicted.

His feelings and thoughts, although filtered through unutterable sorrow, were now more focused. First was the certainty that he could not protect her, despite the fact that she had always protected him. Next came the more painful recognition that he was utterly powerless to coax her back—to make her choose to live. But most painful was the knowledge that he was condemned to watch from the sidelines as she folded in on herself—disconnecting from life, disconnecting from him.

He wasn't sure he could live without her, without her support, without her certainty, without her dreams to guide him. He could not cure her, he could not repay her, and he could not deliver her from her grief. He could only endure without breaking—just as she had.

He decided, as fat, feathery snowflakes accumulated on the brim of his hat, that he would think of a way to honor her. *I will become the man she wanted me to be,* he vowed. *No matter what it takes, my life will emulate the achievements she wanted for me. My life will celebrate hers.*

When he heard the faint knock on his front door, Mitchell Eagan, sixty-two, thought the neighbor kids were playing tricks on him again—it being the day after Christmas.

"Eva, darlin'," he called from the couch, "someone's at the door!" Mitchell heard a second knock, louder this time.

"Damn woman," Mitchell murmured, "probably out back yakkin' with a neighbor."

He heaved himself to a sitting position, grabbed the crutches resting against the arm of the couch, and hauled himself to his feet, instinctively hugging his abdomen with his free arm to lessen the pain—at least he thought it lessened the pain. Then he hobbled to the door and yanked it open.

"This better not be a prank, you little bastards, or I'll whip your behinds," he yelled.

The young man standing on the porch did not flinch but was puzzled by Mitchell's greeting.

"Greetings, Mitch. Came to bring you some holiday cheer," Samuel said, holding up a bottle of good Irish whiskey in his left hand.

"Assuming you haven't given up the drink!"

"It's Sam Wallabee, Mitch. Guido's son. I worked two summers for you in the carding room, remember?"

"Oh, my God! Sammie? Oh my God! Eva come here!" Mitch shouted, forgetting that she wasn't in the house.

"Sammie Wallabee! Come in, come in!" Mitchell hopped out of the way. "Sit," he ordered.

While Sam removed a stack of old newspapers from the only chair in the room, Mitch hobbled back to the couch and fell back into it, replacing the crutches where they'd been.

"I'll be damned," he said, shaking his head from side to side, a big smile on his face. "Look, Sammie, I was sorry to hear about your father, he was a damn good man. We musta worked together what, fifteen years or so before his promotion? And I never begrudged him that," he announced proudly, "not like some of the others. Nope, Guido earned it fair and square."

"Thanks, Mitch." Sam waited, but Mitch had nothing more to say. "Sorry to just drop by like this—didn't know if you still lived here."

"No worries, Sammie. Yeh, me and Eva are still here. How much longer though, who knows?"

Sam pointed at Mitch's cast. "From the fire?" he asked.

"Yep," Mitch said, pulling down the top of his coveralls and lifting his shirt to reveal the dingy bandages surrounding his abdomen. "Lost a kidney too. The leg's broke bad in three places. Doc's not sure if I'll be walkin' any time soon."

"Sorry, Mitch. And Eva?"

"We're just getting by, Sammie, to tell the truth. We get to live here three more months. If I'm not up to working by then, well, who knows? Don't even know if the mill will reopen. Eva don't say much, but I'm sure she's worried sick."

As if on cue, the back door slammed and a female voice from the kitchen yelled, "Hey, hon, I'm back now. Do you need anything?"

"Yep," Mitch yelled, giving Sam a wink, "bring a couple glasses in here, would ya?"

Eva entered the front room, carrying two small glasses in one hand, bewilderment on her face. She stopped short as soon as she saw a stranger sitting in what was usually her chair.

"Eva, this is Sammie Wallabee. Don't think you ever met him. Guido Wallabee's son, you remember Guido?"

"No, don't think so, Mitch."

"Jeeze, Eva, I worked with the guy over fifteen years, the Eyetalian guy?"

"Oh, yeah," she replied unconvincingly. "Hello. How's your father doin'?"

"Eva, for Crissake, his father was killed in the fire!" Mitch looked over at Sam apologetically.

"I'm sorry for your loss," Eva mumbled, clearly embarrassed. "I didn't know."

"Thanks, Eva. Lost both brothers too," Sam added sadly.

"What?" Mitchell cried, his left arm pressed across his abdomen. "Tony and Al too? I never heard that. Jesus Christ, I'm awful sorry, Sammie. I'll take that drink now."

Eva excused herself and Sam filled the tumblers, the first of many times.

"Mitch, I need your advice." Sam stopped, not knowing exactly how to proceed. "Look this'll sound strange, but there's some people who may buy the mill, fix it up."

"Advice?" asked Mitch, squinting, as if the mill news was inconsequential.

"They're offering me a position in the mill, if the deal goes through.

It's a long story. We don't need to get into that now, but I wondered what advice you'd have if somebody did, in fact, rebuild the mill?"

"Advice?" Mitchell repeated, scratching his scalp thoughtfully. "Why the hell would anybody ask me for advice?"

"Jeez, Mitch, you worked there almost twenty-five years! You supervised me when you ran the carding room. You ran the mule spinners after that. I bet you've worked in just about every department there and supervised many of them."

"Just about," Mitch replied slowly. "What's this about, Sammie? They're not going to hire me back, that's for sure. Bein' as I can't walk."

"Do you know what a consultant is, Mitch?"

"Nope, never heard of it."

"Well, I just found out myself. See, when a person knows a lot about something, say carding machines, he can teach others how to run them and get paid for teaching them. That's what a consultant does."

"So?" Mitch emptied his glass and held it out for a refill.

"Mitch, I need some consultants," Sam said, refilling Mitch's glass. "People who know a lot about running the different sections of the mill. Like maybe one day you had an idea about how to improve the carder or you figured out a way to keep the yarns from breaking so easily. Things like that."

"Why me?" Mitchell eyed Sam with suspicion.

"My father respected you, Mitch, talked about you a lot and a few others whose names I wrote here." Sam passed Mitch a piece of paper. "I'd like to meet with these men. I've got questions I need answered before I decide whether or not to take the job they're offering. I'll pay each man for his time."

Mitchell was silent for a long while. He squinted at the list and scrutinized Sam's face. Then he emptied his glass in one gulp and held it out for refilling.

"Will you help me, Mitch?"

"Hell, Sammie! What would your father think if I said no?"

"Great!" Sam felt like he was flying. "Okay, take a look at the names on that list. Would you take any names off? Would you add anybody? I need a cross section of good men, knowledgeable men from every section."

Mitchell studied the list of names again. "Okay," he said, "first off, Danny Holmes, Tom Wright, and Tobias Morrill, they all died in the fire, so . . ."

Mitchell watched as Sam crossed those names off. "Who else? Be honest, Mitch."

"Well," Mitchell seemed uncomfortable and self-conscious, "I don't think much of Frank Littleton, though I know your father got along with him. Most of us didn't. He's a scrappy Yank, always got something to say, mostly complaints. He was good at his job, don't get me wrong, but he didn't think anybody else was good at theirs, if you know what I mean? Not sure he'd have much in the way of good advice to give."

"Okay," Sam said, crossing Littleton's name off. "Let's see who's left. No one can speak about carding better than you. Wheeler and Lescourt are experienced weavers, Sullivan ran the web drawing room, Harding supervised the speeders for a while, Crandall worked in the spinning room, although he wasn't a supervisor, and Luther was a slasher. Are we covered?"

"I don't know whether Lescourt or Luther would be willing to meet."

"Why's that?"

"Both got hurt bad when the fourth floor collapsed. Lescourt's blind and Luther broke both arms."

"Well, Mitch, they can still talk, right? I'm interested to hear what they think. Far as I'm concerned, they both have a lot to offer. If they don't feel up to meeting in a group, I'm happy to meet with them in their homes. Wouldn't hurt to ask, right?"

"No, not at all. Glad you want to include them."

"Any others?"

"Well, maybe, add Lloyd Covell. He worked the second and fourth floors for a while but then got sent to the other building. I know for sure he did some time in sales and maybe purchasing, though I could be wrong about that. I could ask around. Is he somebody you'd want to speak to?"

"Absolutely! Good idea! Let's get started then. Mitch, let's set up a meeting for the day after tomorrow, say around ten thirty in the morning? We'll likely need to meet as a group more than once, depending on how it goes.

"Meanwhile, could you find us a meeting place, large enough for nine or ten of us? And we'll need someone to take some notes during the meeting—I don't want to forget any idea or suggestion. So, could you ask around for the name of a secretary?"

"Sure, no need to worry about a meeting place, St. Mary's rectory's two blocks over. I'll ask Father Montrose, but I'm sure it's okay. Then I'll get word to the guys about the meeting. I don't know no secretary, Sammie, but Eva might."

"Okay, then. See you Wednesday, Mitch. I'll pick you up here about ten fifteen and take you over." Sam pulled on his coat and fished in the pocket for his gloves.

As Sam reached the door, Mitch said, "Sammie, it was real good to see you. Real good. And thanks."

Mitchell Eagan hadn't felt this upbeat in a long, long time. He finally had something serious to do. He was a part of things again, important things, if Sammie Wallabee was anything like his father.

The bitter cold woke Samuel before dawn. He rose quickly, wrapping himself in a worn, woolen cape, which, because of sizable holes, did not provide the warmth it promised. Stuffing his feet into a second pair of socks without noticing they were mismatched, relighting the fire, he paced as he waited for the room to warm.

It was unarguably bad luck to have his entire future depend on a meeting with three strangers, but today he would finally chart his own course. He would step out of the shadows and persuade a few wealthy, powerful, and likely prejudicial men that he was unequivocally capable and experienced.

He was prepared to rebut any narrow-minded skepticism, to expose without confrontation any illusions they might have about textile manufacturing, to refute the prejudgments they'd assuredly made about him. He would not be intimidated by wealth, nor would he let them underestimate or depreciate his experience. Today was heavy with promise.

Never a man who fussed over his appearance, Samuel selected his best clothes, the ones he'd purchased for his father's funeral. As he had on the day of the funeral, he slipped his father's gold watch into the vest pocket, attaching the fob to an upper pocket. The watch had been handed down from Samuel's great-grandfather. With this watch in his pocket, he felt adjoined to something ancient, something precious, something irreplaceable.

As Samuel strode along the familiar sidewalks of his birthplace, with old snow rotting in drifts along the edges, last night's dusting yelped under his resoled shoes. The air, crisper than a new dollar bill, cooler than peppermint, jittered his teeth.

Gas lights, each throwing a perfect halo of light, hissed and burbled as he passed, he was alone in the unsullied stillness of a brand-new morning. Rich, golden rays dripped across the horizon like liquid honey, illuminating the top of one steeple after another, standing there like exclamation points or enormous candles.

The redemptive power of this moment was never lost on him, and he stopped to witness the birth of a new day, unfolding like a delicate flower, so full of innocence and promise. This magical moment when the soft light curves and time seems to move differently, this powerful, joyous sliver of time always persuaded him that nothing was ever out of reach.

He remembered his father plodding home after a ten-hour workday, clenching his lunch pail as if it held all the frustrations and provocations of his day, stopping on every landing to catch his breath, his face blighted by years of unexpressed resentments, unrewarded sacrifices, and unrealized dreams.

And, so too, his beloved mother. Her innate optimism blunted by years of crushing responsibilities, her dreams diminished by opportunities denied her, her spirit numbed by the constant worry of insolvency—of losing everything—until, indeed, she lost everything.

He was the sole survivor, the last of a proud, piteously poor clan. He remembered his brothers' rage at the class prejudice that continually undermined and unmanned them. All of them had patiently played by the rules, deserving so much more than they'd ever received. They were all owed. It was incumbent upon Samuel—his duty as he now saw it—to finally make things right.

Professor Everett had reserved a small conference room at the Mohican where they intended to interview prospective managers for the next few days. Samuel arrived just before his nine o'clock appointment and was relieved to see the professor waiting in the lobby. "Happy New Year!" called the professor. "Let's hope 1873 will be a better year for all of us." They hugged affectionately.

"Wonderful to see you, my boy. Happy New Year!" greeted the professor, looking his protégé up and down. "Perfect choice, Sam, you're looking quite mature and confident. I'd ask if you're ready to face the others, but I can see by the papers in your hand that you are."

"Well, Professor, I did take the liberty of preparing some material, but I would welcome any advice you could offer me."

"Be patient, Sam. These are all accomplished men. Don't assume they realize that running a textile mill is any different from running their own businesses. And," he added waggishly, "I suppose it wouldn't hurt to remember that old men tend to get crotchety when they feel upstaged by younger men, however bright they might be." The professor laughed and clapped Samuel on the back.

"I'll try to remember that, Professor," Samuel said, smiling broadly.

Turning down a narrow hallway, the professor paused at the threshold of a room with gleaming paneling where three men sat expectantly around a carved, mahogany table. The air, though cool, was quite stale, and an indolent corkscrew of smoke rose from a cigar propped in an ashtray.

"Gentlemen," the professor greeted them enthusiastically, his arm around Sam's shoulder, "may I present Samuel Wallabee.

"Sam," he announced, gesturing, "this is Archer Brownley, Jr., vice president of the Fall River National Bank, the oldest and largest in Fall River."

"Pleased to meet you, sir," Samuel said, extending his hand. Archer rose, and, with an eager smile, pumped Samuel's hand firmly.

"And this roguish chap," the professor added playfully, "is Jeremiah Buffington, senior partner at Graves, Buffington and Hill. Their law firm was the first to take offices in the marvelous Granite Block Building."

Jeremiah stood and extended his hand before Samuel could. "Pleased to meet you, Samuel," he said, but his tepid smile belied any pleasure.

"And last, but certainly not least, may I present Colonel Bradford Wheeler, one of the most accomplished shipbuilders on the East Coast and founder of the Fall River Iron Works."

"Sir, it's indeed a pleasure," said Samuel, extending his hand, which the old man pretended not to see. Unlike the others, the colonel remained seated, picked up his cigar from the ashtray, and nodded in Samuel's direction.

Jeremiah suggested—his tone more demanding than requesting—that Archer bring the group up-to-date regarding the sale and rebuilding plans.

As Archer spoke, Samuel studied the three men. Archer appeared the youngest, perhaps early forties, and except for neat muttonchops, he was clean-shaven, his dark hair oiled, as was the custom, and his face, while expressive, was androgynous. Overall, he was impeccably and conservatively dressed but wore a theatrical, royal blue silk tie with a diamond stickpin.

Jeremiah Buffington, on the other hand, was as reticent as his somber black coat and thin black bow tie suggested. Jeremiah's expression was impenetrable and unbecomingly smug. Samuel found his demeanor off-putting. Instinctively, Samuel knew he would not trust this man whose hooded, ambitious eyes hinted at some deceit, at something held back.

In Samuel's opinion, Colonel Wheeler was the oldest, probably in his seventies, and the most fascinating, having about him the gritty cantankerousness that many older men develop. The colonel's appearance was less meticulous than might have been expected of a former military officer. He was compact, top-heavy, and doughy where one might have expected a wiry, flint-tempered, polished man.

For a supposedly wealthy man, his clothing was quite ordinary, even a bit old-fashioned. Samuel noticed that his shirt cuffs were slightly frayed and limp from a lack of proper starching and his outdated waistcoat was missing a button. The knot of his cravat was so off-kilter, it was both comical and plaintive. Samuel wondered whether the colonel was the "crotchety" old man the professor had alluded to earlier.

"Well, I have a question," announced the colonel, diving right in as he might have into a battle and causing the professor to wince. "I'd like to know how the deuces someone your age thinks he can run an operation like this! What experience qualifies you, young man?"

The colonel's tone was as abrasive as his wiry, white beard, and Samuel had no trouble reading the underlying message.

"I believe I'm qualified on several levels, gentlemen," Samuel replied without a hint of intimidation. "I'm more than just familiar with textile manufacturing. In a nutshell, I have, over an eight-year period, worked in every department at the Troy Mill, have experience with every step in the process of producing finished cloth from dirty bales of cotton."

Samuel glanced around the room. The colonel's lips had tightened into a thin line, and his expression was unreadable as he reached for the stub of his cigar with a liver-spotted hand. Jeremiah, pretending indifference, was either inspecting or simply fiddling with his wedding ring. Only Archer and the professor seemed attentive.

Samuel sipped from his water glass until Jeremiah, noting the silence, finally glanced up. Only then did Samuel continue, "I understand the mill's layout. Why, for example, the carding room is always on the first floor and the slashing room is on the fourth." Samuel deliberately mentioned these operations, certain the new owners would be unfamiliar with them.

"At one time or another, I've operated most of the machinery, so I know how each machine works and what skills and strength are necessary to operate them properly. Perhaps, most important, though, is that I've witnessed the circumstances that reduce productivity, which are sometimes in the layout, sometimes in the machinery, and sometimes in the employees."

Almost imperceptibly the colonel straightened in his chair, laid his cigar back in the ashtray, and looked more engaged. Archer sat forward in his chair, elbows on the table, but Jeremiah, unfortunately, was still preoccupied with his wedding band.

"So, Paul, now I understand why you were so determined that we meet this young man," Jeremiah offered, turning to face the professor.

"Knowing Sam as I do, I imagine he came today with questions for us? Am I correct, Sam?" asked the professor.

"Yes, I do. I wonder what your thoughts are about changing the layout of the mill."

"I'm sorry?" Jeremiah interjected gruffly. "But I don't quite understand what you're asking, Sam, or frankly, why it's a concern of yours."

Samuel bristled but refused to rise to the bait. "Well," he replied courteously, "I'm asking because I think it ought to be considered, especially since, as Archer reported, all or part of the mill will have to be rebuilt.

"Let me use the legal profession as an example of what I mean. In the practice of law, one is restricted by the parameters of the law and, to some degree, social custom. Would you agree, Jeremiah?"

Jeremiah nodded reluctantly.

"I would imagine that, over the years, you and your partners have thought of more efficient, perhaps even fairer, ways to do things, but you've been constrained from making changes by an outdated law perhaps or some unquestioned social custom?"

"Well, yes, yes of course," stammered Jeremiah, who now couldn't decide whether to feel flattered or insulted by Samuel's analogy.

"Well, manufacturing, like the legal profession, has its traditions as well. Take carding for example, one of the most dangerous, dirty jobs. It's always on the bottom floor because the machine needs the most water pressure and because a bale weighs about four hundred fifty pounds dry, by the way."

The small gasp Samuel heard reassured him that, as he'd hoped, the new owners did not know the operations as well as he did.

"But, Sam, those sound like a perfectly legitimate reason for locating—*carding*, is that the correct name?—on the first floor," interjected Archer, looking from man to man for affirmation.

"Absolutely," Samuel replied evenly, "before the invention of the steam engine."

Samuel watched the men's faces change and become smooth and blank. No one wanted to ask a question that might expose his lack of knowledge, and Samuel wanted to keep them off-balance.

"Perhaps you might clarify that for us, Sam?" the professor prompted.

"Of course, Professor. Sorry. As you know, the Troy Mill, like most others, is located along a river which provides the power to run it. The mills rely on the amount of water in the river and how powerfully it moves.

"Now, water level is dependent upon weather—how much snow fell in the winter, how much rain fell in the spring, how hot the summer was—none of which we can control."

"Of course," interjected the colonel, nodding vigorously, happy to show he followed the logic.

"But," Samuel cautioned, "the recent invention of the steam engine will change our dependency on these things. It's still a relatively new invention, but it could dramatically alter the manufacturing process."

"But these steam engines are, I would imagine, much more expensive, are they not?" asked Jeremiah peevishly, roundish pink spots appearing on his cheeks. "And," he added in mocking irony, "what assurance do we have that they will be more reliable? Surely, you aren't suggesting that we move the mill?"

"More expensive?" Samuel repeated the one question he'd fully anticipated. "Well, yes and no, Jeremiah. I suppose the introduction of the steam engine could be compared to the army's introduction of the cannon. Would you agree, Colonel?"

The colonel, looking completely baffled and quite uncomfortable, shifted in his chair and reached for his cigar. This was a gamble and Samuel knew it, but he thought it worth the risk. The colonel was the most openly hostile—Samuel needed to get his support.

A silence, complete and impenetrable, shrouded the room while Samuel bit his tongue to keep from prompting the colonel.

"Yes, I take your point, Sam," the colonel finally replied and turned in his chair to face Jeremiah.

"I think Sam's point is this, Jeremiah. Before cannons, soldiers were armed with rifles and swords—that's how wars were fought. But cannons changed that, changed the course of military history, if you ask me. They were more accurate, definitely more reliable, and more deadly at far greater distances than rifles.

"Did they cost more than rifles? Well, of course!" the colonel replied dramatically and held them in suspense while he lit another cigar.

"But," he said, puffing, enjoying the attention, "and this is the point I think Sam is trying to make, cannons end up saving lives because soldiers no longer have to engage the enemy so closely. And battles end more quickly because well-placed cannonballs can kill more people than single bullets and can bring down an enemy's fortification, which a bullet can't do. And it's hard to put a price on these kinds of things, but saving soldiers' lives and shortening wars seemed worth the cost. Have I got it right, young man?"

"Exactly right, Colonel! Thank you." Sam smiled broadly, flooded with relief. Samuel suspected that, as the oldest man in the group, the colonel's input was often overlooked or, worse, devalued. But right now, the colonel appeared insightful, someone with relevant experience—which Samuel hoped might raise his status.

"Getting back to textile mills," Sam continued, "here are the production figures for the years 1850, 1860, and 1870." He passed around a page of numbers and waited until each man had time to read it.

"As you can see, regardless of the year or the number of spindles, four months—April, May, October, and November—are the most productive months. Now, I thought this surprising. In my opinion, it not only confirms the mill's dependency on water and weather but gives us a way to put a price on that dependency."

"Really?" asked Archer, pulling his chair closer to the table.

"Yes. I believe it does. Ice builds up in winter and gradually slows the river, sometimes blocking it completely. Hot summers produce droughts that lower water levels. Typically, there is more rainfall in spring and fall, so there would be more water available in those months, and, as a result, we would expect production to be higher."

"That does seem intuitive, as you explain it," offered Jeremiah graciously.

"But, and this is the real surprise," Samuel added, his excitement growing, "roughly seventy-three percent of total annual production occurs in these four months! Again, regardless of the year or the number of spindles operating."

"What! That can't be!" exclaimed Archer, making another note in a small ledger.

"I've drawn this for you," Samuel said, passing an illustration to the colonel seated to his right. He sipped his water and waited while each man examined the graph.

"So, in answer to your question, Jeremiah, steam engines do cost more than waterwheels. However, as the colonel suggested, there may be benefits that make that investment worthwhile. For example, I would argue that eliminating the mill's dependence on water levels and weather, since neither is controllable, would be a good thing.

"Of course, only the board can determine whether it's a risk worth taking. But it does seem reasonable to assume that, without this dependency, overall production would increase. Surely the eight months of lower productivity would increase—perhaps even to the level of the four most productive months, without making any other changes."

"Hmmm," mused Archer thoughtfully, making more notes, "I understand your thinking."

"So, Samuel, you're suggesting that we rebuild but replace water power, in full or in part, with steam power?" asked Jeremiah without any trace of his former acerbity.

"Yes and no," replied Samuel, laughing. "Mitchell Eagan, a carding room supervisor at Troy for fifteen years, with whom I apprenticed, was the man who actually suggested it. Just as Laurence Crandall, a spinning room supervisor for eighteen years thought that daily removal of lint buildup and spraying individual bobbins instead of the entire room would reduce thread breakage and work stoppages."

No one spoke, each man was lost in his own thoughts, and the room was silent.

"Joseph Wheeler and Francois Lescourt, both expert weavers," Samuel continued, "thought that by following Crandall's suggestion, we could reduce absenteeism from ailments that they have come to believe are related to breathing that damp, lint-filled air.

"While I considered your proposal, I met several times with eight men who have over a hundred thirty years' experience working in the Troy Mill. They represent every operational and one administrative department, and are essentially Troy Mill historians who can tell you, as they did me, what works, what doesn't, and why.

"For me to accept your offer, I would want your permission to rehire them, increase their salaries, and give each sole authority for the hiring and firing in his area.

"In addition, and I know this will be controversial, I want the board to provide some sort of compensation to the families of those who died in the fire."

"What!" Surprisingly it was Archer who interrupted, his face darkened in disapproval. "That alone will undo us! I've never heard of such a thing, and I certainly would never support such an idea!"

"Nor I," Jeremiah stated emphatically.

"Ah yes, compensation," Samuel reiterated. "Such a powerful incentive, isn't it? Giving it? Withholding it?"

"Colonel Wheeler, sir." Samuel turned once again to the military man for assistance. "You've had to lead men into mortal danger again and again, and more than any man here, you've had to face the cruelest possible consequences if you are unsuccessful—the slaughter of brave men, fathers of young children who will never know them, husbands whose widows, now penniless, will slide into society's poorest and lowest class.

"What are your thoughts about support, Colonel? How did you prepare men for battle? To follow your orders without question? To die, if necessary, to complete the mission?"

"Hmm," the colonel said, clearing his throat of phlegm. "Well, I don't mollycoddle them, you can be sure of that!" he said sharply, wanting to make it perfectly clear that he was not one to pamper his troops.

"But expecting men to do their best for you without supporting them is like spitting into the wind. Soldiers must believe they can succeed, and they must feel your commitment to their success. You get them enough food, medical attention when they need it, and arm them as well as or better than the enemy. In my experience, a good soldier doesn't expect miracles, but, and you can believe me on this, every soldier knows if you're committed or not.

"Our most beloved leaders were like that. They showed their men respect, they lived with them, ate what they ate, and their troops walked through fire for them." On this point, the colonel's eyes teared, and he turned away as some unexpectedly powerful memory pulled him back onto some battlefield, somewhere in the rubble of his past.

Again, a heavy silence draped the room.

The professor took off his glasses and rubbed his eyes gently. "I wish you could have heard the seminar Sam gave the executive committee, Jeremiah" the professor replied enthusiastically. "He's incredibly knowledgeable about this business—to the point where he is able to explain these complex processes and complicated machinery to the uneducated.

"As he has today, he does his homework and brings supportive data because he doesn't expect anyone to blindly accept what he says. I've come to know that this is his nature. He abhors mediocrity and won't accept it in himself. He's as respectful and as comfortable talking with weavers and carders as he is with academics and businessmen.

"But the most astonishing thing he gave us was something we hadn't asked for and didn't expect."

Each man looked at the professor expectantly, attentively.

"He painted a grotesque picture of the human suffering and inhumane conditions that existed in the Troy Mill—a picture I will never be able to wash away. I confess it left me feeling soiled and ashamed, though, at that time, I had nothing to do with textile manufacturing. I, for one, would like to see us do better than the prior owners.

"If you're wondering what I think," the professor asked, looking at each man around the table, "I think Sam's a rare combination of intelligence, courage, and humanity. He knows right from wrong and doesn't believe that complaining is the way to change things. Yes, he's a pragmatist and there's no doubt in my mind that he will get the job done for us—but he doesn't suffer fools and won't set himself up to fail.

"He's asking us to give him what he needs to succeed in the job we're thinking of offering him. He's demanding we show him that we are committed to his success. He wants to hire the best men and give them what they'll need to do their jobs well. Is there any one of us who wouldn't insist, hasn't insisted, on the same for himself?

"Jeremiah, he's asking us to believe, as he does, that providing a safer environment and demonstrating some basic human decency for those who work for us, guarantees our success . . . and his.

"Archer, at his core, Sam believes people can be better—he will drive us to be better. With him, each one of us and our mill has an opportunity to accomplish something remarkable.

"Colonel, I trust him, and, despite his age, I think he's as honorable a man as I've ever met, perhaps ever will meet."

"That's kind of you, Professor," Samuel said, rising. "Gentlemen, I imagine you've things to discuss and other candidates to interview, so I will leave you to it. But before I go, let me say this: I cannot accept the position without the contingencies I've laid out.

"Two hundred-seventy people burned to death in that fire, gentlemen. Compensating their families is simply the right thing to do and, yes, it should have been done by the previous owners, but that doesn't absolve us of some responsibility."

"That seems a bit arrogant, Samuel, I must say," Jeremiah chided. "Surely, we weren't responsible for the fire. Why would you take such an inflexible position as this?"

"Because," Samuel replied, gently fingering the watch in his pocket, "my father's body was incinerated in that fire. He worked for Troy Mill for almost twenty-five years. I'm told by witnesses that he stayed behind fighting to get every woman on his floor safely down the only staircase.

"My brother, Anthony, broke windows on the fourth floor and held women over the ledge until firemen could reach them. In the process, he and my brother Alphonso were severely injured and both died in the hospital four days later. This is not just a job to me, gentlemen, it's a sacred trust.

"I do want to thank you for your time," he added sincerely, looking each man in the eye. "It was truly an honor to have been considered." He walked out, quietly closing the door behind him.

8

TRANSFORMATIONS

Two years after the fire, the daily lives of Miranda Davis and Maddy Walker appeared unaltered. They lived together in Maddy's small apartment at St. Vincent's Orphanage, where she was now head nurse. Miranda continued to take the trolley to St. Anne's Hospital every morning and, just recently, accepted a promotion to ward supervisor.

It was a difficult time for the two friends, who were clearly traveling different paths.

Maddy had quietly blossomed into an assured young woman, her adolescent ungainliness somehow buffed smooth, her manner more confident, and even her once coarse, indeterminate brown hair, the bane of her adolescence, now framed her face in lustrous curls. Her trademark optimism and exuberant disposition, however, remained unmarred, which was at the heart of their regular disagreements.

Miranda, on the other hand, was in every way diminished. Her face was pinched with apprehension and impatience. At the hospital, she had become someone to avoid; her irascibility and, at times, her abrasiveness were legendary. An aura of loneliness and indifference shadowed her as she moved about the wards.

What grieved her most was the loss of the dream that had

sustained her since leaving the farm more than ten years ago. It was the only thing she'd ever allowed herself to want, something that had never been hers. She was forced to accept that she would never become a woman of consequence now, and her life would simply be ordinary—piteously ordinary.

"Some of us are heading over to O'Shea's tonight," Maddy said at dinner. "I'd love it if you'd come with me."

"Thanks, but I've made plans."

"And will these plans involve leaving the apartment? Because apart from work, you never do."

"If you've got something to say, say it," Miranda bristled, renewing the familiar undercurrent of discord. "If you want me to leave, just say so, it's your apartment. Whatever you want . . ." Miranda stopped, simply too weary to slog through another confrontation.

Maddy burst out laughing. "What I want? For the last two years, our lives have revolved around you, Mira—what you want, what you feel up to, what you're not ready for, what you need.

"You've made yourself a rather tragic figure, do you know that? You're Miranda Davis, who lost a brother in a terrible fire, though she never told anyone she even had a brother. Or you're Miranda Davis whose handsome suitor died, though she never intended to marry him and most likely never even loved him. The grief, the unfairness, the tragedy—it's become who you are."

"How dare you, Maddy Walker? You've never—"

"I've never what, Mira? Had to grow up without a father? Lost someone I loved? What?"

"I'm just saying it's been a terribly difficult time for me. I'm doing the best I can," Miranda said flatly.

"No! The truth is Mira, you're doing as little as possible. When was it you decided that your circumstances were more tragic than everybody else's and your pain was the most painful? You're completely self-absorbed."

Throwing her napkin down, Miranda retreated to the bedroom, slamming the door so hard the mantel clock rattled precariously.

In frustration, Maddy stormed into the bedroom after her, tired of Miranda deciding when their conversations were over.

"I don't want you to leave, Mira, but I do want you to change. I want things to be the way they were. I can't stand to see you this way." Maddy burst into tears, a release she seldom allowed herself.

The anguish on Maddy's face and the tenderness in her voice mortified Miranda even more than her friend's accusations. Maddy had been, and still was, clearly suffering, but Miranda had been too preoccupied to even notice.

"I'm so sorry, Maddy," she said softly. "I've asked you to be patient again and again and you have, but I can't continue to ask for that. I hardly recognize myself anymore, but I should have recognized what a burden I've become.

"I've never been a brave person, Maddy. Really, as a child I was always afraid of one thing or another, and now I'm so crippled by fear I can hardly take a deep breath. For as long as I can remember, something's felt broken in me—or missing. I'm sorry, I know this can't make any sense to you.

"Truth is," she continued hesitantly, "despite all I'd wanted to do with my life, in the final analysis, I've failed. From the day I was born, I've been thrashing about aimlessly like a reed blowing in the wind. My whole life has been one misstep, one blunder after another."

Miranda's face was streaked with tears tracing the delicate lines of her face. Tentatively, hopefully, she opened her arms, and the two friends clung to each other until the shoulders of their dresses were soaked with tears.

"I'm so very sorry, Maddy," Miranda said softly, breaking the silence. "You're my dearest friend and I've let you down. Worse, I've hurt you. Can you ever forgive me?"

"Some nice gentleman's left this note for you, Nurse Davis," Hannah Nicolls announced as Miranda passed the reception desk on her way to the third floor. Miranda detested Hannah's nasally voice almost as much as she disliked Hannah's proclivity to prattle on about nothing.

"He left," Hannah reported flatly, "but asked you to leave word for him."

"Thank you, Hannah." Miranda took the note, relieved to see that it was sealed. With calculated nonchalance, she slipped it into her apron pocket and, without a word, strode off.

Later, after walking over to The Shelter where she had more privacy, and she could breathe in the softer air of Spring, she opened it.

It was an invitation to join Samuel Wallabee, a man she hadn't seen in years, for tea at the Mohican Hotel—without his mother apparently—on Friday. It was not an easy decision because, although he would never know it, he was intimately connected to the worst tragedy in her life. But in the end, she accepted.

The Mohican's tearoom was so breathtaking, she stopped short at the entrance, dazzled by all the gleaming silver utensils, brilliant white tablecloths, and rows of twinkling chandeliers. The entire room shimmered.

Samuel spotted her before she reached his table and stood quickly. "I'm so pleased you could come," he said, blushing with enthusiasm, surprised at how changed she was.

Had he not stood to greet her, Miranda would not have recognized him. He no longer wore rough work clothes; the awkwardness she remembered had disappeared. He seated her unselfconsciously—seeming neither out of place here nor uncomfortable in any way.

"It was quite a surprise to receive your note, Samuel," she told him, forcing herself to smile.

"A good surprise, I hope?" he asked, flashing her the same brilliant smile she'd so admired in his brother.

"Most definitely a good surprise," she replied sincerely. "I was looking forward to seeing you again, having a chance to catch up. I hope you've been well. I imagine that you've finished college by now?"

"Yes and yes," he replied playfully and was delighted when she blushed.

A waiter, in a starched, pressed uniform, arrived carrying a silver coffeepot and a shorter, rounder teapot. He placed both on the table, adding a silver creamer and sugar bowl.

"Would the gentleman prefer the high tea?" he asked Samuel.

Glancing at Miranda, who raised no objection, Samuel replied, "Yes, we would. Thank you."

Samuel was indeed more polished, she thought, sophisticated even—or at least he'd learned to project these qualities. His perfectly tailored navy suit and simple pale-blue cravat seemed the perfect choice to complement his reddish hair, which fortunately had darkened.

"Let's see," he said, taking a deep breath. "What can I tell you? In a nutshell, after graduating, I took a manager's position at the Troy Mill, which I assume you know has been rebuilt and reopened?"

"Yes, I had heard."

"Anyway," he continued, "it's been a learning experience, working to change the mill's tragic image, adding safety features, and reducing the hours that employees work. Thankfully, it's done well since it reopened, and if all goes as planned, I'll own the mill in two, maybe three years."

"That's incredible, Samuel! What an accomplishment."

The waiter reappeared, bearing a tiered tray of thin sandwiches, miniature scones, and pastries of various shapes and colors. He placed it between them, adding a small pot of jam and a delicate plate with the creamiest sculptured pats of butter she'd ever seen.

"My goodness!" she exclaimed.

"The scones are my favorite. You must try them," Samuel said. Suspecting that she might not know how to proceed, he reached for a scone using delicate silver tongs and settled it onto her plate, adding a scoop of jam and a pat of butter.

"I'm assuming you're still a tea drinker, Nurse Davis?" he asked and without waiting for a reply, picked up her cup and poured from the teapot, leaving her room for milk. She watched him pour himself some coffee, adding a teaspoon of sugar using the darling, miniature spoon provided.

"And you?" he asked. "What's happened to you? I'm assuming it's still Miss Davis, as I don't see a wedding ring." As often as he'd rehearsed this, it still sounded transparent, and he was convinced he was blushing from his neck to the top of his head, a trait inherited from his father.

"Yes, it's still Miss Davis," she replied. "Well, I'm ward supervisor now. And please, Samuel, call me Miranda."

"Well, promoted already, Miranda!" he replied. "That's also quite an accomplishment. May I offer my congratulations?"

"Thank you, Samuel." She hesitated before adding, "And your mother? Is she well?"

"Well, Miranda"—he really enjoyed saying her name—"to tell the truth she isn't. She never really recovered from the loss of my brothers and my father. At first, I thought it was her way of grieving, you know, something temporary. But after a while, I had to admit that she seemed truly lost to me, and, finally, I've come to accept that she won't ever recover. I've had to move her into a small apartment with a full-time nurse."

"Oh, I'm so sorry, Samuel." Miranda's grief-stricken face surprised him. "I guess I can understand her wanting to withdraw from such terrible pain, especially at her age. It must be so hard to watch, though." She hoped she didn't sound clinical.

"Yes, well, I've made my peace with it." He hadn't meant to sound so dismissive, but his own pain and unhappiness had begun buzzing at the edges of his fragile resolve to shut it all out of his mind.

"And what about your family? How are they?" he inquired as much to change the subject as from curiosity.

She felt a slight twinge of conscience for the lie she was about to tell, but she simply had no choice. "I have no family, Samuel. My father died when I was eleven I hardly remember him; my mother died about a year later, and because I'm an only child, I've been on my own for a while." There, it was done.

"I'm sorry, Miranda." He hurried to change the topic, assuming that discussions about her family were as disquieting for her as his family stories were for him.

"Mmmm," he murmured appreciatively. "These little cakes are quite delicious, filled with honey and nuts. Here," he said, choosing for her, "try one."

High tea was, overall, a uniquely pleasant experience for each of them. Both enjoyed talking about their work, the many challenges they faced, and all the ways in which the city was changing and growing.

"My lord," she said, looking at her watch, "can you believe we've been talking almost two hours? Can't remember the last time I did that, but I should go, Samuel. My roommate is expecting me for dinner, although I can't imagine I'll have any appetite at all! Thank you for the invitation. I enjoyed myself very much."

"And thank you, Miranda, for spending such a delightful afternoon with me. Would you consider coming to tea again sometime?"

"I'd look forward to it, Samuel," she replied but was convinced that he was simply being polite.

But she was wrong. They continued to spend time together, strolling the city's parks, marveling at the new growth pushing up everywhere. As it happened, each loved the spring more than any other season.

Occasionally, he asked her to dinner at the Mohican, but she rarely enjoyed herself as much on those occasions, because it reminded her of graduation dinner with Maddy, Francois, Al, and Tony. Only recently had she allowed herself to miss all of them.

Sadly, she would never know how dramatically the fire had changed Samuel, how it had destroyed both their families, because she never got to witness the lovely tenderness he always showered on his mother, the pride he had in his father, or the playful way he teased his brothers.

The Samuel Wallabee that Miranda met for high tea was driven, enterprising, and ambitious. The more time they spent together, the more she noticed how emotionally disconnected he seemed, not unlike her.

They were alike in other ways as well; he was as impatient and as intolerant of mediocrity as she was—which led to some spirited arguments. And, not unlike her, he'd grown accustomed to, and in some ways preferred, his own company.

Unfortunately, they would never recognize their shared demons—the myriad ways each disguised or tried to circumvent the guilt and shame they carried, each adamantly believing that the past could be undone, negated even, by sheer will and determination. As it turned out, this was the most dangerous way in which they were alike.

"We've got to do something about your wardrobe," Maddy announced on a rare Saturday when both were free. "And, lucky for you, I know just the person to help. You've done nothing but save money since you started working. It's time to spend some. And, by the way, you might think about updating your hairstyle too."

Surprisingly, Miranda didn't argue. They rode the trolley to Maddy's mother's dress shop in the old Flint Building, fussily named

L'Elegance, where they flipped through the pages of *Le Follett Courier des Salons*, *La Mode*, and *The Ladies' Treasury*.

"Let's see," said Mrs. Walker as she eyed Miranda. "A young professional woman like you should have at least two fancy dresses for evenings and two or three walking dresses for daytime. Isn't it wonderful that you both wear uniforms at work, so you both have more money to spend on your other clothing!"

Over the next few months, Miranda's wardrobe was completely transformed, and, in a smaller way, Miranda herself was forced to change.

"Miranda Davis, you're a thin girl, too thin if you ask me." Mrs. Walker was fond of saying this. "So, these puffy sleeves you see on other girls and these tiers of ruffles, layers of fabrics, and stiff high collars—you're lost in them. They're just too much fabric for you to carry. And," the seamstress continued, "those dull browns and blacks you seem to favor are not your best colors.

"To me," she explained, "a fabric with a rich color or with an unusual texture will always create a more elegant dress. The current trend of mixing plaids with stripes and tacking on a bunch of trims, flounces, and bows—well, it makes me dizzy!"

The rich, deep-blue taffeta day-dress that Mrs. Walker designed for Miranda took her breath away. The fitted bodice was softly ruffled at the neck, while wrist-length sleeves were fitted and tied above the elbow with ribbon but then flared from elbow to wrist.

Miranda stepped out of the dressing room unable to speak. In fact, all of them were speechless. The color, one she would never have chosen, brought more luster to her pale face and made the gray of her eyes look like velvet. The understated elegance of the design showed off the woman wearing the dress and not the dress itself.

"Now, you must do something with that hair," Mrs. Walker pointed out sharply, clearly pleased with her work. "Maddy, you see that she gets to Mrs. Henry's Salon in the Flint. It's time for you both to learn how to sweep and braid your hair more fashionably.

"I'll leave it to you," she said, looking sternly from one girl to the other, "to buy new button-ups and see if the cobbler can repair the lace-ups you're wearing. Miranda, I won't have you wearing such run-down accessories with my designs. It won't do."

Being a gentleman, Samuel said nothing, though he certainly noticed and admired Miranda's remarkable transformation. Silently and repeatedly, he blessed Mrs. Walker as she expanded Miranda's color palette. He loved that the luster had returned to her remarkable eyes, her ashen skin had pinked, and he was astonished that a simple change in hairstyle could produce such loveliness.

Of all the summer socials, Mrs. Amelia Durfee's gala, always held at the end of the season, was doubtless the most elegant and most prized invitation. The Durfee estate, twenty-two acres in the Highlands, had, in addition to the main house with more than twelve bedrooms, three guest cottages on the property. It was famous for its many superb gardens and a greenhouse filled with exotic orchids.

Strings of tiny candles crisscrossed the magnificent veranda like thousands of fireflies; a string quartet played romantically as satin and taffeta skirts rustled like tender breezes.

Silent waiters slipped among the guests, emptying their silver trays of chilled, fluted champagne glasses before disappearing, just as silently, into the darkened periphery.

Mrs. Amelia Durfee, the evening's rotund hostess, was in her mid-sixties. The only daughter of an old-moneyed family, she had been, from an early age, used to getting her own way and being taken seriously. She was outspoken but never strident or mean spirited. Her peers either admired her openly or belittled her behind her back—she paid no attention to either.

Amelia generously donated her time and considerable financial resources to any of the city's charities which she considered honorable. She sat on St. Anne's Hospital Board for the past twelve years and presided over both the Ladies' Guild and the Garden Society. She was renowned, in fact, for her fundraising because few dared to refuse her.

Her dinner parties were as unconventional as she. Her peers, the upper class as they liked to think of themselves, were naturally invited but only those she actually liked. She always included people she didn't know—usually, but not always, younger men and women who were contributing in some way to her city's betterment. These guests, to the consternation of her xenophobic peers, typically crossed social boundaries.

It was her habit at these affairs to first observe her guests from a secluded balcony above the veranda, her keen eyes gleefully watching the pretty, bejeweled young girls fluttering about like butterflies and finally coming to rest on the arms of their heavier, prosperous, much older escorts. It was from here that she looked for Samuel Wallabee, who she'd met briefly a month or so earlier, and, since then, had heard mentioned in other settings. By placing him at her table, she hoped to learn more about him.

Well, Amelia thought, *I should greet my guests.* She turned and headed down to the veranda, her expansive bulk and the yards and yards of expensive fabric covering it swishing and swaying with every movement. She descended the staircase and slipped among her guests about as gently and imperceptibly as the RMS Oceanic slips into port.

9

DEGREES OF SEPARATION

In October of 1877, with Maddy and Professor Everett as witnesses, Miranda Davis married Samuel Wallabee in a quiet civil ceremony at the town hall, followed by a small, elegant reception at the Mohican. The decision was easier for him than her.

Miranda sensed Samuel wasn't ready so close on the heels of his mother's death. She worried that she was taking advantage. Pursuing him was completely selfish and undignified—not to mention patently dishonest. But part of her had grown weary waiting for the emptiness inside her to fill, and so, just as her mother had many years before, she decided that dignity was overrated.

The engraved invitations had the gossips clucking from Main Street to the Highlands. "Why, they barely know each other!" was the most common response, hinting, of course, at an unacceptable impulsivity. "The bride is simply not in his social circle," opined the bolder critics, buttressing the accusations of impropriety. And, last but not least, "She's a working woman," which was, of course, the pinnacle of rebuff.

Maddy, for one, argued passionately against the match. "Mira, I've lived with you, you know you can be prickly and moody. And Sam? He's perhaps the most impatient person I've ever met. The only things you have in common are that you're equally stubborn and opinionated—and that's not a good thing, in my humble opinion."

In Maddy's view, the fact that her friend failed to see these hazards was inexplicable, except to say that love, truly, must be blind.

Samuel had always imagined his life playing out a certain way. He wanted to be part of a strong, stable family unit and desperately needed something other than work to ground him. He had already achieved more than he'd expected—had made an impact on the textile industry, was making a name for himself, gaining respect.

Two days before the wedding, the professor arrived at Samuel's office and stood sheepishly in the doorframe.

"Professor! Welcome!" Samuel exclaimed, moving quickly from behind his desk, his broad smile a reflection of the warmth he felt for his mentor.

"Ah, my boy, it's so good to see you. Since you're at your desk, can I assume that the wedding plans are all in order? Or are you hiding out, Sam?" The professor laughed heartily, his head bobbing.

"Yes," Sam replied good-naturedly, "make your jokes. So, to what do I owe this unexpected but delightful distraction?"

"I wanted to give you a wedding gift while we had a private moment." The professor passed Sam a thick legal-sized envelope, tightly sealed.

"Well, Professor. I really didn't expect . . . I mean you've already given me so much."

"Sam," the professor began, tears unexpectedly welling in his eyes, "you always tell me how much I've given you, which is very kind. Very kind indeed. But I fear that I haven't told you how much you've given me. Wait, wait"—he raised a hand—"let me finish.

"I didn't marry, though I could have. I chose not to. I was selfish, Sam, wanted a life with very few obligations or responsibilities, except for teaching and traveling the world, and, as you know, I inherited enough money to do that.

"I didn't regret that decision until a few years ago when I was forced to face retirement. It was a very difficult time. I was cranky and maudlin and feeling quite sorry for myself upon realizing how empty my days would be without classes to teach, students to counsel, meetings to chair, or exams to prepare. For the very first time, I felt useless, and a cliché—a lonely old man.

"Then a young student walked into my office and, despite my best efforts, would not be turned away. That he needed my help was obvious. That I might need his was not.

"You have blessed my life, Sam. First, as a brilliant student filled with wonder and curiosity—both things I'd long ago taken for granted. You struggled against so many odds in your young life but still believed in a bright future. You taught me as much, or more, than I ever taught you.

"In so many ways, your friendship changed me, changed the course of my life, and, for that, I can never repay you. Investing in Troy Mill gave me back a sense of purpose and a new direction. I thank you for that, from the bottom of my heart.

"Now I want to pass the mill on to you. We've all been more successful than we'd imagined, thanks to you. I want you to have my shares, Sam. I've had the documents drawn up, it's all in there." He motioned toward the envelope in Sam's hand.

"Sign them and the mill is yours. I'd still like to be involved, if you'd be interested in keeping an old man on the payroll!" The professor smiled, though a tear slipped from his eye.

Sam hugged him tightly. "Professor," he said, his voice cracking, "I cannot accept this. It's too much really. I can't."

But in the end, he did.

At this point in her life, Miranda had made peace with having a certain amount of emptiness as a companion. All she'd ever wanted was to be an independent woman, but finally, she'd seen how utterly impossible that was.

Miranda did not love Samuel and doubted he loved her. Neither, in fact, had ever used the word. And while Samuel did not love her, he needed her and that was something. She thought him a strong, kind man, and she craved kindness so much that she was untroubled by not being romantically drawn to him.

She sensed a stability and purpose in Samuel and believed that, unlike her, he would make something of his life. And in so doing, she dearly hoped, he would increase her prospects and opportunities.

While love has its sweet moments, she told herself, *it is, in the end, an ephemeral state as fragile as an angel's wing.* In this mindset, she was completely unprepared and utterly dumbfounded to find herself adoring her son, Calvin, who was born twenty-two months later in August 1879.

After a taxing pregnancy, she barely survived a life-threatening labor. Soaked in sweat and ravaged by ripping pain, she alternately screamed for Samuel and peered up at her husband through silent, vacant eyes. Finally, a strange nurse stepped out of the mist and placed a tiny baby on her chest. While she was examining the infant's furrowed, blotchy face for any sign of recognition, as if on cue, he howled in protest.

"I know, my darling," she whispered, moving his cheek to hers, "I feel the same way." It was their first conversation.

She felt the injection, and seconds before she slipped into the warm fog of sleep, Miranda knew two things with absolute certainty—she would never do this again, and this precious boy was definitely her soul mate.

Many solitary months passed before Samuel would learn of these decisions. Despite her ordeal, or perhaps because of it, Miranda over-monitored her son, resisting every suggestion to leave him alone. She feared that he was on the brink of some danger that he was too small and too fragile to protect himself from.

Samuel saw very little of Miranda after the birth of their son, and he sorely missed her. He wanted things to return to normal, wanted the rhythm of his old life back: uninterrupted dinner conversations, her interest in his work and in him renewed, and the warmth and softness of her body next to his. It had been months now, so he did not believe that he was being unreasonable.

One morning, Samuel woke to a fat slab of sunlight on his face and the sweet scent of early lilacs outside the window. The silence of the early morning broken only by the songs of wood thrushes and nuthatches and the drowsy sounds of bumblebees. God, how he loved the springtime—that unblemished gemstone between winter and summer.

Every spring was an opportunity to marvel, yet again, at brilliant color—fire engine–red tulips, mustard-yellow daffodils, and deep-purple lilacs—color almost too bright to look at directly after the dreary, dull-brown days of winter. It was in the spring that his life seemed fullest, when he felt the deepest sense of well-being, when the slate was wiped clean and a fresh start seemed possible.

Anticipating a large family, Samuel purchased a house on Rock Street facing the river, a lovely Victorian with cantilevered upper stories, roomy porches, dormer windows with elaborate surrounds, and complex rooflines. Set high on the lot, the moss-green house with Siena-red and burnt-yellow trim was happy and welcoming.

In back, the two-acre property fell off steeply, ending at Mount Hope Bay. The sunniest slopes were dotted with bright colored primroses while masses of dainty white bleeding hearts and pale pink Lamiums lined the shaded areas along the path to the water. Platoons of bees, hummingbirds, and butterflies hummed and buzzed as they worked tirelessly.

As a surprise for his wife, Samuel had a small, covered patio added to the west side of the veranda, with a small fireplace to warm chilly evenings and large terra-cotta pots filled with neat evergreens to create privacy—a protected space for just the two of them.

Sam came home early, eager to see if Antonia, their cook, had carried out his instructions to serve dinner on the patio. The wood fireplace crackled and hissed, filling the space with a rosy glow as the scents of cherry, apple, dogwood, and lilac blossoms drifted up on occasional breezes to sweeten the air.

He and Miranda sipped champagne and quietly enjoyed the view for quite a while. The silky spring air felt moist against their faces, and, after months of biting winter winds outdoors and dry, stale air indoors, it was a tonic for them both.

They sat and ate in silence. Although Antonia's early spring pea soup was exceptional, Miranda found herself tensing a bit more with every spoonful. Finally, setting her spoon down, she turned suddenly. "I think I hear Calvin fussing," she said, pushing her chair back. "I'd better check on him."

"Miranda, he's fine," Samuel cajoled, reaching for her hand. "If there was a problem, Nanny would let us know. Please, Mira, let's enjoy our dinner. I thought this might be the perfect evening for dinner outdoors, just the two of us."

"Yes, Sam, it is," she replied with a weak smile. "It was so thoughtful of you to arrange this with Antonia. It's lovely to get a bit of fresh air." Despite her words, Samuel could hear something unspoken, disapproval perhaps, in her voice.

They sipped more champagne until the second course arrived.

Before Calvin's birth, she had thought it possible that she might, in time, come to love Samuel. Love for Miranda used to be cerebral, a concept rather than an emotion, the result of being raised in a family where affection was almost never displayed and love never discussed.

But now there was Calvin! The joy she felt just looking at him took her breath away, and for the first time ever, she felt an emotion so strong that it overwhelmed her. Finally, it seemed, her life had purpose; in a way this tiny baby had redeemed her.

What she felt for her infant son dwarfed everything she had ever felt before; there was simply no comparison between her feelings for her husband and her feelings for her child. So, quite naïvely, Miranda concluded that she had been wrong; that, in fact, she didn't and couldn't ever love Samuel.

Fortunately for her, Sam chatted through the main course. But she was distracted, only half listening, fretting about a discussion she needed to have with him, one which she'd been dreading and had hoped to put off as long as possible.

Samuel waited until Antonia closed the French doors behind her. He watched his wife pour the coffee before asking, "Mira, where are you?" Even he had noticed her distraction.

"Sam, there's something I need to discuss with you," she announced, pausing to pull her shawl tighter around her shoulders. "I'm dreadfully afraid it will hurt you and that you will misunderstand."

He waited, feigning a calmness he did not feel.

"Sam, I knew when we married that you wanted children. Well, we both did, didn't we?"

"But now, after Calvin, we must face the fact that that isn't going to be the case. And it's totally my fault," she added quickly. "I know I've let you down and I feel ashamed." She was so flustered that ruby blotches began to appear on her otherwise pale face.

"Mira, dear, I do understand," he assured her. "You endured so much to bring our beautiful son into the world. I totally understand that you wouldn't want to go through that again, at least not soon." He reached across the table and took her hand in his.

"Sam, it's more than that," she replied, withdrawing her hand. "I don't want to have another child. Dr. Webber came by today to check on Calvin and me, of course. He told me that I shouldn't even consider having another child, that a second pregnancy would be too much. He said you knew this." She looked at him squarely without expression.

"Dr. Webber might have said something like that during the delivery," Sam confessed warily. "Frankly, I was too concerned about you to really pay much attention."

He waited, not sure what she needed to hear. "I'm just wondering though if we shouldn't put off such a momentous decision until you're completely recovered, completely rested."

"How would that change anything, Sam?" she said, sweeping aside his misgivings.

"I don't know," he admitted. "Everything I've done these past years—the long hours, the hard work, buying back the mill one investor at a time, everything—was for the family we planned for."

Samuel's expression unraveled slowly from confusion to incredulity as he understood the fullness of her meaning, the importance of what she was trying to tell him, and the terrible consequences.

"What exactly are you trying to tell me, Miranda? I want to hear you say it." He made no effort to disguise the bitterness and anger spurting like a nicked artery.

"We cannot risk another pregnancy, Sam. I cannot risk another pregnancy. We have no choice. The church's position is clear on this." She'd decided to take the high ground, though she had no confidence in her choice.

"What the hell are you talking about?" he demanded. "The church's position! I couldn't care less about the church's position on anything.

"Miranda," he asked gingerly, still holding on to the hope that he was wrong. "Are you suggesting . . . I mean, did Dr. Webber suggest that we stop being intimate?" The raspy incredulity and despair in his voice were almost unbearable for her to hear.

"Surely there must be some other way, Mira, you know, to forestall a pregnancy?"

Samuel tried to reason with her, but she seemed immune to reason.

He protested loudly and bitterly, demanding some explanation or clarification. But no matter what he tried, he slammed up against something unyielding in her.

So, on that sweetly-scented spring evening, Samuel Wallabee, not long after his thirtieth birthday, learned that the life he had dreamed about was never going to materialize, his dreams, like his heart, scraped out like seeds from a pumpkin.

His face darkened, he stood and left without a word. For no particular reason, Samuel traveled to the seaport town of New Bedford, where, for days, he seethed at his own helplessness, his disgust as palpable as seasickness. But he found no comfort in anger or self-pity.

No, he wasn't the easiest person to be around; he had his own demons. He'd erected barricades around his heart to protect himself from anything emotional. Under a harsher lens, he had to admit that he had limited experience forging relationships with men and almost none with women. Well, except for his mother, who always seemed to know what he needed and who made him the center of her world, asking little in return.

Had he just assumed that a wife would make as few demands on him as his mother had? Perhaps. Had he assumed that a wife would focus on his needs, requiring as little reciprocity as his mother had? Probably.

Now, when he had or thought he had everything—a wife, a son, a home, a position of authority, financial security—he was powerless and utterly trapped. He was tormented and inconsolable, aching from the failure and shame of it. For reasons he would never understand, he blamed his infant son. And while that seemed indecent and sinful, he did not question it and allowed his resentment, like steam, to build up inside him.

Walking the piers in the thickening dusk, he recalled the heroic self-sacrifice of his parents and felt the heavy mantle of their expectations on his shoulders again. He thought about his beautiful mother who, without a doubt, would tell him to put this heartache behind him, to stop this useless mourning.

By the time he returned home two weeks later, he was greatly altered, his manner more aloof and his heart more protected. Sadly, he'd also become more of what he'd always disliked—more critical, more driven, more bitter.

Miranda tried to prepare for the painful conversation she expected over dinner. When she swept into the dining room, Sam was already seated. She was stunned by the look of him, bleached out, spiritless, his chalky face etched with lines that had not been there before.

She greeted him warmly, but he was dismissive and distracted in return. As he rose to pull out her chair, his eyes brooding and eerily empty, she realized from the fierceness of his glance that he had not forgiven her and never would.

She felt on the verge of something dangerous. Could it be that, once again, she'd blundered and lost something important? It seemed her fate in life was to figure something out only when it was too late to change it.

Once coffee was served, Samuel made the pronouncement he'd come to make.

"Miranda, I've purchased a mill in New Bedford," he told her in a preternaturally calm voice. "It's smaller than I'd like, but plans to renovate and rebuild are being drawn up.

"I expect it'll take a lot of my time, at least for the next few years. Of course, until it's completed," he continued, "I'll need to be on site every day. Because of the distance, I thought I'd look for a small house to stay in during the week and on weekends when I need to."

There, it was done. Her inner trembling stopped and a stillness settled over her.

They would drift apart silently, without any drama, as surely as kites released into a brisk wind. The bitterness she'd hoped would ease was instead cemented for all time.

"I understand," was all she dared to say. And she honestly did.

Samuel was leaving her—unofficially of course, in the only way he was permitted, but leaving her and Calvin, nonetheless. He would live somewhere else; she would have his financial support but would be completely in charge of their son's upbringing.

"Will you need me to send your things?" she asked, feigning indifference.

"No, I've already made arrangements."

"Well then, I guess I'll retire."

How dearly she wished she could tell him how sorry she was, to tell him she'd been wrong, to beg him not to leave, but she said nothing.

In truth she knew. What she'd done was unforgivable. Samuel could never forgive her, and except for Calvin, there was nothing left between them. She had dangerously and foolishly placed their future in jeopardy, and it was still possible, even likely, that there might be future consequences, consequences that she could not, as yet, imagine. The immensity of what she'd done, what she'd discarded so thoughtlessly, terrified her.

Samuel packed methodically, finished by two in the morning, poured himself an especially large bourbon, and sat, drink in hand, in his plush leather chair, looking out onto the veranda and beyond to the city lights. For the first time, the view had no effect on him.

He hauled himself to his feet and up the stairs to his son's bedroom. Carefully closing the door behind him, Samuel stood at the crib, looking down at this vulnerable, tiny infant.

Gathering him up without waking him, he sat in the rocker by the window and, for the first time since the death of his mother, sobbed—wrenching, gulping, silent sobs that convulsed him, leaving him ashamed, dazed, and anguished. Sadly, in the agony of that moment, the father-son relationship was sealed forever, unbeknownst to either.

Samuel kissed his son, placed him back in the crib, and left—for almost twenty-two years.

After an agitated, self-abasing night, when every attempt to sleep quickly unraveled into swirling trepidation, Miranda rose, impulsively grabbed her shawl, and burst from the house, impelled by some unidentifiable malaise, her momentum checked only when she reached the water's edge, where she stood shivering, gasping for breath. She knew she was in trouble.

The thin sun's reflection off the water was surprisingly fierce; persistent winds whipped her nightdress back and forth like an uncoupled sail. She shaded her eyes, bit her lip, stared out across the choppy water, and pretended, in childlike fashion, that she really didn't know what she knew with certitude.

The wind had been gathering force, flattening the water, pulling opaque, clumsy clouds like thick gray blankets across the sky, muting the sun, and lashing the trees along the bank. Without warning, fat, heavy drops spattered her nightdress, and, within minutes, muddy rivulets rolled down the path, quickly deepening into ruts; astonishing blasts of wind brought her to a standstill more than once as she scrambled back to the house.

Heading toward her bedroom, Miranda asked, almost as an afterthought, "Antonia, did Mr. Wallabee have his breakfast this morning?"

"No, ma'am. Mr. Wallabee was nowhere to be seen this morning. I went to the nursery, but Nanny told me that Mr. Wallabee hadn't been there either. Is something wrong, ma'am?"

"No, of course not," Miranda protested more brusquely than she'd meant to, swiping angrily at involuntary tears. She felt no sense of personal abandonment, but she was indignant that he had, so contemptuously, spurned his own son, establishing in her a lifelong asylum for righteous indignation.

She swore now that Samuel's mills would never be her son's inheritance. Calvin would never waste a single day in such a filthy place with such appallingly uneducated people. At this moment, within hours of her husband's desertion, she vowed that her son would never miss out on anything, suffer in any way, or come up short by any measure, for the lack of a father—no matter the cost to her personally. Her son would have the best nannies, would attend private schools, his friends would come from the best families, and his manners would be impeccable.

In Samuel's absence, all invitations extended to them as a couple would have to be declined using one excuse or another, and ultimately few, if any, invitations would be proffered. Since convention dictated that unescorted women were not allowed to attend public events, Miranda was effectively barred from Fall River society—leaving her to cultivate these connections in the only way left her, by befriending women from prominent families. Fortunately, there were many prominent women on the hospital's board and in their various committees.

"Why, Mrs. Durfee!" Miranda declared, as if shocked by their chance meeting in the hospital corridor. "How nice to see you again. You're well, I hope?"

Amelia Durfee, who, by nature, loathed interruptions, grimaced, ambushed as she had been by this blithesome nurse obstructing her entrance into the board room.

"Oh, I'm terribly sorry, Mrs. Durfee. I'm Miranda Wallabee, Sam Wallabee's wife. We met a few months ago at your gala." Miranda tried to sound upbeat, the way one might expect a carefree young woman to sound.

"Of course," Amelia declared immediately, "I remember you both. How is Samuel?"

"Quite well, thank you. And you?" Miranda asked with disingenuous concern.

"I'm very well, my dear," assured Amelia, "just here for a meeting of the board."

"Oh, of course, I'd forgotten you were on the board," Miranda lied convincingly. Then, feigning nervousness, she continued, "Mrs. Durfee, I wonder, could I have a minute of your time? I don't mean to trouble you, it's just that the nuns wouldn't mention—"

"Mrs. Wallabee," Amelia declared petulantly, freezing Miranda with a disagreeable scowl, "if this has something to do with the running of this hospital, I would hope that you'd have felt an obligation to bring it to my attention before this."

"I'm so sorry, ma'am. I didn't know . . ."

"Now then, I will be taking tea at my home this afternoon, and I can assure you that I will not abide having my time wasted. Do you understand, Mrs. Wallabee?"

"Absolutely, Mrs. Durfee."

"Well then," Amelia snorted dismissively and, without another word, waddled into the board room, her skirts swishing mightily.

That afternoon, a genuinely apprehensive Miranda, balanced delicately on an immense Georgian settee, meticulously and patiently presented her case to an expressionless Amelia Durfee. She explained in detail why some of the hospital's surgical equipment was, in her view, dangerously outdated, and illustrated how, if there were another crisis, like a mill fire, the current equipment would prove, once again, to be insufficient and cumbersome and that people would die as a result.

Amelia Durfee listened with unanticipated admiration. She was accustomed to being solicited by men who didn't appear to believe that she was capable of understanding complexity. Amelia was unaccustomed to the potency of straightforward intelligence, heartfelt conviction, and Miranda's mettle, since she would almost certainly be censured for approaching Amelia directly.

Miranda could, as had so many others before her, have simply asked for a substantial sum of money, but instead she suggested a fundraising event, which was admirable. Amelia felt compelled to extend some assistance, so she agreed to host the event, to provide a contact list of her wealthy friends, and to give Miranda the authority to coordinate everything else.

In the end, it was Amelia Durfee who was fully credited with raising almost ten thousand dollars—the largest amount ever raised in a single fundraiser in the hospital's history—praise which, to her credit, she refused to accept entirely without publicly acknowledging Miranda Wallabee's contributions. She praised Miranda's attention to detail, her persistence, and above all her competence—which were qualities, quite frankly, that Amelia Durfee admired in herself as well.

Coming off this success, Miranda received two invitations to ladies' luncheons at the Mohican. The following spring, after Amelia Durfee recommended her for membership in the exclusive Garden Club, Miranda was accepted without discussion.

Understanding the importance of keeping a low profile, Miranda enthusiastically volunteered for projects and committees that other members eschewed. Slowly but surely, over many, many years, she'd managed to ease herself, without resentment, into Fall River society. Miranda was respected for her tireless work serving the less fortunate and for her humility in shunning the spotlight.

As Miranda had hoped, with the help of these new friends, twelve-year-old Calvin was accepted at Andover Academy, where he studied and lived with the sons of the wealthy from Maine to Massachusetts. Miranda enrolled him in tennis lessons on Saturdays, and because he was a natural athlete, he was first tier on the academy's tennis team by the time he was fifteen.

She monitored her son's progress with a keener eye than the dean of students, refusing to accept any grade below a B, even though his professors reminded her, more than once, that her son was not especially gifted academically.

Despite the abundance of structure and discipline, Calvin was rarely discontented with life at the academy. Although he did form some lifelong friendships, he considered most of his classmates, as he brought to his mother's attention innumerable times, overprivileged and under-burdened.

"Mother," he complained bitterly when Miranda chastised him about his grades or pressured him to join another student organization, "most chaps just do the minimum—only what's absolutely necessary."

"And that's exactly why you need to do more, Calvin," she asserted. "They will be ordinary, but you will stand out. The faculty will see that and recommend you for the best colleges. You're forgetting, Calvin, we're not like most families—many still look down on us. You must achieve more to gain their respect and acceptance."

Calvin's impulsive application to Princeton University, which he had absolutely no interest in attending, was, in his mind, a brazen, ingenious stratagem, and, upon acceptance, he felt a powerful exhilaration as if he had repossessed his life and escaped some mortal danger. Finally, he had secreted himself outside the perimeter of her reign, but he had miscalculated—and his new freedom was, therefore, chimerical.

He hadn't fully understood—and how could he—her insatiable need and inexplicable determination to orchestrate the very ebb and flow of his life nor her exorbitant obsession to intrude in his affairs, far and away overstepping her obligations as a mother.

By the time he graduated from college in May, 1901, Calvin no longer presumed that he was, in any way, responsible for his father's abandonment, although he didn't know what was; moreover he strongly suspected that he could never be or do enough to fully satisfy his mother. But most importantly he was beginning to consider that, despite her attempts to persuade him otherwise, it was not his responsibility to fill the obvious void in her.

Three weeks before Calvin's graduation, without explanation, Samuel Wallabee, after more than a twenty-two year absence, decided to return to his native Fall River. He wrote Miranda, telling her of his plan to return, and his intention to take Calvin with him on a business trip to Italy after graduation. Miranda tore the letter to pieces, threw it into the fire, and watched it disappear.

On her own, she hosted a post-graduation brunch at the Princeton Faculty Club, inviting every graduate in Calvin's class, their parents, and many of the faculty. Years of arranging and attending social events had transformed Miranda into an exceptional hostess who greeted guests with special attention, made introductions with aplomb, mingled and conversed effortlessly. Even Calvin took notice and felt a nick of pride.

Raising her champagne flute, she congratulated the parents for weathering the university years, and then the young graduates for their tenacity, and finally the faculty for preparing these young men for successful and honorable lives.

When the cheering and clapping died, she cleared her throat and announced, with the broadest of smiles, to the room filled with hushed, expectant faces that she and Calvin would be exploring the antiquities of Italy for the next four or five months.

It meant, of course, that he would be his mother's companion with all the obligations that such a role entailed. While in many ways still a self-absorbed twenty-two-year-old, Calvin had learned, from the boys of privilege at the academy, to weigh—and tolerate if necessary—a person's usefulness before rejecting them or their ideas outright. He understood that without his mother he could not go to Italy, which rendered her useful.

Florence

They arrived in Florence to absolutely splendid weather—cloudless azure skies, pleasantly warm days with gentle afternoon breezes, and cool evenings beneficial for tranquilizing sleep. Miranda booked rooms, luxurious adjoining suites actually, at the exclusive Principe Hotel in the heart of the city, both with private terraces overlooking the tranquil Arno River, the city's lifeblood, and the handsome Ponte Vespucci.

It was a city of dizzying excess, a place where beauty and sheer opulence ambushed you, where sensuality was palpable and intoxicating. It was a city whose narrow, sometimes-dead-end alleyways and uneven, cobblestoned streets were irresistible, whose soaring marble cathedrals enraptured visitors, and whose bewitching cafés whispered, "Come, sit, relax."

Venice

From the very moment of their arrival, Venice promised to be underwhelming and disappointing, the absolute antithesis of Florence.

They stepped into their gondola on a chokingly hot afternoon, made more oppressive by a spitting rain that curtained everything in murky, melancholic gray, including their sullen gondolier, who wore his distain as clear as newsprint and whose stained jacket, scuffed boots, and greasy hair were proud symbols of his utter indifference.

And Venice stank, especially at low tide, when the decomposing garbage in the canals, the rotting undersides of piers, and the foundations of the spacious but crumbling houses along the canal were exposed—in combination with blistering heat, the foul air became almost too heavy to breathe.

Before the first week ended, Miranda instructed the concierge to rearrange their travel plans, paid their hotel bill in full, and while Calvin slept, had his belongings packed and their luggage conveyed to the train station. Before the hotel's dining room was fully set up for breakfast the next morning, mother and son had boarded the train for Siena and were settling into their first-class compartment.

Siena

The gentle city of Siena—sometimes referred to as the city of contemplation—was a luminous gift just waiting to be opened. Lacking the excesses of its economic and political rival, Florence, and the unseemliness and clutter of Venice, this medieval walled city at the end of an ancient Roman highway welcomed its visitors graciously and unobtrusively.

As their open-air carriage wound through groves of shimmering silver-leafed olive trees and miles of well-tended vineyards backlit by a fiery late-afternoon sun, Miranda's burdensome anxiety diffused enough for her to feel somewhat hopeful. Sight unseen, because she'd felt compelled to leave Venice so quickly, Miranda had chosen the Villa Scacciapensieri, within walking distance of the city, hoping it would be considerably more private and restful than their previous hotel.

Their suites were spacious, charmingly decorated, and quite comfortable. Miranda's balcony overlooked a sprawling perennial garden, while Calvin's view was of a handsomely landscaped swimming pool in the foreground and behind it, from sounds he recognized, a tennis court.

For the first week, they strolled the luxurious gardens, lounged by the pool, or, when the heat prevailed, read in the villa's library, whose cool stone walls were shaded all day. She encouraged Calvin to take up tennis again, which he did immediately. Between daily tennis matches and swimming laps, Calvin was physically exhausted by the end of each day and, thankfully, slept well. By the end of the week, his boyish enthusiasm and joie de vivre had returned.

Architecturally, Siena was a treasure chest of magnificent Gothic buildings, like the breathtaking ninth-century duomo, a marvel of engineering with its alternating jet-black and pure-white marble bands, its towering bell tower, and its zebralike interior overflowing with sculptures, frescos, and bronze panels by Michelangelo, Pisano, and Donatello.

But who could have predicted that the Pinacoteca Nazionale would upend Calvin's life? He returned to the museum, at first almost every day, to study these master painters from different perspectives or in different lighting, watching young people—art students, he surmised—sitting on low stools, attempting to imitate these ancient gods of the art world.

For the rest of his life, Calvin would consider Siena the city of his birth, perhaps because the serenity and acceptance he found there unearthed his passion and revealed his talent for drawing—a precious gift that would comfort him in the darkest periods of his life, an unexpected gift that often made him tearful with gratitude.

One evening, quite late, Miranda noticed a light under Calvin's door. Knocking timidly, she entered to find him sketching under the grainy light of a kerosene lamp. Of course, she lacked any expertise to accurately assess Calvin's talent, but she thought his pencil sketches of bridges and buildings remarkable and encouraged him, quite sincerely, to consider pursuing his interest in architecture more formally.

As was her nature, she acted quickly and without much thought. After submitting a small portfolio of his work and making a formal application to the Accademia di belle Arte di Siena, Calvin was astonished, dazed really, when he was accepted.

Senor Brancia, the villa's owner, was helpful in locating a small room for Calvin at a farmhouse about six miles outside the city, where Calvin could take meals, in exchange for helping the owner with chores. With her son's professional future now more secure, Miranda was finally ready to return home.

The farmhouse he shared with the signora and her two children was clean and simply furnished. While he waited for classes to begin, Calvin helped with morning chores. It was Signora Daniella who taught him to repair pens and fences, to cut and stack hay, and to pick olives and almonds. The physical work hardened and calloused his body but left him with a sense of accomplishment that, except for winning a tennis match, he'd never felt before.

He wouldn't appreciate until much later in life that Daniella was the first adult he ever truly trusted, the first person who didn't judge him, the first person who was never disappointed in him.

What he liked least about her—but what, in the end, benefited him the most—was her outright refusal to accept "I don't know" as an answer, which, while annoying and unnerving, pushed him to think more deeply about his life, his dreams, and especially his feelings.

However, as the months passed, he appeared increasingly disenchanted and withdrawn.

"Calvin," Daniella asked, "you seem distracted these days. What's going on?"

"I'm not completely sure, but I think I've made a mistake," he mumbled, grimacing.

"Everyone makes mistakes, Calvin."

"This is a big mistake, Daniella. A really big mistake, one my parents won't easily forgive."

She decided not to interrupt.

"It's my classes . . . they don't . . . I guess *inspire* is the word I'm looking for, at least not like they did in the beginning." His voice cracked and he paused to steady himself.

"Daniella, I'm so afraid I've chosen the wrong profession. I don't really think I want to design buildings—however beautiful they might be in the end, even the initial sketching, the part I most enjoyed, feels confining now."

Calvin had never admitted this shameful secret, even to himself, but now, having said the words aloud, he knew it was the truth.

"So, what will you do now?"

"I don't know but I've left the Accademia. I stopped going about a week ago."

"Yes, I suspected as much," she said. Because he looked so surprised, she explained, "It's a small village, Calvin. People talk. So, what is it that you do now during the day—when you leave to go to class?"

"Well, at first I went to the park by St. Luke's, just sitting and watching people—mothers pushing their babies in strollers, toddlers chasing pigeons, old men playing chess, lovers walking hand in hand. Suddenly, I realized that the park was alive with life, Daniella, and I felt it too—I felt inspired, or at least what I think inspiration feels like."

She smiled kindly. "I'm happy for you."

A week later, at dinner, Calvin announced shyly but proudly that he'd found a private teacher.

"His name is Paulo Diamonte, he used to teach at the Accademia, but I never had him for any of my classes. He's exhibited at galleries in Siena, Florence, and Rome," he added enthusiastically.

"He stopped taking private students years ago. I met him in the park. He was just passing through and stopped behind me to look at my sketch."

"Ah," said Daniella, "and what did he think of your sketch?"

Calvin cheeks colored. "He laughed out loud and told me my work was technically good but lacked passion."

"And so how did this Paulo become your teacher?"

"Well, first I checked with some of my old professors who described Paulo's work as humbling, overwhelming, and breathtaking," Calvin continued. "So, I went to see for myself."

"And what did you think?"

"Daniella, his work really is humbling. His canvases are large, his brushstrokes bold and thick, and his colors so saturated his work is both physically and visually heavy. He doesn't paint in any particular style, at least not one I recognize, but he paints with emotion and precision. Seriously, he paints feelings. I can't really describe it better than that. His paintings are daring, risky even.

"I stopped by his studio a few days ago, hoping he would remember me, reminding him that he thought my work needed passion. Again, he just laughed out loud. So I offered to teach him English if he would teach me to paint with passion. I knew it was a long shot, but I had to try."

"When do you begin studying with him?"

"In three days."

"So, you figured out what you wanted to do after all? Well done, Calvin," she exclaimed proudly, a broad smile filling her tanned face, causing Calvin to blush from his neck to the top of his head.

Indeed, he felt proud, felt like he'd finally found his way, finally knew what he wanted to do with his life. He wanted to paint.

10

CHOICES

Despite immigrant roots, he was as wealthy now as any in the privileged class—a multimillionaire who chose to live more simply than would be expected; a man who, though incredibly powerful, eschewed the role of powerbroker. An enigma really, esteemed as much for who he was as for who he wasn't.

At fifty-two in 1901, Samuel Wallabee of Lewiston, Maine, bore little resemblance to the thirty-year-old drowning in resentment and bitterness who fled Fall River, Massachusetts, in the middle of the night more than twenty-two years ago.

He was the sole owner of a textile conglomerate, ten state-of-the-art mills from Maine to Massachusetts, and the only man who could truthfully boast, if boasting were in his nature—which it wasn't—that his mills had lists of people waiting to fill any vacancy. He was envied, he was solicited, and, at the end of the day, he was alone.

In the beginning, he'd willingly, eagerly, paid the price for such impressive achievements—grueling fourteen- to sixteen-hour days, an unrelenting focus on innovation, a constant search, often around the world, for quality materials and markets, living his life in the space between unhappiness and happiness and, always it seemed, waiting for something.

Still, he'd managed to learn a few things about himself along the way, painfully and usually in spite of himself. For example, after years of hiring and, subsequently, firing a succession of managers, he was forced to concede that no matter how hard or how creatively he tried, people could not be changed—at least not substantially—so if it wasn't a good fit initially, it would never be a good fit.

In retrospect, he saw how infinitely better his life had become once he'd ceased flailing against people's tempestuous or defensive natures, their deeply ingrained, prejudicial beliefs, or their knee-jerk resistance to even the smallest change. Ironically, it would take him several more years to see the parallels in his own life.

And, like most epiphanies, it blindsided him. He'd just finished dinner, alone as usual, and, as was his habit, retreated to his library, stopping first to pour a generous brandy from its decanter on the sideboard, then settling into his comfortable armchair in front of a crackling fire, propping his stocking feet on a tufted footstool, having earlier removed and set his soggy boots on the hearth to dry. It was at that very moment, as he raised the pale amber liquid to his mouth, that he heard, "I never loved her," and he couldn't decide whether he'd actually spoken the words or simply thought them.

But there it was, as clear as the babbling, mossy-edged brook he loved as a child, and as powerful and dangerous as the thundering Quequechan River swollen with spring thaw.

Indeed, it was not Miranda that he loved, not the socially awkward, secretive, at times prideful, pretty young nurse with the warm gray eyes who stood next to him in front of the justice of the peace. The woman he'd loved was someone else entirely—she was the "ideal" wife, the woman he envisioned Miranda might become under his tutelage. As loathsome as that was to admit, worse yet was the realization that it had been his own totally unfounded preconceptions about women and his romanticized visions of what a family should be that had, in the end, prevented him from ever having a family!

Sometimes something happens—you meet someone, you learn something—and your life can never be the same again because the truth does not always set you free. And so it was for Samuel Wallabee on that introspective evening as he traced the watermarks of his failings through a life, despite its successes, of solitude and loss.

So, late in his life, when there was nothing he could do about it, Samuel Wallabee recognized the dazzlingly simple, heartbreaking truth—that he was to blame for his barren, solitary existence, for the total absence of the thing he used to crave as much as the alcoholic craves drink, the one thing he'd wanted most as a spirited, young man. Nothing now—not money, not power, not pointless penance— could change what he'd set in motion so many years ago. It was irreversible.

So why was he planning to return to Fall River? Perhaps he no longer had reason to stay away, having sufficiently honored the memory of his mother and fulfilled his promises to her. Perhaps he was just curious to revisit the place that had so brutally plundered his family and, as if in reparation, gratuitously launched his brilliant career. "It was time," was what he settled on—that was how he would reply when asked.

Except for a small paunch, Samuel looked much the same physically. He still wore his hair, gray now, short and neatly parted at the side, but, even so, it was, as it had always been, a bit unruly, so like most men he applied pomade liberally. His goatee and mustache were still neatly trimmed, but crow's-feet had settled in the corners of his eyes.

His public persona radiated well-being. He entered business meetings with the nonchalance of someone confident he was among equals, but privately he was a loner, resentful of the relentless demands and the costly sacrifices he'd had to make, all in a quest to accumulate enough wealth and power to insulate him from his past.

Now he was the epitome of gentility, dressed in the European style he'd come to admire, his wardrobe unique in fabrics and design, extraordinary in its attention to detail but never ostentatious.

Before they became popular in America, he wore full-length, double-breasted, fur-collared cashmere coats in winter with a soft, black homburg instead of the customary bowler. He preferred the single-breasted cutaway coat and trousers with pressed creases. And, in what would become his signature look, he always wore a whimsical waistcoat, usually red, and a boldly patterned silk tie.

Arriving home in July 1901, he was neither annoyed nor surprised to learn that Miranda and Calvin were in Italy. In fact, it suited his plans to convert Calvin's old nursery and the smaller adjoining room, formerly the nanny's room, into a master bedroom and dressing room for himself.

Other than appointing a designer, he took no part in this project—made not a single decision, chose no fabric, color, or piece of furniture—since the only thing that mattered was that, in the end, the space was functional.

He felt decidedly different about the redesign of his old office on the first floor, since this was where he intended to spend the bulk of his time when he wasn't at the mill. It needed to be larger and more comfortable, a space where he could work productively, where everything he might need would be close by.

More importantly, it needed to be a private place—a sanctuary of sorts—since he harbored no illusions that living with Miranda again, even after so many years, would be easy. In fact, it would be sadly accurate to say that, at this point in his life, Samuel harbored no illusions, no expectations, and no dreams, having learned, painfully, how easily they can be lost or, in his case, stolen.

The old office was gutted and enlarged. He chose intricate ceiling moldings, dark custom shelving, cabinetry, and flooring. A field stone fireplace anchored one wall and a bank of large, south-facing windows expanded his view of his prized gardens. In front of these windows he placed the immense, handsomely carved, mahogany desk he'd brought back with him.

Two masculine club chairs with comfortable footrests faced the fireplace, each with its own reading lamp and drop-leaf table. A Persian carpet, a gorgeous masterpiece of swirling claret, hunter green, and cinnamon, complemented the rich wood flooring and cabinetry, while the draperies, saffron gold with thin cream stripes, and the blue-and-gold-flecked upholstery lightened the space. It was the perfect room.

"Mrs. Wallabee! Mrs. Wallabee!" Antonia shouted with evident relief from the front steps as Miranda's carriage pulled up to the entrance in late September 1901. "Mrs. Wallabee, he's back. Mr. Wallabee's back! I didn't know what to do, he's made lots of changes. He's at work right now, but I expect him for dinner. Will you be having dinner with him?"

"Antonia, please, take a breath and allow me to catch mine," Miranda cajoled as she was helped down from her carriage. "Yes, of course, I knew to expect Mr. Wallabee," she lied, "and yes, we'll be having dinner together. But right now I need a hot bath and a long nap. Would you see to the luggage and unpacking?"

Although more than twenty years had passed since she'd dined with her husband, Miranda felt surprisingly little apprehension about seeing him again; in fact, she felt a low buzz of excitement. She refused to dwell on the reasons for his return or what she might lose because of it, knowing that whatever Samuel had come to tell her was incontrovertible.

She selected a pale blue taffeta gown from Florence and did her hair in long, soft blond ringlets, which she pulled to one side and fastened with a mother-of-pearl clasp. She chose her rose quartz earrings and, except for her wedding ring, wore no other jewelry.

At forty-nine Miranda was no longer unattractively thin and angular; age had added graceful curves, her skin was as translucent as polished marble, and her gray eyes were soft as velvet. The years served patiently on tedious committees, graciously hosting fundraisers, and the self-effacing charitable work had mollified her restlessness, abraded her ceaseless anxiety, and whittled her malcontent, leaving behind, as glaciers do, a changed landscape—she had become not only someone she could be proud of but, finally, someone she was comfortable with.

Ironically, she too had learned to exude an assurance and confidence that she did not always feel, to move effortlessly among her high-powered guests, to banter easily with total strangers. However, she always fiercely resisted giving out personal information, thereby creating an unintended but nonetheless alluring veil of mystery about her.

Checking her mirror one last time and feeling satisfied with her reflection, she rose to meet her husband for dinner, wondering what he would think of her and genuinely conflicted about what she wanted him to think.

"Good evening, Miranda," he said from his viewpoint at the bottom of the stairs, astonishment evident on his face and in his tone. "I was going to say that you are as beautiful as ever, but, in truth, you are more beautiful. I sincerely hope that you are as well as you look."

She was almost too much for him to take in all at once—luminescent, in a way he couldn't imagine having forgotten, even after all these years. She was dressed unpretentiously, although her gown—or was it simply the color?—appeared diaphanous as she moved with an elegance and grace he'd never observed before.

She descended the staircase leisurely, a gloved hand on the banister, smiled as she took his arm at the bottom, and let him lead her into the dining room. Once both were seated, he lifted his wineglass. "To your health, Miranda."

"And yours, Samuel," she replied, appreciating, how the years had reshaped him. He was ruggedly handsome now without a trace of the old boyish softness, and while he seemed charming and contented, she wondered how deeply the rage he'd left with might be buried and what it might take to loosen it.

"So, tell me about your trip, Miranda. What did you think of Italy? I've only been on business. What's it like from a tourist's perspective?"

Miranda would have preferred to tell him about Calvin right away, but something cautioned her, maturity perhaps, so she set that aside and, in the interest of a pleasant dinner, told story after story about her own adventures, as if she'd traveled to Italy alone.

Intrigued and charmed by her amusing tales and intelligent observations, Samuel stared, humbled by her transformation, one that had been achieved, he was embarrassed to admit, wholly without any input from him, perhaps even aided by his total absence from her life.

"And you, Samuel?" she asked once Antonia had cleared the table. "What have you been doing?"

After providing her the briefest encapsulation of his twenty-two year absence, a skill at which he'd always been proficient, but which nonetheless always annoyed her, he asked, "Would you care to join me for a brandy?"

"Are you inviting me into your new study, Samuel?" she asked with a knowing smile, affirming that, as lady of the house, she was quite aware of his recent renovations. "Yes, I'd like that."

A fire crackled and hissed as they entered, its rosy glow welcoming and warming them. As Samuel poured two glasses of brandy, Miranda surveyed the space he'd created, observing that everything about the room—its ambience, the choice of furnishings, even the scent of cigars and old leather—was a revelation, a manifestation of who he had become: accomplished, prosperous, secure. This was a conspicuously private space, and, in this room, she would always be a guest.

Finally, sitting amiably facing the fire, their feet on stools, sipping contentedly, she was unable to wait any longer. "So," she asked, peering at him over her glass, "what brings you back, Samuel?"

He studied the fire, taking his time. "Honestly, I'm not sure, Miranda. And I've given it a lot of thought. I suppose I've finished what I set out to do or maybe I don't have anything more to prove, but, more likely, it was just time." His eyes never left the flames.

She found his answer both unsatisfying and irritating and waited for him to continue, but he seemed, instead, to recede further and further.

"And what are your plans?" she asked without any hint of the increasing impatience and discomfort she was feeling in this, his space.

"Still sorting that out," he replied sheepishly, turning to look at her, flashing the boyish smile that, despite the passing years, she still found endearing.

"For sure, I'll be taking over the Troy Mill from Eli, who's agreed to take over the Willamette Mill. After that, I'm not sure. From time to time, I've been asked to speak at various business groups and such, but always declined. Perhaps I'll consider doing some of that."

He studied her face, but she remained, as always, inscrutable to him. "You needn't worry, Miranda, I'll stay quite busy. I've no intention of interfering with your plans or daily routines in any way."

"And your son's?" she asked, her tone finally belying her pretext of amiability and, despite her best intentions, loosening a small chip of old anger. "Will you be interfering with his plans?"

He deflected her anger, determined to remain cordial, and with a cautious smile added, "Well, that's up to him, I suppose. I was hoping to get a sense of him over dinner, but I imagine you wanted to keep our first dinner more private."

"Calvin's not here, Samuel," she declared, staring into the fire as he had. "He's in Italy studying architecture. His Italian's fluent, by the way." She'd no idea why she added the last piece of information, maybe to take the edge off news she knew was bound to upset him.

"I don't understand." He was flummoxed, blindsided really, by this unexpected news. "He's already graduated," he protested.

"Yes, Samuel, he finished college and now he's studying architecture in Siena. He submitted a portfolio of his work while we were there and was accepted immediately—he's quite talented," she declared, her eyes still averted.

Words failed him.

"I can hear your disappointment, Samuel, and I'm sorry. I didn't have a chance to tell you because I just arrived home this afternoon. It was my intention to inform you, through your solicitor as you've always insisted. I intended . . ." Her words kept coming, tumbling over themselves like the wake behind a boat.

"But," he interrupted, squinting as if the smoke had irritated his eyes, "I thought he'd be taking over the business, Miranda, starting with the Troy Mill like I did." His irritation was now completely obvious, and the restraint he'd promised himself was quickly ebbing.

"I don't know why you thought that," she declared in a slightly superior tone. "I'm not aware that Calvin has any interest in manufacturing. In fact, I'm fairly confident that my son's chosen something different for himself."

Another angry chip loosened.

"Our son," he corrected her, "and it's quite common for fathers to pass their businesses onto their sons." He exhaled slowly before adding, "Miranda, I wanted to see him graduate and wrote you asking for the date of his graduation. I hoped to get to know him better by taking him to Italy with me afterward. But you never replied to my letter and, interestingly, you whisked him off to Italy yourself."

"I don't know what you're implying, Samuel, or, for that matter, what letter you're referring to." She marveled at how easily, how convincingly she lied. "I took my son, our son, to Italy as a graduation present, a common practice."

She hadn't realized until that very moment the depth of her own anger, understanding now that it must have been simmering all these years and, like a wound left untended, had slowly became infected and was now gangrenous.

By abandoning his family, Samuel had smothered any flicker of hope she'd had for a stable home and a secure place in society. In his wake, he'd left the seeds of bitterness and resentment, which had taken hold inside her like an invasive species. She was, and forever would be, embarrassed by the shocking amount of time, precious, irretrievable time, she'd wasted after he left—nursing her grudges, brooding about the refinement and gentility she imagined was lost forever.

It was tiny Calvin who saved her—forcing her to disengage from the despair she clung to like a life preserver, to abandon the exaggerated hopelessness she carried like a talisman. Motherhood became her tonic. She released her own dreams and watched as they receded further and further until, like balloons loosed into an updraft, only flecks of color remained.

"In fairness," she continued evenly, "I think you would have to agree that I raised him, guided him, nurtured him on my own for over twenty years. Biologically, he is your son, but it was you who chose not to have a presence in his life." She drank the last of her brandy, noticing how chilled and inhospitable the room had become.

"No presence!" Samuel repeated dumbfounded. "Well, unless, of course, you consider that I hired a live-in nanny to help you, I fed, clothed, housed, and educated him since the day he was born. But

I suppose my monetary support was, in your view, solely an obligation—something sterile, not to be mistaken for any expression of feeling on my part. And am I to understand by what you've just said that you share no responsibility for my absence in Calvin's life?"

Waving away his words, refusing to be drawn into a conversation about that night so long ago, she pronounced, "Whatever Calvin thinks about you, Samuel, I assure you that he's formed that opinion on his own. Whether he joins your business or not will be his decision. I have never tried to turn him against you, have never spoken about you discourteously in front of him, though it wasn't easy to explain your absence to a small boy. But the decision not to play any active part in his life was yours, Samuel, totally yours—as is the decision to suddenly interject yourself now.

"I can't imagine," she continued resolutely, "what could possibly be gained, after all these years, by revisiting what happened between us and assigning blame. What's done is done. Let's not pick at those scabs, shall we?

"Calvin's enrolled in a two-year program in Siena, and I'd prefer that you wait until he returns before discussing this with him."

"Yes, well you've left me little choice, haven't you?" Samuel replied, sorely rankled because he'd not even considered this turn of events.

"Good night, Samuel," she said, rising from her chair, having set her glass on the table. "Sleep well," she added, shutting the room's carved door behind her.

He brooded until after midnight, rising only to throw on another log or pour himself another brandy. The juxtaposition of his business and personal personas could not have been starker. In business his life was as rich and fertile as a rain forest; his personal life, on the other hand, was as barren as a desert, littered with failures—one regret, one bitter disappointment after another. How many more, he wondered, would there be?

For this brief moment, he gave himself permission to imagine

Miranda's life after he left, the complete solitude his abandonment would have forced upon her, her very public humiliation with no opportunity for escape.

There was always a noose of sorts around the throats of women—ironclad societal conventions regarding behavior, respectability, and propriety. His abandonment would have tightened that noose, although not because he'd intended it. He'd simply chosen to do what was best for him at the time. In retrospect, what he had done was quite possibly unforgivable.

From that perspective, her need to withhold herself, and especially her heart, from him, as if from a noxious gas, her unbowed refusal to bend herself to better align with the curve of his life, and, most importantly, her inexplicable attachment to their son were all more understandable.

Their final opportunity for reconciliation had been lost because he had overshot—perhaps because of vanity, he hadn't anticipated that she would have so many reasons to shut the door to him so quickly. Perhaps he'd underestimated the amount of courage he would need to make things right.

But a coin has two sides. Miranda's contribution to this lost opportunity was easier to understand. Convinced that what she'd done to him was unforgivable, she perceived retaliation at the heart of everything Samuel did or said—whether or not it was. So, it never occurred to her that there might be any other explanation for his return.

After that night, they could never be lovers again, if ever they had been, but it was certain that they could never be friends either.

Meanwhile, Miranda's anxiety about Calvin had escalated into panic. Of course, she missed seeing him, but, more importantly, she missed feeling connected to him. Each irregular and predictably short letter she received from Calvin seemed a warning that he was building a life without her.

Despite her busy schedule, a hauntingly familiar loneliness began to weigh on her, until, in desperation, she simply made plans for a summer holiday in Greece. She penned letters describing the white-sand beaches, the fiery sunsets viewed from hilltop cafés, the ancient ruins, and the pièce de résistance—they would travel by private sailboat, leisurely exploring the idyllic Greek Isles, stopping whenever and wherever they pleased.

She received Calvin's reply more than a month later on a cloudless afternoon that, despite radiant summer sunshine, was still quite comfortable. She tore open the envelope, pulling out a short note penned on beautiful pale green parchment:

Dearest Cara Mama,

I've tried so many times to rearrange my schedule, but it simply isn't possible to be away during the time you're suggesting. Desperately sorry. Between exams and other commitments, it just won't work this year. I am ecstatic about the trip you're suggesting though. Definitely our best adventure yet! I will be devastated if you go without me because I'm certain next year will be the perfect time.

Amore, Calvin

Cheeks aglow with righteous indignation, her face mottled as if she'd been slapped, she recognized her son's letter for exactly what it was, a rebuke—his insincerity laughable, his lies obvious. He simply did not wish to spend time with her.

And there she sat, for the third time in her life, betrayed by a man she'd loved. But in this case, it was by someone she thought a soul mate, whose rebuke caused more anguish than all the others combined. Oblivious to the tears spilling down her cheeks, she lifted back the fire screen and watched in silence as the pale green parchment floated and swirled, propelled by updrafts, until finally it settled, and the flames devoured it.

If Calvin even noticed that his monthly checks began to be forwarded by his father's accountant, he never mentioned it and continued posting his sporadic form letters, despite the fact that his mother never replied. By then, Samuel and Miranda had established a truce of sorts. Perhaps they had each, separately, found a way to forgive the other or, more likely, to accept the weaknesses of the other, while remaining implacable about their own frailties. They rarely bickered and seemed to have found a way to coexist in harmony, accepting that in almost twenty-four years, neither had changed the other one iota.

Samuel, however, did notice how increasingly edgy Miranda seemed and how seldom she mentioned Calvin. It troubled him to witness how ill-fitting her garments were becoming, how her luster seemed dulled by some deeply burrowed suffering, and it tormented him when she seemed to fold into herself—a terrible reminder of his mother.

Calvin arrived home, quite unexpectedly and without fanfare, on a Sunday afternoon in the summer of 1904, almost a year after he was expected. Involuntarily, Miranda screamed with joy, gushing at the sight of him strolling casually into the sitting room where she and Samuel sat reading. Now a bronzed, handsome man with a confident smile, a mop of unruly hair, the only remnant of his childhood, he reminded her of Michelangelo's *David*, and she could not wipe the broad smile from her face.

Father and son greeted each other with firm handshakes, acknowledging that they were not really estranged as much as they were strangers. Mother and son prattled throughout the entire meal, which sounded more like a fiesta than a traditional Sunday dinner.

The dining room resounded with their flirtatious laughter and raucous interruptions of each other to interject a question or a bit of local gossip. Samuel enjoyed this opportunity to observe them—their easy banter, their riotous laughter, the way each would unmercifully correct the other over some small detail of a story being retold for the hundredth time. Samuel was not expected to participate; he was their audience and played his role enthusiastically without resentment.

"Well, Calvin, what are your plans?" Samuel asked pleasantly as coffee was poured.

Calvin seemed baffled by this question and looked to his mother, who finally asked, a bit too sharply, "What do you mean, Samuel?"

"I was simply asking what his plans are," replied Samuel defensively, trying to keep his annoyance out of his tone. Calvin remained mute.

"I think we've been very generous, Calvin, providing you with an opportunity to see more of the world, to appreciate the culture and history of the land from which our family emigrated. I'm quite pleased to see you so full of life and know that you profited from the experience." Samuel smiled warmly at his son.

"I've been waiting for you," he continued, "really looking forward to the day when you'd join me in business. We've ten mills now in five states." Samuel stopped talking, embarrassed because his son showed no interest in what he was saying.

"Really, Samuel, surely this can wait," Miranda chided in reply. "He's just returned home. Let him get his bearings."

That tone was one Samuel knew well—it meant that this discussion was over. His contribution to keeping the peace in his home was to avoid pushing back whenever Miranda used this tone, and he did so that night.

"You're right of course, Miranda. Let's talk when you're more settled, Calvin. It's wonderful to have you home."

For the next seven months, Samuel did not raise the subject again. Surprisingly, it was Miranda who waited with increasing impatience and irritation to hear what her son had decided to do with his life.

For Calvin, it was a heady time. He continued living as if he were still in Italy—desperate to hold on to the man he'd become there. He drank strong coffee with steamed milk and dressed in the casual style he'd become accustomed to: elegant trousers, linen shirts, cashmere sweaters, and Italian shoes.

On the pretext of looking up some college friends, he escaped regularly by steamer or train, first-class of course, going directly to a part of the city that seemed devoted to the arts called SoHo. There he painted in a fourth-floor walk-up studio on Chelsea Street that doubled as a friend's apartment, where he could leave his unfinished work until his next trip.

When he wasn't in New York, he typically slept until noon, read in the afternoons, and dined at the Fall River Sportsman's Club, playing cards, gambling, and drinking until quite late.

On a bleak February morning, a very hungover Calvin pushed open the dining room door to find Miranda, tight-lipped, at the table with a cup of tea in front of her. *Damn*, he thought, *just what I needed.*

"Mother," he exclaimed, adding as much joy to his greeting as was possible given his state. "What a pleasant surprise. You're usually out and about by now."

He passed behind her chair to pour himself some coffee from the buffet and cursed, under his breath of course, to find that the steamed milk was no longer frothy or even hot.

"Good morning, Calvin, although it stopped being morning ten minutes ago." Her irritation could not be missed, even with so throbbing a headache.

"Sorry it's so late in the day," he said breezily, trying to placate her, keeping his back to her as he stirred his coffee. "Some chaps really got into it after dinner last night, quite a heated argument. Can't remember now what all the fuss was about, something political, I imagine."

It was difficult, but when he joined her across the table, he managed a weak smile.

"Calvin, dear, it's so wonderful to have you home all these months." She tried, unsuccessfully, to keep from gushing like a schoolgirl. "Though I'd hoped we'd spend more time together. You're hardly ever home."

The hurt in her voice was unmistakable, but there seemed to be something more as well—something edgy, something being held back, something Calvin felt a bit thrown off by—so he remained silent.

She held her teacup firmly and continued staring at him, though he averted his eyes. "We've missed some wonderful theater, you and I. You know your father doesn't enjoy that sort of thing, so I must rely on you, Calvin. We haven't really had any chance to catch up. I suppose I'm feeling a bit left out really."

Calvin, looking properly chastened, smiled charmingly and muttered a low "umm," but didn't dare say more for fear he'd get it wrong. He wished he'd not drunk so much; the pounding in his head made it hard to think, and, as always with his mother, he needed a clear head—nothing came from her without strings attached.

"You know, Calvin," she began, "I saw Elizabeth Watts at the hospital yesterday. I believe you and her Robert were classmates? Anyway, he's with Gray, Henderson and Roberts in New York. I wonder, is he one of the boys you've been looking up on your travels there?"

"No," he replied calmly, "I hadn't heard he was there. But I certainly will do so on my next trip. Thanks."

"Well, I was thinking just this morning about the professions the sons of our friends have entered since graduation, and it made me wonder, if I may be quite candid, whether you have any inclination to enter a profession, to actually earn a living?" Her tone vibrated with judgment.

Calvin was totally caught off guard and searched frantically for a way to divert her attention.

"Mother!" he cried, pretending to scold her, "why that's almost vulgar, not up to your usual standard. Can I infer that Father's been complaining about me again?"

"Actually, Calvin, your father's not said a word these many months. Of course, he must notice that you are never up when he leaves for work. Surely, he notices that you choose to dine with your friends most evenings, ironically, at his club. So, except for the rare times when you aren't on some adventure in New York, or at his club, he . . . we . . . don't really see you. I'm sure he's noticed but has, most graciously I must say, remained silent."

"Sorry, Mother, I really must seem thoughtless. Of course, I should have spent more time with you and Father, and I do apologize for my self-absorption lately. I didn't make many friends in college, but I did truly miss the few I had. It's been great catching up."

"Well, dear boy, we certainly don't begrudge you your friends. Good friends are certainly important." She was smiling, but her countenance and her tone did not match. She was studying him soberly with something like recognition, a long time coming, in her eyes.

Although Calvin looked relaxed, his arm slung over the back of the chair, coffee cup in hand, he was anything but relaxed. In truth, he felt overwhelmed, his nerves tingling, unable to shake the feeling that something had changed for her, changed in her, something still out of focus—but, try as he might, it would not clear.

"But surely, Calvin, you must realize that you should have begun to interview for positions by now. Now, I've asked around, there are a couple of prestigious architectural firms in Boston, so I thought we could—"

"Well, that's the thing, Mother," he interrupted quickly, his voice shaky. "I don't want to work in an architectural firm."

Miranda's smile faded, her eyes narrowed. "I don't understand, Calvin. You finished your studies in Siena—in architecture. Was it unreasonable for us, your father and me, to assume that you intended to become an architect?"

"No, no of course not, Mother. I just..." Panic had dried his mouth, forcing him to sip the cold coffee with its disgusting film of milk.

"Well then?" she asked impatiently, her head starting to ache from the tiresome necessity of this conversation.

"I'm sorry I didn't say something sooner, I definitely should have. It's not been easy to find the words. I'm not ungrateful for all your help, Mother, and I hope that you believe that. I adored my time in Siena, you have no idea."

He stopped to catch his breath and pushed on, "I will never lose my respect—my love really—for architecture. I'll always be in awe of those magnificent buildings that we visited. At the same time, I discovered that I didn't want to draw them day in and day out. It all became tedious, boring—well, maybe *uninspiring* is the best word." His words seemed to gush, scattering like inmates unexpectedly released from prison. The cold coffee was revolting, so he pushed the cup away in annoyance.

"You were bored," she repeated, carefully considering his words. "I'm sorry, Calvin, I'm not really understanding. When did you become bored?"

Her tone, while clipped, still sounded more confused than angry. Calvin debated frantically how to proceed. Clearly the old charm wasn't working, and his mother wasn't as forthcoming with her support as he had assumed she would be. As his desperation deepened, he became defensive and then, as was his nature, resentful.

"I don't know exactly, it didn't happen all at once," he replied, not expecting to sound so peeved.

"I understand that it must have been a gradual thing," she said, trying to soothe him, "but at some point, you must have known that this was not your calling?"

"A year ago or thereabouts." He sounded mulish but, quite frankly, no longer cared, having concluded that this conversation wasn't going to end well.

"Mother, I know what you're going to say and you're right. I should have told you, should have sought your advice. I'm terribly sorry. I was worried that you wouldn't understand."

"Well, Calvin, many young people change their minds before settling upon a profession they feel compatible with," she stated, wanting to demonstrate her understanding of these matters. "But," she continued, "when you knew, why did you bother to finish your degree? Why didn't you just come home?"

"I didn't."

"You didn't what?"

"Didn't finish. I just left."

"You left, the Accademia?" she repeated in astonishment. "And so you spent your time doing what, exactly?" Now, she was definitely angry.

"I painted, Mother," he replied haughtily, losing patience, resentful that she didn't seem to get it, convinced that she just wasn't trying hard enough, that she just wanted him to sweat.

"People! Landscapes! Just not buildings or bridges! That's my passion, Mother, that's what I'm cut out to do."

Staring in disbelief, his annoyance stoking hers, she understood for the very first time, and wondered why she'd not recognized it sooner, that Calvin's considerable charm was not only insincere, which was hard enough to bear, but seemed the flip side of a considerable well of anger.

"I studied with an amazing painter, Mother. Paulo Diamonte. He hardly ever takes an apprentice and the most amazing thing happened! A gallery took a few of my paintings—I know, it was probably as a favor to Paulo—but they sold, Mother, my paintings sold—all of them!

"Yes, I should have told you, but I was afraid you'd be disappointed in me. I've always been afraid of disappointing you, and I was convinced that Father wouldn't allow me to stay in Italy and I simply couldn't leave that beautiful place."

He stopped then and waited, like an expectant toddler, waiting for her understanding, waiting for her blessing, waiting for her to share his enthusiasm. Instead, an implacable silence enveloped the dining room, and because he was sorting through his own miasma of feelings, he failed to notice his mother's frozen silence or to detect the tiniest whiff of something dangerous.

"Calvin," she began, her voice heartbreakingly defeated, a lump of something bitter and hard in her stomach, "I can absolutely understand not wanting to speak to your father about this, but me, Calvin, me? We were always confidants, talked about everything, had no secrets. You decided not to tell me until now? Until I forced your hand?"

"Mother, we are close, will always be close, but I want to make my own way in the world, to be my own person. I don't know what I'll do, as you say, to earn a living, but it won't be working in an architectural firm. I'm just not cut out to do that kind of work."

And there it was. She was struck dumb, less by what her son had finally admitted than by what it meant. He wanted to be his own person, but the truth, something she'd been trying to hide from for so long, was that he'd reappraised her and, deciding he didn't need her anymore—perhaps would never need her again—he'd tossed her aside like some old coat he'd outgrown.

She sat silently for a time, her head bowed, forehead puckered, conflicting forces pushing and pulling at her heart like turbulence. She felt bereft, tormented, and worn paper-thin from holding on so fiercely for so long—from desperately trying to keep alive something that was never, it now seemed, more than a pale hallucination.

Her face reddened in embarrassment as she fully understood that all her efforts, all her sacrifices, and the single-mindedness to which she had devoted her life had gone into raising this deceitful child.

He was her life's work—this self-centered, unfaithful young man. Her reward, many hardscrabble years piled with self-denial, restrictions, and obligations. At this moment, from every angle hers had been a wasted life.

The color drained from her face. How was it possible, she wondered, that the thing we prize most, the thing that brings us the greatest joy, can be the very thing that destroys us? It seemed a pattern in her life.

Thankfully, the choking tightness in her chest loosened, but her heart felt like a wind-shredded sail. What a fool she was for thinking, even for a moment, that she had everything when, in fact, she had nothing—she was nothing except a hauntingly empty woman, stricken with desolation, who would never open herself again.

Shoulders stooped, eyes hardened, she made her way to the door before turning to face him—the despair in her eyes, the corrosion of affection, so dazzlingly pure it pierced him.

"Calvin, while you're becoming your own person," she announced, clearly mocking him, "deciding what road to take, I expect you to join your father at the mill." Although he'd made no attempt to interrupt, she held up her hand to silence him, as she'd done so often when he was a child.

"He's been extremely patient and financially generous for years. I expect you to tell him only that you have decided to join him. You will never let him know how dishonorably you've behaved, how long you've been taking his money under false pretenses. No need for him to know, as I now do, what kind of man you really are." Calvin had never heard such contempt in his mother's voice. Her words cut through him as cleanly as a ship's bow sluicing the sea. As the door closed behind her, a funereal silence embraced the room where he sat feeling abandoned and totally unhinged. He would remember it always as the day his life ended.

11

ANNIE'S BEST DAY

She bolted upright, fearing she'd overslept, but thankfully, it was still dark. Listening for any sound that might mean someone else was awake and hearing none, she pulled on the stockings she'd hidden under her pillow, crept across the aisle to her locker, removed the clothing she'd carefully chosen the night before, and carried everything down the long, unheated corridor to the girls' communal bathroom.

She stood on her toes to see herself in the small mirror above the sink, attempted to get a comb through her curly hair but gave up, brushed her teeth, and rolled her toothbrush, toothpowder, and comb into a hand towel.

Carefully, she pulled on her Sunday dress—her only dress actually, a navy-blue sailor's dress with a bright red collar and a flouncy skirt that reminded her of a tablecloth. Not only was the dress out of style, but worse, it was babyish—no eleven-year-old girl would be caught dead wearing a sailor collar with a matching dickey!

To add to her embarrassment, her scuffed, black lace-ups were also out of style, but as the sisters pointed out, they were "still serviceable." She carried them down the back stairs to the mud room, stopping to hold her breath every time one of the old stairs creaked underfoot.

She lifted her brown winter coat from its hook, sighing deeply at the sight of yet another badly chipped button. Checking to see that her knitted cap and mittens were in one of the sleeves, she sat on the bottom step to lace up her shoes before slipping into the adjoining pantry, where she lifted two small cans of stewed tomatoes from the bottom shelf and an apple from a bin on the floor, stuffing them into her coat pockets before slipping outdoors.

The raw April air set her teeth chattering. Moving quickly down the back stairs and around to the far end of the porch, she crouched, removed two rotted slats, and deftly pulled out the small suitcase she'd hidden there the night before. She opened it and stuffed her hand towel and the cans of tomatoes inside before snapping it shut.

Annie Kenny was running away from St. Vincent's Orphanage, where eleven years ago, nearly to the day, she'd been left, according to Sister Mary Thomas, wrapped in a faded blue blanket, in a small cardboard box lined with newspapers and with a note that said only, "Anne Kenny."

In truth, Annie Kenny had been waiting her entire life.

For years, she'd waited to be adopted, but as young couples came and went on visiting days, no one ever chose her, even though she'd done everything the sisters told the orphans to do—look cheerful, speak courteously, smile a lot, and be on your very best behavior. But, like her birth parents, no one wanted her.

So today, on her eleventh birthday, she decided to stop waiting. Her plan to escape wasn't related to any specific maltreatment—she'd been fed, clothed, and schooled—but there hadn't ever been anyone, certainly never any adult, with the time or inclination to listen to her, no one who ever took a real interest in her. The sisters referred to the children as a family, but Annie Kenny was and had always been alone.

She'd never witnessed anyone getting beaten, but if you misbehaved, you wouldn't get supper, which was always a can of stewed tomatoes with a bit of melted cheese on top, two slices of bread, and two mugs of hot, sweetened tea with a bit of milk. On Sunday evenings there would usually be some sort of meat and pudding for dessert, usually vanilla, though on occasion Annie's favorite, butterscotch.

She attended the nearby Ashley School, completing four grades, but hated it because her clothes, never as new or as nice as the other girls, made her stand out in a bad way. In addition, orphans were always segregated on the playground and in the classroom as if whatever had made them orphans was contagious.

At ten-years-old, she was taken out of school to work in the laundry room. Annie would not miss the laundry room, nor having to share an attic bedroom, frigid in winter and sweltering in summer, with twenty other girls, mostly younger. She would not miss wearing dresses and shoes that never fit her because they were never bought for her, but, most of all, she wouldn't miss being invisible, being nobody's anything.

She had a plan, though not much of one really. She was convinced there'd be jobs near the river because that's where the big factories were. Just as she reached Ninth Street, wave after wave of men, women, and children spilled into the street, "mill workers," she'd heard the sisters call them. From a distance, she watched as this flood of people entered an iron gate at the bottom of the hill and disappeared, like ants, into brick buildings.

Like them, she entered through the gate, found an out-of-the-way place to wait, and munched her stolen apple while she thought about what to do next. The only thing she was sure about was that she needed to talk to someone important and impress them quickly, because she doubted she'd get a second chance.

When the bell in the huge tower struck nine, she rose slowly, her knees stiff from the cold. She walked purposely from building to building, reading the signs posted at every entry door until she found one that read ADMINISTRATION. Finally, she thought with relief, this was the door she wanted because, on the wall just outside of Sister Mary Thomas's office was a similar sign—and Sister Mary Thomas, in her view, ran St. Vincent's.

Taking a deep breath, she pulled the heavy door open and entered a room with rail-high wood paneling, a few upholstered chairs, a wooden rack of newspapers attached to one wall, and, on the farthest wall, row after row of framed photographs.

Large windows on either side of the door filled the space with brilliant sunshine, and once Annie's eyes adjusted, she spotted an older woman sitting behind a heavy desk, a typewriter at one end and a huge vase of yellow daffodils on the other.

The woman was engrossed in her typing, and, just as when Sister Mary Thomas typed, this woman's forehead was deeply puckered. Her nameplate said she was Mrs. Grace Doyle.

There were two doors behind Mrs. Doyle that Annie assumed were offices; the door on the right, which was closed, had a brass plate affixed to the left of the door that read: SAMUEL WALLABEE, PRESIDENT. The door on the left was wide open, the room was dark, and the brass plate near the door read: CALVIN WALLABEE, GENERAL MANAGER.

Annie took the chair nearest the president's office, slid her suitcase quietly under it, and waited patiently, not wanting to disturb Mrs. Doyle because Sister Mary Thomas got angry if someone interrupted her when she was working.

"Oh, dear, I'm so sorry," the startled woman said when she finally looked up. "I didn't hear you come in. May I help you?" Mrs. Doyle, who wore her hair in a short, wavy bob, looked at Annie appraisingly but otherwise seemed pleasant enough. Annie wanted so badly to ask how she got her hair so shiny, but even Annie knew that wouldn't be appropriate.

"Yes, please," Annie replied timidly. "I'm here to see Mr. Wallabee, Mr. Samuel Wallabee."

The woman smiled, taking in the small suitcase under the girl's chair. "Do you have an appointment with Mr. Wallabee?" she asked, looking at the calendar on her desk.

"No, ma'am, but I'm sure he'll want to see me." She tried to speak more assertively now, like an adult.

"Really," replied the woman, trying not to laugh out loud. "Well, that's most unusual, and whom shall I tell him is calling?"

"Annie."

"Annie," the woman repeated, still staring at her calendar. "Annie who?"

"Oh, sorry, Mrs. Doyle, I'm Annie Kenny." Annie could feel her hands begin to sweat, and she was sure her cheeks were flushed bright pink.

"And what is this in regard to?" asked the woman, still fighting the pressing urge to laugh.

Annie did not really understand this question but sensed its importance. "It's a very private matter," she replied enthusiastically, repeating the expression she'd heard the sisters use many times, especially when they didn't want to answer her questions.

"I see," said the woman. "And Mr. Wallabee will know what this very private matter is?"

"No, of course not," replied the puzzled girl. "It's private!"

"Yes, I see. Well, miss," replied Mrs. Doyle, continuing to study the calendar in front of her, "Mr. Wallabee's especially busy today. It's unlikely he'd have time to see you. Perhaps, you'd like to leave a message or set up an appointment for another day?"

"No, thank you, Mrs. Doyle. I'll just wait here and stay out of your way. I'm good at waiting."

"As you wish, Miss Kenny," Grace said, shaking her head. "As soon as he's free, I'll let him know you wish to see him."

Annie removed her coat, slid her cap and mittens into a sleeve, and placed it on the chair next to her. Then, straightening her dress and swiping her shoes on the back of her stockings to remove any dust, she sat back down, straight and tall as she'd been taught.

She so wanted to sleep, having barely slept the night before, but hunger and fear kept her awake. She was both determined—a trait the sisters commented upon regularly and not in a good way—and optimistic, believing that anything was possible, which was another characteristic that the sisters mentioned but, again, not in a good way.

After what seemed like hours, the office door finally opened and three men piled out, quickly retrieving their coats and hats from the nearby rack and leaving without a word.

"There's a girl waiting to see you, sir. I tried to send her away, but she refused to go."

Samuel Wallabee, who hadn't looked up from the papers in his hand, asked irritably, "Who is she, Grace?"

"Her name is Anne Kenny."

"What does she want?" he asked without looking up, his tone registering an increasing annoyance at being disturbed.

"I'm sorry, sir, but it's a very private matter."

"It's a what?" he asked, putting down the page he was reading, glancing up with nothing but puzzlement on his face.

"It's a very private matter, sir, that's what she told me when I asked. And she's brought a suitcase with her." Grace Doyle's face remained expressionless.

"She brought a suitcase?" he repeated. "Well, now, Grace, you have my full attention. How old is this girl?"

"I'm guessing about eight, possibly nine. She's really quite small."

"And it's about a private matter, is it?" he said, smiling broadly despite his sour mood.

"A very private matter, sir," Grace replied, correcting him. "Shall I send her away?"

"Absolutely not, Grace. After two hours with three mediocre

salesmen, it might be quite refreshing to have a conversation with an eight-year-old. Yes, quite refreshing. Send her in."

"Yes, sir, right away."

"Mr. Wallabee will see you now," Grace announced, holding the office door ajar.

"Thank you, Mrs. Doyle," Annie said politely, reaching to retrieve her suitcase. "And by the way," she said, turning back to face Grace, "your suit is lovely. It's the very first time I've seen such a lovely color."

Mrs. Doyle's hand could not get to her mouth fast enough to stifle a surprised laugh. "Thank you, Miss Kenny. Why don't you leave your suitcase where it is? I'll be here to see that your things are safe."

Samuel finished signing the letter in front of him before looking up. She was standing in the doorway, a tiny girl, looking quite frightened but also quite determined. He waved her in. "Please, have a seat. Miss Kenny is it? Have we met before?"

"Oh no, sir, Mr. Wallabee, we haven't." In order to keep her feet on the floor, Annie had to lean against the chair in front of his desk, appearing to sit rather than actually sitting. "Mightn't you call me Annie, sir? No one has ever called me Miss Kenny, except for Mrs. Doyle."

Grace was right, thought Samuel, the girl was quite small; he'd be surprised if she were nine years old. Without a doubt, though, she had the curliest mop of chestnut hair he'd ever seen, which she'd tried tying back with a blue ribbon, but, comically, unruly curls had popped out all along her forehead and in front of her ears. She was dressed in what he thought might be her Sunday dress, which, though clean, had been amateurishly patched more than once.

Then, he looked into the bluest eyes he'd ever seen, a startling shade of blue. It wasn't the purple-blue of a clear summer sky in Provence, not the robin's egg-blue of Easter bonnet ribbons, not the Wedgewood-blue of his hydrangeas, or the lavender-blue of his favorite lilacs. He simply had never seen this color before.

"So, Annie," he said without taking his eyes off hers, "I was about to have some lunch. I wonder if you'd care to join me?"

As if on cue, her stomach growled loudly and she grimaced in embarrassment. She certainly didn't need reminding about how hungry she was, but still she hesitated, not wanting to seem needy or—what was that word the sisters used?—precocious.

"Thank you, sir, but I wouldn't want to trouble you, Mr. Wallabee, sir," she replied politely.

"Nonsense, it would be a nice change to have a companion for lunch. I usually eat alone."

"Well, sir, if you're sure, I'd be happy to share your lunch."

"Wonderful!" he said, calling Mrs. Doyle, who appeared instantaneously. "Grace, do you think you could have lunch sent in for Miss Kenny, I mean for Annie and me?"

"Well, I . . . yes, of course, sir," Grace stammered, "if you'd like, but I'd be happy to escort her to the lunchroom, if you'd prefer."

"No, it appears that Annie has something she'd like to discuss in private."

"Yes, of course, Mr. Wallabee."

"Well now, Annie," he said, turning his chair to face her, a broad smile on his face, "what can I do for you?"

"Well, the truth is, Mr. Wallabee, I've come about a job. I'm a real good worker and I'm no trouble. I can take care of myself—even though I look small, I'm eleven. Plus, I can read and write and I'm honest," she announced proudly before blushing deep crimson remembering the apple and cans of tomatoes she'd stolen just that morning.

He hadn't been able to stop staring. There was something unusual about her, this child with the mesmerizing eyes, but he just couldn't put his finger on it. "So you've come for a job? And is that the 'very private matter' you told Mrs. Doyle you wanted to discuss with me?"

"Oh, sir," Annie replied, her eyes filling with tears, as she realized that a job wasn't a private matter at all. What had she been thinking? "I'm so sorry, sir," she said, her voice choking. "I wasn't trying to deceive you. Really, I wasn't. I just thought that if I told Mrs. Doyle I'd come about a job, she'd of sent me away or sent me to talk to someone else."

"But you wanted to talk to me? Why?"

"Because you run the place," she said simply. "You're the boss and people do what you tell them to do. Really, I don't mean to be disrespectful, sir, but that's the truth."

"I see," he said, not having anticipated such candor. "Well, Annie," he began again, "first, I want you to stop calling me sir. Do you think you could call me Samuel?"

"Oh, no, sir, definitely not!" She was appalled by his suggestion. "I couldn't possibly call you that, even if you were related to me. It would be impolite."

Again, he was forced to smile broadly. What a breath of fresh air! She blazed with life. And she was only eleven. Well, that's what she'd said, though she didn't even look nine years old to him.

"I could call you *Mr. Sam*, though, would that be better?" She so wanted to please him.

"Yes, much. So, before we talk about jobs, tell me about yourself."

"Not much to tell, Mr. Sam," she said straightaway. "Well, I don't mean that there isn't much to tell, there probably is, but there's just not much that I know.

"I don't know who my parents are or where they are now but, according to the sisters, they didn't want me. So, who knows? I might have a couple of handsome brothers, a rich cousin or two, or maybe even grandparents out there somewhere. I don't know. I won't ever know." She stopped to take another breath, but this time there was no smile.

"But you do have sisters?"

"No." She laughed out loud, unselfconsciously, at Samuel's mistake.

"Sisters run the orphanage. You know," she said, gesturing, "they wear those heavy, long black robes, cut off their hair, and wear those long black veils with stiff white bibs around their faces.

"Oh, and they wear those awful wooden rosary beads around their waists, as if they were belts! You can hear them coming a mile away," she announced, shaking her head, "what with all that swishing and clacking!" She laughed again, as clear and as uninhibited as, if first impressions could be trusted, she appeared to be.

Involuntarily, he burst out laughing, though never losing his decorum in the process. "Ah," he said, nodding and wiping his eyes, "that explains the suitcase. You've left the orphanage, I take it. Won't the sisters be worried about you?"

"No, Mr. Sam." She spoke simply, without a trace of malice. "I don't mean they don't care about me—well, actually, they don't really care about me, but they do take care of me. There are just too many of us, I guess. I suppose they just don't have enough time.

"No, that's not exactly true," she continued. It was important to get it right. Samuel would come to learn that Annie valued precision not only in what she said but in what she did.

"They're a starchy bunch of women really. Kind of rough for being so close to God. Sometimes, they don't seem to even like kids—well, they haven't really had any, have they?" Again, she smiled.

He marveled at her maturity, how her smile lit up the room, how she seemed to accept what life had dealt her, devoid of self-pity or any hint of resentment, and, despite what she'd been through, she was still able to envision a better future; in fact, she was endlessly enthusiastic about it.

They chatted amiably through lunch, though she did most of the talking since Samuel was unused to the give-and-take of actual conversations, and, although she tried not to, Annie ate ravenously.

"This soup's sure delicious," she announced. "It's got so much in it. What kind is it?"

"It's called stew, Annie. That's why it's thicker than soup and has lots of stuff in it. This one's a lamb stew. I like to take pieces of bread to mop up all the juice," he confided, noticing that she didn't quite know what to do with the gravy left in her bowl.

"Oh," she replied, breaking off a piece of her roll and following his example.

"You're not drinking your tea. Don't you like tea?"

"Oh, yes, Mr. Sam, I love tea. That's all we drink at the orphanage, milk's expensive, but the sisters sweeten the tea and add a little warm milk. This tea's quite bitter."

"I'll have to remember to try that," he said, chewing the last of his bread and pushing his bowl away. "Well, Annie, this was a delightful lunch, but I have a meeting across town, so I need to leave shortly. Perhaps we'll share a lunch again another time. I'd like that."

She was bitterly disappointed, just when it seemed things were going so well. Out of politeness, she forced herself to stand when he did. *Well*, she thought, trying to salvage some comfort, *at least I got a good meal out of it.*

She followed him out to Grace's desk, retrieved her suitcase, and began to pull on her coat.

"Grace, I need your help," he said, his tone serious, businesslike.

"Of course, Mr. Wallabee." Grace stood. "What is it that you need?"

"Well, actually, I don't need anything, but Annie here, who will be your new assistant, needs a few things. Now, Grace, she assures me she's a quick study and a hard worker, so I'm sure you'll find ways that she can lighten your workload."

"But first, she needs a safe place to stay. Please check with the matron at Rose Cottage and see that Annie's moved into a room with girls her own age. Then, Grace, would you help Annie purchase some clothing this afternoon? Otherwise, she'll have to return to the orphanage to get the rest of her things, which I don't think is a good idea," he said, knowing full well that the battered suitcase in Annie's hand probably contained everything she owned.

Annie was stupefied, as was Grace; both stood staring at him, blinking in disbelief.

Glancing from one to the other, Samuel said, "I assume that this arrangement is acceptable, Annie. Grace will give you all the particulars about your salary, work hours, and so forth, and get you settled. Grace, I know this is a lot to ask, so please take the afternoon off. I'll expect to see you both tomorrow morning."

"Yes sir," they replied simultaneously. Finally, Annie had a friend.

Grace Doyle, who was almost thirty, had four children, all boys, and could not have been more delighted at the prospect of shopping for girls' clothing and taking this small child under her protective wing.

They rode the trolley downtown, Annie talking nonstop to hide her nervousness. They stopped first at Wellington's Department Store to choose work clothes: three dark, denim skirts, three plain, long-sleeved cotton blouses, and a pair of black lace-up work shoes.

It was the first time Annie actually got to choose her own clothing, clothes that really fit her and hadn't belonged to someone else first. Even the sturdy, high-top shoes and the thick cotton stockings that Grace selected were, in Annie's eyes, quite beautiful.

"I think your heavy coat will do for a few more weeks," Mrs. Doyle remarked as they left the store. "I'll replace those broken buttons. But soon you'll need something lighter. Do you have a sweater, Annie? You'll be coming to work quite early and the mornings will be cool, even in the summer."

"Yes, Mrs. Doyle, I do," Annie declared, wishing she hadn't packed the ugly gray sweater with sleeves that were too long, but she couldn't lie to Mrs. Doyle.

Since it was a lovely sunny day, they leisurely walked the four blocks to Cherry and Webb's, an exclusive women's store with lifelike manikins in its large, green-tinted front windows. Annie stood rooted to the spot, gazing from one fully dressed manikin to another, studying every detail, until Grace prodded her to enter the store.

In front of her were aisles of marvelous, dazzling displays. Atomizers of at least a dozen different perfumes lined the top of one counter, and on shelves behind the counter were pastel-colored packages of each perfume, tied with matching ribbons, like Christmas presents.

To Annie's right were display cases of jewelry, the jewels twinkling under the rose-colored lighting. It looked to Annie like a field of fresh snow when the sun first hits it—diamond sparkles everywhere.

It was a daunting task to keep Annie moving forward toward the back of the store; she stopped to peer into every case so as not to miss a single thing, and, for the first time all afternoon, she was mute.

Using the Sears catalogue in the customer service department at the rear of the store, Mrs. Doyle ordered three summer dresses that Annie adored. In the shoe department, Grace and Annie settled on a pair of rubber-soled, black patent leather pumps with contrasting tan tops and darling ankle straps.

Then the elevator operator took them to the second floor to a department called lingerie, where Annie was too embarrassed to even touch the strange undergarments. So, guessing at her size, Grace purchased six pastel bloomers with tiny bows on their elasticized waists, three matching crepe de chine chemises, and three pairs of the thinnest cotton stockings that Annie had ever seen. Annie chose a soft blue nightdress with tiny yellow rosebuds, a matching bathrobe, and, for the first time in her life, a pair of slippers.

On the third floor, Annie was introduced to what would become her lifelong obsession, hats. She had never worn anything on her head except a knitted cap in winter; she walked slowly by every single hat.

Some were made of ribbed corduroy or thick, soft velvet, others of rigid felt, and there were even a few straw hats for summer. And the trimmings! Plain or pleated taffeta, satin ribbons in every color, large and small rosettes, bows of every size and shape, even shiny buttons! Because Annie was completely overwhelmed, Grace selected a small blue felt hat with a matching velvet ribbon knotted around the crown and tied into a bow on the left side.

"You can continue to wear your knitted cap to work for a while, but for church and such wear this hat. A girl, like a woman, should always wear a hat, Annie.

"Well," Grace continued as they left the store with their bundles, "I think we've covered most of the things you'll need for now, but come summer, I suspect you'll need a few more things, like a pair of white shoes and a straw hat. I'd be happy to take you shopping again, Annie, whenever you need. It was great fun for me, really, so don't hesitate to ask."

Annie tightened her grip on the shopping bag in her right hand, slipped her left arm through Grace's, and walked arm in arm with her new friend to the trolley stop, beaming from ear to ear. For the second night in a row, Annie did not sleep—convinced she'd wake up to find that all this had all been a glorious dream.

But it wasn't a dream—that day, April 15, 1911, was the day when Annie Kenny's life changed, finally, for the better.

The next morning, Grace introduced Annie to the girls in the cutting room.

"Girls, I'd like you to meet Annie Kenny, who'll be working for me. So in the future, when you need something, if something breaks, if someone's sick, go to Annie first. She'll be at a desk just outside this door. Phoebe, show her the ropes, will you? Where to eat her lunch, where the toilets are, that sort of thing.

"For now, Annie, come with me, let's find you a desk."

Almost every morning Samuel Wallabee stopped at Annie's desk for a quick chat. When Mrs. Doyle instructed her to, Annie would peek into Samuel's office to see if he had any typing for her. Sometimes, in the late afternoon, Annie would bring him a steaming mug of sweetened Irish tea.

Samuel discovered that, among other things, Annie was a born storyteller. Even on the bleakest day, she'd enter his office, a steaming cup of tea in one hand, some letters needing his signature in the other, and regale him with some amusing story that would force a smile out of him in spite of himself and, sometimes, even a burst of laughter.

There was precious little, if any, laughter in the insular world that Samuel inhabited, a world of his own creation to be sure. In the beginning, Annie was like a spring tonic, gently, imperceptibly, soothing an ache so long a part of him that even he had failed to notice it.

For Samuel, this tiny, innocent girl—though she would be offended to be described as either—was a gift. On a morning sweet with jasmine and early honeysuckle, he stood on his terrace, gazing across a field thick with purple and white cosmos. An electrifying sensation overtook him as if tiny bubbles were rising up his spine and bursting in his head like champagne in a chilled crystal flute.

At first, he failed to recognize it, having been so long without it, but it was, most decidedly, joy—unencumbered, unambiguous, uncensored joy. Like the joy of a young boy long ago clutching a bouquet of dripping watercress, a gift for his mother resting on a mossy bank.

Annie's real gift to him, though, was the gift of a second chance. No one, save his mother, had ever done more for him, and, like Angelina, he cherished this exuberant girl who seemed to plunge into life without hesitation. He loved her, really loved her with no wish to change or rearrange anything. Loved her as if she were his own child—loved her more, actually, than he loved his own child.

After a week of strenuous effort, it had become clear to Grace that

Annie was not meant to be a typist, at least not an efficient one, since her tiny fingers did not lend themselves to the bulky typewriter keys. Samuel suggested putting Annie to work with the girls in the experimental cutting room and Grace agreed.

"So, you're one of us now, are you?" asked the oldest girl in the cutting room, who appeared to be in charge.

Phoebe Dougherty was sixteen, spoke with an Irish brogue, and wore clothes that were far too big, not because they were hand-me-downs, like Annie used to wear, but because Phoebe had no sense of style at all.

She had coarse, almost carrot-red hair, which nobody ever dared tease her about because Phoebe was intimidating and not just because of her size. She could give you a look that made you sweat with fear, or she could flash you a brilliant smile that lit up the freckles across her nose. She was unpredictable and hard to read.

"Looks like," replied Annie, smiling. "Show me what needs to be done."

"Well, Annie Kenny," Phoebe said, her brogue as gentle as a caress, "sounds like we're compatriots, so we should get along fine. I'm from County Cork in the south of Ireland. Where're you from?"

"Saint Vincent's Orphanage," Annie replied with a straight face. Then they both burst out laughing.

Though Phoebe was older, it was the beginning of an unbreakable friendship; they were, from that moment, inseparable. Grace Doyle could hear them laughing all the way down the hall and thought that for a girl whose own parents didn't want her, Annie Kenny, bless her heart, managed to bring laughter and sunshine everywhere she went.

Phoebe's fraternal twin, Charlie, less than a minute younger, had the same stocky build as his sister, the same outrageous red hair, and the same smattering of freckles. He worked in the mill's security office across the quadrangle.

The twins differed in only one way, but it was a significant difference. Phoebe had a famously short fuse and an unfortunate habit of telling people exactly what was on her mind, and so would never work in the diplomatic corps. She loved to have fun, the noisier the better.

Charlie, by comparison, was painfully shy, a young man of very few words who deferred to Phoebe in most decisions, and, unless you knew him well, appeared not to take anything too seriously.

Their mother, Jenny and father, Thomas Dougherty, bankrupted by the Irish potato famine, now owned a freestanding, two-family boardinghouse on Whipple Street, which Jenny ran. After Thomas died in an explosion on the docks, the twins, not quite thirteen, were forced leave school and find jobs to help their mother.

Before long, Phoebe, Charlie, and Annie, the three musketeers as they were called, lunched together every day, and Annie regularly joined them for dinner at the boardinghouse, where she was a more talented assistant in the kitchen than Phoebe ever was. Jenny welcomed her warmly and insisted, though she didn't need to, that Charlie walk her home afterward.

"There's some photographer taking pictures," Charlie reported as the threesome arrived at the mill to celebrate the 4th of July, 1912. "Somebody said the boss's here somewhere, no doubt with his insufferable son. I'm going to join the guys at horseshoes, Phee. Back in a while."

When they were toddlers, Charlie couldn't pronounce Phoebe and instead called her Phee, which, to her embarrassment, had stuck.

"You're going to gamble is what you mean, Charlie Dougherty,"

Phoebe replied with a knowing look. He shrugged off her rebuke, winked, and strolled off, waving over his shoulder.

Meanwhile, an overdressed Calvin Wallabee, who hated this holiday more than any other, followed his father around dutifully as Samuel made the rounds. Calvin had absolutely no interest in being introduced to tables of employees with their huge families, overweight wives, and snotty-nosed, bawling toddlers. He had even less interest in shaking hands with groups of sweaty men hurling horseshoes, running ridiculous races, gambling, and telling off-color jokes that his father seemed compelled to laugh at.

Every introduction, every handshake, every fatuous smile felt like another nail in his coffin. Every year it became more and more impossible for Calvin to ignore the truth—without changing course soon, he would lose his chance to live the life he was meant for, the one he longed for, having already sacrificed almost seven years.

Finally, Samuel, who had already removed his jacket and loosened his tie, headed outdoors; the heat inside the tent had become unbearable. Across the way, he spotted his photographer with a trio of young girls under the ancient chestnuts and headed in that direction.

"Ah, there you are," he shouted. Without planning to, all three girls had dressed alike—flouncy, long-sleeved white blouses with ankle-length white skirts, frothy white hats, and newly polished white shoes. The shortest of the three, oddly the one wearing the broadest hat and brightest smile, stepped forward to greet him.

"Well, Mr. Sam, making the rounds, are we?" Annie said, her eyes shining with happiness.

"Ah, Annie girl, aren't you looking as fresh as a daisy in all this heat. Ladies, you're the picture of loveliness!"

Annie, I'd like you to meet my son, Calvin. Annie's smart as a whip, works harder than most men, and, as you can see, has the eyes of a Madonna—she'll melt a lot of hearts in a few years, won't you, Annie?"

"Can't say, Mr. Sam," the girl replied, blushing in spite of herself. "He's a kind man, your father," she proclaimed, turning to face Calvin. "Gave me a job when no one else would, cared about me when no one else did."

Because she was so short, Calvin had to look down to meet her eyes, which were, in fact, the deepest, most vibrant sapphire pools he'd ever looked into.

"Ah, Annie girl, Happy Fourth," Samuel proclaimed, giving her a celebratory kiss on the cheek.

"She's my sunshine girl, Calvin. There's many a day she's popped into my office bringing me a steaming mug of her Irish tea, wearing that lovely smile and entertaining me with a story that left me choking with laughter. I'll tell you, Calvin, she's the daughter I never had. She's rejected every offer I've made to adopt her."

"Well, Mr. Sam, you wouldn't like me as much if you had to live with me, that's for sure! But you're kind to keep asking—it's a great boost to my ego."

At first Calvin thought they were joking, but then, to his amazement and embarrassment, he realized that they weren't. *So,* he thought bitterly, *my father has secretly been begging this girl, this nobody, to join our family, while showing absolutely no interest in me, his own son, his only child.*

Calvin watched them banter. It was obvious that his father loved this small girl, obvious that his father had no trouble interacting with her—his father, then, had simply chosen not to love him and chosen not to get to know him. He was furious.

"Excuse me," Annie heard Calvin say over her shoulder, but he'd already walked away when she turned to say good-bye.

12

THE ARRANGEMENT

Franklin Rowe, enjoying the comfort and solitude of his private club car, rode the train from Providence, arriving a little early at the Fall River Sportsmen's Club to meet Samuel Wallabee, not only one of his favorite clients but a long time trusted friend. On this mid-July day, Franklin smiled in anticipation of a superb lunch of venison stew simmered in red Burgundy, one of the club's signature dishes, followed by a decadent double-Belgian chocolate soufflé and, finally, leisurely puffing on a Cuban from the stash that Sam kept in the club's humidor—all sensory delights unfortunately denied him by his wife, Margaret, who considered them unhealthy and in the case of the cigars, disgusting.

At fifty-one, he was still a handsome man with a thoughtful, earnest face and commanding dark eyes. His wavy, brown hair was salted with gray at the temples, although his thick mustache had not a single gray hair. But, in his view, his proudest accomplishment was that he still weighed the same as he had as a Harvard law student.

Like his friend Sam, Franklin Rowe had been born and raised in one of the poorer neighborhoods in Fall River. In high school, he obsessed about his lack of stature and endured constant teasing from his classmates. To offset this perceived genetic flaw, Franklin became excessively concerned about his appearance. His starched wing collars were always pristine, his distinctive cravats faultlessly knotted, his expertly tailored suit coats fashionably genteel, his shoes always highly polished.

Franklin's father, James Rowe, MD, was a well-liked Fall River physician who devoted his life to caring for the families of strangers but was a stranger to his own family. Franklin increasingly resented the alacrity with which his father left each morning to tend to the pain of others, leaving the care and comfort of his own wife to Franklin.

Instead of medical school, Franklin attended Harvard Law on a partial scholarship and was, not surprisingly, an obsessive student typically reading much more than was required for each class, committing even obscure legal precedents to memory.

It was there he met his future wife, Margaret Elizabeth Laurence, an assistant librarian. As he stood in line to check out some books, he noticed that she was short like him but, unlike him, seemed not to care at all about her appearance. She wore a stiff, high-collared blouse with huge puffed sleeves and layer upon layer of lace ruffles. The extra fabric enhanced her already full figure, and the stiff collar cut into her chin, giving her the appearance of being headless.

Over time and many conversations, Franklin discovered that she was indeed an unusual and interesting woman. She had completed university, was well read, and formed her opinions, which were in his view quite liberal, only after careful analysis. Inquisitive, compassionate, and, at times, delightfully humorous, Margaret was impervious to flattery, impatient with gossipers; she took her work and herself seriously and, not surprisingly, did not make friends easily.

He was fascinated by this unusual woman and, within weeks, was desperately in love with her, proposing on their first official date, a dinner at Parson's Grill the night he graduated. She accepted his invitation to dinner but deferred on his marriage proposal.

Heartsick, he returned to Fall River to open a tiny law office in

The Arrangement

1885. By then, Fall River had become the largest textile manufacturing center in the United States, and he was determined to make a professional niche for himself in this fledgling industry where there were few established legal precedents and even fewer legal specialists. As Franklin saw it, there were only opportunities.

Over the course of a few years, Franklin met with general agents, walked the mill floors with supervisors, and familiarized himself with one manufacturing process after another until he knew them all. Once he felt knowledgeable enough, he arranged meetings with textile mill owners, one of the most progressive was Samuel Wallabee, who, by then, owned two textile mills. Franklin traveled to New Bedford in 1886 to meet Samuel at his new mill there.

Because Franklin possessed such a creative legal mind, he could, on the spot, suggest a legal action to resolve an operational challenge or avert a potential problem. Slowly, he developed a reputation as a specialist in textile law and had earned the confidence of several mill owners who consulted him regularly, including Sam Wallabee.

For the next six months Franklin took the Old Colony Railroad's direct line to Providence, Rhode Island every Saturday morning until Margaret, who still lived with her parents, accepted his marriage proposal. It took two more years but, in the end, Franklin's intelligent manner, his persistence, and his impeccable appearance convinced her parents that he would be a good match for their daughter and an asset to their family. Franklin and Margaret married in 1888 and their only child, Rebecca was born in 1890.

His in-laws introduced him to Henry Appleton, a prominent Providence attorney, whose firm Franklin joined shortly after his marriage. At twenty-six his comprehensive legal and technical knowledge about textiles and his personal relationships with many prominent mill owners made him an invaluable asset.

He was viewed by his colleagues, sometimes begrudgingly, as a man who could exploit an opportunity better than most. By the time he was thirty-seven, Franklin, was the firm's youngest senior partner and financially quite successful.

Over the years, some in their social circle remarked that the Rowes raised their daughter as if she were a son, which was not entirely untrue. Rebecca graduated early from Wellesley College by carrying extra credits each semester, studied violin at the Vienna Music Institute the summer between her junior and senior years, and accepted a junior research position with the *Providence Daily Journal*.

Sadly, however, her parents could never have foreseen how quickly and completely all these gifts would be squandered.

Samuel, who arrived at his club even earlier than Franklin, rose as soon as he spotted his friend being led to his table. "Franklin, it's been too long. Looking a bit pale, my friend. Spending too much time cooped up in your fancy office, no doubt. Good you could get out, breathe some of our country air!" Samuel greeted Franklin with a bear hug, pounding him on the back.

"You know us legal beagles Sam, we'll go anywhere for a free lunch, which of course I'll have to bill you for!"

Both men laughed heartily and sat down as their waiter approached.

"What's your poison, Franklin?"

"I'll have bourbon, double, neat."

Sam shook the ice in his almost-empty glass, "Another one of these, please, Tom."

"Yes, sir," replied the waiter.

As they ate and chatted, Samuel couldn't help thinking about his current situation and wondered how to best explain it. He'd always been a man of little emotion, so he couldn't divulge, even to Franklin, how desperate he was feeling of late, how guilty he felt about his son's unconventional and increasingly embarrassing lifestyle—the expensive trips to New York City, the late nights drinking, womanizing, and gambling.

As Sam's personal lawyer since 1897, Franklin was the only person who knew precisely how successful Samuel had become. In Samuel's view, Franklin was not just his attorney but his friend, someone he trusted completely.

Franklin admired Sam from their very first meeting at Sam's New Bedford Mill in 1886. For the most part, the mill owners that Franklin represented were prestigiously educated, born into money, and politically connected.

Sam was different. He'd come from an immigrant family, actually worked in a mill, could repair a loom, and knew how many yards of cloth a spinner should produce in a day. He was rough around the edges then but had a ferocious drive to succeed. Sam wasn't a talker and certainly not a boaster. He was someone who said exactly what was on his mind, wasn't a flatterer nor a man to skirt an issue—so you always knew where he stood and what he thought of you. Franklin admired him immensely.

As they shared lunch, Sam asked, "Frank, how's Rebecca? Back from Vienna?"

"Ah, yes," Franklin said, beaming, "our girl's back and, frankly, both her parents are breathing easier. Honestly, though, I think she's relieved to be home. She's very much a homebody like her mother."

"I've had the pleasure of meeting her many times over the years—always a pleasure, beautiful girl. What's she up to now?"

"Thank you, Sam. Margaret and I have always been so proud of her. She graduated early and just last January started working for the *Providence Daily Journal*. Loves the work!"

"Well, now, no wonder you're looking as proud as a peacock! That's quite an accomplishment. Give her my best wishes, would you?" Samuel took another sip of his whiskey.

"I'll come right to the point, Frank," he said, clearing his throat and wiping his mouth on his napkin. "You've met my son, Calvin, many times over the years. I wonder what you'd think about them getting together?"

"For what?" Franklin asked, reaching for his drink.

"To marry of course! You know, the combining of two prosperous families."

Speechless, Franklin studied his friend's face. "You can't be serious! No offense, my friend, but arranged marriages are a bit out of fashion, not that fashion was ever your strong suit," he added with a devilish smile.

"I know, I know," declared Samuel, waving his hands in an expression of mock surrender. "Sometimes, the old ways make more sense to me. I know young people today want to marry for love, not to create family alliances. I'm not that out of touch, my friend!

"But, and you know this is true, Franklin," Samuel continued, "the Cabot, Rockefeller, and Lowell kids don't marry for love. They don't marry anyone who isn't in their social class. So don't tell me that arranged marriages aren't alive and well!"

Franklin laughed out loud, nodding his agreement. "Okay, point taken."

Both continued eating amiably. Samuel, understanding that Franklin needed some time to mull this over, talked of other things for the rest of the meal. Finally, as the obligatory cigars were lit, Franklin returned to the subject.

"Sam," he said, choosing his words carefully, "I love my daughter beyond words, as I assume you do your son. Margaret and I have never forced Rebecca into anything, and we never intend to. We've always felt that she should make her own decisions, and, for the most part, she has always chosen well." He drained the rest of his bourbon before continuing.

"Speaking for myself, I have no objections to arranging for our children to meet. Since May, Margaret's been away supervising something or other at our summer house in Narragansett, where she and Rebecca are spending most of the summer and I join them on the weekends. Perhaps Margaret and I could have you, Miranda, and Calvin to dinner one Sunday? But after that, Sam, our children are on their own. Do we agree?"

"Absolutely," replied Samuel, exhaling a thick, gray-blue cloud of smoke.

On the train back to Providence, Franklin tried to assimilate Sam's proposal. One concern Franklin did have was the difference in their ages, but his primary concern was, and he felt guilty even acknowledging it, Calvin's character. Franklin had heard the occasional rumor over the years. But Sam was as honorable a man as he'd ever met, a trusted friend, and a valued client, so Franklin dismissed this concern.

Rebecca and Calvin had, in fact, attended many of the same social events over the years, but had never been introduced as their groups of friends did not intermingle. So it was no surprise that Calvin did not know who Rebecca Rowe was when his father mentioned they'd be joining the Rowes for Sunday dinner in Narragansett.

Rebecca, on the other hand, had heard stories about Calvin Wallabee. She'd heard about Calvin's flirtatiousness, his travels abroad, and some rather reckless feats of bravado, preceded usually by a considerable amount of alcohol. At her age, stories involving adventure and travel were intriguing, and none of the boys in her social circle seemed as sophisticated or, frankly, were as handsome.

Margaret Rowe greeted her guests on a steamy July afternoon with her usual gracious banter, complimenting Miranda Wallabee on her stylish summer outfit—"so airy and such a lovely color, perfect on you"—and her good sense in bringing along an umbrella as "the summer skies can turn so quickly, especially on the ocean."

Immediately, she pressed Samuel to take a turn on the tennis court where her husband was just finishing up his weekly lesson. "I must warn you, Samuel, he's a bear on the court. Drives for every point, but I hear that you're an excellent player yourself, so I don't have to tell you."

"Well, you flatter me, Margaret," Samuel assured her with a smile. "I don't play very often these days, but I'd certainly be up for a match. Care to make it a fourth, Calvin?"

Dinner was the conventional six courses. The food, quite fresh and simply prepared, reminded Miranda of her beloved Florence, a fact she pointed out more than once to Calvin, who was seated across from her. In general, the dinner conversation was subdued, and although there were clearly political differences, the talk never became heated.

Without being prodded, Calvin shared some amusing anecdotes about Italy, mimicking, as only he could, a variety of local accents complete with appropriate hand gestures and shoulder shrugging—all of which caused everyone, including the men, to laugh heartily.

No matter how Margaret encouraged her, though, Rebecca did not reciprocate with stories about her studies in Vienna, which puzzled her father and alarmed her mother, who worried that Rebecca was finding Calvin Wallabee entirely too charming.

Samuel waited for two weeks, then, seated at his desk, watched as Calvin entered his office, stopping just inside the doorway. "You wanted to see me, Father?"

"Yes, close the door, Calvin." Samuel waited for the door to close, which forced Calvin farther into the room.

"Calvin, today is Thursday. I don't recall seeing you at your desk for several days. May I ask where you've been?"

"Of course," the younger man replied congenially. "I had correspondence to catch up on and the end-of-month report to complete, so I decided to work from home. Frankly, there wasn't much here that needed my attention."

"I see. Why, then, do you suppose I left you the year-end projections last week?"

Silence.

"I asked to see you, Calvin, because I wanted to know about the situation in the weaving room."

"I'm not sure I know what you mean, Father," Calvin replied without a hint of anxiety.

"Mrs. Elliot tells me they've been understaffed for nearly a week. Four girls out with some sort of flu, and she had to send two more home this morning."

Silence.

"And the status of the broken looms?" Samuel asked impatiently, although he knew the answer.

More silence.

"Calvin, parts for four looms arrived yesterday, so, with luck, all but one should be up and running before the end of the day."

Samuel stood, turning his back to Calvin, staring out the window behind his desk at the river's swirling, brown water.

Calvin waited, not particularly concerned, because these little confrontations—angry father belittles disappointing son—always blew over. Calvin had learned that it was best to remain silent—which he continued to do. Without turning around, Samuel spoke in a tone of resignation more than disappointment.

"Calvin, as my only son, you've perhaps concluded that you will take over the business when I pass. I think even you would agree that the manufacture of textiles, while not glamorous, is a very profitable business. It has provided our family—all of us—with a good life, an easy life. This has been my life, Calvin, but I don't know that it will be yours."

Whoa, thought Calvin as his stomach lurched, *now this was different*. "Really Father, I think you're overreacting. I simply missed a few days."

"What I'm referring to is so much bigger than some missed days, Calvin, so please listen carefully. You have been pretending to work, yes pretending, since your return from Italy. I fully anticipated that you'd need several years to get up to speed, to appreciate the complexity of what we do, to learn the business, and I was happy to give you that.

"But it's been eight years," he continued, "and, honestly, I've no confidence that you have the discipline or the determination to run this business—a business I've spent my lifetime building.

"You're smart, yes, but that's not enough. I've watched you closely and, so far, haven't seen any desire on your part to really learn much of anything, except for the few things I've put you in charge of, and, even then, your performance has been mediocre—your inability to answer either of my earlier questions, a case in point.

"Calvin, you're thirty-three years old, still single, and, from what I hear, quite the womanizer. You've no serious interests as far as I can tell. You've dabbled in architecture, then in painting. You enjoy expensive wine, fine cigars, and gambling at my club. Why, from what I hear, you'd be the patron saint of hedonism, if there were such a thing.

"You've no goals that I'm aware of," Samuel continued, "you're unfocused and your achievements? Well, let's just say that they've been limited thus far."

Calvin was rendered speechless. He stared at his father, licking his dry lips, unable to process what he'd just heard. He stepped forward, placing his hands on the back of a chair for support because the room seemed suddenly airless. "What is it that you want?"

Samuel's face was full of genuine compassion. "Son, I need to know whether you actually want to take over this business or whether you'd rather be in some other profession. I've waited as long as I can for some sign that you're interested, committed to learning the ins and outs of the business, and that you're really the man to take over the helm."

Calvin eyed him suspiciously but could still think of nothing to say.

"The bottom line, Calvin, is that I want you to grow up. Get married. Raise a family. Behave like a gentleman."

Calvin thought it best to look penitent since he had no idea where his father was going with this little pep talk. Best to say nothing, he decided.

"In fact," continued his father, "I want you married by next spring, next summer at the latest. If Rebecca Rowe isn't someone you feel you could marry, then find someone else. I want you to show up every day for work, to learn every aspect of this business, and to be able to act on my behalf within another year's time. When you have done that, I'll be proud to put you in charge officially and I will retire."

"What? You can't . . . I don't . . . I mean, how? That's impossible!" finally emerged as Calvin's reply.

"Of course, it's possible. But it'll mean you'll have to work long and hard—something you've yet to experience. It'll mean that taking over this business will become your highest priority, assuming it is what you want to do. It'll mean that you will take your place as a prominent businessman in this community, one with strong family values."

"You're not serious? Really? You can't expect . . . in a year?" Calvin flashed his most charming smile, but his father was not impressed. Finally, Calvin collapsed into the chair he'd been holding on to.

"Or what?" he asked, all pretense of remorse dropping away. "If I can't do these things or won't do them?"

"I'll accept whatever you decide, Calvin," Samuel replied sincerely. "I understand that this seems harsh and, under the circumstances, I need to accept some responsibility for the fact that you are so unprepared and so immature at your age." But, in fact, Samuel did not feel at all responsible.

"I need to know who will run this business when I pass. I will not leave my legacy in the hands of anyone incapable or unmotivated to lead it. So, in answer to your question, you have two days to consider my offer. If you decide not to accept it, then you will leave the mill and look for other work."

Samuel waited for this to sink in before adding, "You'll not live at home nor will you receive the carte blanche allowance you've been enjoying. In other words, the kind of life you've been living, which has been fully funded by me, will be essentially over."

Calvin felt beads of sweat trickle down his back, a low humming filled his ears, his mouth was so dry he couldn't form words—assuming he could think of something to say. He was floating and falling at the same time. Cradling his head in his hands, he felt sick, empty, and totally alone.

"Two days, Calvin."

Understanding his son's anger and humiliation at this moment, Samuel stepped from behind his desk and, to give Calvin some privacy, left the room, closing the door softly behind him.

Rebecca Elizabeth Rowe, twenty-three, married Calvin Joshua Wallabee, thirty-four on June 30, 1913. It was anticipated, given their social circle, that the wedding would be an extravagant and elegant event, and, in that respect, it did not disappoint. Elegant it most certainly was—conventional, not at all.

The *Boston Globe*, *Providence Journal*, *Fall River Herald*, and *Narragansett Times* all carried pictures of the handsome couple surrounded by their twenty-person wedding party and flanked by their proud parents. According to newspaper reports, it was a glittering affair with over three hundred guests, including some of the most socially prominent families in New England.

The bridal gown was designed by Jean-Philippe Worth, from the House of Worth, long a dominate force in Parisian fashion whose devotees included the actress Sarah Bernhardt, the singer Lillie Langtry, and more than one of the New York Vanderbilts.

Rebecca chose Jeanne Paquin, another famous Parisian designer who, with her brother owned Maison de Couture, to design her bridesmaids' dresses, insisting that she showcase the slimmed and elongated silhouette that was currently so fashionable in Paris, though not yet in America. Paquin's design, with its raised waistline, close-fitting sleeves, narrow, tubular skirt, and a hemline that barely brushed the floor, was exactly what Rebecca requested and flattered each bridesmaid, whatever her shape.

It was extraordinary that no reporter commented on the bride's choice of a candlelight service instead of the more traditional and some thought more fashionable late-morning service. Predictably, as soon as the groom's parents heard about that decision, they voiced their displeasure because it was their view, and they were not alone in this, that this was just another example of how the Rowes overindulged their daughter.

As it turned out, the day of the wedding was uncommonly muggy, but an hour before the service, gentle breezes lifted the humidity, allowing cooler and drier air to settle in for the evening. Had the wedding been held at the earlier, more customary time, both the church and the country club would have been steamy. It was unlikely, however, that the Wallabees took any comfort from this fact.

In the velvety dusk, as guests drew up to Saint Paul's Cathedral, every stained-glass window twinkled with lit candles. A pair of magnificent urns overflowing with yellow roses and baby's breath had been placed on either side of the massive cathedral doors. A cardinal-red carpet ascended the worn, granite steps—creating an unabashedly royal entrance.

Inside, the setting sun backlit the ancient stained-glass windows and, along with the hundreds of flickering candles, made the cathedral's walls blush. Here and there, along the center aisle, small crystal vases filled with purple lilacs and creamy roses stood atop white pedestals. The scents of lilac, beeswax, and sweet incense drifted among the marble pillars and mahogany pews before settling gently on the shoulders of their prestigious guests.

Instead of white, which had only recently become the more typical color for brides, Rebecca chose the palest of pink silk, a diaphanous material which shimmered as if in moonlight. Rebecca's gown embodied a new, more fluid style and was a distinct departure from traditional American bridal gowns with their enormous skirts, high necklines, layers upon layers of lace, and elaborate trains and veils.

She wore diamond and sapphire drop earrings, above-the-elbow pink kid gloves, and a fresh gardenia positioned over her left ear so that some of the creamy petals gently caressed her cheek.

Most who met Rebecca for the first time thought her an attractive young woman, quite pretty but not strikingly beautiful. Her luxurious coffee-brown hair and her golden-flecked hazel eyes were, undoubtedly, her best features.

Despite her many achievements, Rebecca was still quite impressionable, definitely vulnerable, and had no clear sense of direction in her life. But on her wedding day, the gossamer gown's effect was dramatic: she appeared willowy, and, because of the fabric, her movements seemed fluid, luminous, and powerfully radiant.

By comparison, the man waiting at the altar was the very incarnation of custom and convention. He wore an impeccably tailored, black tailcoat, a white waistcoat with a crisp white bow tie, sharply creased trousers, and a small gardenia boutonniére.

The Arrangement

He was handsome, despite a pale scar across one cheek. His unruly, auburn hair, the one feature he seemed unable to control, was today combed back hard and subdued with hair cream, but even so one small curl had already broken free at his forehead.

What one noticed first about Calvin, apart from his handsome face and athletic build, was his lack of expression. He was emotionally unreadable, and though he rarely smiled, he still managed to avoid appearing unhappy. He looked directly at people when he spoke, appearing both sociable and engaged in any conversation. His slate gray eyes managed to take in everything but reveal little.

Perhaps because of her youth, Rebecca had mistaken almost everything about Calvin, including his interest in her. She openly admired his self-assured, slightly aloof manner, which she considered a sign of his maturity. She could not imagine that it was a ruse, a defense against feeling vulnerable, a disguise for the fact that he never felt quite at home anywhere.

To someone without a strong sense of self, he was irresistibly seductive. Rebecca felt protected by his worldly sophistication, found his attentiveness, which she mistook for intimacy, alluring, and was totally captivated by the aura of mystery that hung about him—never realizing how calculated it was or what it hid. She trusted him when he told her that, because of his increased workload, a honeymoon was not possible.

There were only two people in the world who knew Calvin Wallabee—knew what he longed for, what he cared deeply about, and, most importantly, what he concealed. Rebecca Elizabeth Rowe was not, and sadly never would be, one of them.

So why did Calvin Wallabee marry Rebecca Rowe? It was business, it was convenience, but most of all, it was cowardice.

13

BROKEN PROMISES

"So, you're really leaving?"

"Annie girl! What a lovely surprise!" Grinning from ear to ear, Samuel dashed from behind his desk, wrapping her petite frame in a gentle bear hug. Despite the November chill, her thin coat didn't seem warm enough.

"Sit," he insisted, pointing to a small sofa across the room. "Boy, have I missed seeing your lovely smile almost makes me want to move the cutting room back into this building!"

"Sorry I haven't seen you in a while. It's not as easy to get away now that the cutting room's so far away. Can't stay long," she said breezily. "I'm just on break. Took a chance you'd be in your office. There'll be trouble, though, if I'm late getting back."

"I understand, but please stay a few minutes, won't you? Catch me up?"

"Okay," she said, tempering her impatience while her intelligent blue eyes scrutinized him. Finally, she asked pointedly, "When?"

"Not for a while," he confided, "but that's just between you and me until some formal announcement's made. Annie, I think you're the only one who will miss me when I go."

"That's not true," she countered emphatically. "This is your mill, and you belong here. Does this have something to do with your son getting married?"

"Nothing stays the same forever, Annie, good or bad," he observed, sidestepping her question.

"You're taking Mrs. Doyle with you, aren't you?"

"Yes," he said quietly. "Well, she's been with me for a long while. Calvin will want to choose his own secretary. Do things his own way. And I'll need a personal assistant, someone to keep me on track," he said, flashing one of his big, toothy smiles.

"What would you think about getting back to our waterfront strolls as long as the weather holds, though I do have a couple of business trips I need to schedule?"

"Great! I was hoping we could fit in one more before the real winter weather settles in," she beamed.

It had started a year ago when Annie, who loved to explore new places and sometimes still had enough energy after a ten-hour workday, headed to the waterfront district—by all accounts a motley stretch along Davol and Water Streets. There she uncovered a beehive of activity punctuated by earsplitting whistles, a reverberating staccato of hammers, and the strident scraping of iron against iron.

Surprisingly, the mechanical cacophony was often drowned out by resounding exclamations, raucous shouting, and guttural expletives that filled the air as deckhands, spiderlike, clambered atop and straddled huge pallets of cargo, shoving, spinning, and swinging them over the ship's side and onto horse-drawn flatbeds that were lined up, sometimes two and three deep along the pier. Once the cargo had been off-loaded, the men, exhausted and thirsty, disgorged in packs to the nearest tavern or pub.

Placed at a respectful distance from the dangerous work and the unkempt men, a few granite benches adjoined the docks and became one of Annie's favorite places to relax. She loved the spectacle, the dramatic feel of the action, and the air vibrating with personality.

One day she spotted Samuel sitting motionless on one of the benches, staring out at the bay. As it turned out, Samuel shared her passion for roaming the waterfront, was equally energized by the commotion, and often sat there until well after dark before walking home. Since that day, once and sometimes twice a month—but only if the weather co-operated and his travel schedule permitted—they walked together, sat contentedly, and let the swirling energy of the place revive them. Their outings ended at E. Dunn's Soda Fountain on the corner of Walnut and North Main Streets, where, depending on the weather, they sipped hot chocolate from steamy mugs or slurped chocolate sodas through straws.

One evening, anticipating a spectacular sunset, they sat a little longer than usual, and Samuel began his story about a massive mill fire forty years ago, recalling how even the air was scorched and heavy and how, at midnight when his train pulled into the station, the sky was still dull red.

Once he started, it seemed he couldn't stop, having kept this part of his life a secret for so long. He described how for days, he had looked frantically for his father, searching every hospital, day after day, having his hopes raised then crushed until it was clear that Guido would never be found, his body would never be retrieved.

All the while, his brothers were unconscious in St. Anne's Hospital. He told Annie how his mother sat stoically, day after day, night after night, in the cramped hospital room with his brothers, how she held their bandaged hands and spoke softly to each one, hoping that her voice might wake them. How she prayed for a miracle but both Anthony and Alphonso died four days later.

Tears trickled down Annie's cheeks, splashing onto her blouse until her collar was damp. Samuel too was crying but soundlessly, his shoulders rising and falling, his face contorted with the most profound sadness she'd ever seen.

"I never had a family," she told him quietly. "I suppose I just had to get used to it, accept it somehow, but having a family and then losing them, horribly, in one night—I just can't imagine it, Mr. Sam. I'm so sorry."

She slid closer, linked her arm through his, laid her head on his arm, and let him cry. It was, without a doubt, a transfiguring moment for each, although neither spoke of it again.

Annie's visit today was a total surprise, and Samuel was, as always, delighted to see her. She'd had her hair bobbed in the latest style, which didn't surprise him. She had always been keen on fashion, but her exuberant curls refused to be repressed, which, as always, tickled him.

"I'm glad you're taking Mrs. Doyle with you," Annie confessed. "No offense, but I don't think she cares for your son much."

"Calvin will do a good job, Annie. I'm sure of that or I couldn't possibly think about leaving. Marriage seems to have matured him."

Surely, she thought, he must know that Calvin was not liked or even respected and that wasn't just her opinion. He was prickly, callous at times, and never mingled with employees, at least not willingly. He held himself apart as if they were malodorous.

"But he's not like you," she groused, vexed that he seemed not to know this about his own son. "Why are you leaving? Really, I don't understand, Mr. Sam. Nobody does."

He vacillated, completely caught off guard by the undisguised heartache in her voice, embarrassed by the tears involuntarily forming in the corners of his eyes, and conflicted about which truth to share.

"Because I gave him my word, Annie, and a man's word is his bond. It's as simple as that." But it wasn't really as simple as that.

How could he have foreseen that just when his life was drawing down, when resignation had rubbed away his vitality, when nothing seemed clean or pure, an eleven-year-old girl would walk into his office and, miraculously, into his life?

"Of course, you're right," Annie murmured apologetically, interrupting his train of thought. "Sorry, don't mean to be a whiner. I've you to thank for the incredible changes in my life, Mr. Sam, and I'll never forget it."

"I just gave you a chance, Annie. Everything after that you earned on your own. I do wish you'd believe that. Now, do I remember correctly," he asked, trying to lighten the mood, "did Grace tell me you'd moved out of Rose Cottage?"

"I did," she affirmed excitedly, "just a month ago! Remember my friend, Phoebe? She used to supervise the old cutting room here but left to take a job at Marshall Brothers Hats. "Well, naturally, we were miserable not seeing each other every day, and since her ma runs a boardinghouse, Phoebe convinced her to rent me a room for the same rate as Rose Cottage.

"It's so great. Phoebe, Charlie, and I go everywhere together now—people call us the three musketeers."

"Aha," he teased dramatically, "I thought there must be a boyfriend somewhere in this tale."

"What? Oh, God no!" she gasped. "Charlie's just Phoebe's twin brother. I thought I'd mentioned him. They look alike, for sure, but they're not at all alike, which is good, because I'm not sure the world's ready for two Phoebes!"

Samuel chuckled. "And what does this Charlie do?"

"He works here, Mr. Sam, can you believe it? He's in security, sometimes he works nights and sometimes he's on the day shift."

Finally, she stopped prattling. There was something behind his eyes that troubled her—why hadn't she noticed it before now? And his shoulders, too, drooped as if an impossibly heavy obligation was weighing on him.

"I'm not always good with words, Mr. Sam," she observed tentatively, "but I want to tell you . . . I mean . . . well, you've been so kind. I hope you know . . ."

"I do know, dear girl," he assured her, "but you don't appreciate how knowing you has changed me—for the better."

"You really don't want to leave, do you?" she observed matter-of-factly, again intruding on his thoughts.

Pushing himself up from his chair, he walked wearily to the window that overlooked the invincible Quequechan. He marveled, and not for the first time, at how effortlessly, how uncannily she deciphered his thoughts and how, unlike anyone else, she did so without any judgment—which was reassuring beyond words.

"No, Annie, you're right," he whispered, watching his breath fog the pane.

"I'm afraid I've many regrets," he told her with a sadness so profound it brought tears to her eyes. "Things, so many things, I wish I'd done differently. Of course, I'll miss what's been my life's work—what's been my whole life, really.

"And yes, it will be hard for me to leave, almost impossible, actually, to imagine myself separate from this old mill. Soon it'll be time for me to turn things over to my son—it's his birthright and he's earned it." He turned now to face her, resignation deepening the lines in his face.

"You don't know it yet, Annie girl, but the world out there can be a very dangerous place. I want you to give me your word, here and now, that if you were ever in any trouble, ever needed anything, I'd be the first person you'd call, even after I've left here. Please, would you promise me that?"

"Sure, I promise, Mr. Sam," she asserted easily, "but you must promise not to leave without saying a proper good-bye. I don't want to drop by one day and find your office empty."

"Agreed!" he said enthusiastically, grateful to have something to give back to her. "I promise you that we'll have a proper good-bye."

There was no question that the promises were made in good faith, as both were confident that there was no adversity, no calamity that could ever compel them to renege—but they were tragically wrong.

After his June wedding, Calvin began to focus on minimizing his father's influence in the mills and steadily maneuvered for control of one department after another, one project after another, and one mill after another. From Calvin's perspective, he'd sacrificed everything, fulfilled every requirement, jumped through every hoop his father had placed before him.

Still, the prize, if it could be called that, eluded him, and Calvin was becoming increasingly obsessed about having it—as if it were the only remaining obstacle to his complete happiness. Oddly, Calvin couldn't remember when, if ever, he had decided that he wanted to run the Wallabee Mills.

At year's end, losing all patience and without a word to his father, he hired his own secretary, Miss Irene Lockard, to start on January 3, 1914. The weekend before she was to start, Calvin had the reception area painted the majestic blue of the Mediterranean—a color he still loved, a place he thought about almost every day.

A handsome walnut desk was delivered with new chairs for the lobby in a terracotta colored fabric reminiscent of Siena rooftops. On the desktop, a triangular brass nameplate identified the occupant as Miss Irene Lockard, Administrative Assistant.

On Monday, January 3, a low gray morning, Grace Doyle arrived around six thirty, as she always did, puzzled to see that the office was already lit and the door unlocked. She was startled by the room's complete rearrangement and the unfamiliar red plaid coat hanging on the rack.

The brass nameplate on the new desk was, however, unambiguous. Without removing her coat or hat, Grace walked to her desk, now up against the back wall, retrieved the envelope she saw addressed to her in Calvin's handwriting, and, without opening it, laid it on Samuel's desk before leaving.

Within the hour, Samuel plodded to work through the same frail morning light, lost in thought and with an uneasy foreboding. The future, when he thought about it at all, no longer seemed suffused with possibility as it had only a few short months ago. When he opened the office door, all was confirmed.

As he read and reread Grace's letter of dismissal, Samuel realized that his indulgent vacillation and failure to take decisive action led to this. Samuel understood that he was now redundant, and so, by default, was Grace Doyle. His naïve belief that he might, somehow, reconcile with his son, bridge the schism between them, left a bitter taste on his tongue.

Still, Samuel was nothing if not a man of his word. Decisively, if one could call any action decisive at this point in time, he rose, opened his wall safe, and removed two sealed envelopes and his checkbook.

Pulling a sheet of pale gray stationary from its cubby, he wrote:

My Dear Annie,
I realize now that I've never, ever, been comfortable with good-byes. I'm embarrassed, having promised you "a proper good-bye," to be leaving in this way. Please forgive me.

You saved me, Annie. I was alive but not living. A simple thank you cannot suffice, cannot fully express my debt to you. I tell you this because I worry that you have burdened yourself with an unnecessary sense of obligation to me. It is time for us to wipe that slate clean—the fact is we each gave the other a second chance.

Your love and friendship are gifts I will always treasure, though I'm not sure I was ever worthy of them. It is selfish, but I hope we will remain friends after I leave here—but you must decide what is best for you.

My dearest girl, although you have refused my offers to adopt you, in my mind and heart, you have always been the most-loved part of my family. Please, Annie, accept the enclosed. It is my gift given in friendship and love with absolutely no strings attached. It would mean so much to me to think that in some small way, I was able to help you realize one or two of the dreams that you've shared with me over the years.

I know you will think it too much. It is not and could never be.

Your loving friend,
Sam

Samuel folded the letter neatly, wrote "Miss Annie Kenny" on the matching envelope, inserted a check for $10,000 and a business card with his phone number before sealing the envelope securely.

He opened his office door, gathered his coat and hat from the rack, walked across to the wall of photographs, and carefully removed three.

"Miss Lockard, would you please see that Miss Kenny receives this? I'd like you to give it to her personally, today if possible."

"Of course, sir, I'll do so before I leave for the day," she assured him, taking the envelope.

"Thank you, Miss Lockard," he replied, tipping his hat.

With the photographs tucked carefully under his arm, he left the building, certain his heart would burst from the pain of it, every step away a colossal effort.

By sheer will, he reached the main gate—a gate through which he'd entered and exited hundreds, thousands of times. He stopped to catch his breath and take one final look. Time slowed and expanded as a reel of memories that were his alone played out before his eyes.

He tipped his hat and walked through the gate for the last time

"Good morning, Miss Lockard," shouted Calvin the next morning, struggling to shut the door against the January rain.

"Good morning, Mr. Wallabee. How was your trip? You're quite wet, sir, shall I get you some coffee?"

"No, thank you."

Noticing the empty office, he asked, "My father hasn't arrived yet?"

"No, sir, he left yesterday morning, about eight-thirty."

"Left? For where?"

"I don't know, sir. I assumed he went home."

"I'm sorry, Miss Lockard, I don't understand."

"Well," she reported anxiously, hoping not to offend, "first, he took some photographs off that wall." She pointed to empty spaces on the far wall. "He gave me an envelope to deliver to a Miss Kenny, which I promised to do, then he said good-bye to me and walked out.

"Before leaving for the day, I went in to turn his lamp off and noticed that his wall safe was open. It was empty, as was his desk."

Immediately, Calvin strode to his father's office and switched on the lamp. It was exactly as she had just told him, empty. His father, it would appear, had finally retired—without a note, without a word.

He felt neither guilt nor regret for pushing his father out the door. Instead—and this quite surprised him—he felt rage, an ancient, familiar rage, at having been forced, once again, to follow in someone else's wake, to live someone else's dream. Perhaps, at that moment, he simply wasn't capable of grasping the price he was paying to lead such a false life.

"Miss Lockard," he said, quietly rejoining her at her desk. "I'd like to keep this quiet until I have an opportunity to discuss it with my father and then with the board at the end of the month. But for now, you are to keep this information in the strictest confidence, do you understand me?"

"Yes, sir, of course. Will there be anything else?"

"No, not at the moment," he replied crisply, walking away. At the door of his office, he hesitated, as if remembering something, then turned to face her.

"And did you deliver the envelope to Miss Kenny?"

"Oh, God! No!" she cried, almost in tears. "I'm terribly sorry, sir. It got so busy and then, I just forgot. I'm awfully sorry. I'll do it right now."

"No worries, Miss Lockard," he replied graciously, extending his hand for the envelope. "I'll do it for you."

Closing his office door behind him, Calvin hung his gray cashmere coat and silk scarf carefully on a hanger, shook the wet rain from his hat, and placed it at a jaunty angle on the shelf, then stood beside his desk and emptied his briefcase of the files he'd taken home, dividing them into three neat piles. Removing his suit jacket and hanging it on the hook behind his door, he settled into his chair to begin the day's work.

Hours passed. At eleven o'clock in preparation for his first meeting with supervisors from the Maine mills, he retrieved his suit jacket from its hook and felt the envelope he'd taken from Miss Lockard stuffed into an inner pocket. Without a second thought, he pulled it out, dropped it into his wastepaper basket, and headed for the conference room.

14

NO TURNING BACK

"Enough, Rebecca! Absolutely not! I forbid it!"

With the force of a thunderbolt, Calvin's fist slammed the dinner table, wine sloshed over gold-rimmed goblets, shallow red pools crept and radiated across the bleached white tablecloth, silverware crashed to the floor.

She recoiled, speechless, eyes wide with fear, shocked at this unexpected, explosive eruption—it was a fury of which she would never have thought him capable. His face a dangerous thundercloud, he stormed from the room for the solace of his study. There was simply nothing left to say.

Since his marriage, Calvin never failed to do what was expected—attending to, patiently and conscientiously, his newly incurred responsibilities and obligations. Charming and entertaining at the requisite social and charitable events, provocative and witty at formal dinner parties, and at Sunday dinners with only his and her parents in attendance, he sidestepped, as skillfully as a flamenco dancer, the impassioned, nearly compulsive debating to which his father and father-in-law seemed addicted.

Publicly, he appeared an exceptional husband and an excellent provider, their married life idyllic—but are outsiders ever privy to the true landscape of a relationship?

Like most couples their age, they dined at home most weeknights, but it was Calvin, not Rebecca, who instructed their cook. He disliked dining out because, in his view, even the best restaurants overcooked their vegetables and served fatty cuts of meat camouflaged with heavy gravies and, of course, always some sort of potato—if not fried, then mashed or boiled, but always swimming in butter.

Depending upon the season, he insisted that vegetables be roasted, lightly sautéed in olive oil or thinly sliced in salads. He introduced Rebecca to a variety of pastas—handmade tiny orzo, paper-thin fettuccini, and crinkle-edged raviolis stuffed with mushrooms or delicate cheeses. He preferred, as did their cook, the delicate sauces of the Abruzzi region of Italy rather than the thicker tomato sauces of Northern Italy, which many, their friends included, wrongly considered real Italian.

Outwardly, Calvin remained as amiable as ever, but Rebecca had come, quickly and sadly, to the realization that his amiability was not to be mistaken for the intimacy which it suggested. Still, the first six months of their marriage were enchanting in many ways, except that Rebecca was not yet pregnant, so her joy was less complete. Had she asked, Calvin might have admitted he had no desire to have children. On the other hand, he might have concealed this truth from her, stowing it where he'd hidden so many other truths—truths that would eventually separate them as cleanly as a centrifuge.

He simply could not fathom his young wife's desperation for children—she was only twenty-three for God's sake! Worse, her expectation that he could, or should, do something about this situation was debilitating and hinted that he might be to blame. Although she never accused him outright, there was always a lingering whisper of guilt in the air afterward.

"Mother says there's a specialist at Brigham and Women's who might be helpful," she told him one night at dinner just after the New Year.

"What?" he asked incredulously. "You've discussed this with your mother? Rebecca, this is most definitely a private matter."

"Calvin, there's something wrong with me, I know it. I also know that you find this entire topic distasteful, whereas my mother does not." For the first time ever, there was something sharp in her tone; he didn't like it and was certain his mother-in-law had something to do with it.

"If you want to see a specialist, Rebecca, fine, but I simply won't be part of it. Nothing's wrong with you," he told her assertively, but what he really meant was that there was nothing wrong with him. "I'm just too busy right now."

Starting in February and continuing through the spring of 1914, Rebecca, with her mother in tow, made several appointments with fertility specialists in Boston, listened patiently to a numbing variety of possible causes of infertility, endured a series of embarrassing questions, and many painful examinations. But, in the end, no doctor could find anything obviously wrong.

Calvin, although happily an outsider to the actual doctors' visits, watched unhappily as his wife's hopes were raised and ultimately dashed again and again. Finally, in utter exasperation one evening at dinner, when Rebecca began to describe yet another clinic, this one in New York, and another renowned specialist whom she and her mother intended to consult, he took a firm and unusually harsh stand.

"Absolutely not! I forbid it." He yanked the napkin from his lap, flung it onto his plate, and stormed out of the room for the solace of his study. There was simply nothing left to say.

As a first-year anniversary gift in June 1914, he purchased a small beach house on Cape Cod so Rebecca could have some relief from the fierce summer heat in the city. He arrived, when he could, on Friday nights and returned home on Sunday afternoons.

That fall skidded into an especially bleak winter. Fresh snow arrived at least once a week but turned quickly to slush. The Christmas season came and went quietly, and the winter continued unabated almost without notice. Oddly, the bleakness that had settled so heavily on the Wallabee household could not be loosened, and, ultimately, Calvin was forced to admit that something was not quite as it should be, something had shifted and had not yet righted itself.

Even if he had a detective's temperament, which he didn't, there were few clues to pinpoint what was amiss. Studying her across the dinner table, he decided that yes, she most definitely looked different—more muted maybe, more monochromatic somehow. Listless, yes, that was it—she was listless.

Were this a business problem, Calvin would know exactly what to do, might even consider discussing it with his father, but he would never confide such a personal issue. Instead, he did what so many men did when confronted with marital problems: he worked longer hours and traveled more—hopeful that, whatever it was, would work itself out.

"Calvin," his father said at Sunday dinner in January just after the new year, "I would never have imagined that you would take to the business the way you have. I just wanted you to know how proud I am."

Calvin smiled even as bile rose to the back of his throat. Finally, his father was proud of him! Proud of what? His work ethic, his dedication, his commitment? Ironically, his father was proud of him for doing work that Calvin thought not only demeaning but literally sucking the life out of him.

As they smoked their after-dinner cigars in silence, Samuel's thoughts turned to Annie Kenny, someone he was not prepared to surrender just yet. Though he hadn't heard a word from her since leaving the mill and his check remained uncashed, he'd known that this was a very real possibility. He'd promised to accept whatever she decided, and her silence was unequivocal. Nevertheless, the dissolution of their friendship was a towering sadness from which, although he could not know it then, he would never recover.

"Samuel, I think something's upsetting Rebecca," Miranda whispered at the end of the evening as she and he watched the young couple head home.

"Really," Samuel remarked, "I can't imagine what. They seem quite comfortable together, and the business is doing well."

"True," replied Miranda, closing the door. "But she certainly looked unhappy, hardly uttered a word at dinner. Maybe, I'm reading more into it than there is," she conceded.

"Perhaps," Samuel acknowledged, impatient to return to his study, pour himself a second brandy, and rifle through the recently arrived spring garden catalogs.

On Friday afternoon, April 5, 1915, Miss Lockard slowly opened Calvin's office door and whispered, "Mr. Franklin Rowe's here to see you, Mr. Wallabee."

"Franklin Rowe, what on earth for?" It was a rhetorical question, but Miss Lockard misunderstood.

"I don't know, sir, shall I ask him?"

"Certainly not," Calvin declared impatiently, placing the file he'd been reading on his desk, glancing at the mantel clock. It was already two thirty and he was leaving for Washington at four o'clock.

"Give me a few minutes before sending him in." Then, as an afterthought, he added, "And cancel my meeting with Grayson. I'll reschedule when I get back."

"Yes, sir. Shall I reschedule your driver? Will you be wanting to take a later train?"

"No, I can't change my travel plans, Miss Lockard, everything's been arranged. I'll leave here at four o'clock as planned. Have the driver wait in front. And Miss Lockard, you may as well take the rest of the afternoon off. I won't be needing you."

"Thank you, sir!" she replied, pleasantly surprised to get an early start to her weekend. "I hope your meeting with those southern gentlemen goes well."

"Thank you, Miss Lockard," he replied distractedly, straightening his tie, donning his suit jacket, and eyeing his suitcase, a gift from Rebecca, standing sentry-like at the door.

He didn't need a second acerbic stab in his stomach to remind him how nervous and vulnerable he felt today. There was just no way to prepare for this trip, and the business risk, although hard to determine at this moment, could very well be substantial—might even be disastrous. If the rumors he'd heard were credible, Calvin could only guess what accommodations he might be asked to make, be forced to make by their Southern suppliers.

Recalling that his father-in-law was waiting, he took a deep breath, exhaled slowly, wondering what his wife's father could possibly want—because there was no way that Franklin's unanticipated visit was a social call. Calvin steeled himself for something unpleasant.

Was it possible that Franklin had heard the same disconcerting rumors that southern cotton growers were threatening to build their own mills to avoid the increasing costs of shipping their cotton north? Unlikely, he decided.

"Good afternoon, my boy," Franklin boomed as he entered the office, hand extended, slightly more stooped than the last time Calvin had seen him but his voice still as strong and confident as his handshake.

"Franklin, what a pleasant surprise! So good to see you, please have a seat. Shall I have coffee brought in? Or tea?"

"No thanks, my boy. I'm headed to our monthly meeting at the Mohican, the Rotary you know. Really hope your father will attend this one. Is he planning to, do you know?"

"Sorry, Franklin, he hasn't said anything to me."

"Well then, I suppose I'll just have to wait and see, won't I?" As he stood, despite having been offered a seat, Franklin's smile thinned, then faded as a few awkward seconds passed in silence.

"Well, let me get straight to the point, Calvin." He cleared his throat and shoved his hands into his coat pockets. "Margaret's concerned, distressingly concerned I must admit, about Rebecca. Thinks Becca's in a funk, doesn't leave the house much, hardly sees her friends anymore. What's your take on this, son?"

Christ, thought Calvin, *now her father's involved!* "Well, Franklin," he reported evenly, "Margaret's partly correct. Rebecca has been feeling a bit low lately, not sick, mind you, just fatigued. In my view, she's avoiding anything she thinks might tax her."

"Lately you say!" Franklin sputtered in disbelief. "Why, it's been almost a year!" he said, revealing, as Calvin had already suspected, that his father-in-law knew much more than he'd initially let on.

"And don't think I haven't been made aware of the cause of my daughter's feeling 'low,' as you call it," he added without taking a breath, determined to get this conversation over with as quickly as possible.

"Believe me, Calvin, I hate to interfere and, frankly, I've put Margaret off as long as I can, but something needs to be done."

"And what is it exactly," Calvin asked sarcastically, "that Margaret thinks needs to be done?"

"Look, son," Franklin soothed, shaking his head as if to shake off his distaste for this conversation. "I'm no expert on these matters. But, if it's children my daughter wants... well, if she can't have them, then find another way. But for God's sake, man, do something!"

"With all due respect, Franklin, this is hardly your business or Margaret's. And if I may be candid, I find your raising this private matter between me and my wife an appalling invasion of our privacy."

"I cannot disagree with you, my boy, and you must believe that I am most uncomfortable being put in this position, but she is my daughter, my only child, and something must be done. Do you understand me, Calvin? Something must be done."

Franklin grabbed his hat off Calvin's desk and left so quickly that Calvin, who had turned to check the time on the mantel clock, heard only the soft click of the door.

Calvin stood rooted to the spot, speechless, blinking in disbelief, staring at the back of his office door, incredulous and furious.

"Damn you, Franklin! Damn you, Rebecca!" he boomed, oblivious to the possibility that someone in the reception area might hear him. Enervated and shaky, he fell into his chair, his face deeply flushed and glistening with a thin film of sweat.

Will this ever cease? he wondered. *Or will there always be another demand? Another intrusion into my life? My life*—he snorted in disgust—*when has this ever been* my *life?*

Yanking open his desk's bottom drawer, eschewing a glass, he gulped straight from the bottle of whiskey he concealed there. By three thirty, he was lying across his small office sofa, his narrow feet splayed on its elevated arms, reliving every injustice, every disappointment in the clogged mess that was his life. It was a long list.

Pried free of inhibitions, he admitted for the first time his certainty that he was and had always been damaged. Clearly, neither parent had ever really wanted him. He was, for each of them, such a profound disappointment that a fortune had been willingly spent to groom, educate, and inevitably coerce him into becoming someone he was not, because, apparently, who they thought he was—by temperament, character, or both—was embarrassing, perhaps even contemptible.

Suddenly, as he lay there lugubrious and resentful, a vivid memory returned to him. Happily, serenely, he was standing in a thick field of blazing poppies dotted, here and there, with pencil-thin cypresses; his ears filled with the somnambulant droning of bees flitting and flirting with the yawning red flowers that, with every breeze, grazed his trouser leg, depositing golden specks of pollen.

The torrid afternoon sun seared the back of his neck as he bent over a canvas, sweat stained his shirt along the hollow of his spine, his devoted Paulo stood painting, just a few yards away—all of this so real that he could feel, once again, the tingling sensations of pleasure, could smell the paint on his brush and the sweat on his body.

If there ever had been a moment when he knew absolutely what he was meant to do and what he longed to do, it was that moment. He was meant to be an artist, was determined to live an artist's life without wife or children, without obligations or restrictions, without a luxurious house with manicured gardens.

Instead, he longed for an airy, light-filled studio cluttered with canvases, fragrant with turpentine and softened wax. As he replayed every detail of that blissful, life-changing moment, the huge, heavy tears that had been forming in the corners of his eyes spilled over, and as he wept for only the second time in his life, a blood-red, impotent rage joined the mousy, beige helplessness that always draped him like a favorite winter coat—a dangerous combination.

∼

In the newly furbished cutting room, Annie Kenny was recording the last of the prior month's production numbers into a report that needed to be delivered to Miss Lockard today by three o'clock. Annie was running late; it was almost three thirty, and already the light outside had begun to fade, hinting of an approaching storm.

Annie crossed the field then headed across the quadrangle to the back of the Administrative Building. She broke into a run and a blast of cool air flattened her denim skirt against her legs, reminding her that she should have grabbed her coat.

Pushing through the door to the reception area, she sensed something peculiar. The large room was unusually dim and eerily quiet. Miss Lockard's desk was empty which was odd, but there was a glint of light underneath Mr. Sam's partially closed door.

Dropping the report on Miss Lockard's tidy desk, Annie knocked and pushed Mr. Sam's door open. Her brilliant smile faded and her eyes widened with confusion because Mr. Sam's office was not only completely empty but apparently under construction. Rough boards placed across sawhorses formed a temporary table near the window, and a set of blueprints on top were held open by some rough, faded bricks.

Hesitantly she stepped into the room, silently pulling the door closed behind her, determined to make sense of this—but no matter how she came at it, it remained a mystery.

Ever since the cutting room was relocated so far from the administrative building, she'd not been able to see him with any regularity and he had mentioned that he needed to take some business trips in preparation for retirement. Still, as she perched on the rung of an open ladder, her thoughts swirled as she tried to make sense of this.

When Calvin finally stirred from his drunken reverie, it was into an absolute silence. *Damn*, he thought, *I've missed my train.* He tried to stand and switch on a lamp, but stumbled, tried again, and succeeded. Blinking, because his eyes were hypersensitive even to the soft glow of his desk lamp, he was able to see the mantel clock, which indicated it was three forty-five.

His temples throbbed mercilessly, a sour, sticky film coated his tongue, and he struggled to recall what had happened. Suddenly, he couldn't breathe. Desperate for fresh air, he pulled open his office door and staggered into the reception area, where he immediately collided with Miss Lockard's desk, causing her ivory teacup to crash to the floor.

As he stood there, trying to decide whether or not to pick up the pieces, he had the uncomfortable feeling that hundreds of eyes were watching him, accusing him, taunting him. He turned slowly, his eyes level with the wall of framed photographs taken at the mill's Fourth of July picnics for at least the last ten years.

He didn't know why he reached for a photograph, but he yanked it off the wall and gleefully smashed it on the floor. He laughed then, a barking sort of laugh, before, with equal delight, reaching for and smashing another one.

Annie was uncertain that the first sound she heard was breaking glass, but then she heard it again and again. She dashed out, half expecting to see Miss Lockard, but was bitterly disappointed by the rumpled silhouette of Calvin Wallabee braced against the far wall with a picture frame in his raised hand.

"Who are you and what are you doing here?" he yelled, startled by the shadowy intruder.

"Just dropped off March's report, sir," she shouted back from the doorway of Samuel's office. "Then stopped to say hello to your father, but he seems to be . . ."

"Gone? Ah, yes, the old man's finally gone!" Again, that awful barking laugh.

Unsteadily, Calvin crossed the room, keeping one hand on the wall for support. "And who are you?" he asked as he neared, finally stopping a few feet away, squinting until he recognized her.

"You're that little orphan girl, aren't you? What was it he used to call you? Ah, yes, the daughter he never had! Well, your gravy train's gone, missy! Looks to me like you've been abandoned—again!" This time his laughter quickly dissolved into a consumptive, wet cough, doubling him over and leaving him gasping for breath.

Annie was simply too young and too inexperienced to recognize the danger of her situation. His taunting made her angry, especially because he was clearly enjoying her discomfort.

"I don't believe you," she replied imperiously. "He promised to say good-bye." As soon as the words were out of her mouth, she realized how childish she must sound, and her face reddened.

"Oh dear," he ridiculed her, "has Daddy disappointed you too? You, the chosen one!" He stepped closer and closer, menacingly, forcing her to back up until once again she was in Mr. Sam's office. Then she smelled the liquor on his breath.

"You're drunk," she retaliated, pushing past him in disgust. Her boldness surprised him; unprepared, he lost his footing and groaned when he hit the floor.

Despite how she felt about him, he was Mr. Sam's son, so she turned back to help. It was a terrible mistake.

As she approached him, he sprang to his feet, grabbed her with a fury that surprised even him, pulled her back into his father's office, and slapped her across her face. She staggered back until the temporary table stopped her and, in that split second, she realized that he wasn't finished with her.

"Please," she said, holding an arm out in front of her.

"Please what?" he asked, his voice cruel and hard. "What was it that you did for my father?" He was screaming now and his spittle sprayed her face. "You stole him from me, you little whore."

Again, she tried to push him aside and again almost succeeded, but he managed to grab her hair, spin her around, and, this time, punch her in the face. She heard the muffled crunch just before blood squirted from her nose and ran into her mouth.

Wiping her sleeve across her mouth, she ran full force at him, and this time she slipped past, but he recovered, raced after her, and managed to grab her arm and twist it until she screamed. He dragged her back into his father's office and released her, watching with delight as her body crumpled to the floor.

She lifted her head. He was standing over her, his mouth contorted with fury, his words indistinguishable; her head fell back onto the floor, where she watched his shoes leave the room and knew with icy clarity that he was searching for something with which to kill her.

Clenching her teeth against the stabs of white-hot pain, she braced herself against a table leg and inch by inch managed to push herself to her feet, but it was too late. He was back, his wrath unexpended, his eyes skittering like a madman. Before she could move, he pinned her arms to her sides, lifted her off the floor, and flung her backward onto the makeshift table, which shook violently under her weight. She groaned as her head collided with one of the bricks.

He held her down with one hand and labored to pull up her skirt with the other. She felt his hand on her leg above her stocking pulling frantically at her bloomers. She fought him, kicking and thrashing, and at one point almost managed to sit up, but he slammed her back with such force that her head shattered a brick—then, mercifully, her mind slipped free, releasing her from this terror, welcoming her into a polished blackness.

When he came to, Calvin was propped against the far wall of his father's office, hugging his knees, blood spatters on his shirt, his pants undone, his hands sticky. He was confused at first, but then he remembered when he saw her body on the floor half underneath the table, her arm at a grotesque angle, her face battered.

Slowly, fearfully he slid across the floor until he was next to her.

He shook her, gently at first then harder, but she made no sound, she wasn't breathing. As panic choked him, he shook uncontrollably and then vomited. Slowly, he pushed himself back across the room and used a ladder propped against the wall to pull himself to his feet but lacked the steadiness to stand on his own. Finally, mustering every ounce of discipline he had, he managed, somehow, to get back to his office, zip up his trousers, pull on his overcoat, grab his suitcase and stagger out the door.

"Good evening, sir," the driver said in greeting. "We'll need to hurry, the train to Washington leaves in fifteen minutes. You've cut it pretty close."

"No," Calvin replied, his voice hoarse, "I'm taking the New York train instead."

Calvin would have no memory of that train ride, although he'd had the sense to book a private car, and no recollection of hiring a coach to Soho; he would never remember walking up four flights of stairs and down a long, darkened hallway. He would only ever recall knocking tentatively at first, then pounding on the door until it opened.

"Amato! What a lovely surprise!" cried the older man, opening the door wide, drawing Calvin into his arms and kissing him. His overalls and artist's smock were spattered with paint; his long gray hair was pulled back and tied with a red scarf.

His beard, streaked with gray, was neatly trimmed. Although many years older than Calvin, his face was incandescent with the wonder and delight of a small child who receives an unexpected present.

"Oh, God help me, Paulo!" Calvin sobbed, collapsing into his arms. "I've killed her!"

15

COMING TO TERMS

Surprisingly, Grand Central Station was vibrating with activity even late morning on the following Thursday when Calvin prepared to return to Fall River. Businessmen in pressed trousers and crisp white collars strode briskly along the sullied platforms. Calvin was grateful for the diaphanous curtained windows of his private car screening him from the scrutiny of gawking passengers waiting on the platform, more grateful that it sequestered him from the tiresome curiosity, unwanted conversation, and irritating personal quirks of fellow travelers.

Having boarded the train much earlier in a state that could only be described as debilitated and brimming with despair, he was still incapable of reconciling the respected, dignified man, which is how he used to think of himself, with the violent degenerate capable of such an abhorrent act.

Every staccato of rough footsteps in the passageway was a warning, a heart-hammering reminder that arrest was imminent, that police were searching for him. He groaned aloud when careless passengers thumped and scraped their belongings the entire length of the corridor; he cursed the porters whose ill-maintained luggage carts chattered and squealed in protest; even the rustling and swishing of dresses or petticoats along the uncarpeted passageway disquieted him.

Because he hadn't heard the conductor's "All aboard!" he was unprepared for the earsplitting whistle blast that followed. Snorting and wheezing, the train lurched so abruptly that his hat in the rack above him toppled to the floor.

Sibilant steam billowing from beneath the wheels momentarily fogged his window; the screeching intensity of steel wheels grating against iron track drowned out everything else until gradually the cacophony abated, replaced by a rhythmic *clickety-clack*. Finally, he surrendered to the train's tranquilizing momentum as his private car rolled gently from side to side.

Each mile of track was hurling him closer to abject disgrace—no longer an upstanding pillar of the community, no longer even a gentleman. He would be imprisoned, surely, and there would be a trial. Whether he was acquitted on some technicality or convicted, the end result would be the same: he would be anathema, his auspicious lifestyle, though he'd railed against it regularly, obliterated.

Ironically, just a week earlier, and then only because he'd been under the influence, he'd finally accepted that his parents' disappointment in him was mostly justified. He was indeed deficient in some ways, and, while that was humiliating enough, it now appeared that even that assessment was overly optimistic. He was beyond simply deficient; he was depraved and loathsome.

Despite his considerable lapses in memory, inexplicably one image was forever seared on his brain—those remarkably blue eyes searching his face for some explanation even as blood gushed from her nose. The pleasure he'd taken in her pain was a disgrace so monstrous it could never be effaced.

When he tried to sleep, he heard screams, terrible screams, her screams. Grabbing a cup off the nearby tray, he vomited into it. Resting his head back against the cushioned headrest, he stared out the window at the blurred images flying by, he was sweating profusely. It was much too late of course, but it occurred to him that he might have chosen differently—but he hadn't and the earnest young painter who wanted to make his own mark on the world had ceased to exist a decade earlier. Once again, his stomach lurched; he reached for a cup, but this time it was just dry heaves.

"Good afternoon, Miss Lockard," Calvin said, heading directly for his office, hoping to avoid her questions.

"Good afternoon, sir," she replied as she glanced up from her typing, twisting an errant lock of hair before tucking it behind her ear.

"Why, sir, you look positively ill!" she exclaimed and indeed he did. Heavy purple smudges had settled under his eyes, which glimmered feverishly despite his skin's unhealthy pallor, the corners of his mouth sagged, and his hand shook as he accepted a stack of messages from her.

"Was the trip a success, sir? Shall I bring you some tea with honey?" she called after him but heard only the sound of his office door latching.

Although he'd braced himself for questions about the attack that occurred just a few feet from her desk, she hadn't even mentioned it. He scoured his messages, fully expecting at least one from the police, but there were none; however, there was one from his head of security.

He buzzed her. "Miss Lockard, I see a message from Holmes in security. Please have him come by at his earliest convenience."

"Yes, of course."

Douglas Holmes was a stocky, fiftyish man with a head of thick hair the color of summer hay. He had an owlish look about him, primarily because his small eyes were too closely set, a problem unfortunately accentuated by his thick glasses and narrow nose.

"Greetings, Miss Lockard. Always a pleasure to see you! I certainly hope you're getting on well. I meant to stop by earlier this week, since Mr. Wallabee was traveling. Hopefully, things weren't too dull?"

"Oh no," she replied breezily, "certainly not. There's always something that needs my attention. But it was awfully kind of you to think about me, thank you."

"Miss Lockard, let me introduce one of our junior security guards, Charles Dougherty."

"Good afternoon, miss," the younger man said, tipping his hat. He was as short and stocky as his boss but much younger. Like his boss he was dressed in a dark suit and tie, and his carrot-red hair was neatly trimmed.

"Good afternoon , Mr. Dougherty. Would either of you like a cup of tea?"

"No, thanks," replied the younger man quickly.

"Well then, just have a seat. He'll see you in a minute."

Once again, the front door opened, allowing a gust of wind to shuffle the carefully folded newspapers on the coffee table and signaling the arrival of James Connors, Mr. Wallabee's young chauffeur.

"Hello, doll!" he called, his voice at once too loud and too familiar. "How's every little thing?"

Both Douglas and Charles recognized him immediately because Jimmy Connors had a solid reputation around the mill as a ladies' man—women just seemed to lose their common sense in the presence of those dark eyes and that handsome smile that dimpled his cheeks.

Unlike most men, Douglas and Charles included, he seemed perfectly at ease in the presence of women, young or old. He had perfected, or so it seemed, the art of unabashed flirting. Most men found him annoying, resenting perhaps what they secretly envied.

"Jimmy!" cried Miss Lockard, blushing for no apparent reason. "What brings you by? Mr. Wallabee's not expecting you, is he?"

"Nope. The boss left this on the back seat when I picked him up at the train station this afternoon," he said, passing her an envelope. "Just wanted to drop it by before I got off shift."

Removing his chauffeur's cap, he started to sit on the edge of her desk, but something in her eyes stopped him, so he straightened.

"You know," he told her, "the boss looked as sick today as he was when I picked him up last Friday. Thought he'd puke in the car before we even got to the station. Between you and me"—he leaned in conspiratorially—"smelled like he'd already puked somewhere! Had to keep my window open a crack all the way to the station."

"Oh, Jimmy, stop!" Miss Lockard replied testily. "You're right though, he does look quite ill today. Traveling doesn't seem to suit him like it did his father."

"Well, got to go, doll," he said, replacing his cap, pulling it low across his forehead. When he reached the door, he turned to flash her one of his dazzling smiles and a flirty wink just as her intercom buzzed. She waved him away.

"Gentlemen, Mr. Wallabee will see you now."

"Good afternoon, Douglas," Calvin said without rising. "You wanted to see me?"

"Yes. Good afternoon, sir. Thank you for making the time. Mr. Wallabee, this is Charles Dougherty, the security guard who was involved in the incident I've come to report. I thought it might be helpful to have him here while I filled you in."

"All right," Calvin said tentatively. "Please, both of you, take a seat."

Immediately, Douglas took the chair in front of Calvin's desk while Charles headed to the small sofa across the room and noted, as he sat down, an acrid, off-putting odor.

Douglas cleared his throat. "This will be difficult to hear, sir, so I'll get right to it. Charlie here was on duty last Friday night, and during one of his routine checks, he noticed that the cutting room light was still on. When he entered the building, it appeared that all the girls had gone home by then, but the lights were still on and he saw a single coat still hanging on the rack."

"What time was this, Douglas?"

"About eight o'clock."

"Go on."

"Across the quadrangle he saw a light on in this building, so he came right over and found, quite unexpectedly, that the back door was unlocked. Making his way to the reception area, he stepped on some shards of glass and noticed some photographs lying on the floor.

"There was a single light on in your father's office, and that's where he discovered the body of one of the mill girls lying in a pool of blood. He followed protocol, buzzed the security office for help, then called the police and requested an ambulance. As it happened, I was still in my office and naturally came right over.

"The police and the ambulance arrived together. The girl was unconscious, and Charlie accompanied her to the hospital. The police combed the area for any evidence, interviewed me, and caught up with Charlie later at the hospital. I called a cleaning crew and stayed behind to supervise them."

"I can't believe that this is the first I'm hearing about this, Douglas. Nothing like this has ever happened before!"

"Well, sir, you were traveling and the police took over the investigation immediately. I decided that the fewer people heard about it, the better. But sir, if you think it should have been handled differently..."

"No, Douglas," Calvin interrupted, "I'm sure you did everything by the book. I'm just in shock. What did the police think happened here?"

"They think that there was a break-in and perhaps Miss Kenny walked in on it. Her monthly report was in a file lying on Miss Lockard's desk."

"A break-in? What in God's name for?"

"It's just speculation right now, sir. Nothing, at least nothing obvious, appeared to be missing, but you should check the contents of your safe. There wasn't even anything in your father's old office except a ladder and a table—looked like it was under construction?"

"Yes, it is," Calvin replied dully. "My safe was locked when I arrived this afternoon, and only I have the combination. Are you telling me that even Miss Lockard is unaware of what happened?"

"Yes, sir."

"Was that wise, Douglas? I've been gone since last Friday. She's been alone here all this week. She might have been in danger."

"I did consider that, sir, and rotated extra guards through this building every day while you were away. They were instructed to be as inconspicuous as possible so as not to cause alarm. She was quite safe, sir."

Calvin waited in silence, but neither man had anything to add. Was it possible, he wondered, that she wasn't dead? That he hadn't killed her?

"And the girl?"

"Anne Kenny." It was the first time that the younger man spoke. "She worked in the cutting room. It was her coat hanging on the rack after all the others had gone."

"And where is . . ." Calvin's mouth had become so dry it was nearly impossible for him to form words.

"In the hospital," Douglas replied, anticipating Calvin's question. "She was unconscious when Charlie found her and has not yet regained consciousness."

"And you've checked with the hospital today?"

"No, sir, I spoke with them two days ago. She was still in a coma."

Calvin stood and began pacing behind his desk. "I imagine that the police want to speak with me, Douglas?"

"No, sir, since you were traveling out of town at the time. Captain

Mayfield's in charge of the investigation, he'll let us know when they have a lead. When that happens, no doubt he'll be wanting to speak with you directly."

"What can we do to assist Miss Kenny and her family?"

"She has no family, sir. I understand that she came here from an orphanage. She's worked here for several years now. Apparently your father knew her well. Charlie and his sister also know her and have visited her at the hospital."

"Have you contacted my father, Douglas?"

"No, sir. Didn't feel it was my place. Thought perhaps you'd want to do that."

"Yes, of course, I'll take care of it. Meanwhile, notify the hospital director that we'll take care of Miss Kenny's medical expenses. It's the least we can do."

"Are you sure?" Douglas asked, surprising both Calvin and Charles. "I mean, shouldn't you check with legal first? There might be some precedent we need—"

Calvin raised a hand to silence him and turned to face the younger man. "Charles, I'd like you to meet with the hospital director in person, today. And since you know this girl, please keep Douglas informed if any other assistance is needed."

"Yes, sir, I was planning to go there right after work. I'm on the day shift today."

"No, let's do this now when the director is likely in his office. My driver will take you there and wait for you. Ask Miss Lockard to arrange it. That's all, gentlemen. Keep me informed, Douglas."

"Of course," replied Douglas, exhaling with relief.

Charlie Dougherty waited outside the building for his ride to the hospital, surprised that, for once, the fresh spring air and pale sunlight did not raise his spirits. When the car finally pulled up, he climbed into the back seat without waiting for Jimmy to open the door for him.

"Where to?" Jimmy asked.

"Saint Anne's Hospital."

Charlie rode in silence; something nagged at him—something he couldn't quite put his finger on.

As Jimmy pulled into the hospital entrance and before Charlie could open the door, he turned around. "I'll wait for you in the chauffeur's area. I can see the front door from there, so just wait here when you're ready to be picked up."

"Wish I could tell you how long this will take, but I've no idea."

"That's okay," replied Jimmy. "I'm used to waiting."

"Thanks."

Before asking directions to the director's office, Charlie decided to check on Annie. It was Phoebe's turn to visit, and he hoped his twin would still be there. She could always comfort him when he felt at loose ends, sometimes recognizing what was wrong before he did. As he entered the ward, he spotted Phee sitting just outside of Annie's room saying the rosary, and he smiled with relief.

The curtain around Annie's bed was drawn tight; a nurse and a doctor stood inside while Phoebe and Charlie waited outside. The doctor repeatedly flashed a light into Annie's eyes and listened to her heart; the nurse checked the intravenous line and gently began removing the heavy bandage from the side of Annie's head. Silently, both inspected the angry red, swollen gash, the thin black stitches that held it closed, the clotted blood at the edges, and the sticky yellow pus in the center.

"Make sure this bandage is changed and the wound irrigated twice a day. It's still weeping more than I'd like. If her temperature rises, call me immediately," the doctor instructed.

"Continue checking her eye pressure and her vitals every two hours. If her condition worsens, come find me. I'm on all night."

"Yes, Doctor. Should she have visitors?" the nurse asked, lowering her voice. "These two outside have been here almost every day since she was admitted."

"I doubt it can hurt," he replied wearily. "You might even suggest that they talk to her. We know so little about comas—it might help."

"I'm Doctor Jules Culverson," he told Phoebe and Charlie as he stepped into the corridor. "Are you her family?"

"All she's got. I'm Phoebe and this is my brother Charlie. Annie lives with us."

"How soon will she wake up, Doctor?" Charlie asked, concern etching his face like a spider's web.

"I can't say, Charlie. She's in what we call a coma. Sometimes the body does that so it can heal, especially when the internal injuries are grave."

"What internal injuries?" Again, it was Charlie who took the lead.

"Well, her arm and nose were fractured—those were the things we could see right away and have attended to. The swelling and bruising on her face, which looks much worse than it is, should lessen a bit each day.

"But"—he paused—"she has a severe concussion, due most likely to the deep gash at the side of her head which caused some bleeding and swelling in her brain. We're monitoring that very carefully. It's the injury to her brain that's most concerning, and we can't know the extent of the damage until she regains consciousness."

"What kind of damage?"

"Well, there could be temporary or possibly permanent memory loss, paralysis, difficulty speaking or . . ."

Charlie's face blanched so severely that Phoebe worried he might faint.

"So," she jumped in, "all we can do is wait and pray. You're saying that the most serious injury is to her brain, and when she wakes, you'll know more, but all her other injuries will heal completely in time?"

"Well"—Dr. Culverson hesitated, unsure what more he should say—"I don't know how much you've been told since she was admitted."

He glanced from one to the other, but neither seemed to understand what he meant. "Miss Kenny was raped," he said in a gentle voice, "and given her age, we won't know the extent of any internal damage for a while."

Charlie was halfway down the corridor before the doctor finished his sentence. Phoebe covered her mouth to muffle a cry, her eyes already spilling hot tears.

"I'm so sorry, miss, I thought you knew. I promise to keep a close watch on your friend and will let you know if anything changes."

When Phoebe found Charlie in the corner of the solarium, she knew immediately that he was crying, his thick hands cradling his square face. She pulled a chair up next to him and sat so close that their shoulders touched. She knew that he wouldn't speak until he was ready, and she was prepared to wait, silently, for as long as it took.

"Oh, God, Phee," he said finally, plaintively, his voice cracking, as he fumbled in his pocket for a handkerchief. "If only I'd done rounds earlier, I might have saved her from all this. But I was too late. There was so much blood, Phee, so much blood. Her head was lying in a pool of blood. I thought she was dead."

He blew into his handkerchief, but his tears kept coming. "I held her head in my hands, Phee, tried to comfort her, to tell her she'd be okay, but I couldn't speak, the words stuck . . . then I started to cry, couldn't stop. Oh, Phee, I couldn't do anything, couldn't help her." He was sobbing and trying to cover his face at the same time.

Phoebe lifted one of his hands into hers. He'd not talked about that night since it happened. She couldn't even imagine the horror of finding Annie bloodied and almost dead on the floor.

Of course, he'd never spoken about his feelings for Annie. Charlie never really spoke about feelings, but they were twins—and from birth they always seemed to know what the other was feeling. When he called the boardinghouse after taking Annie to the hospital, Phoebe heard the stark terror and anguish in his voice and knew he loved Annie, had known it for a while, but doubted that Annie did.

"I know you, Charlie Dougherty," she told him, "better than anybody, and you're a good man. I know you did everything you could. In fact, if you hadn't found her when you did, she might have died alone on that floor. Thinking that you should have done something more, could have done something more is idiotic—it won't help her . . . or you. She'll need us to be strong when she wakes up, and that's exactly what we're going to be."

He dabbed at his eyes, tried to pull himself together, to rise to his sister's challenge. "Mr. Holmes and I met with Mr. Wallabee this afternoon." he told her after a bit, "and he sent me here to tell the hospital director that he wants all Annie's medical bills forwarded to him."

Phoebe nodded. "Well, see, that's something then. You'd better head over there now, and I'll see you at home later. Ma said she'd sit with Annie tonight."

When his brief meeting with the director ended, Charlie stood, as instructed, on the hospital's front steps, and, as promised, in less than a minute Jimmy pulled the car up.

"Thanks for waiting. Sorry it took so long."

"Not a problem. When the boss says wait, I wait."

"I'm Charlie by the way."

"I'm Jimmy."

"You were right, you know," Charlie began once they'd left the hospital driveway. "I overheard you telling Miss Lockard that Mr. Wallabee looked ill today. I was there and he certainly looked under the weather to me."

"Boy, that's the truth!" Jimmy confirmed, grateful to have someone to talk to. "He looked awful bad last Friday too. When he climbed into the back seat, he smelled so bad I thought he was hungover. Like I told Miss Lockard, I thought he was going to puke right there in the back seat."

"When was that?"

"Umm, let's see, I had to be there before four o'clock because he wanted to leave for the train station around four, but he didn't come out until after four thirty. Actually, I thought he might miss his train, he'd cut it so close."

"But he made it in time?"

"Turned out he'd changed his mind. As soon as he got in, he said he wanted to take the train to New York instead."

The hall telephone rang just after six. Phoebe got there first, lifting the earpiece as Charlie stood beside her, his hands stuffed into the pockets of his bathrobe.

"May I speak with Mr. Charles or Miss Phoebe Dougherty?" a woman's voice asked politely.

"This is Phoebe Dougherty speaking," she said, trying to keep her voice calm while bracing herself for the worst possible news.

"Miss Dougherty, this is Sister Margaret at St. Anne's. You asked to be called if there was any change in Miss Kenny's condition. I'm calling to tell you that Miss Kenny regained consciousness about an hour ago. We're waiting for her doctor to look in on her, but I thought you'd want to be here."

"Oh, thank God! Thank God!" Phoebe cried. "Thank you, Sister Margaret! Of course, we'll be right there!" Phoebe replaced the earpiece, laughing and crying at the same time.

"She's awake, Charlie!" she shouted, jumping up and down before throwing her arms around his neck. "Annie's awake!"

When Dr. Culverson pulled the curtain back, he was not surprised to see them standing in the corridor, their faces eager for news. "Well," he said as he approached them, "it's a good sign. Definitely a good sign. She hasn't spoken yet but was able to nod yes or no to a few questions we asked. She's a bit confused, which is quite normal.

"I've explained the cast on her arm and the bandage on her head. She knows she's in the hospital, but I haven't mentioned the attack and she didn't ask.

"Her vital signs are better. Let's give her some time to get oriented. I'll drop back later —she might be more coherent then."

"Thank you so much, Doctor, we're so relieved. Can we see her now? When do you think we could take her home?"

"Not for a while, I'm afraid," the doctor said firmly. "She'll need much more time in the hospital before she's stable enough, and even after that, she might need round-the-clock care. Remember we aren't sure yet that she can walk or talk. It's likely that she'll go from here to a convalescent home until she is able to do everything for herself.

"I'll arrange for her transfer but only when I'm certain that she can tolerate the move. I understand that her medical bills are being taken care of, and I'll send her to the best facility available. But for now, she needs to stay put.

"Yes, you can see her but don't stay long. And please don't pressure her to remember anything. We must let her take her own time with that."

16

RESTITUTION, BUT A GIFT NONETHELESS

Floating. That was the only way to describe it. Wherever she was, time slowed and expanded deliciously, surging and ebbing wavelike beneath her while she floated peacefully inaccessible and insensate—right up to the moment when, quite involuntarily, her connection ruptured.

Unlike most comatose patients who feel blessed to regain consciousness, Annie felt bitterly disappointed. She prayed that someone would come soon—there was a foul-tasting, thick coating on her tongue, her skin itched relentlessly, and even she knew she reeked of sweat and infirmity.

Thankfully, she didn't have long to wait. Within the hour, a parade of surprised and solicitous nurses and doctors were fussing over her, bringing warm broth and cool water, taking her temperature and blood pressure, redressing her wounds, bathing her, and changing her soiled sheets.

Her physical pain teetered on the razor's edge of unbearable, which to her surprise she couldn't tell them because she had no voice, couldn't make a sound. The heavy cast on her arm was a mystery. The thick bandage and throbbing pain in her head—another mystery. A swarm of angry bees seemed to have taken up residence in her ears, tears dripped involuntarily from her right eye like a leaky faucet, and for some reason she couldn't breathe through her nose. She had no explanation for any of this.

Day after day, week after week, she prayed and waited expectantly for the pain to ease, for her muddled thoughts to stop drifting like snow, and for a nugget of memory to dislodge.

Meanwhile, she cherished the daily visits of Phoebe and Charlie, whose presence soothed her increasing panic. Without them to rein in her creeping despair, she would have abandoned hope entirely. Truly, they kept her alive. Their unabashed affection swelled her heart with a gratitude she knew she could never fully express—even if she could talk—and certainly never repay, which brought her to tears every time.

True to her nature, Phoebe glossed over the obvious seriousness of Annie's condition in pursuit of any kind of silver lining, no matter how feeble. Daily, for example, she reminded Annie that the most important thing, the thing to be most thankful for, was that she, Annie, was alive.

Phoebe's repeated admonitions that Annie just needed to try a little harder, force herself to eat more, or adapt a more positive outlook made Annie want to scream—so she supposed it was providential that, at least for the time being, she had no voice.

In her heart, Annie understood that Phoebe was just . . . well, being Phoebe—her loyal, well-meaning, and opinionated friend whose abrasiveness set Annie's teeth on edge with distressing regularity.

Fortunately, Phoebe's brother was her antithesis, and how they could possibly be twins, Annie would never understand. Once Charlie transferred to the day shift, he sat with her for hours, reading from newspapers, avoiding any story he thought might distress her, avoiding any mention of the Troy Mill.

Every evening dutifully refilling her pitcher with fresh water, gently lifting the pillow from beneath her head, and replacing the soiled pillowcase with a freshly laundered one.

When it was time to leave, he kissed her cheek as softly as the grazing of a butterfly's wing. "Goodnight, Annie girl," he would whisper, "tomorrow will be better."

Finally, after six weeks of disturbing images that flitted in and out and rattled her sleep, Annie woke with her first memory.

"I shouldn't have called him a drunk." Seven words spoken as softly as a lover's whisper but as electrifying as a bolt of lightning.

"Why did I do that?" she croaked, again astonished by the effort it took to speak. "I provoked him."

And with that crossing of the Rubicon, a thundering tidal wave of emotion and memory split off from whatever had been holding them in check and roared down on her, stripping her of every protection. It felt like drowning. Her stomach clenched, pushing bile up into the back of her throat, her chest constricted painfully until she was gasping for each breath, in terror her bowels emptied, and sweat matted her hair. As she rang for help, she vomited.

Despite her attempts not to, she thought about Mr. Sam often, wondered whether he ever thought about her. She relived the heartbreaking moment when she discovered he'd left—without explanation, without saying good-bye—and then the tears would start. While she couldn't have known it then, this particular grief would never leave her. This betrayal would never be forgiven, and this mistake, she promised herself, would never be repeated. She had trusted him completely. Admired him. Loved him.

But, in fairness, he'd given her, a total stranger, the only chance she'd ever gotten to rise above her circumstances. Without his amazing kindness, his unfettered generosity, she knew exactly what kind of life she'd been destined for.

He had given her a job; more likely he created a job just for her and placed her under the caring, watchful eyes of Grace Doyle—the closest thing she ever had to a real mother. He gave her a safe place to live with girls her own age, and he never, ever, asked for anything in return. Not once.

At the end of the day, Calvin was Mr. Sam's only child, and, despite the animosity between them, they would always be connected—they were family. Of course, Mr. Sam would never have imagined that Calvin was capable of such violence but—and she was absolutely certain of this—he would unquestionably blame himself, would hold himself responsible, and would view it as confirmation that he'd failed as a father—and the shame would crush him.

In the court of public opinion and despite his inculpability, Mr. Sam would share his son's public disgrace, and although Calvin would spend the rest of his life in jail, Mr. Sam would live the rest of his imprisoned as well. His entire life's work, all his accomplishments and successes, his generosity and many kindnesses—everything would be overshadowed by this one despicable act. Calvin's depraved act would become Mr. Sam's legacy as well.

Despite Calvin's brutality, despite the pain he'd inflicted, despite the emotional repercussions that were certain to follow her all her life, she had a debt that needed to be paid. And that was how it began, the birth of the lie she believed would release Mr. Sam from shame, the lie she thought would protect them both—the lie that once set in motion could never be recanted.

Charlie sat reading her an article from the *Fall River Herald* about the launch of a new steamship that reduced the once overnight trip to New York to a mere five and a half hours. The article described all the new ship's amenities and, of course, its lavish furnishings.

"Fun."

It wasn't much, a tiny word spoken in an equally tiny voice, but Charlie heard it plainly, lowered his newspaper, and looked into the expectant blue eyes staring back at him.

"Yes, Annie," he stammered, "it was fun, our trip to New York. Do you remember dancing?"

She nodded almost imperceptibly. "Polka." Again, a single word in a hoarse, croaked voice, but it was her voice.

"Yes," he agreed, almost overcome with emotion. "You, Annie girl, were the best dancer on the floor!"

A thin, wan smile lifted one corner of her bruised mouth, and even that seemed to take an enormous effort, but it was the first time he'd seen any expression on her face, and he was overjoyed beyond words.

"Thanks," she said slowly, carefully forming the word.

Charlie ran to find a nurse, a doctor, anyone!

To: Mr. Calvin Wallabee, President, Troy Mills
From: Captain Ernest R. Steiner, Chief of Police
Date: June 30, 1915
Re: Miss Anne Kenny

Sir, this notice is to inform you that we have closed our investigation into the attack on Miss Anne Kenny which took place on April 5th inside the Troy Mill. Detective Ellis McMannis has questioned Miss Kenny on three separate occasions since she regained consciousness, but at no time was she able to provide any details about her attacker other than to say it was quite dark at the time.

Mr. Jules Culverson, MD, her attending physician, has concluded that her memory of the event is blocked and likely will remain so given the level of physical and emotional trauma that she suffered.

If this situation changes in any way, you can be assured that we will reopen the case immediately.

Sincerely,
ERS, Cpt

Slowly, methodically Calvin read and reread the undeserved, inconceivable, but indisputable reprieve that had just been hand delivered. He was exhausted by weeks of anticipating an arrest that would dismantle his life and expose him to horrifying public humiliation, and a moan heavy with guilt and shame escaped from some closeted place deep within him and morphed into shuddering sobs.

"I've been given a second chance," he repeated incredulously over and over as he sat at his desk, unaware of the passage of time or of the deepening darkness outside his window. But why?

With rapier-like clarity, he was stung with the realization that he had the life he had because he hadn't fought for the life he really wanted. *I am the man I am today*, he finally understood, *because I hadn't the courage to be the man I wanted to be.* Calvin knew that he now stood precariously at a crossroads.

I will not make these mistakes again, he promised himself. *I will not let this chance for a new beginning slip through my fingers. I will*, he decided adamantly, *sweep my house clean.* The obligation to make restitution settled on his shoulders like new fallen snow hangs, scarf-like, along a ridge.

July 1, 1915

My Dearest Paulo,
Something remarkable has happened! I am, incredibly, a free man.

By some miracle, my shameful secret is safe. I am determined not to squander this gift, this reprieve, which comes, at the very least, with an obligation to make myself worthy of it, does it not?

Paulo, I need to be a better man. You know that I accepted certain responsibilities in my life with no intention of honoring them. I chose to accept them when I could—and certainly should—have refused. Now, I'm resolved to relinquish everything that has kept me from acting more honorably.

How many times, dear one, have we reminisced about returning to our beloved, Siena? Of standing again knee deep in poppy fields drunk on the scent of the ripening lavender? How many times have you wished to see your home, perhaps even your old studio, before you die?

I want this for you, Paulo, but cannot go with you. You must return. Otherwise I will never have the strength to do what I must. My heart is breaking with a sadness the depth of which I have never felt before.

Know that you will always have my heart and that I will never forget you.

Ti Amo,
Cal

Mr. Calvin Wallabee
President, Wallabee Mills, Inc.
Fall River, Massachusetts
July 16, 1915

Dear Mr. Wallabee,
Our hospital director, Mr. Elias Northrup, has informed me that you wish to be responsible for the continuing care of Miss Anne Kenny. While she has made tremendous strides these few months with us, she continues to need very specialized care in order to facilitate a complete recovery.

Dr. Jules Culverson, her physician, requested my assistance in locating a rehabilitation center that will adequately meet her needs, and, in that regard, I am recommending that she convalesce at the Convent of the Sacred Heart in Brattleboro, Vermont.

The beautiful mountain environs will certainly be curative. Many of our young novices live there, so Miss Kenny will have girls her own age as companions. I can assure you that their medical staff is expertly trained and will provide exactly the care she needs right now.

With your permission, I will make all the arrangements. Please feel free to contact Mother Superior at the Convent with any questions or concerns. I will send her contact information once the arrangements are finalized.

Sincerely, Sister Margaret Thomas, Head of Nursing
Saint Anne's Hospital

Sister Mary Magdalena, Mother Superior
Convent of the Sacred Heart
Brattleboro, Vermont
July 30, 1915

Dear Mother Superior,
I am writing on behalf of Miss Anne Kenny who will be arriving next Saturday on the 12:40 train. I am pleased to hear that arrangements have been made for her rehabilitation at your convalescent home.

Miss Kenny will be traveling with two friends, and I wonder if you could have a driver meet their train and arrange for them to stay overnight in order to help Miss Kenny settle in.

She has suffered a great deal and requires, as I am sure you are aware, the quiet solitude and safety of your convent and the compassionate nursing care of the good sisters.

We are all grateful to be able to rely on you for her physical and spiritual care. As she is an exceptionally proud young woman, I would ask that my assistance in this matter remain private, and I would appreciate an update periodically on her progress.

Sincerely,
Calvin Wallabee
President, Wallabee Mills, Inc.

Fatalistically, Annie slumped in her window seat, staring into the sunlit emptiness of the early morning, trying to resign herself to the fact that her life was no longer her own. How she hated having to rely on others to help her with even the most mundane activities.

Despite having endured tremendous suffering without complaint, despite appearing a model of perseverance to everyone around her, Annie was nonetheless enormously changed. Her effervescent joie de vivre, that delightful quality that drew people to her, had been squelched as cleanly as a sudden gust extinguishes a candle's flame.

Once the train chugged into the weather-bleached Brattleboro station, emitting a final gasp of steam, they disembarked into crisp, clean mountain air, which, despite its energizing effect, could not lift Annie's spirits. Standing on the platform, she and Phoebe watched Charlie approach a young man in faded work clothes standing, hat in hand, near the ticket window. After a brief discussion, Charlie gestured for them to join him.

"Annie, Phoebe, this is Jonathan Watts. He's come to collect our things and drive us to the convent. Don't worry, Annie, it's only a short ride." It was an attempt on his part to allay Annie's trepidation, but it just seemed to deepen her sadness. In desperation, he looked to his sister, but Phoebe, uncharacteristically, had nothing to offer.

The Convent of the Sacred Heart did not resemble a church, which

Phoebe had worried about, nor did it look like a hospital, which Annie had expected. Instead Jonathan pulled up to a three-story red-brick house with a brilliant white-columned wraparound porch, a wide entrance door with a row of bullet-glass windows along the top, and an imposing brass knocker in the shape of a pineapple—the New England symbol of welcome.

Almost an acre of freshly mowed lawn sloped from the front and sides of the convent before running into dense woodland and steep mountains in the distance. As Phoebe, Charlie, and Annie stood in the driveway surveying their surroundings, Jonathan quietly unloaded their suitcases, but before he could knock, the front door opened.

"Hello, I'm Helen," announced an eager, pleasant-faced girl with intelligent, brown eyes who appeared to be about Phoebe's age though a bit taller. She wore a plain black shirtdress that hung to her ankles, exposing black cotton stockings and black shoes. Her brown hair was tied back, and a small gold cross hanging from a thin gold chain around her neck hinted that she was a novice. Charlie introduced himself and the girls.

"Welcome," Helen said matter-of-factly. "Phoebe and Charlie, Jonathan will take your things to the guest cottages. Sister Elizabeth has prepared lunch for you in our refectory, which is on the way. Jonathan will see that you get there.

"Meanwhile, I'm going to get Annie settled and bring her some lunch. But then she'll need to rest. Why don't you stop back around four o'clock? Perhaps Annie will feel up to taking a short walk by then. Dinner is at six o'clock sharp," Helen informed them.

Without waiting for any reply, Helen linked her arm carefully through Annie's and gently escorted her into the convent's handsomely furnished but, at present, completely deserted parlor, then past a small library, empty as well.

A faint aroma of incense still lingered in the air outside the chapel doors, and although none of the overhead lights were on, a lovely stained-glass window over the altar was beautifully backlit.

Helen led Annie to her room, which, because it faced south, was already flooded with sunshine. It was not a large space, but, without feeling cramped, there was room for a bed, a bird's-eye maple writing desk, and a comfortable chair with a tiny footstool at the only window, which overlooked the rolling front lawn.

"The water closet is three doors down on the right," Helen explained. "It's a shared WC and right now you're sharing it with two other women. The bath is at the end of the hall, but you cannot take a bath without a nurse present. Use the buzzer on the side of your headboard to call the nurse's station whenever you need help.

"Now, I'll let you unpack while I fetch your lunch," Helen said, swinging Annie's bag onto the bed. "I won't be long, Annie. Is there anything you need my help with right now? Do you have any questions?"

Annie shook her head. She had lots of questions but none that this young novice could possibly answer.

Dinner was a simple and hushed occasion. All the sisters and novices sat quietly at two long tables in the center of the refectory, and if they did speak to one another, they spoke in whispers. The food was simple: bread and a clear soup, followed by roasted chicken with thin carrots and small onions and finally roasted apples stuffed with vanilla pudding and sprinkled with cinnamon.

After dinner, the threesome headed back to the comfortable Adirondacks and watched the tiny white moths flirt with the porch lights. Despite the heat of the day, the air cooled quickly once the sun sank behind the nearest mountain.

"I'd like to say our good-byes now," Annie told them bluntly. "It'll only be harder in the morning." She took a deep breath. "I cannot thank you enough and I'll never be able to repay you for all you've done for me. Without you I would certainly have died." Her voice caught in her throat and she stopped to compose herself.

"Phoebe, you are my best friend, and I wish I could be livelier when you're around, really I do. Charlie, my dear friend, I wish I could look happier. I know that's what you both want for me. But I can't and I'm sorry for letting you down."

For perhaps the first time in her life, Phoebe was afraid to speak, certain she would say the wrong thing, something that would hurt Annie rather than help, and she couldn't bear to leave her best friend like that.

"Give yourself more time, Annie," Charlie said softly. "We understand, as best we can, that you're carrying a terrible sadness. Right now everything must look so dark. Truly, you've thanked us enough now. Please, just concentrate on getting better, getting stronger, and coming home. That's all we want."

He stood, tenderly pressed his cheek against hers, and gently kissed her on the forehead. "Goodnight, Annie girl. I will not say good-bye." He quickly turned away and headed back to the guesthouse, hoping she'd not seen his tears.

Phoebe, still speechless, stood too, kissed Annie on the cheek, and gently squeezed her hand. "Good-bye for now, my dearest friend," she whispered. "Please come home soon."

It was barely light at five thirty when Annie woke. Dazed and glassy-eyed, she slid to the side of her bed and awkwardly, using the headboard for leverage, pulled herself up. From her window, she spotted Phoebe and Charlie climbing into Jonathan's carriage for the short ride back to the train station. She felt relieved; they would never understand how this solitary place was truly a gift. In this serenely quiet place, she would finally be left alone, would not have to disguise her lethargy, repudiate her disinterest, or conceal her depression.

Here her days would be meticulously choreographed: morning prayers, breakfast, physical therapy, short walks with Helen, lunch, rest, more physical therapy, more time with Helen, dinner, free time, and then in bed by eight. She welcomed this strange routine primarily because she didn't have to make a single decision, didn't have to plan anything, and, most importantly, didn't have to think about anything.

August 15, 1915
Mr. Calvin Wallabee
President, Wallabee Mills, Inc.
Fall River, Massachusetts

Dear Mr. Wallabee,
As you requested, I am writing to update you on Miss Kenny, and I'm afraid that the news is not good. We've been concerned since she arrived that she might be suffering from influenza, but our physician, Dr. Amos March, confirmed that Miss Kenny is pregnant.

Since her arrival, she has been quite withdrawn but, given the circumstances, that was understandable, even expected. Unfortunately, the news of her pregnancy has distressed her so severely that I have assigned one of our novices, Helen Riley, to be her full-time companion so Miss Kenny is never alone. We will watch her carefully.

Dr. March, an experienced obstetrician, is doubtful that Miss Kenny will carry this pregnancy to term given the extent of her injuries, but that, of course, is in God's hands.

Should Miss Kenny carry to term, we will place the child with St. Joseph's Orphanage in Stowe, Vermont. In the event that she needs time to recuperate after the birth, be assured that we are pleased for her to remain with us for as long as necessary.

All of us at the convent are most grateful for your generous support, which allows us to continue our work and service to God.

Yours in Christ,
Sister Mary Magdalena, Mother Superior

August 20, 1915
Dear Phoebe and Charlie,
By now you've received Sister's letter with the news. I hope you will not think me ungrateful, but I cannot bear to see either of you right now. I certainly cannot bear to talk about what has happened.

Please, don't waste your hard-earned money by coming to visit me here. I will not see you. Honestly, I don't know how things will turn out for me or where I'll go from here. In fact, nothing in my life is certain anymore. I so wish things were different. Please try to understand.

Your grateful friend,
Annie

"Can you believe this?" asked Phoebe indignantly, tossing the letter back to her brother who'd read it earlier. Having just returned from Mass, they sat in the boardinghouse's small but tastefully decorated parlor, waiting for Sunday dinner.

"She's ashamed, Phoebe," Charlie replied, removing his suit jacket and slipping it over the back of his chair. He was first surprised but then irritated that his own sister could not see something so obvious. Sometimes, and this was one of those times, her insensitivity truly vexed him—sometimes, he hated to admit, even embarrassed him.

"No doubt, she's thinking she's to blame for all that's happened, and I just bet those sisters have her convinced that this is God's punishment for something or other. She shouldn't be there, Phee," he said, crumpling the letter into a ball and angrily tossing it onto the floor. "We shouldn't have taken her there."

"What's wrong with you, Charlie Dougherty?" Phoebe asked curtly, partly because his accusatory tone had indeed stung and partly because she was exasperated by his increasingly short temper and irritability. Usually, Charlie was soft-hearted and conciliatory, but lately he had been unpredictable and easily provoked.

"You've had something stuck in your craw for months now! Ever since Annie went to Vermont—no, now that I think about it, even before that."

Charlie felt a stab of guilt because his sister was right. He'd been debating for weeks about whether he should tell her what was on his mind, whether he could convince her of something he was certain she would not want to believe. But he'd never kept a secret from Phoebe and was certain that Phoebe had never kept one from him.

"Phee," he said quietly, "I think Annie knows who did this to her."

"Don't be daft," Phoebe blurted out, shaking her head in disbelief, her eyes wide with surprise. "If Annie knew, she'd tell us. She wouldn't let him get away with it."

"Not if she thought no one would believe her."

"And why wouldn't we believe her?"

"I think she's protecting Mr. Wallabee," Charlie said, relieved to have finally spoken the words out loud.

"Mr. Sam! Really, Charlie, have you gone 'round the bend?"

"No, not Mr. Sam," he replied in frustration. "Calvin Wallabee."

Incredulous, Phoebe laughed out loud but stopped short when she saw the look on his face. "Okay," she said slowly, "let me get this straight. You're telling me that you think the president of Troy Mills attacked our Annie? Why? Have you proof?"

"Not much, Phee, I admit," he said, his tone belying the anxiety and frustration he felt. "There's a string of contradictions in what he's said about that night. And I've a strong feeling in my gut that he's the one."

"Charles Dougherty! You're accusing someone of a terrible crime when in your own words you have very little concrete evidence! Accusing a man like Calvin Wallabee. My lord, Charlie!"

"Exactly," he said, chafing, "that's my point, Phee! You don't believe me and Annie didn't think anyone would believe her."

As Phoebe considered what at first seemed unthinkable, she felt her anxiety ratcheting. "Okay," she said flatly, hesitantly, "what doesn't add up?"

Charlie took a deep breath. "Well, in the first place, I overheard Jimmy Connors telling Miss Lockard that Mr. Wallabee was disheveled and sick when he picked him up the night of Annie's attack. He said that Mr. Wallabee smelled bad like he was hungover or had just puked on himself. Those were his exact words."

"So that's it?" Phoebe asked. "He was sick?"

"No, let me finish, Phee! Mr. Wallabee lied to me and to Mr. Holmes. Told us he'd left for a scheduled business trip to Washington DC and that he was picked up before four in the afternoon. But Jimmy said that it was after four thirty when he came out. And Mr. Wallabee didn't take the train he was scheduled to take—he had Jimmy change his ticket at the last minute. He went to New York instead."

"Okay, so Mr. Wallabee was sick and decided to take a different train. How do you get from that to him attacking our Annie?" she asked, genuinely puzzled.

"I know I haven't told you much about that night, Phee, and I'm sorry. When I found Annie, she was lying in a pool of her own blood, and there was some vomit on the floor near the wall behind her, not hers."

Definitely alarmed now, Phoebe sat silently for a long, long time considering whether such a thing was even possible. Could Calvin

Wallabee have attacked Annie? Why would he do such a thing? Her heart raced and her thoughts swirled and it was hard to think clearly, but one thing she knew for sure—her brother would never accuse anyone of something unless he was convinced it was true.

Her alarm escalated to foreboding. If Charlie pursued this, Calvin Wallabee would have him fired and blacklisted in every mill town up and down the coast. But Phoebe was not naïve. Calvin Wallabee was a powerful man, and if he was capable of rape, then he was capable of anything and Charlie would be in grave danger. She decided then and there to protect her brother at all costs.

"I think you're dead wrong, Charlie!" she told him in blunt Phoebe fashion. "And I hope you're not seriously thinking about accusing Calvin Wallabee of attacking Annie based on what that sleaze Jimmy Connors told you. God, Charlie, he's a laughingstock and a liar! Everybody knows that!

"And besides, right now," she said, deliberately shifting topics, "we need to be much more concerned about Annie. She's all alone and she's in a bad way, Charlie. We need to do something."

"Let her be, Phee," he replied. Had they not been so emotionally connected from birth, he might not have understood what Phoebe was thinking despite what she'd said. In all likelihood, she believed him but feared for his safety—which was something he'd been thinking about for weeks. If he tried to get justice for Annie, especially now, he could easily make things even worse for her—and him.

"What we think doesn't matter, Phee," he said gruffly. "What matters is how Annie feels, and right now she doesn't want to see us."

"So, what do you suggest we do?" she asked irritably.

"Wait," he replied evenly, "she'll tell us when she's ready."

17

ANNIE'S SECRET

Lured by the irresistibly private semi-circle of woods and abetted by a surprisingly audacious novice, Helen Riley, Annie planned her escapes for the end of breakfast when the sisters and novices, preoccupied with daily assignments and chores, returned their dishes to the kitchen and scattered in different directions like dry leaves in an autumn wind.

Beleaguered and unable to acculturate to either the regimentation or the abstemious ways of convent life, Annie slipped into the woods behind the refectory where, for a few hours at least, she was free to choose her own path.

Not only was the forest's chimerical landscape the antithesis of the convent's stony austerity but it was truly a magical place where downy mosses carpeted the forest floor, blanketing and camouflaging even the massive trunks of fallen trees. It was an aromatic place where the shifting breezes could carry the sweet, heady fragrances of pine and cedar, the nose-tickling mustiness of rotting leaves, or the pungent odor of moist earth.

Panting from the exertion of the trail, her blouse stained with perspiration, she finally reached the edge of a wide, sunny meadow filled with arching grasses in hues of yellow from sulfur to straw, browns from burnt sienna to russet, and burnished vermilion.

Some had flowered into head-high feathery spikes that appeared downy but were, in fact, as coarse as sandpaper. Others produced seed heads, airy wheat-colored panicles as delicate and intricate as any lace she'd ever seen. Without trees to block or redirect the wind, the entire meadow undulated like ballet dancers in unison with the slightest breeze.

Mysteriously, a collection of thin, chiseled boulders stood silently, huddled together like cows in a snowstorm. They were ancient and undisturbed for hundreds of years except for curlicues of pale green lichen resembling hieroglyphics. Annie returned here many times, drawn by the permanence of these ancient stones with their indecipherable secret messages.

In late September, by heading south and following the faint sound of water, she discovered a waterfall that had, in the process of carving a path through the cliff above, dislodged a section of granite, pushed it over the top, and deposited it in the riverbed below. Years, centuries perhaps, of running water had smoothed and polished the side that remained in the water, but because the opposite end rested on the river's bank, it remained quite jagged. Annie discovered that these jagged edges were perfect handholds for climbing to the top, where she would sit for hours, arms wrapped around her knees. The gentle lapping of water below her was a balm that nourished her deeply. She felt safest here.

One bright afternoon, as she lay on this rock letting the sun's thin rays warm her expanding belly, Annie heard shuffling from the brush below and braced herself for the interruption she was sure would follow.

"Ah, there you are! I see you've found my secret hiding place," called Helen, hauling herself up the final few feet. "You missed lunch again," she announced, winded and huffing.

"I wasn't hungry," Annie replied flatly.

"Here, I've brought you a sandwich," said Helen, shaking some errant pine needles from the front of her skirt before sitting.

"I'm really not hungry, Helen, but thank you."

"Well, maybe the baby's hungry."

"Is that supposed to be funny?" Annie replied, bristling, bracing herself for an argument, a lecture, or both.

"Just trying to make conversation, Annie. Are you always so prickly? You make it hard for anyone to get to know you."

"The way I see it, Helen, you really don't need to get to know me. I'm a fifteen-year-old girl that no one wanted who's now in trouble—all of which you know. Seems to me you know enough."

"You mean you're pregnant?"

"What?"

"You're pregnant, Annie. You're not 'in trouble' as you put it and you're not at fault." Helen was determined to push Annie to face the reality of her situation by forcing her to use the correct terminology or, as Helen's mother used to say, to call a spade a spade.

"You don't know that," Annie objected stubbornly.

"Well, let's see. I know you were beaten and raped. I know you fought back, tried to get away, but he overpowered you. And now, still a child yourself, you've learnt that you're pregnant. I can't even begin to imagine what you must be feeling or what you've had to go through before coming here. But I do know for sure that you are not to blame."

"So why would you need a secret hiding place?" Annie asked, changing the subject, trying to deflect her embarrassment that a total stranger had correctly guessed so much of her story.

"Because sometimes I feel unsure or overwhelmed or unworthy—you name it, Annie, I've struggled with it."

"So, you're not sure you want to be a nun?"

"Most days I am," Helen answered honestly, "but living a nun's life faithfully requires more than just abstinence. Sometimes I'm not so sure I can do it. Sometimes I'm not even sure I want to.

"On those days, I come here. I discovered this lovely spot about a year ago. I feel that I can talk to God here."

"And has God answered?" Annie asked without bothering to conceal her skepticism.

"Do you ever talk to God, Annie?"

"No, I suppose not. I'm not sure I ever really believed there was a God."

"Maybe that's something you could do here," Helen suggested, ignoring Annie's agnosticism for the time being. "You need to talk to somebody, that's for sure."

"I don't feel like talking."

"Yes, you've made that pretty clear and I'm sure you have your reasons, but I think you're afraid?"

"I'm not afraid. I just don't want to talk about it."

"Annie," Helen said, her voice filled with kindness, "what happened to you must have been terrifying. You must have asked yourself a thousand times, 'Why me? What did I do?'"

"Other girls like you who've stayed with us over the years said they felt ashamed or guilty because they were convinced that what happened to them was somehow their fault. So they were afraid to trust anybody, to tell anybody, because they were certain that whoever they told would discover that terrible truth."

Silence.

"And now you've learned you're pregnant," Helen continued, "as if you needed a daily reminder of that terrifying night, of that contemptible man. As if you haven't suffered enough. You're right to think it isn't fair, that life isn't fair, because it isn't."

Unexpectedly, Helen stood, brushed off the back of her skirt, and laid her hand on Annie's shoulder before starting back down. On the river bank, she spied a perfectly flat stone. Annie watched as she picked it up, studied it, then skipped it brilliantly across the river, grinning from ear to ear like a toddler. To Annie's surprise, she was grinning as well.

Before disappearing into the tall shrubs, Helen called back, "See you at dinner, Annie."

Because she was such a light sleeper, Helen heard the soft, urgent tapping. Turning on her lamp, she saw that it was two in the morning. "Come in," she said softly.

The door opened slowly, revealing a form wrapped in a blanket from head to toe, and although the sound was muffled, Helen recognized the sound of sobbing and the worn blue slippers.

"Annie, what is it?" she asked, full of concern. Annie pushed the blanket from her face; she was indeed crying and must have been crying for a while because the collar of her nightgown was damp, her nose red and runny, her face swollen and blotchy.

"I can't stop," Annie sobbed, her eyes wide with fear.

"Come," Helen said gently, lifting a corner of her blanket and sliding over in bed. "Get in. It's time, Annie. I won't leave you and I'll listen to whatever you want to tell me."

"Good morning, Mother. You sent for me?"

"Yes, Helen," Mother Superior replied, rising from her chair with some difficulty. "I want to know how Miss Kenny's doing. Please sit," she said, gesturing to the chair at the side of her desk.

"I notice she's taking her meals regularly again, but it seems she continues to miss morning prayers."

Mother Superior, formerly Sister Mary Magdalena, was seventy-seven years old, had been a nun for nearly sixty years, and had lived in this convent, serving in one capacity or another, for the past twenty years.

Her reputation, at least among the novices, was as someone who censured emotional outbursts, someone to whom canonical rules were imperatives, a woman of ineloquent candor, on occasion offensive but never imperious. Sister Mary Magdalena was perfect for her chosen vocation and for her current position.

"Yes," replied Helen, "I'm pleased to report that Miss Kenny is eating better, though, by the look of her, I doubt she was ever a big eater. She's just starting to reveal more about herself, and, like most of the girls who've stayed with us, she's burdened with shame and guilt. Physically, her nausea's gone, as Doctor March predicted, but she's starting to have lower back pain and that keeps her from sleeping soundly."

Impatiently, Mother continued, "Have you spoken to her about the baby, Helen? Have you and she talked about what she'll do after the birth, assuming that she carries to term?"

"No," replied Helen, taken aback by the question. "It's still so hard for her to get through each day, she's so depressed, Mother. I was waiting until she felt a little—"

"A little what, Helen?" Mother asked, raising her voice. "She's only fifteen! How could she possibly raise a child?"

"I understand, Mother, but she's so fragile right now, at times even hopeless. I just don't think she's—"

"Helen," Mother interrupted, "Miss Kenny's five months pregnant. Has she any relatives who could or would be willing to raise this child? Would she even want this child raised by a relative?

"Perhaps, an orphanage would be a better choice," Mother continued. "Miss Kenny would never have to see the child. Of course, she would be conflicted about this, given her history."

"I don't agree, Mother. I'm older than Annie, but in many ways, many very unfortunate ways, she's experienced more of the world's cruelty than I ever will. I, for one, can't imagine how it would affect me to have never known my own parents. Wouldn't I always wonder why neither of them wanted me? How does one ever heal from that?

"Neither you nor I can ever understand what she's going through. But we have seen enough girls over the years to know that the feeling of defilement doesn't seem to go away. And now she's pregnant! At fifteen.

"With respect, Mother, I'm not concerned that she doesn't attend morning prayers. I'm concerned about keeping her and that baby alive.

"Wandering about the woods seems to give her some relief. I don't understand it, but when she returns, she seems a bit stronger, less despondent. Mother, I don't mean to be disrespectful or contrary, but you told me to take care of her, to watch out for her, to determine what she needs. I need you to trust my judgment as I have learned to trust hers."

With great effort, Mother stood, shuffled to the window, and surveyed the peaceful surroundings beyond the convent. "I suppose you're right, Helen," she said softly. "We are fortunate, insulated as we are from the real world. Neither of us will ever have to endure the torment that Miss Kenny has and likely always will have to endure. I appreciate you reminding me of that, however difficult it was to hear.

"I do need to trust you in this, Helen, and so I will. Let me know what any of us can do to help. Miss Kenny surely deserves that. You may go."

Much sooner than expected, Annie became oppressively fatigued. As her pregnancy advanced, its stigma and her belief that it was deserved punishment became more and more tangled in her mind.

Her own mother had not wanted her, and Annie was about to give birth to another unwanted child. She was being encouraged to place this child into an orphanage where Annie knew exactly how meager and parsimonious life would be, knew firsthand what this child would never feel and, more tragically, what he or she would always feel. Insufficient.

On the first day of December, winter arrived in full force. Annie woke to a gloriously sunny morning. From her partially glazed window, she looked out over a resplendent snowscape, a totally white masterpiece. She heard Jonathan's shovel scraping beneath her window. How he'd managed to get to the convent, given that the road looked impassable, she couldn't imagine but recognized, sadly, that walking outdoors, even where Jonathan had cleared some narrow passageways, would be treacherous.

In midmorning Helen chanced upon Annie pacing the first floor's labyrinth of corridors, hands cradling her belly, a woolen shawl cinched around her shoulders, her ubiquitous blue slippers scuffing.

"There's nothing to do, Helen. I don't dare take a walk outdoors. I need a job, a real job. There must be something I could do around here to be helpful?"

"Maybe," Helen answered thoughtfully. "Come with me."

"You've got to be kidding!" Annie whispered as they entered the convent's kitchen saturated with the savory aromas of roasting meat and the sweet fragrance of baking cinnamon bread.

"Good morning, Sister Agnes," Helen called to the thin, black figure furiously chopping on a thick, worn butcher block.

Laying aside her knife, Sister Agnes looked up, welcoming them with a beatific smile. "Helen, how lovely," she said, her voice still thinly edged with an accent despite having left Belfast over twenty years earlier.

"And this must be our last boarder, is it?"

"Yes, Sister, this is Annie. As you can see, she's very pregnant and the recent snow has made getting outside dangerous. She is desperate for something to do, something to keep her mind occupied and her hands busy. I wondered if you might be able to find something for her in here."

Sister Agnes studied Annie carefully. "Can you cook, dear?"

"No," Annie replied flatly but then remembered, "I did help in a kitchen for a while, but it was a long time ago."

"Well then, let's get you started, shall we? I'll be happy to give

Annie a try for a week, maybe two, depending on how she feels. How would that be, Helen?"

"Wonderful, Sister. You're a great help as usual. Annie, I leave you in good hands." And without waiting for any objections from Annie, Helen left.

Her labor started in the early afternoon on January 15, 1916 and seemed to galvanize the convent. Eight hours later, Annie was barely dilated, her blood pressure was seriously elevated, and the baby's heartbeat was starting to be erratic—all symptoms of what Doctor March called failure to dilate.

Helen stayed at Annie's side, wiping her face with a cloth dipped in lavender water and whispering encouragement while Annie lay panting and exhausted. Suddenly, Helen's eyes widened as a bright red stain spread across Annie's sheet.

"Nurse, we have to take the baby," Doctor March announced, his voice clipped with tension.

"No!" Annie moaned, her face distorted by the pain of another contraction.

"Don't worry, Annie," Helen soothed, "many young women deliver by Cesarean."

"No!" Annie thundered, the effort splitting her badly chapped lower lip, causing a garnet drop of blood to trickle down her cheek. "I won't survive," she added without further explanation, her eyes bulging with fear.

Lowering her face until she could feel the heat and dampness rising from Annie's face, Helen said firmly, "Annie, you've got to be brave now. I'm telling you that you'll be fine. This is not unusual. I'll be right by your side."

"Helen!" Doctor March said gruffly, clearing his throat. "We need to take her in." The urgency of his tone confirmed not only that Annie's condition was deteriorating but that the baby's was as well.

As the nurse wheeled her bed toward the door, Annie cried out for Helen.

"I'm right here," Helen said, running to her side.

Panicked, Annie gripped Helen's hand ferociously. "If it's a girl," she said, panting, her color rising, "I want to name her Helen Rose Kenny. Promise me, Helen, that you'll put that name on her birth certificate."

"Of course, but—"

"Give me your word, Helen."

"I promise, Annie."

Just over an hour later, Dr. March found Helen still sitting outside the operating room. "It's a small but healthy baby girl," he told her. "Nurse is cleaning her up. We'll keep her in the nursery at least overnight. You can see her if you'd like."

"Annie?" Helen asked, her fear visible.

"The pregnancy took a heavy toll. She's very weak, lost a lot of blood. Hopefully, she'll regain her strength, but frankly I can't guarantee that she will. Her uterus was damaged either from her pushing or from the internal injuries she suffered during the rape. I can't say for sure, but there was no choice except to remove it. Tragically, she cannot have more children."

"Doctor," Helen pleaded as fat tears sluiced her grief-stricken face, "please wait until she's much stronger before telling her that she can't have more children. I don't know that she would survive that news now."

"Of course, Helen," Doctor March replied, removing his glasses, wiping one lens on the sleeve of his jacket, "I understand."

18

THE TRUTH DOESN'T ALWAYS SET YOU FREE

From the parlor chaise where she'd been lazily watching dusk purpling the late June sky, Rebecca Wallabee chuckled at her three-year-old's unrestrained exuberance and knew by the staccato clatter of tiny shoes across the wooden floor that Gwendolyn was running full tilt, as she always ran full tilt, her skinny arms outstretched, her hair ribbons flapping like flags, and a sunbeam of a smile on her face.

As her garrulous daughter climbed the stairs to her nursery with Calvin, her adoring father in tow, Rebecca felt indescribably happy with her life, though that hadn't always been the case.

This was her favorite room with its abundant afternoon sunlight and distant views of the bay. The parlor was the heart of their home with its stone fireplace and a fan-shaped top which nearly reached the ceiling. Calvin was overjoyed to finally have a place to display the rosewood mantel clock that he'd lovingly carried back from Italy so many years earlier and for the stunning pair of jade vases they'd received as a wedding gift.

Opposite the fireplace wall, two fairly large canvases hung side by side. Row after row of perfectly mounded, purple-blue Spanish lavender (although Calvin insisted that the field itself was in Italy) completely covered the first canvas; on the other, a large field of flaming-red poppies drenched in sun was interrupted, here and there, by pencil-thin, emerald-green cypresses—you could almost feel the heat.

The muted sounds of Gwendolyn's animated prattle and Calvin's baritone laughter brought Rebecca's thoughts back to her daughter, who was the very center of her life. Gwendolyn was taller than most girls her age but more delicate in build. Her thicket of auburn curls absolutely defied combing, so Rebecca insisted, at least for now, that it be kept short. Fortunately, she was even-tempered, giggled easily, and was, in general, a funny and contented child.

To her dying breath she would always remember the evening when Calvin asked, "Rebecca, I've been thinking and . . . um . . . we haven't discussed it for a long while, but well . . . I was wondering if you still felt the same about having children."

To his credit, Calvin had indeed noticed how changed his wife was becoming—how she'd seemed to have lost her vibrancy, becoming more and more muted. And while the lovely violet gown she was wearing showcased her beautiful gray eyes, it also accentuated her increasingly unhealthy pallor.

"What are you asking me, Calvin?" she asked flatly, dislodging a tiny nugget of irritation.

"Well . . . I'm asking if you still thought about having children."

"And why are you asking me this now, Calvin?" she demanded, narrowing her eyes as the flush on her neck crept onto her face.

"I'm not exactly sure, to be honest, but I've been thinking about this and well . . . it occurred to me that we hadn't ever considered adoption."

"Calvin, I really don't know what to say," she stammered. "I always imagined that you wanted your own son, an heir. You never mentioned adoption before . . ." Her voice trailed off.

"To be honest, Rebecca, I'd always thought adoption was something . . . well, frankly . . . not something people like us did."

"Oh, Calvin," she cried, "let's not have this discussion, please. It's taken me so long to accept our . . . my . . . situation. I simply cannot . . ."

Her face was contorted with pain, and the sorrow he saw etched there shamed him until he could no longer bear to look at her.

"I'm so very, very sorry, Becca," he said softly, his voice catching. "I've watched you withdraw further and further from me. I'm ashamed to admit that I didn't know what to do, so I did nothing.

"Maybe I'd hoped that time would make things better—isn't that what everyone says? But, of course, it hasn't. I can't really put it into words except to say that you're not the same . . . and we're not the same." His eyes shone with tears.

She was speechless, touched and undeniably skeptical about what he'd just revealed, despite the fact that she'd longed for such emotional connectedness for years. As was her nature, she remained silent.

"You still haven't answered my question. Do you still want children?"

She looked away as tears slipped over her eyelids. "Yes," she said softly without rancor.

"Then we shall," he replied.

"What? I don't understand." She stood so suddenly that her chair toppled behind her. "How? Calvin, are you sure? What would we do?"

"I'll speak to your father," he said, smiling broadly. "He'll surely know someone who can handle this for us. But, Becca, I don't have any idea how long something like this might take. Your father might be able to shed more light on that, but meanwhile you'll have a nursery to plan, people to hire, decisions to make. Are you sure you're up to it? Shall I ask Mother to help?"

"Oh no, please! I want to take care of everything," she said quickly, her wide smile and tear-stained face a visual paradox.

The Truth Doesn't Always Set You Free

"Rebecca, please, I'm ashamed that my selfishness caused you so much pain. I never meant to hurt you. Please believe that. Hopefully, becoming a family will set things right again."

It was a statement as well as a question.

Late afternoon on Valentine's Day 1916, Calvin, Rebecca, and both sets of parents nervously awaited the arrival of Mrs. Christina Merriweather from Fall River Social Services. While they waited, Rebecca proudly showed her mother and mother-in-law the recently completed nursery.

They marveled at the pale, butter-yellow walls and the violet-blue ceiling with soft cottony clouds floating across it. A white sleigh crib with a soft pink blanket stood in the center of the room, a handsome rocking horse waited nearby, and, in the corner, a miniature table for two was already set for an elaborate tea party.

The three men remained in the parlor, enjoying the warmth of the roaring fire and their snifters of brandy. Rebecca's father, Franklin, now fifty-six, paced between the fireplace and the window, observing fat snowflakes spilling out of the low gray sky.

"What time is it?" he asked bluntly. "It's really coming down out there."

"Franklin, sit down, man! Relax. You act like you're the one having a baby!" chided Samuel, who still loved teasing his oldest friend. "At my age, I can't afford to get too excited, but I have to admit I didn't think I'd live to see a grandchild."

"I'll just be glad when this is behind us," Franklin said tersely, almost to himself.

With the melodic chime of the doorbell, everyone's life was transformed. Rebecca ran to open the door. With damp snow on her shoulders and bonnet, Mrs. Merriweather gratefully stepped into the entrance hall and began stamping the fluffy snow off her boots.

"Good afternoon, everyone," she said, beaming. "I assume you are the new mother," she said, placing a pink blanketed bundle carefully into Rebecca's outstretched arms.

"And you must be the father," said Mrs. Merriweather as she handed Calvin a thick envelope. "Unfortunately, I must be off. I wish I could stay and chat a bit, but the snow's really starting to pile up and my driver's quite nervous."

"Oh, I almost forgot," she called back when she reached the curb, "Happy Valentine's Day!"

"Calvin, look how beautiful she is!" Rebecca cried, lifting a corner of the blanket as he closed the door behind Mrs. Merriweather.

"Hello, my darling girl," Rebecca whispered to the baby.

"Such tiny fingers!" she exclaimed, heading into the parlor with her pink bundle.

As the parents gathered round smiling and cooing over the baby, Miranda Wallabee asked, "Rebecca dear, what have you decided to call this child?"

"Her name is Gwendolyn, Mother. Gwendolyn Elizabeth Wallabee," Calvin announced proudly.

In the sanctuary of this parlor now overflowing with benevolence and rose-colored dreams, it would have been impossible to imagine that this child's future would never mirror the comfort and abundance that her fairy-tale nursery promised.

19

DOING THE RIGHT THING

"You asked to see me, Mother?"

"Yes, I wanted an update on Miss Kenny's condition."

"Well," replied Helen, "her extreme postpartum depression has lifted a bit. Given the amount of blood she lost during delivery, we'd anticipated this extended recovery time, and her health has improved. In fact, Doctor March released her from his care.

"Emotionally, though, she's as withdrawn and undecipherable as when she first arrived here. The only time she seems content, even at peace, is when she's working with Sister Agnes—who sincerely enjoys her company, I must say."

"Yes, I've heard that as well," agreed Mother Superior. "Isn't it a blessing that Miss Kenny has some innate talent in the kitchen. I'm not the only one to appreciate that our simple meals, while still simple, are more flavorful. Frankly, her day-old bread puddings are heavenly!"

Unexpectedly, she laughed heartily at her pun, which startled Helen. She couldn't remember hearing Mother Superior laugh, ever.

"My concern, Helen," Mother continued, "is that she's become too comfortable here. Unconsciously, I think she might be hiding here. It's June, she's six months postdelivery, and unless she's planning to enter the convent, which I doubt, she shouldn't still be here. Miss Kenny needs to return to the outside world to face her very understandable fears."

"I've broached the subject with her, but obviously, Mother, I need to be more direct. I was considering giving her an actual date—to make the reality of her having to leave us more concrete. What do you think?"

"I'll leave that to you, Helen. I'll support whatever you decide. If you need more advice later, I'm quite happy to talk again."

"Thank you, Mother. I appreciate your counsel."

Neither Mother Superior nor Helen Riley could have foreseen that the decision about when Annie Kenny would leave the convent would not be made by them—nor by Annie.

"Sister Agnes, you're looking positively beat! The heat's terrible today. Here," Annie said, handing Sister Agnes a glass of cool water. "Sit for a bit, why don't you? In fact, why don't you take a break, the arbor should still be shaded. I'll handle things here."

"Ah, Annie, aren't you an angel," Sister Agnes exclaimed, gulping down the water. "I really do feel a bit off my game, as you young people say. A cool drink and a sit down will do me good."

Annie continued preparing for lunch. The chickens, roasted earlier, were cool enough now to begin removing the meat for a chicken salad. She'd already chopped celery, snipped chives, and whipped mayonnaise. The loaves of baking bread were nearly finished, so she opened the oven door and basted the tops one last time.

She was shredding lettuce when she sensed a presence. Myra Talbot, the youngest, shyest novice, was standing silently in the doorway, head bowed, hands folded, waiting to be noticed. Finally, Annie asked, "What is it, Myra? Sister Agnes's resting if it's her you're after."

"Nn . . . nn . . . no," Myra said forcefully. "It's for y . . . y . . . you."

Impatiently, Annie called back, "Really, Myra! I've work to do. What is it you need?"

"You," she replied plainly. "Helen . . . ne . . . ne . . . needs you in the p . . . p . . . parlor right now." With that, an exhausted Myra padded down the hallway, relieved to have delivered her message without incident.

Removing the scented loaves and setting them on the counter to cool, Annie turned off the oven, hung up her apron, washed her hands, and headed upstairs to meet Helen.

In an effort to keep the convent cooler during the summer months, the sisters always drew the curtains over every window and the parlor, which had the most windows, so it was especially dim, but considerably more comfortable, than most other rooms.

Stopping at the entrance to allow her eyes time to adjust, she couldn't immediately see the person sitting across the room.

"Annie girl," a familiar voice said.

"Charlie?" she asked, squinting. "Oh my God, it is you!" she cried, running across the room and throwing her arms around his neck.

"It's been so long I was afraid you mightn't recognize me," he said with the familiar grin that started in his eyes, then spread to the rest of his face.

He sat at one end of the couch while she sat at the other. For a while, they didn't say a word but stared at each other, searching for the much-missed, familiar flaws and the ways that each seemed the same or different.

"You look well, Charlie. Are you?"

"Mostly," he said flatly, clearing his throat. "Annie, I'm afraid I've brought bad news."

Annie inhaled, stiffened, and gripped the arm of the couch.

"We buried Ma three weeks ago. She died of influenza."

"Oh God! Oh no, Charlie! Not Jenny!" Wiping her tears with the sleeve of her dress, she added, "Oh, Charlie, I'm so very sorry. Jenny was so good to me."

"Ma loved you like you were her own daughter, you know. She wasn't one to hand out the compliments, but she thought the world of you, always thought of you as family."

"And Phee?" Again, Annie braced herself.

Charlie sighed deeply. "Phee's another story, Annie. She blames herself. Not for Ma getting sick but for going to work and leaving Ma alone the day she died."

He stopped abruptly, doubled over, placed his elbows on his knees, and rested his head in his hands. He was silent for a long while, and once he regained his composure enough to look up, his face was a mask of suffering.

"She won't listen to me, Annie," he said softly. "She nursed Ma day and night. Ma really did seem better on that last morning, and she insisted that Phee get back to work. She was convinced Phee would lose her job if she stayed home any longer. When we got home that night, we found her.

"Now Phee refuses to even enter Ma's room. She cries constantly. She's got black circles under her eyes, hardly eats. Out of respect the boarders are staying with a neighbor, but we can't impose on Mrs. Abbott for much longer."

While she listened, Annie had drawn up her knees, laced her arms around them, and rocked back and forth as a rivulet of tears slid down her face.

"Oh, my poor, dear Phee! And poor Jenny!" Annie sobbed and continued rocking.

When her waves of tears ebbed, Charlie handed her his handkerchief. Annie furiously wiped her eyes, blew her nose, and asked in a whisper, "What can I do, Charlie? Please tell me. How can I help?"

"Well," he replied after taking a few deep breaths, "you know Phee, Annie. She'd sooner die than ask for help. She needs you—we both

Doing the Right Thing

need your help—nothing I've tried has worked. Come back home with me, help her get on her feet. After that, if you want to be here, I'll bring you back myself."

Five minutes earlier, Annie honestly had no intention of ever leaving the safety of this convent; the very thought would have sent her spiraling into panic. But her best friend needed help, as Annie had once, so despite her almost-paralyzing apprehension, Annie could not refuse.

"I can't leave today, Charlie," she told him, unable to disguise the trepidation in her voice. "I need to serve lunch, pack my belongings, and say my good-byes. Will tomorrow morning be okay?"

"Of course," he said, flooded with relief. "I took a room in town. I can meet you at whatever time on whatever day you want."

"Do you have tomorrow's train schedule?"

Charlie pulled a piece of paper from his inside pocket and unfolded it. "There's one at 7:10am and another at 2:35pm."

"I'll ask Jonathan if he can take me to the station for the earlier one, and I'll meet you on the platform. Would you purchase a ticket for me, Charlie? I'm sorry but I have no money."

"Of course," Charlie answered, dizzy with relief. "Take all the time you need."

Heart jittering and thundering in her chest, Annie stood on the platform and dried her sweaty palms on her skirt. Jonathan spotted Charlie easily, handed him Annie's bag, and helped Annie board before waving good-bye.

Shepherding her down the aisle, Charlie stopped in front of a half-glass door with a handwritten RESERVED sign taped to it.

"Charlie?" she asked.

"I told the conductor you were leaving the convent hospital for the first time in over a year, asked him if there might be a quiet car he could recommend because you needed to rest. He was kind enough to help."

The private car was roomy and immaculate. It had large windows that could be opened for fresh air, the upholstered couches were extra-long so each passenger could stretch out or even lie down, and thin pillows and blankets were neatly stacked on an overhead rack.

As usual, neither felt uncomfortable with the silence between them, but both were visibly relieved to hear the warning whistles and feel the train lurch forward on the track.

As soon as they left the station, Annie slid open her window and gulped fresh air, hoping that the turbulence might smooth out the buzzing in her head. Like a boomerang, she was hurtling back to the city of her rapist without warning; she was careening toward a place where unimaginable brutality, though it hadn't killed her outright, had ended her life nonetheless.

"It was a girl," she said, finally breaking the silence. "I had a baby girl."

Charlie glanced up at her, his eyes filled with benevolence without a sliver of judgment.

"They took her away. I didn't even see her. Can you believe it? Doing the same to her as was done to me." The tears that had been filling her eyes spilled over.

"You did what you had to do, Annie. There were no other choices." He hoped that over time his assurances might alleviate some of the guilt he knew she carried. "I will pray that a loving family adopted your little girl."

"Helen. I named her Helen Rose. Then I sent her away."

"I'm so sorry, Annie. You both deserved better."

There was nothing left to say, and once more a blanket of soft quiet fell over them. In the daylight, the swollen, plum-colored circles under his eyes looked like bruises, and his suit jacket clearly hung off his shoulders as he dozed on the opposite couch.

As the train pulled into the Fall River station, Charlie stirred. Rubbing his eyes, he retrieved his hat and her luggage from the closet and, once the train stopped completely, escorted her down the aisle to the stairs, where a conductor on the platform offered Annie his hand.

"I'll find a car to take us home," Charlie told her.

Recognizing them as private car passengers, the conductor flagged the stationmaster, who started toward them. "No problem, sir," the conductor assured Charlie. "The stationmaster will find one for you. Just follow him, please."

As they pulled up to the boardinghouse, the black funeral wreath on the front door made her heart ache. Setting her purse down in the foyer, Annie headed directly to the kitchen, where she found Phoebe slumped over the kitchen table still in her robe and slippers, her hair uncombed and wild. Phoebe glanced up with eyes that were vacant and bloodshot.

"Phee," Annie said quietly. "Don't worry, Phee, I've come back to help."

Phoebe stirred, but her eyes registered only confusion. Annie pulled up a chair and gently took her friend's hand and kissed it.

"Annie?" Phoebe finally asked, her voice breaking. She began to sob uncontrollably as if she'd been saving up her tears. Annie left her side only to fetch a glass of water and a cool washcloth.

When Phoebe finally stopped, Annie quickly filled the kettle, set out cups, and checked the icebox. She fried some eggs, toasted some bread, and found a small tin of butter and a nearly empty jar of strawberry jam. By the time the water had come to a boil, she'd set out a small lunch for the three of them.

"Phee," she said kindly but firmly, "I want you to eat this and then I want you to sleep. After that, we can have a long chat, just like we used to."

Phoebe said nothing, just stared at the food in front of her as if unsure of what to do. Annie spoke to her as if she were a child, which ordinarily would have gotten Phoebe's back up, but without a word Phoebe ate the egg, drank the tea, and let Annie tuck her into bed. As she pulled the covers over her friend, Annie whispered, "I know you miss your Ma, we all do. Take a bit of rest now."

Charlie hadn't moved from the table. Annie returned to find him staring into his teacup looking as lost and bereft as his sister.

"Charlie," Annie said, taking charge. "I'll make a list of groceries I'll need you to fetch. Afterward, you should take a rest this afternoon as well. Meanwhile, I'll give this kitchen a good cleaning. At some point, I'll need a place to stay. Is there an empty room?"

"I'll move upstairs. You can have my room," he replied in a voice layered with exhaustion and sorrow.

Until now, he'd not allowed himself to feel the full weight of his mother's death. How strange, he thought, to be sitting in Ma's kitchen—a place he'd sat in hundreds of times—without hearing the sounds of her chopping something, scraping out some heavy frying pan, or her infamous off-key, albeit enthusiastic, singing. How many times had he and Phee teased her about that?

"Let's take tea in the parlor," Annie suggested after a dinner of barley soup and bread. "Phee, bring in the biscuits, would you? Charlie, fetch cups and saucers. I'll fill the teapot and be right there."

"There," she said, pouring them tea and settling into the large armchair across from them. "Now I want to hear everything. I want to hear about every problem that needs sorting."

"I can't think where to start," Phoebe said hesitantly, her voice unusually timid, "so much has happened."

"I want to hear it all, then I won't feel so disconnected, Phee. Start when I left."

In the nearly two hours that followed, Annie learned that the day after Charlie left her at the convent, he quit his job at the Troy Mill. Quitting was so entirely out of character for him, and his explanation didn't really make sense, but she decided not to press him.

He found work at the newly opened Firestone Mill that ran twenty-four hours a day producing special tires for military vehicles. Although he hated working nights, he accepted a position as director of security on the night shift, but, finally, after applying three times, he was moved to days.

Despite Phoebe's obvious grief, her enthusiasm for hat making had not waned, and, except for peak manufacturing times when everyone felt overworked, it never really felt like work to her because each day and each hat was different.

As a confirmation of her talent, she had been recruited to the company's small group of elite designers—one of only six in the whole factory—and promoted to assistant designer.

"It was very unexpected," Phoebe said, still furiously kneading the white handkerchief in her hand. "It's really exciting and the other girls are great to me. I'm the youngest." She stopped talking then but never stopped kneading the handkerchief.

"Phee," Annie asked, "why do I get the feeling that there's something you're not telling me?"

Phoebe immediately looked to her brother, but Charlie's expression neither encouraged nor discouraged her from continuing. "Well, it just doesn't seem right to talk about it now, Annie," she explained, "what with Ma's death and us thinking we'll need to close the boardinghouse. And it's all up in the air anyway."

"What's up in the air?" Annie prompted.

"Thomas and I."

"Thomas?"

"Thomas Sullivan. He was my supervisor at the factory, but he transferred into sales. For sure, he's a good man, smart too, but it won't work."

Annie searched Charlie's face for confirmation, for disagreement, for any reaction at all, but there was none. "And why won't this work?"

"Ma's death changes everything. We were planning to get engaged and hoped to live here after we married so I could help Ma and we could save some money."

"But you didn't get engaged?"

"No, we didn't. Before we could tell her our plans, she got the flu. I stayed home to take care of her and sometimes Charlie did too, but ten days later she was dead."

Forgetting her handkerchief, Phoebe used her sleeve to wipe her eyes, reached for her tea, and took a few sips before she could continue.

"I just couldn't go back to work after Ma died. Couldn't face Thomas."

"Does he even know?"

"Yes," Charlie interjected. "I told him. He came to the funeral but hasn't come round since then."

"I don't even know if I still have a job there. It's been almost a month," Phee confessed.

"And if you don't have a job, what will you do, Phee?"

"It doesn't matter to me, Annie. I'll probably run the boardinghouse. That's what Ma would have wanted." Again, she had to stop, wipe her eyes, and collect herself.

"We've discussed selling, Charlie and me, but . . ."

"But?"

"Well," Charlie explained hesitantly, "it turns out that Ma didn't own the boardinghouse like we always thought. There's still a mortgage on it with at least three years left. It took the rent from three boarders just to cover the mortgage payments.

"We had absolutely no idea, Annie, but she was barely scraping by. And she never said anything, never complained."

It was clear from his tone that Charlie was embarrassed and ashamed that he hadn't known of his mother's plight.

"What did the doctor say, Phee?" Annie asked, hoping to stem the tears by changing the topic.

"He came twice," Charlie explained, "thought she had a better chance to recover if she stayed here. He prescribed medicine, which Phee made sure she took, and he warned us about dehydration."

"She had no appetite," Phoebe chimed in. "I had to threaten her just to get her to take a few sips of tea or broth. Last time the doctor came, she was having trouble breathing."

"He said Ma was obese," Charlie recalled sadly, "and that was why so much fluid was collecting in her lungs. Every day we were supposed to make her walk, but she got too weak to even stand."

"That last day she seemed better, didn't she, Charlie?" Phoebe asked. "Like she'd turned a corner. For the first time, she ate a little toast and finished almost a whole cup of tea. But she insisted I go back to work, convinced I'd lose my job if I didn't. I shouldn't have gone . . . and because I did, she died all alone."

"I'm so sorry, Phee," Annie said sincerely, "I loved Jenny, but once she made up her mind about something . . . and her health was never good because of her weight. It doesn't sound like there was any more either of you could have done. The odds were against you.

"I understand how badly you wish you could have been with her at the end. I wish we all could have been with her, Phee," she added.

They were exhausted, totally wrung out, all of them.

"Are there any boarders now?" Annie asked after a while.

"Three. They're staying next door with Mrs. Abbott until the end of this week. She wanted to give us time to plan a wake and have the funeral."

"Well," said Annie, standing, "I'm worn out. You must be too. I'll sleep in Charlie's room tonight. Charlie, I moved a few of your things into the empty room upstairs.

"I'll make us breakfast in the morning, but then both of you need to go to work. Phee, you and Thomas need to sort out where you stand. We'll talk more at dinner tomorrow."

The next evening they gathered in the parlor again. Less exhausted, Phoebe had a bit of color and her fiery hair was neatly pulled back and gently twisted into a figure eight, but as soon as she was seated, she tugged her boots off and massaged her badly swollen feet, evidence that she'd worn real shoes for the first time in weeks.

Charlie sat in his shirtsleeves, resting his head on the couch's back; his stubbled, heavily lined face and the dark circles under his eyes aged him ten years. He and Phoebe stared at her like small children who hoped their broken toy could be fixed. In their minds, she was the key to something good happening.

"Well," Annie began, "I've come up with a plan to get us through the next few months and give us some breathing room before any big decisions have to be made.

"If, as you said, you need three boarders to cover the mortgage, then we've already got that, so we need to get them back into their rooms as soon as possible.

"Both of you have good jobs and we need both incomes, so, at least for now, the two of you should keep working. Unlike you, dear Phee, I think I could run this boardinghouse—at least for a few months.

"I can make simple breakfasts and dinners. I know how to change linens and clean, even how to do laundry. Whether I'd be good enough to satisfy your boarders, I can't say, but I'd be willing to try."

They were speechless. Phee actually thought Annie was joking.

"Charlie," Annie continued, undaunted by their silence, "could you keep track of what monies come in and what go out for the next few months? Then we'll have a better idea about whether to keep the house or sell.

"I don't need a salary, at least for a while, but I will need some cash to buy food, supplies, stuff like that. I've no idea how much Jenny spent, so we'll all have to be as frugal as we can."

Both continued to stare at her blankly.

"Well, say something," Annie said sharply.

"Well . . . I just don't know what to say," Phoebe finally replied. "I don't think we can let you do this, Annie. It's too much work. And without a salary? Absolutely not!"

"You're being too generous, Annie. Phee's right," Charlie agreed, shaking his head.

"Put that aside," Annie said, determined to move them forward. "Have you other objections?"

"No," Charlie replied carefully. "Well, at least I don't think so. Truthfully, Ma handled everything, so neither of us really has any idea how much money was needed or where it went.

"But," he added, "if you're asking whether your plan's worth a try? Absolutely! But not paying you still seems wrong to me, Annie."

"Fine. Then how about this? If—and it's a big if—if there's money left over at the end of each month, let's put it aside for me, but I'll not use it for a while in case something unexpected comes up. By the end of four or five months, we should know one way or the other."

"Agreed!" Phee and Charlie cried in unison, their voices awash in hope.

And that was exactly what happened. In fits and starts over the next four months, Annie learned the rhythm of running a boardinghouse. It was definitely hard work and she made many mistakes, but they lost only one boarder during that time. Secretly terrified that she might have to look for work in another mill, Annie was incredibly motivated to succeed.

With a limited number of dishes in her repertoire, she formed an alliance with Maria Gesmondi, the grocer's wife, who was at least as old as Sister Agnes. Maria taught her how to identify the freshest meat and fish and how to prepare it.

"Simple is always best," she counseled Annie, "and you must always buy the best ingredients too. Remember you get what you pay for."

Slowly, Annie added lamb stew and braised beef to her repertoire of hearty soups and roasted chicken. She learned how to make tangy pies and tarts using whatever fruits were in season. She baked bread or scones every morning before anyone woke, and the fragrance of cinnamon, apples, or sweet buttermilk wafting throughout the house was more effective than any alarm clock for getting people to the breakfast table on time.

By March 1917, they'd finished their first house project. One by one the bedrooms upstairs had been repainted pale blue with crisp white trim. Comfortable armchairs were moved up, and Charlie found small reading tables in a secondhand shop which Thomas refinished admirably.

Annie bought new linens and pillows, and, borrowing Mrs. Abbott's sewing machine, she made snow-white curtains for each window and set a potted fern on each sill. Thomas made simple headboards, which he secured to the wall and painted white to match the trim. Phoebe found colorful travel posters, which she framed and Thomas hung above each of the new headboards.

Once the three rooms were finished, they raised the rent and all three rooms were rented out by mid-May. Jenny's Boardinghouse was full once again.

The following month Phoebe and Thomas became engaged. Thomas, who was quite good with tools, spent hours making flower boxes, attaching them to the front porch railings and filling each box to overflowing with a riot of colorful annuals.

He had a real knack for fixing things, which, in the day-to-day running of a boardinghouse, was invaluable. He won people over with his surprisingly gentle manner—a good foil for Phoebe's irascibility and bluntness, which, surprisingly, he never seemed to take offense at.

In June 1917, Phoebe and Thomas Sullivan were married in St. Paul's Church, with a small afternoon reception at the boardinghouse catered by Maria Gesmondi.

Annie made Phoebe's dress, a simple, cream-colored, satin A-line on which she hand-stitched faux pearls across the bodice and along the edges of the three-quarter-length sleeves.

On her wedding day, staring wide-eyed at her reflection in the mirror, Phee burst into tears, hugged her friend, and whispered, "Annie I've never, ever felt beautiful until this moment. This dress is so perfect I can never thank you enough."

Then Phee carefully removed a wide-brimmed ivory hat covered with gorgeous beaded ribbons and swirls of ivory netting from a blue-and-white striped box, placed it at a jaunty angle on her head, and pinned it in place with her ma's silver hat pin. At that moment, she was the happiest and prettiest she'd ever been in her life.

On the newlyweds' return, the entire house and all its occupants settled into a comfortable, predictable routine. Breakfast was served at six, and by six forty-five, every boarder, along with Charlie, Phoebe, and Thomas, set out for work, and Annie had the house to herself until suppertime.

Typically, she made a fresh pot of tea and ate whatever was left over from breakfast. Then, carrying her last cup of tea into the parlor, she sat at the window, observing the pedestrian traffic and letting her mind wander.

With regularity, she circled back over past sorrows. Wistfully, she thought about the enigmatic Mr. Sam but could never think about him without recalling his son's savageness, which led to thoughts of the tiny daughter she'd abandoned. On these occasions, a melancholy and blistering self-reproach would torment her. She was inconsolable then, sometimes for days at a time.

Understandably, the birth of Phoebe's first child, Robert John Sullivan in March 1918, was a bittersweet event for Annie. Inexplicably fatigued for months, Phoebe was listless and even more cranky than usual, so the care of the new infant fell to Annie, who adored him.

One bright Sunday afternoon in late April, Thomas convinced everyone to go for a walk. After several blocks, Thomas stopped in front of an abandoned storefront. It took Phoebe a few seconds to notice the handwritten sign taped to the smudged window announcing the coming of "Phoebe's Hats."

"Oh, my God! Oh my God!" she screamed in delight. "Thomas Sullivan, what have you done?"

"Well," he replied grinning sheepishly, "you always said you wanted your own shop. There's even a workroom in back where Bobbie can sleep. Here"— he pulled a key from his pocket—"let's take a look!"

It was dingy and dark inside and the air was terribly stale, but the space was perfect and Phoebe had no trouble imagining her hats on display in the window. There was plenty of counter space, and the workroom in back was more than adequate. The tiny washroom was a bonus.

"Oh, Thomas," Phoebe said, hugging him again and again. "It's perfect! And there's space for the baby to sleep while I work. It's just perfect!"

Leaning against a dusty counter, Thomas beamed in admiration as his wife walked round and round, inspecting every nook and cranny, peppering him with questions. Secretly, he'd been putting money aside for years while searching for a space close enough to

Doing the Right Thing

home so she could walk to work. In July, 1918, Phoebe's Hats opened for business.

As word spread, a new customer appeared at Phoebe's shop almost every month. The demand for hats was cyclical—there was a huge demand in the months before Easter Sunday, again in June because of weddings and graduations, and finally around Christmas. Phoebe worked feverishly during these times, often late into the night, so her front window was always an alluring garden of unusual, extravagant, and tempting blossoms.

On a lovely spring day when Gwendolyn was five, Rebecca decided to take her to purchase a new Easter hat. On the subject of hats, Rebecca had strong opinions: hats were *de rigueur* for every well-bred lady, and she wanted to instill in her daughter the importance of wearing "just the right hat." Several months earlier, Rebecca discovered the unusually charming hats of a talented young milliner who recently opened a shop near South Park.

"Where to, ma'am?" the driver asked.

"Three hundred South Main," answered Rebecca, retying, for at least the third time, the pink satin bow in Gwendolyn's hair.

Twenty minutes later the driver pulled up in front of a royal-blue-and-white striped awning shading a spotlessly clean window-display of colorful hats perched on manikin heads or jauntily propped on elaborate hatboxes.

"Thank you, George," Rebecca said, sliding out and reaching back to help her daughter.

The retail space with walls painted the color of ripe peaches glowed from the combination of natural light, countertop lamps, and some overhead fixtures. Some hats were backlit on tall stands, while others, particularly those with colorful glass beading, were set directly under an overhead fixture so they glittered like stars. The whole room had an air of whimsy.

"No one's here, Mama," Gwendolyn observed, her disappointment evident.

"Hello! Good morning," Rebecca called out.

"I'll be right there," replied a voice from a back room, where bolts of fabrics and boxes of buttons—sorted by color and size—were neatly lined on shelves. Feathers, especially peacock feathers, boxes of glass beads, a myriad of buckles, and silk flowers were heaped on a single table along the wall.

"Well, hello there, Mrs. Wallabee," Phoebe called as she entered, still wearing her bulky work apron and a measuring tape around her neck.

"And didn't I put aside something with you in mind just the other day?" she continued with a conspiratorial wink.

Of course, Phoebe hadn't really put something aside, but she liked her customers to think that she'd designed something especially for them.

"And who have we here?" Phoebe asked, removing her apron, noticing a child half hidden by her mother's pleated skirt.

"Oh, Phoebe, this is my daughter, Gwendolyn," replied Rebecca proudly. "Gwendolyn, say hello to Mrs. Sullivan."

"Hello," Gwendolyn replied shyly, stepping out from behind her mother.

Startled into silence, Phoebe stared into the bluest eyes she'd ever seen. "Hello," she finally managed to say, "I've a little one at home, but I bet you're older than him—my Robert's three."

"I'm this many," said the girl, holding up five fingers proudly.

Phoebe continued to stare at Gwendolyn's eager expression until finally Rebecca broke the silence. "I was hoping you might have some scraps of fabric that Gwendolyn could play with while I try on some of your lovely hats? It's nearly Easter!"

"Oh yes, of course," replied Phoebe, reluctantly prying her eyes from this child whose pink satin ribbon was unsuccessful in holding her hair off her face.

Relieved to have an excuse to leave the room, Phoebe strode to her workroom and into the washroom, where she splashed cold water onto her face again and again. Light-headed, she held onto the sink with one hand, took deep breaths, and toweled her face dry with the other. *This is not the time to try and sort this out*, she told herself.

"Will this do, Mrs. Wallabee?" Phoebe asked, returning to the sales floor with a box of large colorful buttons that she handed to Gwendolyn, who gleefully dumped them all onto the countertop.

"Now," Phoebe said crisply, "let's get started, shall we? I've lots to show you."

Almost an hour later, having decided on two new hats, Rebecca rallied her daughter while Phoebe encased each hat in tissue paper and settled each into a blue-and-white striped hatbox.

"Come, Gwendolyn," Rebecca said cheerfully, "it's time to go. Wait 'til you see Mama's new hats."

"Just a minute please," Phoebe said, hurrying into her workroom and returning with a length of grosgrain ribbon. "Here," she said, kneeling in front of Gwendolyn, removing the satin ribbon, and replacing it with the one in her hand.

"There," she said, standing. "That satin ribbon's too slippery, which is why it keeps coming untied. This one should stay put better. Hope you don't mind pink?"

"Oh, no," replied Gwendolyn, beaming, "I love pink."

"Well, it's definitely your color," Phoebe assured her. "Hope you'll come back soon. I'd love to make a hat just for you—pink, of course."

"And thank you, Mrs. Wallabee," Phoebe said, opening the door for them. "Wonderful to see you again. Happy Easter, Gwendolyn!"

Long after mother and daughter were seated comfortably in the back seat, after the chauffeur had secured the hatboxes, even after he slid into the driver's seat and pulled away from the curb, Phoebe hadn't moved. She stood holding her shop door open and staring after them in disbelief. It couldn't be, she thought. And yet . . .

After the war the chemise dress became the iconic prototype of the era and was paired with an equally simple, helmet-style hat called a cloche, which was an overnight success—a statement of understated chic that women flocked to. It was quickly mass-produced using felt, which was easy to shape and decorated simply with feathers or ribbon.

Phoebe refused to use felt and instead experimented with sisal, a fine straw, which she either braided or, using a special hand-blocking technique, made into thin, artful ridges around the circumference of the hat—a uniqueness that mass production could not duplicate.

She also designed small-brimmed cloches so that the brim could be turned up or not. She used unusual fabric combinations like rich chocolate or ebony velvets lined with iridescent gold or silver lamés that sparkled when the brims were turned up.

When she added decoration, Phee avoided using ribbons or feathers, preferring instead jeweled stick pins, antique fobs, or art deco appliqués. These unusual cloches appealed to more style-conscious women who were willing to pay a premium.

At Thanksgiving in 1926, everyone gathered around the beautifully decorated table—Bobby, now eight was seated next to his father, Tommy, Phoebe's second son, now six, sat next to his mother and the two-year-old twins, Seth and Paul squirmed in their highchairs. Thomas and Phoebe sat at the heads of the table while Annie and Charlie sat on either side.

Unexpectedly, Charlie rose and seemed for a few seconds at a loss for words. "I want us to lift our glasses," he said with a quiet sadness, "to Jenny Dougherty, our Ma, who worked every day of her life to keep me and Phee safe and put a roof over our heads.

"I wish she'd lived to see her darlin' grandchildren, to meet Phee's husband, Thomas, who's like a brother to me, and to welcome Annie back." He stopped because his eyes had filled with tears.

"We can never repay her for the sacrifices she made," he continued. "Yesterday, I made the final payment on her mortgage, Phee. Ma's house is now legally ours. To Jenny," he said, raising his glass and wiping tears away with the back of his hand.

"To Jenny!" everyone repeated, clinking their glasses.

"I know what you're up to Charlie," Phee announced as they walked to the trolley stop the following Saturday morning. "I saw you coming out of Kellerman's yesterday."

Charlie blanched. "Phee, you didn't say anything to her, did you?"

"Of course not. I'm not daft! When are you planning to ask her?"

Something in his sister's tone disquieted him. "What's on your mind, Phee?"

"I just wonder if you're doing the right thing?"

"By proposing to your best friend?"

"She's my best friend for sure, but you're my twin. I'm just being protective. I don't want you to get hurt."

"Hurt how?"

"She's not the same girl, Charlie. That convent changed her."

"Being raped and nearly beaten to death, that's what changed her!"

"I'm sorry, Charlie," Phee said, ashamed to have caused the sadness she now saw on his face. "Of course you're right. I didn't mean to sound so callous. What happened to Annie was unimaginable, unforgivable . . . I'm just surprised that you—"

"Don't tell me you never guessed I was falling for her. Really, Phee?"

"Of course, I did! I'm just saying that the girl you fell for was a free spirit, full of fun, ready to take life by the horns. I used to think she'd be a great match for you—might even loosen you up a bit. She's not that girl anymore, that's all I'm saying."

"You're right about that, Phee. Annie lost everything but still came back here to take care of us in our time of need. It was her loyalty and generosity that saved us—and Ma's boardinghouse. My heart breaks when I see how tenderly she cares for your children every day, despite having lost her own.

"Is Annie hard to read? Yes. Does some terrible sadness overcome her sometimes? Yes. But nothing's changed for me. I want to help her feel safe again—safe enough to laugh out loud like she used to, safe enough to love without fear."

Phoebe looked at him with pride and kissed him on the cheek. "You're a good man, Charlie, and Annie Kenny, more than anyone I know, deserves a good man."

After midnight Mass that Christmas Eve, sitting in front of the cozy fire, sipping mulled cider with fresh cinnamon sticks, Charlie proposed.

"I can't," Annie told him softly.

"Why?"

"I just can't," she repeated, her discomfort obvious.

"I'll wait then," he announced without rancor.

"No, Charlie, don't wait!" she pleaded. "You're such a kind man. You deserve someone better. I'm sorry but I just can't give you what you need."

"You don't know what I need, Annie," he said, sensing her loneliness. "I intend to wait. I'm in no hurry. Besides, sooner or later my Irish charm and devilish good looks will win you over," he said, grinning from ear to ear.

20

LOVE UNRAVELED

Despite a cooler than normal breeze and an inordinately blue sky that looked like polished marble, the early May 1927 morning began unremarkably with no warning of the imminent danger or of the unimaginable treachery ahead—all because of Gwendolyn's new hats.

"Damn!" Phoebe exclaimed. It was almost ten-thirty, the glue still hadn't fully dried, and she was running out of time.

Scrambling from kitchen to parlor, she hastily laid out cups and saucers, a sugar and creamer, and a few of Annie's homemade ginger cookies on her best porcelain tray.

"Napkins!" she cried, rushing back to the linen closet, pulling out and scrutinizing every napkin until she found two that weren't badly stained or frayed.

Her head throbbed. Seth, her youngest, had the croup and had been up most of the last three nights. Luckily, she'd been able to work from home, but, as a result, the parlor was littered with bolts of fabric, supplies, and the tools she needed to finish the three hats now perched on manikin heads along her worktable.

She rechecked the glue on one. "Almost dry," she said aloud and decided to move that hat to an open window in the kitchen.

The doorbell chimed. Phoebe stopped abruptly in the foyer, took a few deep breaths, and re-pinned an errant strand of hair.

"Good morning, Mrs. Wallabee," she said, opening the door. "I'm so glad you got my message. Sorry to bring you all the way out here, but my little one's been up all night with the croup and I daren't leave him."

"No bother at all, Phoebe!" Rebecca Wallabee replied graciously. "It's just a few blocks from your little shop."

"Please come in. I'm nearly finished. I've just made tea."

"Oh!" Rebecca exclaimed as she entered the parlor and spied one of Gwendolyn's hats on a manikin head. "This is just darling! Gwendolyn will love it. She's so excited about going to Rome. These colors go beautifully with the snippet of dress fabric you had to work with. Really," she said enthusiastically, "it's splendid!"

Phoebe poured Mrs. Wallabee a cup of tea. "Thank you," she replied, trying, though not quite succeeding, to match her client's excitement. She was simply exhausted.

"This one's finished," Phoebe said, lifting the hat off the manikin. "It's the newest summer color called 'orange sherbet,' and the trim, as you can see, is the exact pink of her dress."

"Yes," Rebecca said, nodding. "I've never seen that color combination before, but it's so delightfully fresh and chic."

"Now, Mrs. Wallabee, this hat's meant to be worn low. With Gwendolyn's curls I know it's difficult to keep any hat on her head, and at eleven she's much too old for a chin strap, so I've hidden two tiny loops, one on each side, where you can secure the hat."

Rebecca beamed as she held the hat to the light. It was fun and sophisticated and she had the perfect hat pins for it. "Gwendolyn will be over the moon, Phoebe. She'll feel so grown-up. And the other?"

"It's in the other room. I'm just giving the glue a few extra minutes to dry. Excuse me while I check on it. Please help yourself," she said, pointing to the tray of cookies. "My friend Annie's ginger cookies are famous."

While she waited, Rebecca rose, poured herself a bit more tea, and wandered to the end of the worktable to inspect a woman's hat on the last manikin. The fabric itself was extraordinary, a crisp ivory jacquard with silver threads woven through it. Slowly, she turned the manikin, watching how the threads caught the light, imagining how it would sparkle in sunlight, moonlight, even candlelight—like a crown.

On the table next to the unfinished hat lay a small bolt of the most delicate, ivory lace she'd ever seen. "Stunning," she said aloud, gingerly fingering the lace.

"What a magnificent hat!" she cried, settling back onto the couch as Phoebe returned carrying Gwendolyn's second hat.

"Thank you, Mrs. Wallabee. It's for my dearest friend. She's getting married soon. Now," she said proudly, holding up a child's hat for inspection, "what do you think?"

It was a pert, deep-purple oval hat with a bouquet of pale-pink pansies surrounded by green leaves attached off-center. "I just need to tack the braid. It'll only take a minute."

"It's a lovely color, Phoebe. Very regal. At first, I thought it might be too plain, but now that you've set the dress fabric in front of it, I can see that the hat's simplicity is what makes the combination so elegant! I would never have thought these colors could be so companionable."

Setting the hat on her lap, Phoebe threaded a fine needle and began attaching the marvelous braid she'd made using ribbons in all three colors.

"Phoebe, you're right—these cookies are marvelous," Rebecca said, helping herself to another.

A few minutes passed in silence as Rebecca watched Phoebe concentrating on each stitch. "So, you've a friend getting married soon. Well, her hat is stunning, and if her dress is half as lovely, the groom will be simply speechless."

"Yes, ma'am," Phoebe said, chuckling as she slowly pulled the stitch through. "It's my brother she's marrying."

"Oh, my goodness!" exclaimed Rebecca. "Isn't that wonderful! Well, I wish them every happiness."

Were she not so bone-weary and stressed, Phoebe would have thought more carefully before replying, "Yes, well our Annie certainly deserves a bit of happiness!"

Setting the hat aside for a moment, Phoebe filled her cup and began the story of how she'd met Annie Kenny the day after Annie, who was only eleven at the time, had decided to run away from the orphanage where she'd been left at birth.

Phoebe went on to describe how happily they'd worked together for years, what a special friendship they had, and how it was she who introduced Annie to her terribly shy but handsome brother who was a security guard at the mill.

Squinting to rethread her needle, Phoebe recounted painfully how her brother found Annie on his rounds one night, beaten, raped, and nearly dead with a head injury so severe that she was in a coma for weeks.

"I doubt he'll ever forgive himself. He still thinks if he'd done his rounds earlier . . ."

In a softer voice, she recalled how awful it had been to take Annie to the Sacred Heart Convent hospital in Brattleboro and leave her there because, even after months in the hospital, Annie still required specialized care. "So far away," Phoebe mused sadly, "and all alone.

"I'll never forget the day the letter arrived telling us that Annie was pregnant." Phoebe's voice caught in her throat. "Can you imagine? She was only fifteen!"

Rebecca was moved to tears; her face reflected the outrage and genuine sadness she felt for this young girl—someone she'd never even met.

"My God, how absolutely tragic," Rebecca said, "that poor, poor girl. And no family to help. I certainly hope the police caught her attacker?"

"No," Phoebe said sadly, carefully knotting her thread, "they never did."

"I can't even imagine how she endured. But isn't it marvelous, Phoebe, she's finally found happiness and with your brother!"

Because she had to concentrate so completely on each tiny stitch, Phoebe did not look up but offered her view. "Yes. But she's not the same girl anymore," she said sadly. "Before that happened, Annie was one of those people who grabbed life by the tail. Now she just seems to . . . I don't know . . . endure it."

Rebecca, who typically found silences a bit unnerving, asked, almost as an afterthought, "What happened to the child?"

"Well," Phoebe replied matter-of-factly without looking up, "Annie certainly couldn't raise a child then, could she? She was only fifteen. She had to give her up."

Snipping the last knot as close as she dared, Phoebe said proudly, "There, we're done!"

Although Phoebe hadn't heard her, Rebecca had gotten up from the couch and was standing at the front window, watching the pedestrian traffic.

"Lovely," Rebecca said, turning to look. "Would you wrap them separately, Phoebe? I need to be getting along. There's still so much to do before we leave for Rome."

"Of course," Phoebe replied, pulling two blue-and-white striped hatboxes from under the worktable along with a thick stack of tissue paper the color of cotton candy.

Meanwhile, Rebecca struggled to understand her sudden agitation. Had she forgotten something? There was definitely something troubling her out on the edge of her awareness, something shadowy and drifting.

Resolutely, she gathered her coat and gloves from the couch.

"The hats are marvelous," she said quietly. "Thank you for the tea, Phoebe, and those delicious cookies. I'm certain your friend's wedding will be lovely, and she certainly deserves to be happy."

With her head buzzing and her skin tingling, she felt as if she might be coming down with something, which, since they sailed for Rome in one week, only made Rebecca more nervous. Bending to retrieve her purse, Rebecca's arm stopped midair as a most appalling thought slipped into her consciousness and literally took her breath away.

In a tiny, slightly tremulous voice, she asked, "Where was she, by the way?"

"I'm sorry, Mrs. Wallabee"—Phoebe glanced up from the pink cloud of tissue paper—"what?"

"I asked what mill it was. Where your friend worked?"

"Oh," Phoebe replied, still trying to settle the first hat gently into its box, "the Troy."

Rebecca's usually erect posture collapsed under the weight of the name she feared most; she slid back onto the couch in a daze, her mind a hive of questions. Simultaneously, her hands felt numb and icy while her face felt scorched. Her stomach twisted and she quickly grabbed a handkerchief from her purse and pressed it tightly against her mouth.

Oblivious, Phoebe was carefully nesting the second hat into its box when the sound of the front door opening startled her.

"Sorry it took so long, Phee," a voice called from the foyer, "but I managed to pick up everything, even your dress! I'll just hang it here for now."

Moments later, flushed from exertion, Annie hurried in with a stack of gaily bundled packages in one hand and a small bag of groceries in the other.

"Oh Phee, wait till you see—" Annie stopped short. "Oh, I'm so sorry. I didn't mean to interrupt. Hello," she said, carefully resting her packages on the arm of the couch and extending her hand, "I'm Annie Kenny."

Rebecca would never forget how it felt to be staring into eyes that were a most unusual shade of blue—a shade she'd seen only once before—and to recognize the familiar auburn curls that, despite being carefully bobbed, flaunted their irrepressibility.

She tried to speak, her mouth opened and closed several times, but no sound came out. Instead, her face which had been crimson slowly paled to the color of chalk, and her eyes widened as if she'd seen a ghost.

Bewildered, Annie turned to Phee, hoping for an explanation, but, surprisingly, Phee seemed unable to speak as well. Fortunately, the awkward silence was obliterated by the hoarse, plaintive cry of a sick child.

"I'll get him," Annie said, dropping the groceries on the table and heading toward the bedroom. "I'm right here, Seth," she called out.

The early afternoon train rocked from side to side, which, on a different day, might have been soothing but today just seemed to make her tears more copious, and since she was alone, she made no attempt to rein them in.

As the conductor announced the Brattleboro station, Rebecca stepped into the washroom, splashed cold water on her puffy eyes, patted her face dry, and applied fresh powder and lipstick. She pulled her hat low across her forehead, grateful for the netting that would partially shield her face. Smoothing her skirt, she picked up her gloves and looped her purse over her elbow. She had no luggage; there hadn't been time.

Immobile on the platform, Rebecca had absolutely no idea what she'd say when she got there or even how she'd get there, but as she approached the ticket counter, she watched a taxi driver depositing a suitcase next to a well-dressed man who seemed in a rush to purchase his ticket.

Rebecca waited nearby, her head bowed, her heart racing.

"Can I help you, ma'am?" the driver asked, approaching her.

"The Sacred Heart Convent," she asked softly. "Is it far?"

"No, ma'am, just a few miles. I can have you there in a jiffy."

"Thank you," she replied so softly he barely heard her.

It was bigger than she supposed but not imposing. The front door opened almost immediately, and a young novice with a wide smile that lit up her freckled face asked, "May I help you?"

"I hope so," Rebecca said, trying to sound self-assured. "I'd like to see the person in charge."

"You must mean Mother Superior," replied the novice, smiling. "Do you have an appointment?"

Rebecca shook her head.

"Please, come in. May I bring you something to drink, a cool glass of water perhaps?"

"You're very kind but no thank you. I'm fine."

But even the young novice could see that Rebecca Wallabee was not fine.

Standing outside the closed door of Mother Superior's office, once again Rebecca felt horribly nauseous. She hadn't completely formulated a plan but knew that if she didn't act quickly, she would lose her nerve entirely.

She knocked forcefully and entered immediately without waiting for an invitation. "Mother Superior," she said a bit louder than she intended, "thank you so much for seeing me. No doubt you're very busy and I've come without an appointment, so thank you for taking the time."

"My name is Margaret Laurence," she lied. "I'm an only child and my mother recently passed. At the reading of her will, I learned that

I have a younger sister, and, according to my mother's executor, this girl, my sister, spent some time here in the hospital. As you might imagine, I'm desperate to find her. Just think after all these years alone, I have a sister!"

Mother Superior sat calmly listening to a well-dressed, obviously nervous, but nonetheless pleasant woman who had turned up, totally unannounced, looking for a sister she'd never met. *Well, this was a first!* she thought.

"Well, I don't know how I can help you, Mrs. Laurence. As you might imagine, our records are confidential since the young women who stay with us are usually pregnant. So . . ."

"You're saying that I might have a niece or nephew as well? How wonderful!" Rebecca interjected excitedly.

"No, Mrs. Laurence, I'm not saying that you have a niece or nephew since I don't know whether or not the girl you're looking for was ever here."

Refusing to be denied, Rebecca pushed on. "Her name is Anne Kenny and according to my mother's executor she was likely here between 1915 and 1916."

"Then I cannot be of any assistance," Mother Superior concluded definitively, "since I didn't come here until October of twenty-one, which, as it turned out, was the worst winter in the history of Vermont! I'll never forget it." She shook her head. "Not at all a pleasant beginning for me."

"Please, Mother, there must be someone here who knew my sister, perhaps even kept in touch with her? This is my only chance." She sounded so desperate, and indeed she was, but not for the reasons she'd given Mother Superior.

Pushing her intercom button, Mother spoke to someone on the other end. "Would you check on Sister Agnes? See if she's up to a visitor? I'll walk Mrs. Laurence back to the foyer and you can take her to Sister Agnes—but only if she's up to it. Thank you, Jean."

Back in the sitting room, Rebecca waited and paced until finally, a young novice, presumably Jean, stood in the doorway. "Sister Agnes will see you but she's not entirely well, so I must ask you not to wear her out. Please, follow me."

"Sister Agnes?" Rebecca asked the hunched black form slouched in a chair near a sunny window reciting her rosary.

"Yes, dear? How can I help you?" Her voice was fragile but clear.

"Mother Superior seemed to think that you knew a girl who stayed here several years ago. Her name was Anne Kenny. Did you know her?"

Sister Agnes shifted in her seat; her rheumy eyes gazed out the window for a long while. Finally, a contented smile lit up her weathered face. "Oh, yes," she said happily, "she used to help me in the kitchen. Lovely girl. How is she?"

"I'm afraid I don't know, Sister Agnes. I just learned that she's my sister, and all I know about her is that she stayed here some years back. I was hoping you might know how I might find her."

"Oh no, dear! I'm afraid I've no idea where she went."

"But you remember her being here?"

"Oh yes, clear as a bell. I taught her how to cook! She was quite a good little cook when she left. Just a tiny wisp of a thing when she arrived. Never talked much. Seemed terribly sad."

"Sister Agnes, was there anyone else who knew her well? Someone she might have kept in touch with."

"No, I'm sorry, dear. That was such a long time ago. My memory isn't what it once was. Though . . ." She sighed deeply and shook her head as if whatever she was trying to recall might somehow fall out from her jumbled memories.

"There was a young novice here at the time," she said slowly. "Yes, they seemed friendly, but I wouldn't know if they kept in touch."

"Oh, Sister Agnes," Rebecca pleaded, growing more desperate and more impatient, "what was her name?"

Two or three minutes passed in agonizing silence while Rebecca silently clenched and unclenched her fists, afraid to say or do anything that might interrupt Sister Agnes's train of thought. But as the minutes ticked by, she wasn't convinced that Sister Agnes was still trying to remember the novice's name and hadn't, as many elderly people do, slipped into some other place, some other time, some other memory.

"Riley! That's it, Helen Riley!" Sister Agnes beamed in triumph, though clearly the effort had drained her.

"Thank you. Thank you so much, Sister." Flooded with relief, Rebecca took Sister Agnes's hand and kissed it. "I'll leave you to rest now."

As promised, Jean was waiting in the parlor. "Any luck?" she asked.

"Oh, my yes! Can you take me to see Helen Riley, Jean?"

Looking perplexed, Jean replied, "There's no Helen Riley here, at least not that I know of. But if you'll take a seat, I'll go ask someone who might know."

Again, minutes seemed like hours as Rebecca waited and paced.

Jean reappeared with such a solemn look on her face that Rebecca assumed the worst.

"We don't usually give out such information, but Helen Riley was a novice here. She chose the name Sister James Miriam when she took her vows."

"And?"

"Sister James Miriam stayed on for only a few more months after Annie Kenny left, then revoked her vows and left the convent."

Rebecca was crestfallen, and her eyes filled with tears. She slumped into a chair and sobbed with exhaustion and frustration.

"Please, Mrs. Laurence," Jean cried, "I wasn't finished. When Helen Riley left here, she took a position at a local elementary school. As far as we know, she's still teaching there. I can run you over if you'd like."

Helen Riley, formerly Sister James Miriam, was sitting alone in the school's library, furiously grading papers with a red pencil, a steaming mug, and a plate of digestives untouched on the table beside her, disappointment on her round face.

Briefly, Jean explained why she'd brought Mrs. Laurence and then left the two of them alone.

"Ah yes," Helen said, sitting back in her chair, grateful for the respite. "Yes, Annie and I did become friends when she was here. But I haven't heard from her since she left—not that I thought I would. So I can't really help you on that score."

"Mother mentioned that she had a baby?"

"Yes, a little girl."

"Could you tell me what orphanage the baby was sent to? Perhaps they can help me locate Anne."

"Yes, well, that was a bit odd. Annie's baby didn't go to an orphanage, even though that was the convent's policy. Poor Annie! She was so conflicted about sending her child to an orphanage—she'd been left at one herself you know.

"Whenever I tried to raise the subject, Annie would clench her jaw and refuse to discuss it. To be honest, she came to us so broken, in pain, and terribly depressed that I was afraid to pressure her. Then one day some man came to the convent asking to see her—by name. If I recall correctly, she was six maybe seven months into her pregnancy by then.

"Anyway, it turned out he was a lawyer and left with Annie's signature on adoption papers! We were all shocked, but Annie looked relieved not to be sending her child to an orphanage. We never spoke about the baby again."

"Do you remember his name?"

"Who?"

"The lawyer who came to see Annie?"

"No, can't say that I do," she said, bringing her chair upright again. I really only spoke with him briefly but . . ."

Helen pushed back in her chair and stared at the ceiling, her eyes closed and her forehead furrowed. Finally, Helen smiled sheepishly. "But I do remember it had something to do with a boat or maybe water. I remember kidding him about it. I'm afraid I was a bit cheeky in those days."

"A boat?"

"I know it sounds awfully silly now, but that's all I remember. Sorry I can't be more helpful."

"Rowe?" Rebecca asked, forcing herself to say the name clearly. "Could his name have been Rowe?"

Helen's eyes widened in disbelief. "Oh my, yes, that was it! 'Row, row, row your boat!' You know like in the old nursery rhyme?"

The train ride back to Fall River was entirely different. Her heart galloped, her palms sweated, and her mouth was dry as toast—but not a single tear was shed. For a while, her thoughts whirled and twisted uncontrollably but gradually tapered until only a single, shocking thought remained—her father knew!

It's an unhinging revelation to discover that a beloved parent has intentionally betrayed his child—it's a narcissistic injury to the soul from which few children recover, and while it left Rebecca with an indescribable emptiness, it also stoked the fire of her fury.

Would it ever be possible, she wondered, to reclaim the self-reliance and self-confidence of the girl she had been when she graduated college, now a dim and distant memory. She'd been an A student, an astute reporter, one of very few women reporters, an accomplished violinist with a large circle of loyal friends. That was when life seemed full of beginnings and possibilities. It was embarrassing to recall the pieces of herself she'd forfeited so easily in her marriage.

And, yes, in hindsight, she'd absolutely had suspicions about her husband—his mysterious trips to New York and his convoluted explanations that never seemed completely believable. She remembered thinking, more than once, that he was lying and that he was having an affair, but she never confronted him.

More humiliating, she never questioned his out-of-the-blue interest in adoption, even though the reason he gave was patently false. In retrospect, she'd just wanted it to be true—she was so desperate for a child that she pretended to believe him.

Holding up the mirror of truth, she could see herself clearly. She was a foolish, romantic girl who had squandered her precious education and let herself be shaped into the passive, deferential, self-sacrificing woman that her mother had always crusaded against. Rebecca flushed with shame.

By the time the train pulled into the station, she'd decided to leave her marriage, the web of Calvin's lies, and, despite the inevitable social repercussions, she would divulge the secret that her husband had spent years concealing.

Arriving at her parents' home in the evening, Rebecca barged into her father's study hatless, face flushed, almost vibrating with agitation.

Margaret Rowe, sixty-five, sat nearest the door, reading. Apart from gaining twenty pounds over the years, nothing about her had changed. Franklin Rowe was seated across the room, writing at his desk, an open briefcase overflowing with legal documents on the floor and his nightly snifter of brandy in hand.

"Rebecca, darling!" cried Margaret, clumsily removing her wire-rimmed glasses. "What a lovely surprise, we weren't expecting you. Have you had dinner? Shall I—"

"No." Rebecca's tone silenced her mother mid-sentence. It was at once contemptuous and suggested, correctly, that she was barely holding herself in check.

"Is something wrong, Rebecca?" her father asked, looking up. "You seem—"

"I seem what, Father?" she asked icily.

It wasn't just her tone that unnerved him, although it did make the hairs at the back of his neck stand up. It was the loathing in her eyes that immediately filled him with dread.

"You knew, didn't you? All along . . . you both knew?"

"Knew what, dear?" her mother asked, genuinely puzzled by such obtuse questions. "Franklin?" She turned to face her husband. "What's going on? Why is our daughter so upset? Did you say something?"

Rebecca's laughter teetered on the narrow edge of hysteria, but she managed to pull herself back. "No, it wasn't anything he said, Mother. It was something he did. When he arranged for us to adopt Gwendolyn, he knew full well that she was Calvin's illegitimate daughter."

Margaret blinked several times, quite certain that she'd misheard her daughter.

"Rebecca, dear, I don't understand. How could Gwendolyn have been . . ."

"Do you want to tell her, Father?"

"Rebecca, please. Let me try to explain," her father pleaded. "Calvin came to me. He was desperate for my help. I didn't think I could refuse him."

"Would someone please tell me what's happened?" Margaret exclaimed, having become quite annoyed with both of them.

"It's about Calvin," Franklin told his wife, standing, removing his suit jacket, and placing it neatly over the back of his chair. "He'd gotten someone pregnant and came to me wanting to adopt the child without the mother knowing."

"Oh," replied Margaret, although her husband's explanation only exacerbated her confusion.

"No," Rebecca scoffed, "Calvin didn't just get someone pregnant, did he, Father? He raped someone!"

"I didn't know that, Rebecca!" Franklin asserted boldly. "How could I have known such a thing? I just handled the legal end of things . . . the paperwork and such."

"Liar!" Rebecca screamed at him.

"Rebecca! Please calm yourself," Margaret said firmly. "Your father's trying to explain . . . something."

"Rebecca, I was trying to help your husband out of a mess he'd gotten into. I was trying to protect you!"

"Ah! You were trying to protect me! When you learned that my husband had impregnated another woman while married to me, you didn't think I deserved to know?"

For the life of him, Franklin couldn't find the right words, and although he had known this day might come, he hadn't prepared. His thoughts tumbled as he desperately considered one explanation after another but could not find a single one that would exonerate him, so he simply stared at her.

"You knew Calvin raped that girl and beat her nearly to death."

"No!" Franklin protested, slamming his fist on his desk. "I absolutely did not know that, Rebecca," he shouted. "He didn't tell me that. How could I have known?" He sat back in his chair like a balloon deflating.

"When you met her, of course! When you traveled to the Convent of the Sacred Heart to do my husband's bidding. You asked for her by name. She was just a child, only fifteen!

"Somehow, you tricked her into signing adoption papers. Perhaps you told her some story about a loving couple who couldn't have children. Good people who would save her poor child from life in an orphanage.

"You let me bring that infant into my home to raise as my own. You said nothing. You knew I was married to a rapist and you said nothing. And now you want me to believe you did all this to protect me?"

Margaret turned to her husband. Surely, he would deny such unthinkable accusations. But he didn't.

"I'm going home now," Rebecca said, facing her father, "to confront my loving husband. But rest assured, Father, I will never forget what you did and will never see you again. I will despise you for the rest of my life."

Rebecca stormed out, leaving behind the furious rustling of petticoats and the contemptuous clip of heels on their marble floor.

Margaret slumped in her chair. Never had she seen her daughter so unhinged, but what she'd accused her father of was simply impossible, absolutely unthinkable.

"Franklin?" she asked fearfully, total incomprehension on her face. Stunned, she watched as he cradled his head in his hands and began to sob.

"Oh Margaret, I didn't mean . . . I didn't . . . please don't think . . ."

"It was you who encouraged our child to marry this boy, this son of your friend," she said curtly as she stood to her full height. "And when you found out how utterly despicable he was, you didn't rush over there and drag our daughter back. Instead, you chose to help him to betray her?"

She heard only a muffled moan. "Answer me!" she screamed.

"What else could I have done, Margaret? Expose Calvin? Report him to the police? Watch our daughter's reputation be ruined along with his? Become part of the scandal ourselves? I was trying to protect her."

"That's a lie!" Margaret screamed just as her daughter had done minutes before. "You did this because you hadn't the courage to do what was right. And you've been telling yourself that pathetic lie ever since. I suppose when you're rich enough or arrogant enough, you feel entitled to take such liberties with the truth. Your daughter knew it was a lie as soon as you uttered it—and so do I.

"You will leave this house tonight," Margaret told him. "And don't you dare call Calvin to warn him before our daughter gets there. Perhaps your good friend, Samuel, will take you in. I'm assuming he's known all along about your deception?"

Franklin's head snapped up, and, from the stark panic on his face, she understood then that Samuel Wallabee was, as she had been all these years, in the dark. She felt truly sorry for Samuel because, at nearly seventy-nine, he was about to learn something that no parent would ever want to know about their child.

As the years passed, Calvin had become secure in the belief that his ugly past was securely hidden. And the price he'd paid was formidable. He had to surrender every dream, every aspiration he'd ever had in order to remake himself, and in the end, he'd had to abandon everything and everyone he loved.

It was not an easy transformation, but he succeeded in becoming an adoring and doting father to Gwendolyn, an attentive, thoughtful husband to Rebecca, and a tireless crusader for better working conditions in the mills.

However, as his wife exploded through the door of his study, her face contorted in rage, hurling accusations at him so forcefully that her spittle exploded with every ugly word—"Rapist! Betrayer! Liar!"—he realized it had been a false sense of security.

She came at him like a raging storm, howling and pummeling him, wave after wave, until she was spent, and at the end, everything he thought he'd earned, every hope he'd had for redemption—vanished.

Rebecca took refuge in her bedroom; bolting the door, shutting off all sources of light, and curling into a fetal position. Her mind stumbled and tripped again and again over the same questions, unable to answer any of them.

She bitterly regretted accepting the life her parents had chosen for her without ever correcting their assumption that she wanted it as well. Why hadn't she? And why hadn't she ever objected when time and time again Calvin's decisions limited her and denied her access to opportunities and experiences that she craved?

It became painfully clear now that her present situation was her fault, and her life at this very moment, curled up on her bed, was truly the product of her own decisions. She wondered if anyone else had ever been so utterly ashamed and disappointed with their choices. It was she who'd sacrificed her own ambitions and dreams, she who'd dutifully accommodated so often the expectations of others that she had lost herself and lost her way. No matter how she measured it, she was a failure.

Surreptitiously, Calvin had begun filling his briefcase with documents from his office, then packed suitcases for himself and Gwendolyn. He called for his car to be brought round and instructed that the suitcases be stowed in the trunk and the blankets arranged along the back seat.

At two in the morning, he gently roused his daughter, who wrapped her thin arms around his neck as he carried her quietly to the car, thankful that, although she mumbled, she did not fully wake. Like a thief in the night, he drove away, leaving his distraught wife alone. He had no choice. He had to protect his daughter—she was the only thing he had left.

Negotiating his car through the damp, blustery May morning that ripped wet leaves off trees and plastered them onto the slick roads,

Calvin returned two days after spiriting his daughter away in the middle of the night.

He ran straight up to Rebecca's bedroom, but he'd waited too long. She looked as peaceful as a sleeping toddler curled up on her bed, her pale face emptied of all rage, her hair fanned across her pillow, a thin blanket tucked under her feet, an empty pill bottle in her hand.

Suddenly, he began pacing, his terrible grief and guilt momentarily pushed aside by an inexplicable rage. How could she have done such a thing? He would never have thought her capable of such selfishness. She had chosen to do something that would shame and punish them all, that would leave an innocent girl with a dreadful, scarring legacy.

Given the social prominence of both families, the obituary in the *Providence Daily Journal* was oddly brief:

> *May 9, 1927: Rebecca Elizabeth Wallabee, 37, daughter of Franklin and Margaret Rowe of Providence, Rhode Island, died yesterday at her Fall River residence after a short illness. She is survived by her husband, Calvin Wallabee, and her eleven-year-old daughter, Gwendolyn Elizabeth.*

Nearly half a decade would pass before Gwendolyn would tragically stumble upon the truth about her mother's death.

Two months later, on a muggy July afternoon, after visiting her only child's grave in the plot beside her own parents, Margaret Rowe stood in what had once been her daughter, Rebecca's favorite room, which, because the lights were turned off and the drapes tightly drawn, was layered with gloom and the stale air of loss.

Eventually, growing accustomed to the dark, she could see a huddled shape on the chaise—a gaunt, hollow man who looked more like the unhealthy, unbalanced homeless men she sometimes passed on the street rather than the successful businessman he'd once been.

Hollowed-eyed, Calvin stared unblinkingly at the two side-by-side paintings of lavender and poppies on the wall nearest him as if they were lifelines to the solace of a cherished memory. She waited in silence.

She'd taken no delight in learning that Calvin's parents had completely disowned him once they learned what he'd done or that Samuel Wallabee had suffered a massive stroke and was completely bedridden with little hope of recovery.

Clutching an empty bourbon bottle, Calvin felt the subtle movement of air across his bare feet. "Who's there?" he called out, his voice gravelly and tentative.

"Calvin," she replied, coming closer, her voice measured and cool, "I've just sent Gwendolyn off to school with Nanny Bernadette."

He stared blankly, unable to comprehend why she of all people was standing before him, the man who'd killed her daughter.

"Except for Gwendolyn," Margaret continued, "I've lost everyone I loved. I cannot imagine ever forgiving you, but I cannot let Gwendolyn be lost to me as well.

"She is the only thing that unites us," she said slowly, as if forming her thoughts took tremendous energy. "Ensuring her happiness, protecting her as much as possible from the scandals you've created are all that's left me."

"Why would you..."

"It was entirely too easy to blame you for everything," Margaret said sadly, her voice catching in her throat. "My daughter left unfinished business and questions I shall never find answers to. She was always an ideal daughter and, in my opinion, a loving mother, and yet what she did was unspeakably cruel. I cannot stop thinking that I failed her in some way, that I should have done something more the night I learned the truth.

"But you needn't worry. I will never reveal the truth to Gwendolyn. I will raise her as my daughter would have wanted. And you, Calvin, will be an exemplary father. You will pull yourself together. I don't care how. You will return to work and I will take over the running of this house."

He stared at her as if she were an apparition until Margaret strode across the room, grabbed the empty bottle from his hand, and threw it into the fireplace.

As it shattered, she said, "Starting right now, I will live here. I will be here when Gwendolyn goes to and returns from school every day. She and I will spend time together until you return from work. Dinner will be served at the usual time. This house and everyone in it will return to normal."

"Margaret . . ." he stammered. "I—"

"Stop!" she shouted in a voice reserved for small misbehaving children. "We will never discuss this again."

And for the next five years, they never did. Like most wounds, scabs formed, fragile at first, but over time sturdy enough to hide what was underneath. Together, Calvin and Margaret cobbled together a facsimile of a normal family, but there was always something missing. Even Gwendolyn felt it in the dense silence between them.

Calvin recommitted himself to raising his daughter, making her the center of his world, attending ballet and music recitals, helping to organize her yearly birthday parties, and spending summers with her at their beach cottage.

Margaret provided a woman's perspective on the social customs and behaviors expected of young ladies her age, but most importantly, she held Gwendolyn tightly whenever she was frightened, soothed her when she was upset, and encouraged her when her confidence wavered.

The custom of using a girl's sixteenth birthday to mark her transition from girlhood to womanhood had its beginnings in the Deep South, but genteel northern families also adopted it, referring to it as the girl's "coming-of-age"—the day that launched their daughters into high society and signaled their availability for marriage.

Not surprisingly, the preparations for Gwendolyn's sixteenth birthday party were elaborate, and although the January day was quite cold, there was no snow in the forecast. Sitting in front of the fire that afternoon, Gwendolyn seemed unusually quiet.

"You seem especially pensive, dear," Margaret prodded.

"I'm missing my mother, Mimi. Don't misunderstand," she pleaded, "I love you to pieces and don't know what I'd have done without you."

"This is a very special day, dear girl, and of course you wish your mother could be here to share it with you. I miss her too and especially today. You remind me of her in so many ways."

"Oh, Mimi," cried Gwendolyn, hugging her grandmother fiercely, "I wish you'd tell me more about my mother. Father only tells me stories about where they met and things we all did when I was a baby."

"Yes, well," Margaret replied pensively, "I suppose some things are just too painful to talk about. Losing a child or a spouse is one of those things." Margaret's eyes brimmed with tears.

"Well," she said, standing and brushing the wrinkles from her skirt, "I should see to the floral arrangements. I see that their truck has arrived."

"Oh, Gwenie, how absolutely stunning you look!" Margaret said, entering her granddaughter's room as the guests began to arrive downstairs.

Gwendolyn stood in front of a mirror. Her violet organza gown had turned her blue eyes into the smoky, purple-blue of the lilacs that lined their driveway every spring. It was an off-the-shoulder couture garment with gossamer capped sleeves, a full skirt, and none of the ruffles or fussy things that she hated.

Unexpectedly, she looked taller; her long, auburn hair had been loosely plaited and held in place by several dazzling emerald clips, a few soft ringlets framed her face, and a tiny comb held a bouquet of violets over her right ear.

"Thank you for letting me choose this dress, Mimi. I know you weren't crazy about it, but I just love it!"

Beaming, Margaret handed her a small, blue-velvet jewelry box. "These were your mother's," Margaret said simply. "She wore them on her wedding day."

"Oh, Mimi! Aren't they gorgeous?" Gwendolyn cried. "Are these real diamonds and emeralds?"

"Well of course, dear child! Would I have saved them if they weren't?"

Margaret watched with mixed emotions as Gwendolyn, who'd turned in order to face the mirror, gently positioned each earring, then tilted her head from side to side to see the light bounce off the dangling stones—exactly as Rebecca had done on the morning of her wedding.

Sensing that something was wrong, Gwendolyn turned to see a profound sadness etched on her grandmother's heavily lined face, tears welling in the corners of her eyes.

"Oh, Mimi, what's wrong?" she asked fearfully.

"It's nothing, dear," Margaret replied with the wave of her hand. "I'm just a foolish old woman thinking about things that happened a long time ago. Now," she said, shaking her head as if to rid herself of those memories, "I should go down and check that everything is as it should be. I'll come back when it's time for you to make your grand entrance."

Standing at the top of the stairs, Margaret and Gwendolyn were dazzled by the beauty of the scene below them. A lavish garland interwoven with iridescent pink bittersweet, alabaster hydrangeas, and dainty pink pansies edged the banisters of the marvelous double staircase. Eight-foot candelabras stood on either side of the bottom stairs, illuminating urns overflowing with mounds of ivory damask roses and bundles of Spanish lavender. Identical combinations of candelabras and urns were positioned in front of mirrors around the entire perimeter of the room, which turned it into a dazzling mirrored ballroom.

As Gwendolyn descended the staircase, slowly and deliberately the way she and Mimi had practiced dozens of times, she looked quite regal. Surprisingly, when she reached the last stair, she flashed a triumphant smile, and her guests applauded her perfect entrance.

Throughout the evening as he stood on the perimeter, Calvin was totally unprepared for how powerfully the rich aroma of the lavender, as if a custodian of memories, transported him back to Siena—the place that opened him to passion and desire. The place that unearthed and nurtured his talent and gave him the courage to be who he was.

Despite decades of resignation, repression, and blatant denial, his pertinacious yearning for those magical years in Siena had incredulously survived. No memories were more cherished or more indelible than the sweetness of Paulo's kisses, the gentleness of his touch despite callused hands that always smelled faintly of turpentine, and the rhythm of their bodies under pale yellow moons and millions of glittering stars.

But this was his life now—alone, standing in the doorway of an opulent ballroom ribboned with flickering candles and lush floral arrangements. A room swollen with jeweled, moneyed, self-important guests. In disgust, he emptied his tumbler in one gulp and signaled the waiter for a refill.

This was never the life he wanted. Siena had taught him that, but the bold dreams and plans of those heady years were gone, leaving him to live, if one could call it that, someplace between memories and regret.

"Oh, Mimi," Gwendolyn gushed, "what a lovely night! Honestly, I wasn't looking forward to it. I thought I'd be too nervous to really enjoy myself, but I was wrong! Thanks so much. It was a perfect birthday!"

"You're very welcome, my dear."

"You look so tired, Mimi."

"I am dear," she replied, wearily lifting the comforter so Gwendolyn could slide into bed. But in truth, she was more anxious than tired.

Before her daughter died, Rebecca left a letter in Margaret's care and asked that it be given to Gwendolyn on her sixteenth birthday. Of course, Margaret saved the letter and intended to carry out Rebecca's wishes, but now indecisiveness scraped against her. Was this really the right thing to do?

In the end, she decided that regardless of the outcome, this had been her only daughter's last request and she, Margaret, was duty-bound to honor it.

"There is one last surprise, dear girl. Before your mother died, she asked me to give you this letter on your sixteenth birthday. I'm sure she felt such sadness knowing she would miss such an important day in your life, and I'm certain this was her way of sharing the day with you, at least in spirit. Perhaps you should read it in the morning when you're more rested."

"I understand, Mimi. I'm pretty tired. Thanks again for everything."

"Well then, I'll kiss you goodnight, dear girl, and wish you sweet dreams."

Snuggling more deeply under her comforter, Gwendolyn yawned and stretched.

Reaching to turn out the lamp, she noticed the envelope on the night table. Perhaps Mimi was right that it would be better to save it for the morning—like another present. Unfortunately, patience had never been her strong suit.

May 8, 1927

My dearest Gwendolyn,

I hope with all my heart that this day, your very special day, was, despite my absence, as beautiful as you have always deserved.

I'm sure you've been told by now that when your father and I learned that we couldn't have children, we adopted you, my darling girl, within days of your birth. I wanted to tell you about the adoption so many times but was always cautioned to wait at least until you were a little older.

What I just learned, however, is not something I can keep from you. Gwendolyn, I feel duty bound to tell you that your father is, in fact, your biological father, who forced himself on a mill girl younger than you are today.

You may judge me harshly, but I can never forgive him. I am tormented by what he did. As far as I'm concerned, there is no way for him to atone for his brutality and deception, but God will be the final judge.

I sit here humiliated and disgraced. I know I am flawed, but I cannot look at you without being reminded of what he did—to me, to you, and to your fifteen-year-old mother.

My darling Gwendolyn, I love you and have since the moment you were placed into my arms. My only option is to leave you and pray that someday you might understand and forgive me.

Rebecca

Wide awake now and determined to get to the bottom of this, she strode into her father's study. He was standing in front of the fireplace, his back to the door.

"What is this?" Gwendolyn demanded, shaking the letter at him. "Since when am I adopted?"

"What in the world's wrong now, Gwenie?" he shouted, his frustration and emotional exhaustion getting the better of him.

The raised voices alerted Margaret, who hurried downstairs to find Calvin standing at the fireplace flushed, wild-eyed, barely able to stand. She thought he was drunk.

"What in God's name is going on here?" Margaret demanded, striding through the open doorway, cinching her robe.

"You told her!" Calvin exclaimed, pointing an accusatory finger at her, his fury barely suppressed.

"I most certainly did not!"

"I'm adopted, Mimi! It's here in this letter," Gwendolyn shouted petulantly, snatching the letter from her father's hand and giving it to her grandmother.

"Oh my God," Margaret moaned, eyeing the familiar blue stationary. Her mind stumbled and careened as she struggled to understand what her daughter, Rebecca, had done. Her own daughter! Unimaginable.

"Is it true?" asked Gwendolyn.

"Yes," Margaret whispered miserably, collapsing into a nearby chair. "Truly, Gwendolyn, I had no idea," she said sorrowfully. "If I had, I would never have given you her letter."

Wrapping her arms tightly around her chest, Margaret began to rock as shame, utter disbelief, and grief settled on her face.

"How did she die?" Gwendolyn asked. "She wasn't ill, was she?"

"No," her father admitted.

"She said that she found out you had betrayed her. Did she kill herself?"

"Yes," Calvin whispered.

"So, it's true what her letter says? And how did she find out? Did you tell her, Mimi?"

"No, dear, I never knew. I knew you were adopted, of course. But I didn't know what your father had done or that your grandfather had helped him until Rebecca told me."

"So that's why grandfather went away?"

"Yes, I couldn't stand to look at him after what he did."

"So, I'm adopted. Somehow you tricked Mother into adopting me but hid the fact that I was really your daughter. Somehow she found out the truth and killed herself because she couldn't stand to look at me anymore."

"No, Gwenie!" Calvin protested. "No! Your mother loved you. Please let me—"

But she wouldn't let him because once trust is broken, it can never be repaired. That door is forever closed.

"What kind of man are you?" she asked, disgust rising off her like dampness off a lake.

"Everything I believed about myself . . . everything you told me about my family. . . all of it was a lie."

The silence that followed was horrifying and deafening.

Gwendolyn ran from the room, stomped up the stairs, and, forgetting caution, furiously slammed her bedroom door, the sound reverberating back at them like a slap in the face.

"Well, Margaret," Calvin said sarcastically, "you've finally taken your revenge. Get out! I want you out by the morning. I don't care where you go."

Dazed and needing both arms of the chair to help her stand, Margaret managed to leave the study without collapsing. Somehow, though she had no memory of it, she ended up in her bedroom, wrapped in a blanket, sobbing and staring into the pitch-black, starless night. Just before dawn, she heard a light tapping on her door followed by a whispered, "Mimi."

Margaret shuffled to the door, eyes red and swollen, face mottled, and opened it, allowing Gwendolyn to quickly slip inside.

"I need your help, Mimi," she said, gasping for breath. "Take me with you. I hate him and I hate my mother. You're all I have. Please, Mimi, you've got to help me."

About an hour later, Margaret with Gwendolyn in tow stood in the doorway of Calvin's study. He was sitting in the same chair with his head in his hands, and from the look of him, he'd not slept either.

"What are you still doing here?" he asked, his voice as cold and unforgiving as his eyes. Then he noticed Gwendolyn, who was standing behind Margaret, wearing a coat and hat.

"Where do you think you're going, Gwendolyn?"

"She's coming with me, Calvin."

"No, she's certainly not going anywhere with you! I forbid it!"

"Yes, I am," Gwendolyn declared curtly. "I never want to see you again. I hate you!"

"Please, Gwenie, let me try to explain what happened."

"No!"

"She's my daughter, Margaret. I'll fight you on this."

"No, you won't because if you do, it'll all come out—the whole sordid story. And as much as I would like the world to know the kind of man you are, your disgrace will tarnish Gwendolyn as well, and neither you nor I want that to happen."

"Where will you go?" he asked bitterly, his face a picture of searing pain.

"I'm not sure at the moment. But out of respect for my granddaughter's wishes, you will never be welcome there."

21

FORGIVENESS LOST

It was Mimi who saved her by spiriting her out of the country when she was sixteen, and it was Mimi who brought her back to Fall River in March 1940. At twenty-five, Gwendolyn buried her beloved Mimi in the Rowe family plot in Rhode Island, where thirteen years earlier Mimi had buried her own daughter, Rebecca.

Gwendolyn promised to follow her grandmother's instructions to the letter and she did. There was no religious service, no notice appeared in any newspaper, and, except for the minister, she was the only person standing watch at the grave.

A week after the funeral, she arranged to meet Alfred Burrows, Esq., Mimi's attorney for almost thirty years, and learned to her complete surprise that Mimi had been a woman of significant means.

When Mimi's husband, Franklin, passed—an event she never mentioned—his considerable assets, since they never divorced, were left to Mimi, who, for her own reasons, had no interest in them and had put them all in trust for her granddaughter. Upon Mimi's death, Gwendolyn became the beneficiary of that trust and her grandmother's surprisingly sizable estate as well.

"I don't know what to say, Mr. Burrows," Gwendolyn admitted, her face dull with grief, her eyelids swollen as much from lack of sleep as from crying. "I really had no idea Mimi was so wealthy."

"Margaret was my dear friend for many years," he said, trying to offer some comfort, "and she spoke of you often, Gwendolyn, with immense pride."

"And I'm so grateful to you for arranging our transport back from Paris and for taking care of all the funeral arrangements," Gwendolyn replied, trying to steady her emotions. "I really don't know what to do now," she confided in a hoarse whisper.

"It will be a hard time for a while, dear girl, I won't lie to you. The best advice I can offer would be to avoid making any big decisions right now. Perhaps there's a place that holds a few happy memories for you? You might consider going there, where you can grieve in private and take time before deciding what your next step might be."

After several months, Gwendolyn decided to settle permanently in the small coastal town of Ocean Grove, Massachusetts, where a few wide-set summer bungalows with shady porches remained scattered among the dazzling white sand dunes. Built at the turn of the century, the beach abutting them was private property, so the annual influx of summer tourists would never disturb the residents.

She selected the only cottage built on a spit of land facing the ocean, and, like most of the remaining bungalows, it needed considerable renovation. Determined not to change the original footprint, she had a foundation added and every exterior wall doubly insulated. Every window was replaced, the plumbing was updated, and central heating was added so she could live there year-round.

The original stone fireplace, the wide-plank flooring, and the hand-hewn ceiling beams were saved. The only major renovation was to the kitchen, where newer appliances and additional storage space were desperately needed. Finally, a small loft studio with sky lights was added above the living room.

Combining furniture from Mimi's old house, which had been in storage for the last thirteen years, with a few pieces Gwendolyn had shipped back from their lovely Paris apartment, the cottage became a curious amalgamation of Queen Anne and Art Deco—the end result, a total redefinition of "beach bungalow."

In Mimi's storage, Gwendolyn discovered a silver-framed photograph of her grandmother in her early twenties, which she lovingly placed on the mantel next to the framed photograph of the two of them standing near the Eiffel Tower.

More than any other event in her life, the death of her grandmother shattered her. Weeks passed when she didn't leave the cottage because even the smallest decision overwhelmed her. Days passed when she didn't get off the sofa even to prepare a meal or when she stayed in bed without bothering to get dressed. Memories haunted her.

Slowly, silently her apathy and lethargy lightened with the greening of the dune grasses the following spring. As she swept out the sand that had breached even the new doors and windows, pulled down the cobwebs of hibernating spiders, and draped winter blankets over the porch railing to air, she knew with certainty that she would endure just as Mimi always had.

Finally, she began painting the things she loved—the glove of fog that rolled off the ocean at dusk, the early-morning dew beaded like pearl necklaces on the dune grasses, and the curious flotsam that washed up after raging storms. She loved the feel of things at the ocean's edge, the coarse, damp sand under her feet, the nuzzle of cool morning mist, the tangy edge of salty air that she imagined came from faraway, wondrous places.

The artist's solitary life suited her perfectly. Anonymously, and without fear of reprisal, she could release onto each canvas small scraps of the suffering she'd always concealed. It was from this place that her incredibly moving paintings were birthed—opaque, muted, swirling with emotion.

The life she chose was predictable and steady until she received notice of her father's death in March 1948. She had absolutely no curiosity about her father or his passing, but she could not avoid his lawyer's repeated insistence that they meet.

Despite his new client's indifference, he was relieved to have secured her cooperation but modulated his confidence because there was still a chance, a very real chance, she wouldn't come.

George Brownley, fifty-five, had been Calvin Wallabee's attorney for the past fourteen years. When they met, Calvin was fifty-four and physically still a lithe, agile man with close-cropped, curly, graying hair and a neat auburn goatee just starting to gray.

When Calvin turned sixty-eight, his health severely declined and he asked George to prepare a will. This was the first time George learned of a daughter named Gwendolyn—a daughter whom Calvin hadn't seen or heard from in fifteen years.

"I'll leave finding her up to you, George," was all Calvin said by way of explanation.

Finding her, informing her of her father's death, and getting her to agree to a meeting took George eight and a half months. She tentatively agreed to meet him here this December afternoon. She was late.

From the front door sidelight, George watched as a 1941 two-door Chevy with gleaming chrome and spotless whitewalls pulled up to the curb. A full minute passed before a woman got out, leaned against the passenger door, lit a cigarette, and stared grim-faced at one of the upstairs windows as if she expected to see someone there.

At thirty-two, she was unmarried and an artist, though neither decision had been easy. That she was unmarried, whether by choice or misfortune, seemed to make people wary, as if she were defective or had a contagious disease. Harder still was her decision to pursue art when nursing and teaching were far more respectable occupations for women. But despite occasional loneliness, she had no regrets.

Meeting her for the first time, people generally commented on the color of her eyes because they were not a shade of blue that was easily described. The second thing she was sure people noticed was her hair, although most were too polite to comment on the wildly tangled, reddish-brown curls which she pulled back with a headband or hid under a scarf.

She dressed simply, as she had this afternoon, in navy blue, wide-legged cuffed trousers, a pale blue cardigan, and loafers.

With relief, George watched her stub out her cigarette and start up the walk. Despite being angular and tall like her father, she moved with a suppleness and fluidity that was lovely to watch.

"Thank you for agreeing to meet me here today, Miss Wallabee," he said, stepping aside so she could enter.

"I understand you have some papers that require my signature, Mr. Brownley," she replied tersely, "but as I told you on the telephone, I really would have preferred to meet in your office."

"Yes, you said that on the phone, Miss Wallabee. I tried to explain that as sole beneficiary—"

"And, as I told *you*, Mr. Brownley," she interrupted, "I want you to sell everything!"

By now, George had become familiar with her flashes of anger, which were an undercurrent in every conversation he'd had with her, but he decided to shrug it off.

"Because you haven't been here for many years, I wanted to be certain there was nothing you wanted to keep or perhaps give away before putting the contents up for auction."

Pacified, at least momentarily, Gwendolyn brushed past him into the grand hall. As if it were yesterday, she saw herself playing on the colorful oriental carpets. On the staircase to the second-floor rooms, her impatience got the better of her, and again her anger flashed.

"Look, Mr. Brownley, I really don't want to traipse through every single room in this house. I will sign whatever is required in order for you to sell everything at auction."

Nearly at the top of the stairs, George Brownley stopped abruptly and sighed heavily. He was, finally, out of patience. "As you wish," he replied a bit more stiffly than he'd intended.

As they started back down, he decided to try one more time. "And do you wish to keep any of the paintings?"

Gwendolyn grimaced, dramatically rolling her eyes at the dusty portraits of strangers that lined the walls. "God, no! I can't imagine keeping any of these!"

"I'm sorry, Miss Wallabee, I didn't mean these," George replied with more condescension and smugness than he knew he should. "I meant any of the other paintings."

"What other paintings?" she asked, stopping abruptly.

"The ones in your father's studio."

"My father's studio?"

"Yes, on the third floor."

"The third floor?"

Gwendolyn turned and took the stairs two at a time. She couldn't recall the house even having a third floor when she lived here, and she was absolutely certain there had never been a studio!

She shoved open the door at the end of the second floor hallway, climbed a few stairs and immediately had to shield her eyes from the thick slabs of sunlight pouring in from skylights which helped warm the room. This must have been the attic, she thought.

Four easels held canvases of various sizes and in varying stages of completion, and although she'd never been in this room before, there was an eerie familiarity about it. The smells of linseed oil and turpentine, the sight of palettes flecked with dried paint piled in a corner, tubes of paint scattered on a table—some full but others squeezed paper-thin—it looked and smelled like her own studio.

But it was the sheer number of paintings propped against every wall and the colors—bold, audacious, and defiant—that left her mute.

"These are my father's?" she asked, finally finding her voice.

"Yes, miss."

"And when did my father take up painting?"

"It is my understanding that your father trained at the Accademia in Siena, Italy just after completing university. He wouldn't have even been twenty-five then, so quite a bit younger than yourself, miss. I understand that you are an artist as well."

"Yes, but my father wasn't," she insisted. "He managed textile mills. He did not paint. He was not an artist. I would have known if he were an artist."

This, she thought . . . all of this . . . was impossible. In the first place, this could not be his work. Her father was not this fearless . . . or unrestrained. This was the work of a nonconformist, an audacious risk-taker, someone who bore no resemblance to her father and, in fact, was the antithesis of her father.

"If you don't mind, Mr. Brownley, I'd like you to leave. I'll show myself out when I'm finished."

"As you wish," he replied, handing her a set of keys.

Sitting cross-legged on the floor studying a group of nearby canvases, she finally picked one up and balanced it across her knees. As much as she wanted to look away, she couldn't. For the first time in sixteen years—Mimi's death being the only exception—a giant tear rolled silently down her cheek and plopped onto the canvas, followed by another and another until she was forced to wipe her eyes and nose with the sleeve of her cardigan.

Gwendolyn stared at the little girl whose clear, blue eyes were wide with excitement, whose curls were in complete disarray, her skinny legs running at full tilt with outstretched arms. That little girl was a blur of movement, enthusiasm, and happiness.

There was no one else in the painting, no hint of who or what the girl was running toward, but Gwendolyn knew instantly and her heart ached for the knowing. Gently, she laid the painting aside.

On another canvas, an elegantly dressed woman stood behind a terra-cotta pot bursting with red geraniums, shielding her eyes from the sun while surveying a well-tended perennial garden that was a pandemonium of colors and textures. Although the woman's face was completely hidden, Gwendolyn recognized the violet dress and the gold bracelet her mother always wore and sometimes even let her play with.

Her father's studio was a family album—reality one step removed. Painting after painting chronicled their lives together, not just the early years when they were a real family, but the years after her mother's death as well.

She found bundles of beach scenes: a two-year-old toddling along a curved stretch of sand wearing a bright pink bathing suit, lugging a bucket half-filled with shells or sitting on the sand, shovel in hand, surrounded by at least a dozen sand castles.

Against another wall were a cluster of winter scenes: a girl in a pink snowsuit, standing on tiptoes with a bright orange carrot in her mittened hand, smiling at the snowman beside her who wore a decidedly, off-kilter bowler hat.

Or a six-year-old laughing gleefully, her nose and cheeks as pink as her snowsuit, while her mother in a long fur coat with a blazing red scarf around her neck pulled her through the snow on a shiny red sled.

But the largest painting stood alone, taking up almost one third of the last wall. It was a full-length portrait of her on her sixteenth birthday wearing her lilac gown, every detail captured exactly as it had been, including the sparkling emerald clips in her hair and her mother's shimmering diamond earrings. She was luminous, lit from behind, descending a lavish staircase. This was his final painting. He had nothing left.

He'd never once painted himself. Never once put himself in a painting, as if afraid or ashamed to show his face. Despite his use of brilliant color, a palpable longing whispered off every canvas. With so much obvious talent and passion, she wondered why her father had given up painting. It was inconceivable that he would choose instead to work in filthy mills. How could he have ever been happy there?

Despite being melancholic, her own canvases were as ostentatiously dramatic and emotionally charged as his. While her work was brooding and funereal and his canvases were sumptuously colorful and buoyant, it was not difficult for her to spot the shared undertone of remorse in their work.

She'd never forgotten that he'd tried to explain, but she'd refused to listen, preferring to harbor her anger. In exasperation, just a few months before she died, Mimi chastised her: "You need to find a way to forgive him, Gwendolyn, and your mother too, because forgiveness is where grace is. Otherwise, I'm afraid there will come a day when you'll terribly regret your stubbornness."

Huddled on the floor, Gwendolyn stared through the window at the velvety, starless night and wept inconsolably for herself, perhaps even for her father, but most definitely for her beloved grandmother who had warned her that "bitterness, like acid, corrodes."

"Oh, Mimi," she cried in grief that was now mixed with shame, "you must be so disappointed in me."

Her return to her father's house had been, in her mind, a total waste of time until she stood in the thick silence of her father's studio surrounded by images of what had mattered most to him. Painting after painting of his most cherished memories of her were captured in perfect detail and showed that he'd never forgotten her, told her in the only way left to him, that she was loved. It was a heartbreaking, life-altering moment.

At the end of December, on a cold, blustery afternoon, the sky leaden and threatening, a courier delivered a box of documents from her father's lawyer: the contents of her father's safety deposit box, a formal itemization of what had been placed in auction, a financial accounting of all of her father's assets, and various forms that required her signature.

She lit the fire, made herself a cup of strong tea to which she added a bit of whiskey, and, pulling Mimi's throw over her shoulders, opened the box. Her hands were unsteady as she sorted through the contents because there was one document she desperately hoped to find, and when she saw the creased, official-looking envelope, she pushed all the others aside.

"Helen," she whispered after reading her adoption decree, "I'm Helen Rose Kenny and my mother is Anne Kenny."

Finally, she'd found herself.

Alfred Burrows, Esquire
300 Waterfront Square,
Providence, Rhode Island
December 28, 1948

Dear Mr. Burrows,
I hope that you can assist me with two requests.
   Enclosed is my birth certificate. I want to change my name legally to Helen Rose Kenny, which is the name my birth mother gave me.
   Secondly, I would be so grateful if you could try to locate

my birth mother, Anne Kenny. Unfortunately, I cannot provide any clues as to her whereabouts, but perhaps my grandmother told you more about her.

After so many years, I realize that there is little hope of finding her. Nonetheless, I would like very much to try.

Thank you for any information that you can provide.

Most Sincerely,
Gwendolyn E. Wallabee

22

THE FINAL DREAM

She's dying. My mother's best friend who raised me because my mother could not. This tiny woman placed at birth in a cardboard box and deposited without a second thought on the steps of an orphanage—unwanted, unloved, and left to the care of strangers.

Now, in May 1971, marching toward the end of her life, she is again alone, having mourned, one by one, the loss of her dearest friends and her adoring husband, once again in the care of strangers with only smudged memories and a few faded photographs for comfort. She deserves so much better than this, my beloved soul mate, Annie.

Remarkably, despite the precariousness of her daily existence in the orphanage, she clung vehemently to an improbable belief that a better life was possible and, at just eleven years old, risked everything to find the life she dreamed about instead of accepting the life she'd been handed. Without a doubt, she's the most courageous woman I know.

Annie's sitting in a wheelchair placed in front of the window of her hospital room, and, despite pillows stuffed on either side of her, she's leaning like a dinghy slowly taking on water. Standing at the door of her room, it's impossible, even from this distance, not to notice how she's losing ground, caving in on herself.

As a slab of late-afternoon sun spills across her lap, she's tracing the embroidered yellow rosebuds on her housecoat, both hands ribboned with new and fading bruises and the skin of her arms sagging from the quicksand of her seventy-one years. I can't help smiling, though, watching her cup her fingers as if to gather the sunshine pooling on her lap, reminding me of her love affair with the sun. But I'm getting ahead of my story—or rather hers.

Officially, we met the day after a fierce winter snowstorm. As Uncle Charlie, her husband, tells the story, fat snowflakes started in the morning on December 20, 1933. The evergreens in South Park, many already trimmed with holiday lights, had a lovely, confectionary-sugar dusting along their lacy boughs, and the grimy surfaces of the city's sidewalks were temporarily spotless.

Exiting trolleys and trains, commuters, who typically headed straight home, lingered to allow the plump flakes to collect in the brims of their hats and on their shoulders, drawn like children to resplendent shop windows filled with tempting holiday delights—boxes of handmade chocolates, bundles of red-and-white candy canes, fruit cakes nestled in foil.

During the night, though, a nor'easter blasted through, its howling winds swirling the snow into fanciful shapes, pelting windowpanes with flakes of ice, and blanketing the city with nearly two feet of snow.

Sometime just after ten o'clock the next morning, while comfortably enjoying the pristine view from her parlor window, Annie had a frightening premonition. Leaving her cup of tea on the windowsill, she pulled on boots, tied a scarf under the collar of her tweed coat, corralled her auburn curls into a felt toque, and grabbed mittens that were warming on top of the radiator.

Heading out to our boardinghouse, she had to pull herself up Division Street using the fence along the sidewalk. When she finally reached the top, she saw, unhappily, that the sidewalks of

South Park had not been shoveled and were, in fact, completely indistinguishable.

Gingerly, she picked her way through the park, trying to find the hidden sidewalks without tripping over their metal edgings. Finally reaching the far exit, she crossed the trolley tracks and started up our street, where sidewalks fortunately had been shoveled. Sopping wet and chilled to the bone, she opened our front door to find my mother barely conscious on the parlor floor, her breathing shallow and fast and a small red stain forming on the carpet beneath her.

After calling for an ambulance, Annie pulled cushions off the sofa to raise my mother's head and shoulders in an attempt to ease her breathing, then wrapped her in blankets. Lying together on the floor, their foreheads nearly touching, they held hands as my mother drifted in and out of consciousness.

According to Uncle Charlie, no matter how many times Mother insisted on getting up, Annie somehow managed to keep her on the floor—which was hard to believe because my mother was, as he was fond of saying, "a big woman," while Annie was barely five feet tall!

According to the doctor who arrived a few hours later, moving my mother, even to the nearby sofa, would have completely ruptured the umbilical cord and the resulting hemorrhage would have killed her and most likely her baby—which was me.

Despite the loss of blood, my mother survived but remained in the hospital for weeks, and Annie moved back into our boardinghouse to care for me. By the time my mother was strong enough to return to work, Annie and I had formed what was to be a lifelong, unbreakable bond. I adored her.

Although she had come into the world unloved, receiving little, if any, from the stern caretakers of her youth, Annie knew instinctively what love was and loved me from the moment I was born. Not in the syrupy, wistfully romantic way portrayed in movies—Annie's love was ferocious, unwavering, and at times, impatient.

In hindsight, I believe the blueprint of my life was at least partly determined by the circumstances of my birth on that snowbound afternoon and, more importantly, that my mother's inauspicious absence right after my birth foreshadowed a deeper absence in all the years that followed. Be that as it may, this much is indisputable—without Annie, I wouldn't be me.

According to my mother, Phoebe, she and Annie were best friends from the very first day they met in the cutting room of the Troy Mill. Annie had lugged a battered suitcase all the way from St. Vincent's Orphanage to the Troy Mill, a distance of about three miles, looking for a job.

Whether genuine or feigned, Annie's confidence convinced the mill's president, Mr. Wallabee, who, fortunately, was a kinder man than most mill owners, to meet with her. Perhaps it was her curious combination of bravado, naïveté, and humor, but Annie not only landed a job in the mill but also a place to live in Rose Cottage, the mill girls' dormitory.

Although my mother was five years older, the two of them were inseparable, and soon my mother's twin brother, Charlie, joined them—they became the Three Musketeers. Eventually, Annie moved into and managed our boardinghouse while my mother opened a small hat shop and Charlie continued working in security at Firestone Tires.

My mother was pregnant three times. Those pregnancies had been fairly uneventful, but she was much younger then. She was thirty-eight at my birth and according to her, this pregnancy was different. She suffered with throbbing headaches during her first trimester, and, by the end of her second trimester, back pain forced her to temporarily close her shop to stay off her feet. A month before her due date, she started having what the doctor explained was false labor. On December 21, two weeks before her due date, she felt what she assumed were more false labor pains and, because of the snowstorm, decided not to bother Father at work. But an hour or so later when she began to bleed and cramp, she hurried to the phone but never reached it. Annie's premonition saved my life.

Annie looked after me every day until I entered the first grade. Weather permitting, Annie, with me in tow, shopped for food nearly every day, and she steadfastly refused to step foot into the new stores called "supermarkets," despite my mother's assurance that food there was much cheaper. Enigmatically, Annie also repudiated frozen foods that were staples in many homes, mine included, and absolutely refused to use the butter substitute called margarine, which she considered both unpalatable and toxic.

"You always get what you pay for, Rosie," she told me confidently, and I believed her. In fact, I never doubted her because, even as a youngster, I could tell that Annie had the gift of seeing things that were not always visible to other people.

In retrospect, Uncle Charlie and Annie always seemed to have a happier life than we did, even after the Depression. Unlike my parents, who seemed embittered and addicted to want, Annie and Charlie never seemed to want more than they had—it was always a relief to be in their apartment, which was the only place where I honestly felt completely safe.

Although my mother was a creative woman with many talents, the gift of a nurturing temperament, however, was never one of them. Opinionated, prickly, and corseted by bitterness, she hoarded words of sympathy and praise as if they were precious jewels and was convinced, until the day she died, that her glass was always half, if not completely, empty.

Returning from school when I was about eight, I overheard my mother arguing with Annie in the kitchen. "Well, if you ask me," my mother said, "she's totally to blame for this mess. That woman doesn't deserve your help and frankly, you shouldn't have gotten involved."

I'd learned by then that whenever Mother started a sentence with,

"Well, if you ask me . . ." it always ended badly, so I pressed myself up against the kitchen door and held my breath.

"For the love of God, Phee," Annie replied, her voice flaring with indignation, "you've no right to tell me who I can help or criticize me for trying to help someone." The only sound after that was the back door slamming.

Complaining during dinner about her earlier altercation with Annie, my mother must have been surprised that my father, who ordinarily let her complaints roll off his back, was uncharacteristically out of patience and soundly defended Annie's right to help whomever she pleased.

For the first time in my memory, he scolded her for forgetting Annie's generosity over decades, pointing out how Annie's self-sacrifice had literally saved our boardinghouse and how Annie's incredible kindness after the birth of each baby allowed my mother to continue working.

Then, lowering his voice, he added angrily, "Have you forgotten what Annie's gone through, Phee? The pain and humiliation she's had to rise above? Will you ever learn to keep your opinions to yourself?"

I thought my father was talking about the orphanage where Annie was forced to live, but as it turned out, Annie had been keeping a painful secret all those years and fooled everyone, even Uncle Charlie, who we all thought knew her best.

"Hi, there!" I call, entering her room. Although her eyes are closed, I pull up a folding chair so we can sit side by side at the window.

Eventually, the sun shifts, so I rearrange her wheelchair to keep her face and hands bathed in sunshine. Opening her eyes, she glances at me briefly. Once resplendent, blazing sapphires, her eyes are now leached of light, as if her very spirit is being drained.

It's difficult to explain her addiction to the sun, but it was as important to her as food. Craving it like an opiate, wherever we went, whatever the season, she always gravitated to the sunniest spot, whether a chaise on an outdoor patio, a chair bathed in the afternoon sun, or a sunny window seat in a restaurant.

My fondest memories are wondrous days at the beach, just the two of us. Because Annie never learned to drive, we used public transportation, and our favorite destination was the white sand of Horseneck Beach. The details are still as sharp as a razor's edge.

We couldn't have been more different from other beachgoers arriving in wood-paneled station wagons with passengers who leapt out and, with the speed of Indy pit crews, unloaded their car's contents onto the side of the road, after which the driver sped away to join the long line of other gutted vehicles circling the parking lot.

Annie actually prided herself on traveling light, carrying just one old blanket and a couple of seriously ragged towels. I can still see her, struggling to walk on the sand in her open-toe pumps and nylon stockings, her summer dress flapping at her legs like a useless sail and one hand anchoring her wide-brimmed straw hat to her head.

Once she found the perfect spot, she snapped that blanket two or three times, and I watched in admiration as it floated down, landing perfectly opened without a single grain of sand on it. Finally, she plopped down in the middle of it with a contented, albeit unladylike, grunt before lifting her chin to the sun. I sat next to her on the blanket playing with my paper dolls or squatted in the sand digging holes with clam shells.

On occasion, what Annie did made absolutely no sense to me. I mean, who wore shoes and nylon stockings to the beach? Why did she bother going since she never actually went into the water and to my knowledge never owned a bathing suit? And sometimes, when I thought we were having fun, a look of undisguised disappointment and obvious pain would cross her face, erased quickly by resignation.

"I wish the Good Lord would take me, Rosie," she says, finally breaking her silence with what has been her mantra for many months.

Knowing her as I do, I know that this is neither a ploy for sympathy nor self-serving drama. I believe she knows she's broken in a way that cannot be repaired and she doesn't want to be here anymore, plain and simple. I search for even a mustard seed of comfort to offer her but cannot find one.

Life is about choices and Annie seems to have made peace with hers. What she wants now is to sever her fragile thread to life. Despite being, by nature, a survivor and despite her church's position on such matters, if she could do it herself, she most certainly would.

She sighs deeply and her mood shifts. Turning away, closing her eyes, she drifts off, leaving me guessing—is she napping, luxuriating in the sun on her face, or, in fact, dismissing me? As always, I sit and wait—for what, though, I'm never sure.

Minutes pass, stirring old memories. According to my father, Annie used to be a courageous adventurer who planned to travel the world and was always the life of the party. I was also told that "Annie had a very hard life," but the specifics of that "hard life" were never forthcoming.

Although I won't ever know what tragedies befell her, it's clear, from knowing her now, that whatever happened to her changed her profoundly. Her regrets, her grief, her unanswered prayers can be read, like text, in the deep lines and creases on her face. Did her life measure up to the life she hoped for the day she ran away from the orphanage? I wonder.

Especially now, as the shadow of death waits a stone's throw away, I wonder, for the very first time, whether Annie was ever truly happy and must conclude that, for at least the years that I've known her, she never appeared so; she seemed to endure life instead of celebrating it.

What I dearly wish I knew about is the battle that Annie did not survive, the event or events that caused what Uncle Charlie used to call Annie's "blue days"—days when she simply couldn't get out of bed. I dreaded them because I wasn't allowed to see or talk to her, which was worse than punishment.

I never really believed, and still don't, that Annie suffered from some physical ailment on these days, which is what I was always told, but rather that she was sick at heart—weighed down by a grief so heavy she literally couldn't stand.

What event so tormented her that she could never suppress it or prevent the recollection of it, I will never know. Whatever it was, it haunted her; she never recovered from it. It marked her permanently like an oil stain on gravel.

What I do know is that there's almost nothing about who I am that cannot be traced back to her. I am forever rooted in her. Only in hindsight, can I see how she taught me important life lessons without ever talking about them directly.

For example, my first day of school—we trudged, hand in hand, to the schoolhouse attached to St. Anne's Church without uttering a word. I wasn't even buoyed by the fashionable, navy-blue sailor's dress with red stars on the collar or the shiny new Buster Browns that Annie bought me to wear.

I can still feel how cool it seemed and how dark and eerily quiet it was inside the school's foyer. As my eyes adjusted, I could make out the shapes of two women in long, black dresses with faces cinched, like tourniquets, by stiff, white fabric that curled up on either side of their chins, like wings.

"Welcome," the taller one said grimly. Despite her thin smile, her dead eyes frightened me and I looked up at Annie, who wasn't smiling either. Sensing something wrong, panic erupted in the pit of my stomach, and I squeezed Annie's hand with all my might.

Stooping down, Annie gently brushed a stray curl out of my face, handed me my lunch bag, and said softly, "You're a big girl now, Rosie."

At that very moment I understood that Annie wasn't going to stay with me and my heart began pounding so hard I was sure Annie could hear it, but I didn't cry because, as Annie had just pointed out, I was a big girl now.

Similarly, when I was eight, I got a fire engine–red Flexible Flyer for Christmas. Now, I never had any desire to try sledding, but there we were, Annie and I, the very next day, trekking through fresh snow to the hill behind the Pavilion.

When we got to the top, Annie waited for me to catch up, while carefully positioning the sled near the crest. "Get on," she shouted over the noise of other kids and parents on the hill, but fear glued me to the spot.

"Okay," she said without judgment, "I'll go myself."

Then she totally surprised me by plopping onto my sled and grabbing the steering bar. Now let me be clear, Annie wasn't the shrunken woman propped in a wheelchair next to me today. When I was eight, she was quite rotund and the added bulk of her brown winter coat and floppy knitted cap made her look like a humpbacked whale with black boots dangling off the back of my sled.

"Coming?" she asked without looking at me.

Hesitantly, gingerly, I lay down on top of her, wrapping my arms around her neck. Given our combined weight, I've no idea how she got that sled to slip over the edge. All I remember is how tears formed in the corners of my eyes and froze as we swooped down that hill and how at the bottom, we both rolled off onto the soft snow, breathing hard and laughing.

"Let's go again!" I shouted, grabbing the sled's rope.

That was quintessential Annie! She didn't offer up platitudes about the value of taking risks nor did she promise me any reward for doing something I was afraid to do. No psychobabble about self-worth—she just offered me a chance to face my fears.

Although my mother never seemed to tire of pointing out that I was "afraid of everything," Annie never criticized me for being so dreadfully apprehensive; in fact, she never mentioned it. Instead she showed me, time and time again, that facing fear head-on was the key to feeling better about myself, to feeling proud.

After what I convince myself is an appropriate amount of time waiting, I stand to leave just as Annie opens her eyes.

"I'm going now, Annie, but I'll come again soon."

"Rosie, help me!" she pleads, grabbing my hand in a surprisingly strong grip as a single tear drops onto the collar of her housedress.

She's never done anything like this before and it totally rattles me. My stomach's in knots just like it was on my first day of school.

"Bye, Annie," I say, quickly leaning to kiss her cool cheek.

At the door, I look back; I've never seen Annie look so vulnerable or desperate and admittedly it really unsettles me. Obviously, she needed something or needed me to do something, but I didn't even try to understand.

Back in the safety of my blue Ford Mustang, the tears start and quickly build to racking sobs, forcing me to roll down my window, light a cigarette, and watch as the little scarves of smoke swirl and ripple not unlike the whitewater of memories engulfing me.

One of my favorite photos of Annie is one she showed me on my twelfth birthday because in it she's twelve and enjoying the Troy Mill's annual Fourth of July celebration. Thinking about it now, it's noteworthy that Annie's shared only two stories about working in that mill—both about the mill's owner, Samuel Wallabee, or as she called him, Mr. Sam.

From her tone, it was easy to hear how much she really liked and admired this Mr. Sam. It was surprising to hear that, on occasion, he invited her to share lunch in his office, ordering food from the executive dining room which was delivered on trays with, as she put it, "real silverware." Chuckling, she confessed that her recipe for lamb stew, for which she is famous, was actually given to her by the chef at the mill.

She told me how they both enjoyed walking down to the docks after work to watch the huge cranes lifting pallets of cargo from inside the giant iron ships that scraped unmercifully against the docks. She and Mr. Sam would sit on a bench observing the activity and drinking hot chocolate until dark.

The other story she shared was so inconceivable that I assumed, I'm not proud to admit, that it was wishful thinking on her part. In a surprisingly soft voice layered with sadness and regret, she told me that Mr. Sam had wanted to adopt her! That, in fact, he had actually asked her more than once.

Perhaps Annie hoped I would ask for more details, but I could see that something about this story in particular made her quite sad. More importantly, I doubted that such an incredible story could be true. I mean, really, what young orphan wouldn't have jumped at the chance to become part of a family, especially a family like Mr. Sam's? So why would she refuse him?

It's astonishing that I could know so little about someone I've known for so long. She certainly looked happy enough at twelve standing between two girls, my mother on one side and another mill girl on the other.

All three girls dressed in white—high-collared, starched blouses with banana-boat sleeves, long skirts with cinched waists, and lace-up shoes. According to Annie, white was the quintessential color of summer, at least in those days. Although she's the smallest of the three girls, she's wearing the biggest smile and the biggest hat, which is the other constant in our years together—the splendor of Annie's hats!

Despite an untamable mass of auburn curls, Annie had a passion for magnificent hats in a symphony of unexpected colors, with swirls of netting, ribbons, beads, silk flowers, and antique pins or fobs.

Unfathomable to me, since in every other aspect of her life, Annie not only preferred but insisted upon simplicity and abhorred fussiness in the food she prepared, the clothing she wore, and the people she spent time with. Nothing about her was overdone or flashy.

My mother, a milliner, never designed a single hat for the average woman. Her unconventional, prodigious hats were one of a kind. She never made the same hat twice, which was exactly the kind of exclusivity that appealed to the fashionable, socially prominent women in town who happily paid a premium for the assurance that no other woman could ever wear the same hat. As Mother was fond of telling them, "You won't see this hat coming and going."

It took time, but eventually her fashion-forward hats were considered chic, and, by association, the small but loyal circle of women who wore them were assumed to be connoisseurs of refinement and good taste.

Like them, Annie and I made twice yearly pilgrimages to Mother's shop, where, as a toddler, I sat on the counter playing with boxes of buttons. Despite their size and delightful whimsy, my mother's hats possessed a graceful fluency and an unexpected airiness, and when Annie wore them, she appeared—no actually became—regal, confident, and serene.

Nonetheless, I found them distasteful not only because they were unconventional but because, in my view, these hats were the antithesis of who Annie really was—introverted, accustomed to suppressing her thoughts and feelings, and shackled by social prescriptions for women of her class.

It was years later before I considered the possibility that these larger-than-life hats were Annie's alter ego—as unrestrained as she was reticent, as joyful as she was ponderous, as extroverted as she was standoffish.

Wearing these hats transformed Annie, albeit temporarily, into a woman of substance, a woman with a presence and a voice in a world where she was mostly silent and unnoticed. In other words, the kind of woman she dreamed about but was never allowed to be.

We were truly two peas in a pod. Perhaps because we were so much alike, Annie understood me better than anybody else and never needed or wanted me to be different. Unlike my parents, she never took my preference for silence as a personal affront. Annie was always my true north.

Only now, sitting in my Mustang, do I appreciate how obstinately and unconditionally she loved me, imperfections and all. It couldn't have been easy for her to dedicate so much of her life to me, no doubt she had to make many sacrifices. I just wish I'd told her that she'd always done the right thing, the honorable thing, and how I wanted to be just like her.

Without fully understanding why and without any plan, I hurry back to her room where a dinner tray has been left on the table next to her wheelchair.

Her expression is indecipherable, but she watches attentively as I pull the tray table between us and sit down. I honestly can't tell if she even remembers my visit less than a half hour ago.

"I'm back, Annie," I say cheerfully. "Thought we'd have dinner together tonight."

Her eyes smile.

Peeling back the sticky Saran Wrap from a plate of mashed potatoes with gravy puddled on top and a wafer-thin slice of roasted chicken isn't easy, but separating it from a steamy bowl of clear broth and a cup of chocolate pudding takes me several minutes. How is Annie expected to do this herself?

I offer her a spoonful of potato and, surprisingly, she accepts it;

then I try a sliver of chicken dabbed in the gravy, which she also accepts but chews so slowly it's almost like she's forgotten how. Meanwhile, I prattle on about this and that with no expectation that she's even interested.

The young aide is startled when she returns to remove a nearly empty tray.

"They've forgotten Annie's tea," I tell her. "Would you please bring a very hot cup of water, a tea bag, three cubes of sugar, and a small pitcher of milk?"

When it arrives, I'm delighted to watch Annie fix her tea exactly the way she likes it and drink it with obvious pleasure. While she sips, I read her an article in the outdated *Reader's Digest* on her night table. She listens with some enthusiasm to the story about a family lost in the Vermont mountains for four days before being rescued by a man out hunting with his teenaged son.

"I'll get her ready for bed tonight," I inform the night nurse making her rounds, and she wearily raises no objection.

Filling a basin with warm water, I give Annie a sponge bath like I used to when she could no longer climb into the claw-foot tub in her apartment. After drying her off, I finish up dramatically patting her back and shoulders with a powder puff full of her favorite scent, Evening in Paris, then dabbing her wrists with perfume of the same name from the cobalt bottle I've seen on her dresser since I was a toddler.

Helping her into a clean nightgown, gently brushing the tangles from her hair, and straightening out her bed linens, I ring for an aide to help me get Annie safely back into bed.

Pulling a chair right up to the side of her bed, I ask, "Do you remember any of Pa's silly jokes?" *Pa* was what she always called her husband, Charlie.

At first, she looks quite puzzled but then says, "Pa had lots of jokes."

"Well," I continue, "remember the one where he'd say, 'Rosie, ask me how I feel.' So, I'd ask him how he felt and he'd say, 'Like the inside of a furnace—grate!'"

She actually chuckles.

"Or sometimes he'd say, 'Like seven days, week!'"

She's nodding now, there's a lovely smile on her face, and her eyes brighten when she says, "He was a good man, Rosie."

I start to say something, but she interrupts.

"No!" she says emphatically. "Nobody knows what a good man he was. I was no picnic, even your mother tried to warn him off me."

"My mother tried to stop you from marrying her brother? That's unbelievable!"

"There are things you don't know, Roseanne," she scolded me. "Phee could sure get my goat and did many, many times, but she was a loyal friend. You've no idea what she went through for me."

The night nurse pushes a cart of medications into the room, pours water into a glass, and hands Annie a tiny paper cup with three pills in it. She watches Annie swallow every pill before leaving to continue her rounds.

I break the silence with, "Annie, remember our trips to McDonald's?"

"Umm," she replies so softly I almost don't hear it.

Once I got my driver's license, Annie and I were free as birds—no longer limited by bus routes and time tables. Sometimes, we just drove around like teenagers on the loose—just because we could.

One summer afternoon about six months after I passed my driver's test, Annie suggested we ride out to Ocean Grove to visit a friend of hers. She gave me the address, and once we got into the town, I pulled into a garage to ask for directions.

"Stay on this road till it ends," a rumpled mechanic said, "then get on the unpaved road . . . probably all the way out on the spit."

I followed his instructions and found the old beach road that coiled through sand dunes, exposing a few summer cottages in various states of disrepair along the way.

At the very end there was what looked like a narrow driveway, although the house itself was completely hidden. Fortunately, an old mailbox mounted to a weathered post confirmed that the house number was 180.

The serpentine driveway of crushed sea shells was entirely screened on both sides by dense, overgrown shrub roses and misshapen scrub pines twisted and stunted by years of unwanted salt spray and harsh winds.

"I won't be long," Annie said nervously. "Just having a cup of tea and a short visit. Here"—she handed me a dollar—"why don't you get yourself a soda at the pavilion we passed. Pick me up in an hour." She stepped out and headed to the front door.

When I returned, Annie was staring out at the ocean from the patch of grass that separated the end of the driveway from the beginning of the beach. She looked as if she'd been crying, but when I asked, she denied it. She said nothing and pretended to sleep on the drive home.

The following week, she suffered the first of three strokes. Inexplicably, Annie refused to go to a hospital where we all knew she would get better care. Stopping by every day after school, I led her through the series of exercises the doctor had suggested, made sure she'd taken her medicines, and heated up the food Charlie bought for supper.

Within a few weeks, Annie was up and about and wanted to go on an outing. She suggested, of all things, driving to McDonald's for lunch! I didn't even know she knew what McDonald's was. The woman who'd shunned all but the freshest food now wanted to try "fast food"!

From her very first bite, Annie was head over heels for McDonald's cheeseburgers and fries, ate them with unbridled enthusiasm, but never really cared for Pepsi. After that she agreed to any outing I suggested—so long as we went to McDonald's for lunch.

Nine months later, she had a second, more severe, stroke; her recovery took longer and left her with a permanent limp, but her third stroke, which happened on the drive home from Uncle Charlie's funeral, was the worst. This time she had no choice about nursing care. It took her nearly six months to recover her speech, and she was left unable to walk without assistance.

Two weeks ago, she stopped eating the McDonald's cheeseburgers I brought her, and, according to the nurses, for the last two days she refused to eat much at all, although she still loves her sweet tea.

"How many cheeseburgers do you think we ate?"

"A million," she says with a wan smile.

I stand to kiss her cheek. "I love you, Annie."

"Stay," she says in a voice both weak and vulnerable.

"Sure, I'll stay until you fall asleep."

"Roseanne," she says reaching for my hand, "I always did the best I knew how."

"Of course, you did. Without you I don't know where I'd be, Annie. You were my mother when I desperately needed one and then my best friend."

I'm puzzled by her sudden agitation and try to calm her, but she persists.

"Sometimes, Rosie, things turned out wrong, but I always tried to do my best." Her voice and her eyes seem to plead for something.

"Annie, I'm so grateful you were there for me, always protecting me, always loving me. I know you always did what you thought was best."

"Roseanne, listen to me!" Her voice is no longer weak and her tone takes on a strange urgency. "I need you to find Helen. Tell her how sorry I am. Make things right."

I don't know who Annie's talking about or what she means, so I am silent.

Annie, eyes wide with trepidation, struggles to sit but can't. "You

The Final Dream

have to find her, Rosie! Tell her I thought I was doing what was right. You have to promise me!"

"Annie, it's not good for you to get overexcited like this." I wrap her hand in mine and kiss her cheek. "Now, please, try to rest a little. I'll stay right here and when you wake, we'll sort this out. I promise."

But Annie never woke up. An hour later, with her hand in mine, she lowered, like a pilot light—dying exactly the way she lived, quietly and without fanfare. It was May, 1971.

It's impossible to describe grief. It empties you until you are almost transparent and the outside world suddenly becomes a dangerous place. Everyday there is something, a woman on the street, or the aroma as I pass her favorite bakery that reminds me of what I've lost. Sometimes, I hear the sound of her voice so clearly that I turn to look for her, and for that briefest of moments I am happy—until I remember.

It's an early morning in August before I find the courage to open the package sent from the nursing home after Annie's death.

Annie's engagement ring with its tiny diamond chip slips out first, followed by her worn, black rosary beads and finally her gold wedding band. Holding these, her most precious possessions, I try to remember her face and the things we did together, only to realize how fragile the past becomes when we try to touch it.

Her Bible and two sealed envelopes remain in the package. Opening the thicker envelope on which Annie has written my name in her familiar scrawl, I find photographs, some very old by the look of them.

In the first, a young, unmistakably annoyed teenage girl slouches in a doorway next to a young novice who is fingering the small gold cross around her neck. Surprisingly, on the back of the photo in my mother's handwriting is: "Annie and Sister Helen, 1915." I've never heard of a Sister Helen.

The next photograph is the one with three girls in white dresses that Annie showed me on my twelfth birthday which I feared was lost.

The smallest photograph is of a tiny newborn swaddled in a pink blanket, lying in what looks like a hospital bassinet. On the back, someone, but neither Annie nor my mother, has written: "Helen Rose, January 15, 1916. Another person I've never heard of, another puzzle to solve.

Next is a badly creased photograph of Annie and Uncle Charlie on their wedding day—both so young, their eager faces filled with hope and promise. On the back is written: "Our June Wedding, 1927."

The final photo is also one I've never seen before. Annie, smiling broadly, holding an infant wrapped in a pink blanket on her lap. "Me and Roseanne, December 28, 1933" is scrawled on the back.

These photos chronicle the important events and people in Annie's life, and I know them all, except for the two Helens. Rechecking the dates on the back of both photographs, infant Helen and teenage Helen, I realize that they cannot be the same person. As I slip them back into the envelope, I remember Annie begging me to find "Helen." Which one? Why?

In the second smaller envelope, creased and yellowed with age, is a letter.

Alfred W. Burrows, ESQ.
300 Waterfront Square
Providence, Rhode Island
February 21, 1949

Dear Miss Anne Kenny,
A couple of months ago, Miss Helen Rose Kenny wrote me

The Final Dream

requesting my assistance in locating her birth mother. She was born at the Convent of the Sacred Heart in Brattleboro, Vermont, on January 15, 1916, and adopted shortly thereafter. According to the convent's records, a baby girl was born to Miss Anne Kenny on January 15, 1916, and, according to the birth certificate, was named Helen Rose Kenny. You are, I believe, my client's biological mother.

Adoption laws are quite strict. I am absolutely precluded from passing any information about you to my client, which I have thoroughly explained to her. That said, I am enclosing her name and address on the back of my card should you wish to contact her or me.

Please understand, Miss Kenny, that you are under no obligation to contact her; in fact, you may not wish to see her at all. Rest assured that I have not, nor will I ever, share any information about you with my client. Your privacy is completely protected.

Most Respectfully,
Alfred Burrows, Esquire

It feels as if all the air has been sucked out of the room. Checking to see if the date on the back of Helen Rose's baby picture matches the date in this letter, I am baffled because the dates are the same. If the infant, Helen Rose, is, in fact, Annie's daughter, then Annie would have been about fifteen when she gave birth and that is simply not possible.

I drive immediately to our boardinghouse where my oldest brother still lives, hoping that, as the oldest, he might know more about Annie's past. He's at the kitchen table finishing breakfast when I enter.

"Hey, Rosie, you're up early."

"Did you know that Annie had a daughter that she gave up for adoption?"

"I thought she couldn't have kids," he replies, scooping the last bit of fried egg into his mouth.

"That's what I thought! But I just found out she had a daughter when she was about fifteen. Did you ever hear our parents mention this?"

"To me? No, but why would they? Maybe they didn't know."

"They had to know! All four of them lived together for a decade. I just can't believe it. I can't make sense of it."

"Does it matter?" he asks in his usual, infuriating, nonplussed way, as if we were discussing the weather.

"Are you kidding? I looked up to Annie all my life. She never told me about a baby."

"So?" he asks. "How does that change anything? Obviously, she made a mistake when she was a teenager. Jesus, who didn't? This has nothing to do with you, Rosie."

He wipes his plate clean with the last bite of toast and gulps down the remaining coffee. "Sorry," he says, shrugging. "I've got to get to work. Nobody's perfect, Rosie."

I sit at the kitchen table, feeling and no doubt looking like an abandoned child—lost, confused, and scared.

Then, I remember Annie's "blue days."

EPILOGUE

Weeks are lost trying to answer unanswerable questions like, "How could Annie have done such a thing?" or "Why?" But, in the end, my brother had the right question: "Does it matter?" Annie loved me completely and fiercely. I loved and am literally rooted in her. Nothing's changed except that now she's gone.

With increasing anxiety, I pull off the highway and drive slowly onto a lesser-used road lined with sand dunes and summer bungalows. Rechecking the address on an old business card as I drive. By the time I reach the end of the road and see the narrow driveway still overgrown on both sides, I know for sure that I've been here before a very, very long time ago . . . with Annie!

I roll down the window and take deep gulps of sea air. Confused and anxious, I recheck the address—yes, this is it. Like everything else, the house is a bit changed; a wide deck has been added to one side, a row of skylights can be seen along the roof line, almost a dozen large, colorful pots, filled to overflowing, soak up the sun on the porch and at either sides of the front door, and a set of weathered Adirondack chairs face the ocean.

Deciding to use the side door instead of the front, I step out of the car before the last of my courage evaporates. With my heart in my mouth, my first knock on the screen door is tentative, but I knock again, louder.

A tall, fiftyish woman comes to the screen door, wiping her hands on a smelly rag. She's wearing paint-spattered overalls and what looks like a man's long-sleeved denim shirt and is barefoot. Her cropped auburn hair is a mass of curls. Definitely Annie's hair.

Her round face, oddly pale for someone who lives at the beach, is sad and resigned, but it's her eyes that take my breath away—pools of liquid sapphires—Annie's incredible eyes.

"Yes?" she asks, keeping the screen door between us. "May I help you?" She studies me, but whether it's with contempt or curiosity, I can't tell.

"Hi, you don't know who I am," I stammer, "but I wanted . . . to . . ." I can't stop staring into her eyes. Embarrassed and nearly in tears, I know I have to push ahead.

"Look, she asked me to make things right and well . . . you're Helen, right?"

On the other side of the screen, she sighs and covers her mouth with both hands. Wordlessly she shakes her head back and forth, and finally, she clears her throat.

"You're wrong. I do know who you are, but I doubt you can make things right."

"I don't know if I can either," I admit, somehow finding my voice. "She was the one person I loved most in the world, she was the person who loved me the most, and now she's gone. Without her, I'm lost.

"You look so much like her, Helen, it's uncanny. Annie used to tell me, 'You either open doors or you close them—those are our only choices.'

"All I know for sure is that, if you send me away, if you close this door, it'll be like losing Annie a second time --for both of us."

Helen's face is heavy with suffering; her mouth opens but no words form and tears silently slide down her cheeks unnoticed. Without a sound, she reaches for the handle and holds the screen door open for me.

ACKNOWLEDGMENTS

None of us gets where we are in life by ourselves—this could not be truer for *The Mill of Lost Dreams*.

As a rookie author, I discovered that writing is a lonesome business and, at least for me, a high caloric business. As soon as I finish, I'll join a gym and hire a personal trainer.

In the beginning, I wanted to tell a story about my grandmother, Anne Kenny, who was an orphan and started working in a textile mill when she was eleven. Unfortunately, I knew nothing about textile manufacturing or her experience as a "mill girl"—and thus began five years of research.

Between 1870 and 1900, twelve million people immigrated to America. Hundreds of thousands of them came to work in the textile mills of Fall River, Massachusetts, which by 1876 was the largest textile manufacturing center in the United States and the place where my grandmother lived. Before writing anything, I needed to learn what working in textile mills was like for all these immigrants who risked everything they had for the singular dream of building a better life.

I wanted to know about the pressures and challenges of mill culture, the dangerous process of turning 450-pound bales of cotton into yards of fabric, and, more importantly, what happened to the people whose dreams of a better life were irreversibly lost.

I am eternally grateful to my grandmother, who sacrificed so much in order to care for and keep me safe. She taught me that, in a successful life, truth trumps all; that facing what we fear is the only way to grow straight and strong; and that you always get what you pay for. Without her I could not be me; I am rooted in her and draft off her courage every day.

My awesome friend Barbara Freedman Wand is as instrumental as I am in getting this story told. She read every chapter and gave me valuable feedback on my characters. As importantly, she counseled me to be patient, never my strong suit, during the many emotional ups-and-downs of writing and guided me in the search for an editor. Her encouragement never wavered. I've added her to my will!

I see that most authors thank their spouses and/or family, but, seriously, I am so grateful for my husband, Rod, who stood by me in every struggle. His patience, which, no doubt, was stretched almost to the breaking point on more than one occasion, made this book possible. He brought me meals and a constant supply of vanilla lattes, did the laundry and grocery shopping, and solved every frustrating software problem and the all too regular computer glitches. He is my knight in shining armor.

I want to express my appreciation to the Fall River Historical Society for their incredible collection of materials and exhibits related to textile manufacturing: fabric samples, historical photographs, stories penned by mill workers, and architectural plans.

Similarly, I am deeply indebted to the Lowell National Historic Park, where the Boott Cotton Mill was built in 1835 and is still running by a canal power system! The entire first floor is filled with dozens of looms, and when staff turn on only a few looms, the noise is absolutely deafening—which helped me understand why the women in so many historical photographs had cotton in their ears.

Acknowledgments

Thanks to the brave souls who wrote firsthand accounts of the work and the culture of textile mills: *So Far from Home: The Diary of Mary Driscoll, an Irish Mill Girl* by Barry Denenberg; *Eight Hours for What We Will: Workers and Leisure in an Industrial City, 1870–1920* by Roy Rosenzweig; *The Lowell Mill Girls* by Alice K. Flanagan; and *The Belles of New England: The Women of the Textile Mills and the Families Whose Wealth They Wove* by William Moran. Your candid, powerful writing taught me so much.

I live half the year in Whistler, British Columbia, and am indebted to my cheerleaders there whose encouragement and support fueled me. Mary Forseth and Deborah Brown, you have no idea how much your enthusiasm, unbridled excitement, and friendship kept me sane. I couldn't have done it without you.

Thanks to everybody on the She Writes Press team: editors, project managers, proofreaders, and designers, each making the manuscript better, and especially to Brooke Warner, publisher, and Samantha Strom, editorial manager, who patiently guided this novice through the process.

Please remember that *The Mill of Lost Dreams* is a work of fiction. Names, places, events, and characters are products of my imagination. Any resemblance to actual persons, living or dead, or actual events is purely coincidental.

About the Author

© Bob Keene, Keene Vision Photography

Lori Rohda an MBA and PHD psychologist, is a former Assistant Dean of Students at Boston University and, as President of King Walker and Associates, was a management consultant to Fortune 500 companies.

She divides her time between Boston, Massachusetts where she loves to golf and design perennial gardens and Whistler, British Columbia where the skiing and hiking are unsurpassed.

SELECTED TITLES FROM SHE WRITES PRESS

She Writes Press is an independent publishing company founded to serve women writers everywhere. Visit us at www.shewritespress.com.

Eliza Waite by Ashley Sweeney $16.95, 978-1-63152-058-7
When Eliza Waite chooses to leave a stagnant life in rural Washington State and join the masses traveling north to Alaska in 1898 during the tumultuous Klondike Gold Rush, she encounters challenges and successes in both business and love.

The Vintner's Daughter by Kristen Harnisch $16.95, 978-163152-929-0
Set against the sweeping canvas of French and California vineyard life in the late 1890s, this is the compelling tale of one woman's struggle to reclaim her family's Loire Valley vineyard—and her life.

The Rooms Are Filled by Jessica Null Vealitzek $16.95, 978-1-938314-58-2
The coming-of-age story of two outcasts—a nine-year-old boy who just lost his father, and a closeted young woman—brought together by circumstance.

Lum by Libby Ware $16.95, 978-1-63152-003-7
In Depression-era Appalachia, an intersex woman without a home of her own plays the role of maiden aunt to her relatives—until an unexpected series of events gives her the opportunity to change her fate.

The Sweetness by Sande Boritz Berger $16.95, 978-1-63152-907-8
A compelling and powerful story of two girls—cousins living on separate continents—whose strikingly different lives are forever changed when the Nazis invade Vilna, Lithuania.

Tasa's Song by Linda Kass $16.95, 978-1-63152-064-8
From a peaceful village in eastern Poland to a partitioned post-war Vienna, from a promising childhood to a year living underground, *Tasa's Song* celebrates the bonds of love, the power of memory, the solace of music, and the enduring strength of the human spirit.